GOLDEN REICH

by MARK DONAHUE

D!
DONAHUE
LITERARY PROPERTIES

GOLDEN REICH
LESTER'S WAR

ISBN s/b: 978-1-7349711-7-0 (Paperback)

This is a work of fiction. The characters, incidents and dialogue are products of the author's imagination, any resemblance to actual persons, living or dead, is entirely coincidental. Any references to historical events, real people, or real places are used fictitiously.

Front cover design by Marsha Donahue. Illustration by Mary Sue Oleson, bludesignconcepts.net
Published in the United States of America by Donahue Literary Properties, LLC
www.donahueliteraryproperties.com

Dedicated to
Tom; for all the adventures we never went on. Yet.

ACKNOWLEDGEMENT

IN 1995 I WENT TO THE Holocaust Museum in Washington D.C. In 2005 I went again. Again in 2009. Again in 2012. Each visit haunted me for days. Each face I saw was etched in my brain. Especially the children. How could the Nazis...children? Or women? Or anyone? How?

I determined it had started with lies. But in reality, lies are not a bad thing, we hear them every day. The lies remain harmless unless people swallow them, digest them, ingest them, and by doing so, they metastasize into people's mental and emotional hard drives, gestate, and ultimately emerge as a horror.

There can never be repayment for that horror. But we must be ever vigilant for the lies. We must be mindful that there are some who eat those lies, relish those lies, and will, if opportunity presents, act on those lies.

Those who perished in Auschwitz, Bergen-Belsen, Buchenwald, Dachau, Gross-Rosen and the others deserve our vigilance. It can happen again.

"He didn't know how to speak properly, how to walk properly, how to comb his hair, and she felt embarrassed for him as he shouted about restoring jobs and national honor, about a better and splendid Germany. The mob applauded, shouted. Did people really believe that he wanted what was best for Germany?"

— Ursula Hegi, *Children and Fire*

BOOK ONE—LESTER'S WAR

PROLOGUE

SCOTTSDALE, ARIZONA PUBLIC LIBRARY

BEN SMITH AND HIS DAUGHTER, Samantha, known as Sam to family and friends, were giving a presentation at the Scottsdale Public Library on local Indian culture. "You don't have to have Indian blood in your veins to realize the connection between the Earth, the sky, and the things we feel or sense as human beings. It's just that my Navajo ancestors cultivated those feelings more than the white man did. You know what they say, 'use it or lose it.'" Ben said.

An audience of about fifty local attendees leaned forward in their seats and hung on Ben's words. While her father spoke, Sam operated a computer-generated overhead projector that showed images of the Indian culture of which Ben spoke.

Off to one side of the large well-lit room, a plainly dressed woman in her eighties hugged a tattered leather binder against her chest while she sat quietly and listened. She also watched as Ben and Sam smiled patiently as they spent nearly an hour responding to a myriad of questions from the rapt audience.

After the last question had been answered, and the audience gone, the father/daughter team gathered their presentation materials and did not at first see the old woman who approached cautiously.

"Mr. Smith?"

"Yes ma'am, please call me Ben. You have a question?"

The old woman hesitated. "Well, I read about you and your daughter and how you study the history around these parts and wanted to talk to you about something my husband left me."

As she spoke, Sam noticed the old woman wore a faded blue cotton dress with a worn leather belt that was cinched tightly around her thin midsection. The woman's gray hair was pulled up in a bun, and her tanned leathery hands tightly gripped the binder that contained faded yellowed papers sticking out haphazardly from its edges.

"I guess Sam and I could be called local amateur historians. What did your husband leave you that you wanted to chat about?"

At first it appeared the old woman was going to walk away. Sensing her discomfort, Sam approached her. "Hello ma'am, my name is Samantha Smith, but you can call me Sam. If you'd like to sit down, my dad and I would be happy to answer any questions you have."

The old woman appeared relieved, smiled warmly at Sam, pulled out a chair, and sat down at a large circular oak table. Sam and Ben sat on either side of her. In a clear strong voice, the old woman said, "My husband, who disappeared over thirty years ago, left me this here book. It's kind of a diary, I guess. I can't prove everything he wrote in this book is true, but I know one thing, he weren't no liar, and he weren't one to make up no tales neither. I think maybe you two might want to take a look at it. At my age, I could drop over tomorrow, and no one would ever see this and try to figure out what it all means."

The elderly woman slid the binder to her right toward Sam, who gently accepted what was clearly very old and precious to the gray-haired octogenarian. The binder was worn and brown with age like the old woman's hands. The papers that stuck out were ragged, and some were torn at the edges. The binder smelled old.

Carefully, Sam opened the binder and began reading while Ben and the old woman chatted. As she slowly turned the pages, Sam's eyes narrowed in concentration, the space above her nose furrowed, and her cheeks flushed.

After several minutes, she turned to Ben and said, "Oh my God, Daddy, you've got to see this. We were right!" Ben rose from his chair and made his way to the seat on Sam's right. Sam moved the binder in front of him and said, "Look at the dates."

As Ben gently turned the pages, he too became immersed in what he was reading. For the next hour, Ben and Sam pored over the old binder, entranced by the tale that unfolded in front of them.

Finally, Sam and Ben looked back at the old woman, ready to ask her a thousand questions. Maybe a million.

She was gone.

CHAPTER 1

BERLIN, GERMANY—1940

THE BLUE WOODEN SANDBOX IN which four-year-old Ari played was littered with the small steel toy trucks given to him by his older sister Anna as Hanukkah gifts months earlier. When Ari drove them over imaginary roads, he vibrated his lips and made motor sounds that caused spit to drop onto his red cotton shirt forming a wet six-inch teardrop pattern below his chin. His dark brown hair was matted with sweat from his focused efforts in the midday sun. His beige shorts, white socks, and canvas shoes were covered with fine gray sand.

Ari looked up from his diligent work and squinted in the sunlight when he heard the rumble of three tarp-covered military trucks pulling up in front of his parent's large Tudor-style home in an affluent neighborhood outside Berlin.

While the truck engines idled, Ari excitedly bounced up from his sandbox and ran toward the large swastika-emblazoned vehicles, his favorite red toy truck clutched in his right hand. When he crossed over the circular driveway and approached the front gate, he was intercepted by his mother who swooped him up on a dead run. When she turned back toward the house, Ari wailed in protest and dropped his toy truck in the grass. "Mama, mama, truck, truck!"

His mother, Rebecca, a slender, attractive, raven-haired twenty-six-year-old, ignored her son's protests. Instead she ran toward the garage where her husband David held the side door open. Inside the cool garage a dark blue 1937 Cadillac sedan sat in the shadows. After David slid in behind the steering wheel, Rebecca moved into the passenger seat. She held their only son who had grown quiet sensing his parents' curious emotions.

David pumped the accelerator pedal twice, turned the ignition key, and the V-8 roared to life. He reached for the driver's side door handle to go open the garage door. But Rebecca grabbed his right arm and held him back.

"Rebecca, we must leave now! Out the back gate, there's no time!"

"David, where can we go? Where can we hide?"

"We can…we can go to my brother's house; he will hide us!"

"And who will hide him, David?"

"But we can't stay in here or we'll…"

"When they take us, they will separate us, like they have all the others. Let's stay together. Just the three of us…here."

For several seconds, amid the low murmur of the V-8, David pondered Rebecca's meaning. "What about little Anna?"

"My sister will understand and watch over her. You know how

Anna loves her and they'll be safe in Zurich."

"But…are you very sure we should…?"

"Staying together is best, David." Rebecca slid next to David and placed her head on his shoulder, with Ari on her lap. Ari appeared confused. He looked between his mother and father for some kind of explanation. Instead, David rolled down the driver door window and kissed his son's forehead. He wrapped his arms around his wife and child.

Ari was still confused. "Papa?"

"We love you, Ari." David explained.

Exhaust fumes rose from the Cadillac and within minutes the car was enveloped in a dense gray fog. From outside the garage, smoke could be seen seeping from the bottom of the garage door and floating skyward in a series of specter-like wisps.

Inside one of the trucks waiting in front of the house, a young German soldier grew concerned. "Sergeant, they aren't coming out of the garage. Should we go get them?"

"Private, you're too impatient. They make our job easier. Relax, we have plenty of time. The Jews go nowhere."

Inside the Cadillac, Rebecca, Ari, and David appeared asleep in each other's arms. Thirty-minutes later, a hulking young German soldier, a handkerchief held over his nose, opened the door and entered the smoke-filled garage. He made his way through the gray haze until he could see the Cadillac's left rear bumper. He felt his way along the side of the car, found and opened the driver's door. He reached over three bodies and turned off the ignition.

After he left the garage and allowed the smoke to clear, the soldier returned several minutes later to "clean up the mess," as his sergeant had ordered. He pulled David and Ari from the car and haphazardly dropped them to the floor of the garage. He turned back to reach for Rebecca and saw her dress hiked up. The soldier could see her smooth thighs and white panties visible in the half light.

For several seconds, the soldier was entranced by Rebecca's sad, lifeless eyes, still moist with tears. Unable to take his eyes off her, he slid into the seat next to the dead woman. After a full minute, he reached out and tentatively fondled her right breast with his left hand, as if in fear she would awaken and slap him for such temerity.

When she did not, he moved his hand down to her thigh. Then between her legs. All the while he gaped at her large dark brown eyes in fascination. He began to breathe heavily and sweat beaded on his forehead. He looked through the narrow back window of the Caddy and the open garage door. He saw no one. *Why not?* He shrugged his shoulders and unhooked his belt. But seconds later he heard sounds from the front yard. Cursing the noises and a lost opportunity, he rehooked his pants, pulled

Rebecca from the front seat of the Caddy, and tossed her on the floor of the garage next to Ari and David.

The soldier slid back into the Cadillac's front bench seat and sat behind the wheel of the high-priced American symbol of luxury and affluence. He stroked its fine leather seats and ran his hands over the shiny black steering wheel, imagining a drive in the massive car to his girlfriend's house near Munich. His thoughts about his newfound respect for American engineering and design were interrupted by an impatient sergeant. "Private, I told you to move that rubbish out of here and pull that car into the driveway. General Eck has made a request for that make and model. Make sure it's cleaned inside and out."

"Yes, sir."

After the soldier removed the bodies from the garage, six more men entered the large three-story home. They began their systematic task with the care of professional movers. That was partly due to the fact that four of the men had been professional movers in civilian life. Yet they had never experienced as much work as they now had. Nor had they moved people and furniture from such grand homes.

At the bottom of the stairs leading from the large veranda-style front porch, the sergeant inspected the loads carried by his men. He made detailed notes in a thick notebook that included a description of each item confiscated. He also listed the names and addresses of the Jews who had *donated* to the Führer's cause. He wanted to make sure all the Jews in the neighborhood had an opportunity to pay their fair share. He also had a message for his men. "After we're done here, I'm going to search each one of you, and if I find you've taken anything for yourself, you'll get a year in solitary."

A strapping young soldier presented a large jewelry case made of mahogany. "Sergeant, I found this in a closet."

"Let me have it."

Opening the box, the sergeant saw several rings, bracelets, gold watches, and other pieces of jewelry. After he made his notes in the binder, he lifted the contents from the box, and placed them in a large wooden barrel that sat by the side of the stairs. However, the sergeant did reward himself for work well done by palming an elegant man's gold Rolex. After checking to be sure he could not be seen, he slipped the timepiece into his pocket. "Thanks, Jew boy. You had good taste."

The soldiers methodically emptied the house except for specially requested items that were on a list provided by the next inhabitants of the Tudor home—a Nazi general, his wife, and three small children. In addition, they searched the grounds, the garage, and the storage bins around the house for valuables. One soldier found a red toy truck in the grass and tossed it in one of the barrels at the bottom of the stairs.

By the next afternoon, the Nazi general's children were playing in their new blue sandbox. In it they found a small brown canvas shoe and two toy trucks.

CHAPTER 2

BERLIN, GERMANY—1943

SS COLONEL KURTIS ROLLE LOOKED older than his thirty-three years. It wasn't just his close-cropped hair, receding hairline, and pale skin that prematurely aged him; it was the way he carried himself on his six-foot-two-inch frame. He emitted an air of self-confidence that made him appear at least ten years older.

However, it was more than his mature appearance that had garnered Rolle the attention of the senior leadership of the Nazi Party. He also had a solid academic background and had worked his way up the Party ladder by doing good work and keeping his mouth shut. Most importantly, he displayed an almost maniacal loyalty to the Führer, even for a Nazi.

Sitting in a straight-back red leather chair in SS General Heinrich Becker's waiting room, Rolle appeared at attention. His back was rigid, his cap was in his lap, and his eyes were riveted on something. After ten minutes, Becker's secretary approached. "Colonel, the general will see you now."

Without speaking to or looking at the attractive young woman, Rolle rose from his chair and followed the secretary into Becker's lavish cherry wood paneled office. Rolle's first impression of the office was its smell. It reeked of cigar smoke and expensive men's cologne. The odor and fragrance fought each other for supremacy.

As he stood at attention in front of Becker, Rolle noticed how the general's desk and chair were raised several inches off the floor. He also noticed Becker was a small man— a small, distasteful, rude, and vain man. Rolle immediately disliked him before Becker said a word.

For nearly five minutes, Becker ignored Rolle while he read some paperwork his secretary had placed on his desk when she had brought Rolle in from the waiting room. Rolle remained at attention and stared straight ahead while he waited to be recognized. Finally, Becker looked up at him, a smug smile on his face, as if he had won some sort of competition. "Colonel Rolle, it is a pleasure to meet you. You are well, yes? Please be seated." Becker pointed to a large soft-cushioned chair that forced the occupant to look up at him. Rolle sat.

"Thank you, I am well. How may I be of service?"

"Your reputation for getting to the point is refreshing, colonel. Very well then, to the point. What I am about to discuss with you is to be kept in strictest confidence. Breaking that confidence is a crime punishable by death, is that clear?"

"General, the information I see every day is of the utmost sensitivity. I am quite familiar with such responsibility."

For several seconds, Becker stared at Rolle, then rose from his chair, turned his back and looked out his ten-foot high window onto a small park surrounded by government offices. The gray buildings were being pelted by a cold, heavy rain that turned their color a slate black.

Without being asked to, Rolle left his chair and joined Becker. The two men looked out across the street in silence. In the park they saw an old woman with a gold star pinned to her worn wool coat. She pulled a child's wagon that carried her food rations for the week. After another minute of silence, Becker said, "Colonel, the war is lost. Eventually, the Allies will march into Berlin and everything we have worked for and dreamed of will be gone."

"General, I am aware of the realities we face. Everyday our resources ebb, and soon we will have nothing to fight with. The bravery of our men is not enough."

"Yes, it is an unfortunate truth."

As the men continued to look out into the pouring rain, three teenage boys entered the park and saw the old woman as easy prey. They knocked her to the ground and viciously kicked her in the head until she stopped moving. The boys took her food but instead of running away, they casually stood over her body and ate from her basket of groceries. Becker and Rolle saw what had happened but did not speak of it.

"Colonel, with the war lost, we must now redirect those limited resources you spoke of in order to further the Führer's vision."

"How can I help that cause?"

Becker turned back to his desk, picked up a thin report, and handed it to Rolle.

"Take responsibility for this."

Rolle took the report and saw *OPERATION REBIRTH* stamped in red ink across the top. In the middle of the page, "TOP SECRET" was written in thick block letters with the Nazi seal at the bottom of the cover.

"What is Operation Rebirth?"

"It is a general strategy to perpetuate the Führer's vision after the war and even after his death. And no, the Führer will not survive the war. If the Allies do not kill him, then the assassins within Germany will. There have already been over forty attempts on his life."

"I have heard of such attempts but had no idea there had been that many."

"What you hold, Colonel, is a basic plan. We need someone to fill in details to ensure the plan's success. Without such details the plan is useless talk."

Rolle opened the report and read silently. After several minutes, he looked up at Becker with a look of disbelief on his face. "Whose idea was this plan? And do they have any idea what this strategy would do to our war effort?"

"This plan was crafted by party loyalists, men who want to perpetuate the world vision of the Führer over the next hundred years, including the total elimination of the Jews."

Rolle did not immediately respond to Becker. Instead he looked out the office window. He saw the motionless body of the old woman and the boys who continued to dine on her rations.

"Colonel Rolle, does your lack of a response indicate a lack of enthusiasm for this proposal?"

"General, the need to perpetuate the Führer's goals is clearly of primary importance, but the execution of this plan, while we are at war, could prove catastrophic."

"Colonel, to throw more resources at a war already lost is equally catastrophic and foolhardy. It would also deprive the world of benefitting from the Führer's genius. Do you not believe we have a duty to see his vision expanded around the world?"

"Yes of course, but this plan ensures we will lose the war sooner and perhaps valuable concessions from the Allies. There are so many questions that need to be answered before…"

"Colonel, your questions are well founded and at this point unanswered. That is why you have been selected for this assignment. You are to be the chief architect of Operation Rebirth."

Rolle looked at the report in his hands one more time and then to the dead woman across the street.

CHAPTER 3

ARIZONA DESERT—1980

THE FADED BLUE VAN PULLED into the highway rest area off Route 60 east of Phoenix. A tall rail-thin old man lingered in the idling vehicle for a few minutes. He needed to gather his strength. He knew that once he left its air-conditioned coolness, he would face hours of unrelenting heat and utter exhaustion.

Finally, he switched off the ignition and gathered his army surplus backpack that was loaded with a canteen and his usual lunch. When he stepped out of the van onto the already simmering asphalt of the rest area parking lot, the old man took a breath, but the searing dry air instantly parched his throat. He coughed several times before a drink from his canteen allowed him to breathe again. But the cool water did not assuage the pain in his back. Nothing would.

Ignoring the pain, he squinted against the late morning sun but opted not to wear his aviator wire-rimmed sunglasses that remained on the van's front passenger seat. He was afraid that his already fading sight would miss something. He needed to see things clearly.

When he had made the treks in the cool of winter over the years, it helped a bit, but they still beat the hell out of him. Yet there were times he had no choice but to enter the summer desert cauldron. This was one of those times.

It wasn't just the heat and the four-mile walk that was exhausting, it was also the weight of what he carried on the return trip. The old man, with skin the color and texture of a dried maple leaf, would hike across the Arizona desert for two miles, pick up his load, and lumber back to the van laboring against fatigue and heat. But now, the ever-expanding pain that had invaded his body over a year earlier made this trip even more arduous.

Over three decades, he had made hundreds of hikes into the desert. There was a time when he recorded every single trip in his journal. But as the months rolled into years, he had gotten a little careless with his record keeping. The trips now just seemed to blend into a single fogged memory.

As usual, he wore khaki pants from Sears, a dingy gray sweatshirt to protect him from the sun, old Nike running shoes, and a yellow Panama hat his wife had given him for Christmas. He checked his Timex and noted it was just after 11:00 a.m. when he set off north across the muted brown desert, under a clear cobalt sky.

The path he followed had a slight two-degree rise that led to several plateaus nearly two miles into the distance. If he kept to his usual schedule, it would take about ninety minutes to reach his destination. It would take another half hour to gather up his load and have some lunch. He would rest for a few minutes before starting his return trip, which would take about two hours. His oft repeated routine was embedded in his brain, and he performed his task with military efficiency.

Weaving through the cacti and low-lying scrub, he walked at a slow but steady pace. He made it to the undistinguished flat spot in the sand in just over ninety minutes. As usual he stopped a quarter mile from the site, took out a pair of binoculars, and looked around the desolate desert landscape. He looked for the glint of a car or pickup truck reflecting in the sun. He looked for men on horseback, motorcycles, or hikers. He even looked skyward to make sure there were no low-flying planes or helicopters. He looked for anything and everything. If he saw something, he would stop and wait until whatever he had seen disappeared before he retrieved his load. On that day he saw nothing.

After he picked up his load, he stopped at the same place and ate the same lunch he had eaten on every trip: Two hard-boiled eggs, orange slices, rye bread, two slices of Velveeta cheese, and four Oreos. They were all wrapped around a dozen ice cubes and eaten in order. His dining area was under a covered rock ledge, overlooking a dry creek bed. The niche was seven feet high, twelve feet deep, and eight feet wide. He had discovered it thirty years earlier when trying to escape a torrential downpour that folks outside Arizona never thought took place in the desert. Since then he had used it as a halfway resting place to escape the unrelenting sun.

The old man sipped water from his canteen, cracked open his first egg, and thought of his wife, who would be getting up at about that time after a particularly long night. The thought of her made him smile. He looked forward to getting back home and seeing her one more time. He figured his coming home might even surprise her.

He sat Indian style against a rock at the back of the niche he had leaned against for most of a lifetime. He gazed out over the Arizona desert. It was a sight that still filled him with awe after all the years. He saw the heat rise like dancing, sensuous phantoms, distorting the monochromatic landscape behind them. He could smell the creosote bushes. He could hear the hum of insects. The familiarity that surrounded him was comforting. He felt a little better. Even the pain in his back seemed to dissipate just a bit.

Sitting in the cool darkness of the covered niche, he realized this would be the last shade he would be in for the next two hours, and he rested a little longer than normal after lunch. He dreaded the long walk facing him. He wondered if the trip back in the hundred- degree heat was even worth it given the circumstances. Maybe it would be better for everyone if he just stayed right where he was.

As he contemplated an answer to his own question, he lifted his canteen for a last swig of water after he had downed his final Oreo. That is when he saw it out of the corner of his eye.

He had seen them many times before over the years but had always been warned away, and either sidestepped them or stood still until they crawled back under a rock or bush. This time, since he wasn't wearing his hearing aid, he hadn't heard its warning. It was now just four feet to his right and its tongue darted, as it tasted the air for scent. He saw it coiled and poised. He faintly heard its four-inch rattle. He knew his only hope was to remain as still as possible and pose no threat.

The old man ever so slowly lowered the canteen and tried to position it in a way to deflect a strike if it came. Staring into two unblinking black eyes, he remained motionless for over two minutes as rivulets of sweat ran down his arms and face. At last, it began to move sideways toward the back of the small cave, never taking its lifeless eyes off him. Watching it silently slither into the shadows, the old man exhaled in relief not knowing how long he had held his breath.

Finally free to move, he kept his eyes focused over his shoulder into the darkness at the back of the small cave. At the same time, the surge of adrenalin that coursed through the old man's body caused his heart to pound and made his senses razor sharp. Yet for some reason, he also realized he was no longer in pain. He felt invigorated. He felt young. Yet again, he had survived.

With a self-satisfying half grin on his face, and a renewed energy to return home to his wife, he had just gathered up his backpack and canteen when he was hit. The first strike sank deep into his left cheek piercing the skin and stopped when it hit the enamel of his lower molar. Almost simultaneously, he was hit two more times, once in his left thigh and then the left arm. Knocked to his right by the force of the hammer-like blows, he moaned in pain as the combination of fang, poison, and shock hit his body like 400 amp electric current.

Without a cognitive thought to do so, the old man began to crawl on his stomach toward daylight and the opening of the niche. As he did, he felt two of them squirm wildly beneath his weight. He spilled out of the cave entangled in his backpack and canteen strap.

He careened down the embankment leading to the creek bed seven feet below the rock ledge. When he landed face first in the sunbaked dirt, he gasped for air. He did not understand that his lungs were already constricting from the venom and had been smashed empty by the force of his fall.

He attempted to clear his mind and regain control of a body now out of control. He tried to rise but could only make it to his knees. As he sat on the red hot baked earth, he detected movement and felt searing pain in his left leg. He looked down and gagged in revulsion at the sight of the third one writhing, trying to free its left fang still embedded in his blood-soaked thigh. He stared at the snake in what appeared to be idle curiosity for several moments. Then nonchalantly he reached down, grabbed it by the back of the neck, and yanked it from his throbbing thigh.

With his vision blurred by a nervous system gone haywire, he had placed his left hand too far down its neck. As soon as it was free from his leg, the rattler pivoted nearly 180 degrees and sank its one-inch fangs deep into the flesh that formed the V between his thumb and forefinger.

With more instinct than thought, he picked up the heavy object that had fallen from his backpack in his right hand. He methodically brought it down and smashed the head of the snake and with it several bones in his left hand.

Now feeling no pain, the old man gaped at the dead snake on the ground and the two bones that protruded from his hand. He tried his best to take stock of what had just happened, but his brain refused to think. He gasped for breath and spat up blood that spilled down his whiskered chin onto his dingy sweatshirt. Dizziness and nausea swept over him like a wave, but he fought it. He got on all fours and crawled over the hot gravel and retrieved his scattered belongings, including his yellow panama hat. In his right hand, he tightly held onto what had brought him to the desert.

The old man called on all his remaining strength and staggered to his feet. He steadied himself and began to walk. It was time to get back home now, he thought. He desperately needed to see his wife. She would take care of him.

Moving without seeing, he listed to his left with each step and within ten yards he fell to the ground again, this time onto razor-sharp cacti. But the numbness that was slowly overtaking his body now protected him from the pain. He began to convulse and choke on the vomit that rose in his throat. Still holding onto what he had come to the desert for, consciousness left him and was replaced by a peacefulness he had never known before. He had one final thought that led to a hoarse whisper, "Ain't 'sposed to be this way." A breath later, all the pain was gone.

CHAPTER 4

MANHATTAN, UPSCALE STRIP CLUB—2006

AS MARVIN GAYE'S "LET'S GET IT ON" simmered in the background setting the stage for late-night sexual healing, thirty-three-year-old Jon Cole considered his many options for the night. Option one, and currently ahead in the polls, was the tall brunette who had slithered on stage and immediately focused on Jon's $500 haircut, $2,000 Armani suit and $26,000 Patek Philippe gold watch. She was also armed with and charmed by the knowledge that Jon had that very afternoon closed a Wall Street mega-deal that had netted him a $22,000,000 commission. In fact, everyone at Jon's table had shared in that deal, but Jon was The Whale. The Big Kahuna. The Man.

Jon was also tan, slender, Rob Lowe good-looking, and kind of funny in a Midwestern sort of way. All these attributes made the brunette thankful that her shift allowed her to place her spectacular breasts only inches from Jon's face.

"Wow, what a set of tits," one of Jon's cohorts noticed, a statement so ridiculously obvious as to be both redundant and rhetorical at the same time.

As he stared at the flawless brunette, Jon nevertheless continued to mentally weigh his options. "You should see her sister."

"You mean this is the ugly one?"

"Let's just say the sister...is more eager to please."

Finally making the only logical executive decision he could, Jon stood and whispered a suggestion into the brunette's ear and slipped her a wad of cash.

"But I don't know where she is."

"She's your sister, for heaven's sake. Where are your family values?"

"I'll find her. You at the Sofitel?"

"Room 1004. Here's the key."

The brunette smiled, then blew a kiss to Jon as he moved toward the strip joint's front door and waved his coworkers a fond farewell. He also, to the glee and expectation of all, picked up everyone's tab.

On his way out he thought he saw a familiar face among several large men stuffed shoulder to shoulder in a booth. Given other priorities, Jon decided that any further thought as to whom the familiar face might be would only divert his attention from focusing on the brunette and her red-haired sister. He deduced that he would soon know which one colored her hair and who didn't...maybe...unless. That possibility made him walk a bit faster down West 44th.

Back at Jon's table, another coworker mused about Jon as he saw him exit the club. "Guy's got it made. What'd he make last year, twenty-five extra-large?"

"Yeah but he'll double that this year. And he looks like a fucking movie star. Hope he at least has a small dick."

Overhearing the comment, the brunette said, "Sorry, boys."

"How the fuck did he pull off that equity deal? No one saw it but him."

"Other guys saw it but didn't have the balls to go for it. You're fucking with the feds on that deal. You mess up and get accused of stealing widow's pensions, it's ten years guest of Uncle."

Looking up at the still hard-working stripper, a third coworker proffered a logical and heartfelt question of her. "So, what's your interest in an average-looking guy with a small dick and just two mil in the bank?"

"I keep Thursdays open for my pity cases, but I'll need an upfront deposit and a month's notice."

The sound of his coworker's laughter did not stop him from removing his wallet from his Brooks Brothers inside suit coat pocket.

––––––––––––––––––––

At the other end of the club, the five men that Jon had seen on his way out crammed into a booth were engaged in what appeared to be earnest conversation. In the middle of the group was a tall man in his early thirties. He was Tom Patrick, former Princeton Tiger and New York Knicks power forward. Tom was at that moment all ears listening to a huge, squat man with bad acne and worse breath wearing a dark blue sharkskin suit. The squat man was talking to him nearly nose-to-nose in a most sincere way. Tom was particularly focused on what the man was saying. That was because a second equally squat man in a black sharkskin suit, who apparently went to the same dermatologist as the first, sat on Tom's left and had a Smith and Wesson .38 snub nose revolver stuck in Tom's crotch. It was uncomfortably near his left ball.

The man in blue voiced some heartfelt concerns. "You know, Tom, I'm a little worried you may not understand our deal."

"No, no, I understand our deal. Like I said, I'll have your two hundred grand by next week, really."

"Tom, Tom, Tom, I *knew* you didn't understand our deal. See, you owed us two hundred grand last week. This week you owe us two-hundred-twenty-five grand. Next week two-fifty. You see how this works now?"

"Ah, interest. I did forget the interest. You know, you guys need to be careful because you might be close to breaking some usury laws that could land you in big trouble with the Feds. Just trying to help."

The man in the black, with the gun stuck in Tom's crotch, thought he detected just a tad of sarcasm in Tom's rejoinder and took exception. "You tryin' to be funny, puke?" I'll blow your ball sack off if you're tryin' to be funny."

"No, please." Tom presented a newfound sincerity in his voice. "I'm just trying to bring some levity to the situation given my current lack of funds that leaves me temporarily, and I emphasize the word temporarily, unable to repay my debt that would eliminate the need to have you shoot off my best friend."

Looking back at the blue suit, the black suit asked, "What the fuck did he say?"

"He said, since he can't pay us, he's going to help us reach out to some college boys who always need extra spending cash and explain to them that shaving points isn't really cheating, it's really just a way of making the games more exciting. It also insures that when we bet the spread, we win. Right, Tom? Because if that isn't what you're saying, Sal here is not only going to remove your nuts, he's going to put a slug in each knee so you won't be able to walk or fuck."

Now showing enthusiasm for the plan presented by blue suit with deteriorating breath, Tom was effusive in his support. "Unbelievable! This is incredible!! That's exactly what I was, with some great difficulty I might add, trying to say. How did you know what I was thinking and trying to articulate? You, sir, have a gift."

"By the way, Tom, we have really good memories about deals we make and who we make them with. We never forget, Tom. Never."

Tom forced a smile. "That's very reassuring."

CHAPTER 5

CALIFORNIA FEDERAL PRISON—2008

JON EXPECTED HIS FIRST NIGHT in prison to be awful. He underestimated. The noises, the waves of smells, and the utter fear he experienced overwhelmed him. He couldn't help but think of the film *Stir Crazy* when Richard Pryor and Gene Wilder went nuts when they realized where they were. But this wasn't a movie. It was real, and Jon was not at all sure he could survive. Or if he wanted to.

Within ten feet of entering the echoing din of the cell block, Jon received his first formal invitation: "Hey baby, come on and bring that fine, tight white ass on over here, I got a little sumthin', sumthin' for ya."

The second offer, only six feet later, was even more enticing, "Hey white boy, don't listen to that ho' he got the crabs and clap. I got what you need."

As Jon continued down the block toward his cell, he heard the wails of desperation from men absent of all hope. He also smelled pine-scented Lysol trying its best but failing to hide the stale stench of dried urine, sweat, and too many men. Yet, for some reason it was at that very moment that Jon realized it had been two years to the day since his romp with the twin sisters. It was the same day he had received his $22,000,000 commission all of which was now gone. In fact, everything was gone.

Later that night Jon, along with four other men, was placed in a twenty-four-hour holding pen until his permanent cell could be assigned. As he lay in the darkness, he heard the sobbing and incoherent mumblings of men going or gone mad and thought of the whirlwind of events that had brought him to prison.

The Cole Commercial Real Estate Investment Trust that he founded had been a great idea. The *Wall Street Journal* called it "the fastest rising, best-run REIT in the country, maybe the world." It was, for a while.

Jon had seen signs of pending disaster early on. But by then he was deeply immersed in trying to prop up existing projects by selling new projects to investors who were not paying attention to what was happening in an unfamiliar market. All they knew was that Jon's firm had been paying investors big returns, and they wanted their piece of the action. They were not interested in the details, which is where the devil lay in wait.

When the Feds finally knocked on his door, Jon was almost relieved.

Jon's position was not helped when the judge and jury learned the details of his well-publicized income and lifestyle, which included lavish parties, luxury cars, a jet, yacht, LA condo, beachfront home, and New York City apartment. They saw the trophy wife/wannabe actress who escaped prison herself only by putting on an Academy Award–worthy performance in front of the jury. She claimed she knew "absolutely nothing about what Jonny had been doing in business." A fact which both Jon and she knew was utter bullshit.

Out on bail and two weeks before he turned himself over to federal authorities to begin his sentence, Jon came home and found his wife giving a rather energetic blowjob to their landscaper on the deck of their Santa Barbara beachfront home. Rather than being at least concerned at being caught in the act, she casually defended herself by saying it was her way of dealing with stress. On top of which, she explained, as she continued to hold onto the landscaper's still very erect member, they owed this very patient landscaper over $2,000 for a new tree he had planted by the driveway and there was no money in the bank since the court had frozen their assets. "Like, what was I supposed to do, Jonny?" she had logically asked.

The landscaper, not at a loss for understanding the ways of commerce, also provided helpful detail by saying, "It was a very beautiful orange blossom tree which I sold to your wife at a discount." Jon tried to file for divorce the next day only to find his wife had beaten him to it.

Jon's attorney had suggested that if he pled guilty to all charges, agreed to forfeit his remaining assets, assisted investigators, surrendered his securities license, and acted contrite in front of the judge and jury, it was possible he might get a "light sentence" of say eight to ten years. Given that Jon was charged with felonies that could have amounted to over 100 years in federal prison, eight to ten years did, at first, seem reasonable.

The judge accepted the plea deal and sentenced Jon to ten years in a medium- security federal prison in central California. Jon's attorney called the sentence a "victory" and pointed out that with good behavior Jon could be transferred to a minimum-security prison in a few years and out on parole in maybe eight. As a result, he would not be appealing. Besides, appeals cost money, and Jon David Cole, Princeton grad and Wall Street wunderkind, had none.

As Jon lay on his metal bunk his first night in prison and heard the moans and cries of the men around him, he thought back exactly seven hundred and thirty nights…and the redhead. She was his favorite. He also wondered how his ex-wife had paid the guy who cleaned the pool.

CHAPTER 6

BERLIN, GERMANY—1943

AFTER MONTHS OF EXHAUSTIVE PLANNING, Rolle sat in front of his unlit fireplace and stared into the empty hearth. He wondered what he had overlooked. His elderly housekeeper, Rachel, kept bringing him his favorite wine as she had done every night for years. He drank it without tasting. She had also prepared braised beef tips, fresh carrots, and potato salad for his dinner, yet the plate sat untouched on a table next to him.

"Kurtis, you must eat, you are losing too much weight. It is not good."

"They think me a fool. They think I believe Operation Rebirth is to perpetuate the Führer's legacy. I know better."

"Would you like me to warm up your plate? The food is cold now."

"They want me to execute a plan that will destroy Germany for decades. I know what they are doing. But to whom do I turn? Bormann? Himmler? Becker?"

"Kurtis, please eat something. You need your nourishment."

"They're all part of the cabal. Yet, I will be the one hung with piano wire if the plan is discovered. I, the loyalist."

"Kurtis, if you are not going to eat, it is time for you to go to bed. No more wine, please."

Emptying his glass in a single gulp, Rolle, with Rachel's help, rose from his chair and headed for the bedroom. But his slurred monologue continued. "I created the plan for them. But I also created a second plan. My plan. It will ensure Germany will not be destroyed and those who tried to deceive her punished."

With Rachel's help, Rolle fell into bed. She removed his shoes and pants then covered him with a quilt she had made for him on his tenth birthday.

"That's fine, Kurtis. You sleep now and when you awake, I'll have breakfast ready for you."

"My plan will protect Germany. My plan will save Germany."

"Good night, Kurtis." Rachel turned off the light and shut the bedroom door.

The next morning Rolle entered the kitchen and appeared rested. "Good morning, Rachel."

"Good morning, Kurtis. Did you sleep well?"

"Yes, but I do have a bit of a headache."

"I tried to get you to stop after that first bottle but..."

"I shall listen next time."

"What time is your train?"

"Noon."

"And when will you return home?"

"Rachel, I have waited till now to tell you, but it may be a long time, many months, before I return."

"Many months? But where are you...?"

"I cannot tell you where I am going or when I shall return. I've left money for you next to my bed. I have also alerted Dr. Dyke to look in on you. You'll be fine."

After several minutes, Rachel asked, "Is this part of that Operation Rebirth plan you spoke of last night?"

Rolle froze when he heard Rachel's question.

"I mentioned Operation Rebirth? What else did I say?"

"Only that you felt there were those who were using you to..."

"What else?"

Rachel tried to change the subject. "Nothing. Nothing else. Would you like more coffee, Kurtis?"

As Rachel spoke, Rolle rose from his chair and stared at Rachel. "What else did I say? You must tell me."

"Nothing, Kurtis, you told me nothing more." As she spoke, Rachel tried to move away from the kitchen table, but Rolle grabbed her arm. As he did, a look of resignation came slowly over her face. "I knew this day would come. After you turned your parents in to the Gestapo, I did not have the heart to abandon you. Even after what you had done. But I knew if you could do that to them..."

"My parents were threats to our cause..."

"But they loved you, Kurtis, as do I..."

"You have treated me kindly, Rachel, but I should not have said... what I said...if

others learn..."

Rolle rose from his seat and moved directly behind Rachel where he could smell the perfume he had purchased for her as a Christmas present years earlier. She had worn it every day since. He moved his hands to her shoulders, then her neck.

"Will there be pain, Kurtis?"

"No pain, Rachel." Rolle quickly twisted Rachel's head until her neck snapped with a loud crack. "See, Rachel. No pain at all."

CHAPTER 7

BERLIN, GERMANY—1943

AT PRECISELY NOON, THE GLEAMING black train lurched from the station. Rolle glanced at his watch and smiled at the irony. The country was losing a war, but the damn trains still left on time.

"Colonel Rolle, it's very good to see you. Would you mind if we shared the ride to Paris?" An overly polite and slightly effeminate SS Major Berne stood next to Rolle's seat and hoped his question would elicit an invitation. The major was wearing a new, freshly pressed black with red trim Hugo Boss–designed SS uniform. He had seen Rolle as he entered the train moments before. He had concluded that sitting with a colonel for a few hours might be a career-enhancing exercise.

Rolle had also seen Berne as he had entered the train. He remembered he had always thought him a fool. Rolle also suspected that Berne was homosexual and wondered how he had escaped a trip to a prison camp years before. Not looking up at the smiling Berne, Rolle replied in a low, disinterested monotone, "I prefer to sit alone, major, but I do admire your new uniform. Quite fetching."

"Certainly, Colonel Rolle, as you wish," replied an embarrassed yet still smiling Berne as he backed away from Rolle's seat with a slight bow. He wondered if he would still be a major by the end of the trip.

The *Brandenburg* was Hitler's personal train and preferred mode of ground transportation. It was used exclusively by the Führer, except for this trip. The train had been originally named *Amerika* but after the United States entered WWII, Hitler had renamed it. The unmarked train was powered by two sleek black locomotives, which pulled eight heavily laden freight cars along with two luxury club cars that carried forty passengers and crew.

Several minutes after leaving the station, the *Brandenburg* slowly picked up speed as it clamored west through the expansive railroad yard. It rumbled into the industrial section of Berlin and finally broke free of the dirty gray buildings into the lush green German countryside.

The steel wheels clattered over the tracks and produced a repeatable white noise that had a sleep-inducing affect on most people. But Rolle knew sleep was impossible. Instead he remembered, as he did almost nightly, the first time he had seen and heard Hitler speak in the late summer of 1926. Rolle was sixteen years old and spellbound by a man who spoke directly into the hearts of every German patriot.

Yet Hitler's words and plans were more than jingoistic rhetoric. They were a clearly defined road map. They were specific, concise, and fearless. His words were quite simple and brilliant.

As a teen Rolle had joined the Greater German Youth Movement later named the Hitlerjugend, League of German Worker Youth. His every free moment was spent furthering the growth and development of the Nazi party. However, he realized his father, a respected history professor at the University of Berlin, was vehemently opposed to Hitler and everything he stood for. To avoid confrontations, Rolle did not tell his father of his decision.

Rolle's mother tried her best to avoid the political arguments that grew louder and more intransigent each time they occurred between father and son, and inevitably, led to yelling and door slamming.

In 1932, Rolle, armed with two college degrees and with the recommendations of several of his commanding officers, was hired into a low-level position within the government's economic operations department. By the mid-1930s, and despite his youth, Rolle was given ever more responsibility in helping reorganize Germany's fragile monetary system.

Rolle quickly became respected as a young man with both superior intellect and devotion to government. Long hours, coupled with brilliant suggestions that led to many innovative and successful programs, helped define him as an "insider," someone to be admired, reckoned with, and even feared.

Power was not something Rolle sought. He used it only when he felt it necessary to achieve a goal he knew was in the best interests of Germany. Rivals soon realized they could challenge him only so far because of his power. Many learned too late that to push him was to put their careers or even their lives at risk.

Rolle reveled in his status and responsibility. At the same time, he regretted that in over seven years of meetings with the Führer, including several at the Berghof, Hitler's Bavarian retreat, he had not spent any time alone with Hitler. Yet, at early group meetings with the Führer, Rolle was struck by Hitler's reserved nature. His questions were thoughtful and to the point. He seemed to grasp whatever Rolle or others presented. He was also courteous, polite, and always thanked Rolle for his efforts.

Things changed in early 1943 when Rolle confirmed that the rumors he had heard over the previous five years were true. His country was indeed killing millions of its own. Even though they were Jews, and Rolle did not deny they had to be removed, why not simply deport them and send them to Jew-loving counties like the United States or Great Britain?

Rolle felt the killing was pragmatically inappropriate. It was not that killing for a cause was not a valuable tool in running a government; it clearly was the best tool in many cases. But the mass murder of men, women, and children was fraught with unneeded political risk, especially if the international community discovered such actions.

What troubled Rolle more than the mere killing of Jews was the knowledge that many of his superiors were stealing millions of Deutschmarks from the German government, seemingly with the approval of their superiors.

By the fall of 1942, Rolle was aware that millions in cash had been transferred to checking accounts in South American banks. In addition, regular trips to Switzerland by couriers taking with them cash, gold, and securities under the guise of "investments on behalf of the German people" had become commonplace. Rolle was told by his immediate superiors that these investments were legitimate, but he knew better.

Yet, his options were limited. If he went to Bormann with this information and the investments were indeed authorized, Rolle's career and perhaps his life would be in jeopardy, for he would be charged with going over the heads of his immediate superiors.

If Bormann himself had authorized such theft, it was likely Rolle would have been shot without ever leaving his office. What Rolle knew for certain was an army of individuals who cared little for their country, and much for their own wealth, were sucking his beloved country's resources dry. And he was powerless to stop it.

It was obvious to Rolle by the spring of 1943 that Germany was going to lose the war. Not for lack of will or brain power but because his country was running out of money.

CHAPTER 8

ARIZONA MINIMUM SECURITY PRISON—2012

AFTER SPENDING FOUR YEARS IN three different prisons within the federal system, Jon Cole's hair displayed a touch of gray that went nicely with his orange prison jumpsuit. At thirty-nine he was still in good shape due to his daily visits to the weight room and his three-mile jog around the prison grounds. But the previous six years, including the pressure of the trial, had taken a toll on Jon physically, emotionally, and mentally. He had changed. He recognized those changes but had not yet determined if they were for the better.

Given the unrelenting boredom Jon faced every day, he had developed a tendency to daydream. "Hey Cole, you been hanging on the damn broom for ten minutes. Get the hell back to work." The gentle suggestion was made by an overweight prison guard with greasy slicked-backed hair.

"Oh yeah, I need to finish here so I can get back to washing underwear."

"Oh no, is Mr. Ivy League bored? Not enough mental stimulation for you? Well, look at it this way, you only got what, three and half years left? Shit, that's easy time, boy."

Jon used a dustpan to pick up crap and tossed it into the trash bin. "Three more years and I'll be qualified to pick up trash in any city in America."

"Heard you were lucky you didn't get fifty years in the Big House."

"Yeah, ten years was a real gift. I hardly noticed the lifestyle change. And how can you beat all the great food and wine?"

"So, how much did you hide on the outside? Tell me where it is, and I'll make sure the next three years are real easy on you. I'll take half and leave the other half for you. How 'bout it?"

"Wow, really? Let me think it over. But just to show your good faith, you get me a blonde, a case of Coors, a large pizza, and computer sent to my cell tonight, you'll be rich by Tuesday."

"Smart ass. Just 'cause you one of them white-collar-crime assholes, you think yer shit don't stink." The guard kicked over the trash bin that Jon had filled and spilled the contents all over the floor.

Jon quietly swept the trash into a new pile that the guard walked through. "I want this shit picked up in five minutes, and your ass back in the laundry in six."

"Guess this means no ESPN and beer tonight," Jon whispered to himself.

Several hundred yards away at the prison's front gate, a van idled in the blazing Arizona sun and waited for the thirty-foot high gate to be opened. Carrying five new arrivals, the van finally entered the prison grounds and was directed to the north end of a courtyard where the prisoners would be let off. Among the group of five was former Knick and Princeton grad Tom Michael Patrick, who had proven to be an utter failure in his efforts to convince college basketball players to shave points.

That failure led the guys in silk suits with bad skin and breath to become very agitated with Tom. In fact, they had expressed enthusiasm for removing his favorite body parts with a rusty knife. He finally decided to go the police for his own protection. But despite turning state's evidence, he learned he was going to have to do some time too. The judge suggested five years in a place far, far away.

On the bus ride from a California medium-security lockup where he had spent three years prior to the long-awaited minimum-security facility in Arizona, Tom sat next to a young black man named Marcus who updated Tom on his well-rounded criminal resume. While clearly less than unsuccessful, the young man's career was indeed varied and colorful. Especially the part that had led to his latest arrest. "They wouldn't give me the money, so I cut 'em,'" he calmly explained to Tom.

Almost afraid to hear the answer, Tom felt compelled to ask, "You mean your grandparents?"

"Yeah, I mean they knowed I was in need, cuz I wuz shakin' and sweatin' like a motherfucker and they still wouldn't give it up so…"

"So…of course…you…cut 'em. I mean what else could you do?"

"Yeah, right. That's what I told the judge. Funny thing was after I cut 'em up and they wuz lyin' on da floor yellin' and bleedin', and all that shit, I got hungry."

"Always makes me hungry too, especially when grandparents are involved."

"Yeah, I mean I ate everything in that kitchen. Ate like a motherfucker. Ate till the cops came. Couldn't believe my ma-maw pressed charges. Damn, that wuz cold."

"When you can't trust family…"

"Yeah, that's what I said too…damn."

"How did you end up in a minimum?"

"Hell, what you sayin'? I didn't kill nobody, biggin'. Just cut them up a little."

"Of course, what was I thinking?"

When the men exited the bus in handcuffs, Tom coughed several times, not used to the hot, dry air that parched his throat. Even as he and the other men stood in the shade next to one of the six buildings that made up the prison, the oppressive heat overpowered them.

Inside the building that the new prisoners stood next to, Jon threw dirty laundry into a washer and looked into the prison yard at the new arrivals. One of the men, a tall white guy, looked familiar.

Three days later, Jon entered the cafeteria where he saw the tall man eating alone. He passed him and glanced down at Tom. Tom did not look up. Later the same week he saw Tom in the library reading. Tom noticed Jon, but the men did not speak.

It wasn't until Jon saw Tom on the basketball court and recognized his jump shot that he remembered where he had seen the tall guy before. That night at dinner, with no invitation or introduction, Jon sat down next to Tom and asked, "So, how many points did you score against Harvard at home your sophomore year?"

Not looking up from his meal, Tom didn't miss a beat. "Twenty-one but sat out ten minutes with foul trouble."

CHAPTER 9

AS THE *BRANDENBURG* MOVED STEADILY southwest through small German villages toward France, Rolle stared out the spotless passenger window. He recalled when he first heard of Becker's plan months earlier. His initial response was that the plan was utter folly, created by a group of military barbarians wishing to retire as wealthy men living in South America. Upon further consideration, Rolle realized the plan was also treason of the highest order.

While officially a colonel in the SS, Rolle was never particularly fond of the German military, either as an institution or as an effective tool in getting Germany to where he wanted to see her on the world stage. First of all, he knew it was money that fed the military both literally and figuratively. Without the shrewd planning of men like him, and adequate financial resources, the military would grind to a halt in days. Further, the strutting and pomposity of the generals, who for years guaranteed victory over the Allies, was, in Rolle's opinion, no more than schoolyard boasting. Rolle knew that America's financial resources were, in the long term, the realthreat to Germany, not its military strategy and weaponry. When presented with Operation Rebirth by General Becker, Rolle was, to say the least, more than skeptical.

Rolle saw Becker as a plodding dolt who fancied himself as a short-of-stature Germanic Don Juan. And who, for reasons not consistent with his IQ and known only to himself, always saw himself as the smartest person in every room. Rolle doubted Becker would be the smartest man in a room in which he was alone.

Rolle did not believe Becker had the intellectual horsepower to come up with even the fake general plan he had shared with him. He was simply too stupid. But the uniqueness of the tale Becker had related to Rolle, no matter who designed it, was the audacity of its sheer scale.

Days after that original meeting, Rolle had posed a question to Becker: "Does the Führer support this plan?"

"The Führer has many things on his mind at this time, but his overriding commitment is the perpetuation of his vision. As men dedicated to his vision, we must create strategies that achieve his goals. The Führer does not want to know specific details, only that we are successful."

"And Secretary Bormann, is he supportive?"

"Of course, in fact he personally recommended you given your past work for him."

Rolle realized the unanswered response to his first question was, no, the Führer did not know of this plan, and that Rolle was being lied to. Again. In terms of Bormann's involvement, Rolle was not certain if he would support such a venture or not. But Rolle could not risk going directly to the unpredictable secretary, challenging the chain of command.

Rolle remembered Becker saying, "Operation Rebirth is certainly not without risks Colonel Rolle, but what are we supposed to do? Think what the Soviets and Americans will do if we stand by and do not execute this plan?"

"Why not prolong the war to perhaps increase our chances for fair treatment by the Allies?" Rolle had suggested.

"Operation Rebirth is, in the long term, far more important than a war already lost. We have supporters all over the world who will carry the message of the Führer into future decades. When the time is right, they will resurrect his dreams into reality. These groups need our support for recruitment, training, and weapons."

More lies thought Rolle.

Yet the plan on its surface was not without merit, if in fact, it would create what would become a Fourth Reich in the future. But Rolle had surmised in the first ten minutes of his initial meeting with Becker that this was yet another scheme, albeit on a colossal scale, to help destroy Germany from within by crippling her ability to wage war.

But Rolle also knew his own position was precarious. If Becker suspected his true feelings or Rolle's own already developing options for Operation Rebirth, he knew he would be eliminated immediately. Becker would have no choice. The sheer magnitude of his plan made it clear that only a handful of individuals were involved and at a level just below the Führer.

One of Rolle's options would have been to go directly to the Führer himself, but that assumed Hitler would have been coherent enough to understand what was happening. It was rumored, and in his few meetings with the Führer over the previous several months Rolle had confirmed, that his behavior had changed. He was erratic, paranoid, and trusted no one. He had created an environment of fear around him. His closest aides were afraid to bring him news of Allied victories or report that the questionable battlefield strategies that the Führer had ordered, over the recommendations of his generals, had once again failed. They feared that as the bearers of bad news they would be ordered shot on the spot.

As bad news begat bad news, the Führer had become at times melancholy and almost childlike in his response to the disaster befalling Germany. But those moods were interspersed with periods of violent and terrifying behavior. Like many others, Rolle had been surprised when Hitler ordered the elimination of Field Marshall Rommel and other loyal patriots for even suspected disloyalty.

After the initial meeting with Becker, Rolle realized he had few options and could trust no one. He was on his own to try to save Germany. He also knew that even the slightest miscalculation on his part would mean immediate death.

As the train moved toward France and the setting sun bathed the German countryside in an orange hue, Rolle had set in motion two plans. One he had shown to Becker. A second plan was being assembled in his mind that would truly serve Germany and help her achieve her goals.

He calculated that what rested inside the enclosed cars being pulled by the *Brandenburg* was the only hope for Germany's survival and the only hope for the creation and perpetuation of Hitler's Fourth Reich. A Reich that would be led by those yet unborn into a new millennium. That glorious thought brought a smile of contentment over Rolle's face. But it also raised the all too familiar fear and nagging doubt in his mind. What if he failed? What if the cargo only yards behind him did not make it to the destination?

Rolle rose from his seat and moved to the back of the train. He needed to look at the cargo once more. He needed to be sure.

"Halt!" the taller of two young soldiers said, as Rolle approached the first cargo car.

"Oh, Colonel Rolle, it is you. I'm sorry…"

"Sorry for what? Following orders?"

"No sir, I meant I did not recognize you…and…"

"Do not let anyone enter these cars."

"Sir?" the shorter one asked. "What if a ranking officer wishes to enter?"

"Shoot him… here." Rolle placed his forefinger between the lieutenant's eyes.

"Because if you don't, that is precisely where your comrade here will shoot you."

After he entered the car and shut the door, Rolle knelt to one knee next to a green canvas covered steel pallet that held a wooden box. Untying the ropes, he used a claw hammer to lift one end of the box. As the top gave way under the pressure of the hammer, it squeaked in protest then slowly revealed what Rolle knew was the future of Germany. As the contents came under the glow of his flashlight, tears glistened in his eyes.

CHAPTER 10

ARIZONA MINIMUM SECURITY PRISON—2012

THE MEN SAT ON A PICNIC table adjacent to the prison exercise yard while Tom recounted when he'd first recognized Jon. "I thought you looked familiar after I saw you a few times but wasn't sure from where. After turning state's evidence on the boys in Jersey, I was a little careful who I talked to."

"I saw you your first day here from the laundry window and knew I'd met you before too. Was afraid you might have been an old client. Never thought it was school. Did we know each other back then?" Jon asked.

"I knew you because you paid me big bucks to get you some tests in history when I was a prof's aide."

"That was you? Damn, I hated history."

"Yeah, and I hated math and bought some tests from you." Tom said. Both men laughed at their memories, but soon the conversation became more serious.

"Ever think we'd end up here back in our Tiger days?" Jon asked.

"I thought I was too smart. But once I got hooked up with the Mob Squad, I figured it was just a matter of time before I got nabbed. I was afraid I might get involved in someone getting hurt or even killed. Figured I'd turn myself in and cut my losses. They were bad guys."

After more than a minute of silence, Jon looked around the prison yard and said, "I had an idea I'd end up somewhere like this as soon I got into the money biz. I mean what we were doing was wrong, and once it hit the fan a lot of us went down."

"Any wife or kids?" Tom asked.

"Had kind of a wife once, but no kids, thank God...you?"

"No. Just glad my mom and dad didn't live to see where I ended up. They died when I was still in high school."

"Not close to my parents, never was." Jon said unemotionally. "How many places you been before here?"

"Two. Utah and California."

"This is my third. All were bad."

"How much longer?" Tom asked.

"Three and change if I'm a good boy. How about you?"

"About two and a half."

After more silence, and a challenge in his question, Jon asked, "Ever play chess?"

"No, but I could learn to beat your ass in a week."

Over the next several months, Tom and Jon became inseparable. When they had free time, they'd while it away in the library, workout areas, or just sit and talk, mainly about all the stupid things they'd done to deliver them from an Ivy League campus to an Arizona State prison.

Their conversations would also morph into more esoteric pursuits including sports, women, politics, world events, women in sports, women in politics, and women on CNN.

Beer was also a frequent topic of discussion that would lead to discussions about food and wrap up with what they were going to do their first night out of prison, which included lots of beer, food, sports, and women. Jon also told Tom about a woman he suspected was a true redhead he had once known in New York.

CHAPTER 11

BRANDENBURG TRAIN—1943

THE TWO HUNDRED TONS OF gold that Becker's group wanted to move from Germany had been amassed over a five-year period from various sources: French, Hungarian, Austrian, Dutch and Polish banks; German vaults, as well as thousands of items confiscated from the homes, businesses, and safe deposit boxes of Jews who now waited to die in the ovens or at the hands of firing squads in concentration camps.

What had once been coins, jewelry, or various sized gold bars from throughout Europe had been melted down and recast into twenty-pound, ten inch by three inch by two inch ingots, and stamped with several different identifications including "Property of US Treasury Department," "Property of Australian Government," or "Property of Mexican Government," among others. There were also four steel reinforced wooden barrels that contained miscellaneous pieces of gold that had not yet been melted down.

Under Rolle's personal direction, the bars were stacked cross-hatched on heavy gauge steel pallets with one hundred ingots per pallet, each pallet weighing one ton. The pallets were placed in wooden containers with identifications on the side that falsely indicated the boxes contained various Swiss machine parts. The pallets along with the four barrels were loaded as equally as possible onto eight oversized, steel-reinforced railroad freight cars, each car carrying twenty-five pallets or just over fifty thousand pounds per car. Draped with green tarps, each car carried three armed guards who were ordered to shoot anyone attempting to open the cars without Rolle's personal authorization. This included high-ranking German officers.

Becker had given Rolle total authority over virtually every detail of Operation Rebirth and a virtually unlimited expense account to accomplish his task. All he had to do was adhere to the general plan of getting the gold from Berlin to the initial distribution area. At that point Becker would take over the plan and the responsibility of getting the gold to Nazi supporters around the world who were supposedly waiting for the arrival of the resources needed to begin the task of the global expansion of the Fourth Reich. At least that was the story Becker told Rolle. But Rolle knew that after he completed his part of the plan, he would be considered expendable, and the gold would eventually make its way into the hands of Becker and his cronies.

Twenty-four men had been handpicked to provide the support Rolle would need for the operation. Those men would accompany the gold for the entire trip from Germany to the initial distribution point. The men had been chosen for their size, strength, intelligence, loyalty, multilingual abilities, knowledge of the United States, ability to use weapons, and most importantly, for the fact that they understood they would likely never return to Germany dead or alive.

Managing such a large number of men concerned Rolle, for he feared that he would not be able to control their actions relative to the project. More importantly, he wondered if he would be able to implement his own plan under the day-to-day scrutiny of twenty-four dedicated and heavily armed Becker loyalists.

Trusting no one, Rolle saw to every facet of the operation. The size and strength of the rail cars, the route the train would take from Berlin, the forged passports, foreign country identifications, and the ship that was to take the men and the gold to their initial debarkation point. Fearing someone would learn of his alternative plan, Rolle agonized over every aspect of the project and as a result labored under constant fatigue and often suffocating stress.

As the train slowly gathered speed, Rolle tried to stay awake even though he needed rest badly. But after thirty minutes. the sound of steel wheels on the steel tracks created a soothing background noise, and despite his efforts to stay awake, Rolle drifted off into a vivid dream. He was on a similar train ride with his parents from years before. "Father, I heard a man on the street…"

"You mean the house painter? He's a fool. Don't listen to such trash. He and his scum will make things worse not better. They will ruin Germany if we let them."

A young man in a seat across the aisle from Rolle's father heard his warning to his son. He had a warning of his own. "Herr Professor, I am returning from the Bamberg Conference and heard our leaders describe our glorious and exciting future. You would be wise to keep such derogatory comments to yourself, and not pollute your son's mind with untruths."

Looking across the aisle at the young man, Rolle's father said, "Untruths? Hitler is a buffoon who uses fear and lies to infect the minds of the uneducated and unstable. Thank God our country is too wise to allow such a dolt to rise to meaningful power."

As the train pulled into a stop, the young man rose and glowered down at Rolle's father then hissed a response close to his ear. "There will be a day, and that day is soon, that men like you will learn painful lessons. You will learn, my friend, that such vile as you speak, will not be tolerated."

Rising to face the young man, Rolle's father said, "Then that is a day I hope I shall not live to see."

"As you wish, professor. As you wish."

Less than six months later, sixteen-year-old Kurtis Rolle turned his parents over to the Gestapo for "undermining the efforts of the Reich." On the day his parents were led away, he attended a rally demanding Jews pay higher taxes. On his return home, Rachel silently served Rolle the strudel his mother had baked that morning that was still on the cooling rack. He had his strudel with milk after eating a cold roast beef sandwich and went to bed after he found the uniform his mother had hidden from his father. He was glad to see it had been ironed before she left.

CHAPTER 12

AT SIX FOOT EIGHT AND 250 pounds, with shoulder-length hair he usually wore in a 1970s ponytail, Tom Patrick was a large, powerful, and at times, intimidating physical specimen. He was also a contradiction.

Able to quote Shakespeare, Franklin (Aretha and Ben), John Adams, and Lenny Bruce when appropriate—or even not appropriate, depending on the social setting—he was also extremely valuable to have on your side in a bar fight, which, in Tom's case, was not an infrequent occurrence.

A brilliant student with a double major in English literature and history, Tom not only completed his undergraduate studies at Princeton, but he later returned to campus after a knee injury ruined a promising NBA career and obtained his master's in American history. Of course he did get to keep the $12,000,000 signing bonus he had gotten from the Philadelphia 76'ers...for a while. But after taxes, some unwise investments, his agent's 8%, and three years of serious partying in Manhattan, the money had disappeared. Unfortunately, his desire for partying and dating New York models did not. He always said he just liked having fun and liked tall women, and models happened to be tall.

It also didn't help Tom's net worth that he liked to gamble, an avocation he was not very good at. His problems began when he started gambling with other people's money and lost that as well. That was why he had been approached in a New York City strip joint by four men representing the best interests of two New York bookies who offered him an interesting proposal. He could repay them the $225,000 he owed them, at that very moment, or they would kill him. Or worse, shoot off his dick. Or, he could help them reach many of the East Coast college basketball players he knew in New York's no-nonsense summer leagues and convince them that "point shaving" was an easy way to earn that always hard to find extra spending money. If he would be kind enough to reach out those players, they wouldn't kill him or shoot off his dick.

Tom listened extra hard to the not killing him/keeping his dick option, which made a whole lot more sense than the killing him/shooting off his dick option. After all, he had attended Princeton. Tom decided to give crime a chance.

He proved to be a failure at crime. Within six months of the first few games he tried but failed to fix, he was arrested. Though he cooperated with police in their investigation of organized gambling, he was still sent to prison in California for five years.

At their first meeting, Tom and Jon became friends. It wasn't something they talked about or had to work at…they just became friends, it was easy. They talked about the financial world, history, politics, analyzed various poets, overstated and embellished sexual conquests, even connived ways to be assigned together on various work details.

Their friendship, despite their similar educational backgrounds, was in reality, the coming together of opposites. Jon had always had a plan for his life, goals he wanted to reach even if upon reflection late at night those goals now seemed shallow and childish.

Tom had no goals. His epicurean approach to life was based on both his supreme confidence in his intellectual ability and a firm conviction that having fun today was a way better idea than maybe having fun tomorrow.

Jon and Tom both had Ivy League smarts, but their intellects were in fields the other could respect but not relate to. Yet, they saw things in each other that probably would have been overlooked in the outside world. They each had fully developed, some called bizarre, senses of humor, and they made each other laugh. Both, despite their bravado to others, grew to hate what had become of their lives and how they had wasted some of their best years by being immature, short-sighted, and unappreciative of their gifts and abilities. Each had plans for when they got out of prison, and neither wanted to repeat the mistakes of their past. Yet both men, despite the jokes, were embarrassed by their pasts and afraid of their futures.

The Arizona State Penal Farm (ASPF) outside Phoenix was a minimum-security prison that most of the inmates had "graduated" to by demonstrating in other facilities that they were neither dangerous to themselves or others nor likely to try and escape.

In the prison world, places like ASPF were considered "soft time." That was because inmates, even though they worked six nine-hour days per week, had large amounts of free time for reading in the library, watching TV, working out, playing basketball, or even being allowed to leave the facility on work details.

While Jon had a financial nest egg waiting for him since he had hidden away over $250,000 from the IRS in cash in two Cayman Island banks, his thoughts were of more than money. Bankruptcy, a failed marriage, a fortune earned and lost, eight years in jail, and he wasn't even forty yet. He had been thinking about what had gone wrong with his life. In short, what was wrong with him?

While there were always people who apparently cared about him, he never seemed to be able to keep friends or family close. With his looks and wit, women were also available, but his relationships were vague and shallow. Even when he found his wife on her knees servicing the landscaper, he realized he had only been mildly annoyed by the event. He wondered why he had not felt hurt, betrayal, or even rage. The answer was simple; he never truly loved his wife, or for that matter, anyone else. But why? Was he incapable? So motivated by the urge or need to make money that he was oblivious to anything else? His answers to his own questions did little to allay his fears about the kind of person he had become.

CHAPTER 13

BRANDENBURG TRAIN—1943

AFTER BEING JOLTED AWAKE BY the train as it moved over a rough section of track, Rolle looked out the window as the *Brandenburg* slowed. In the distance, he could see the vague outline of the Eiffel Tower in the "City of Lights" only eight miles away in the fading sunlight.

He rose from his seat and went to the train's forward bathroom, relieved himself, and splashed water on his face. He looked in the mirror, which reflected a weary man whose biggest challenges lay ahead of him. He wondered if he had the strength to carry out his task.

When he moved from the front of the train toward the cars that held the gold, Rolle spoke briefly to two guards who told him the pallets and barrels were not shifting and the reinforced steel girded floorboards were holding up well.

Rolle knew that as long as the train maintained its slow speed, there would be little chance of a pallet tipping over or falling through the floor of the car and sending millions in gold over the German countryside.

Over the previous weeks, Rolle had kept his distance from the guards. First of all, it was his fundamental philosophy to always maintain a strictly professional relationship with subordinates. No idle chatter, no small talk about the weather, or families. There was no time or need for that.

Second, he didn't trust any of them and wondered which one had already been given the responsibility to kill him when he had served his purpose. For that matter, how would they kill him? Gun? Knife? Garrote? Poison? Or would they just throw him off one of the many high bridges they would cross in the next two days? All effective, yet it may be too soon for any.

For the time being Rolle felt a certain security based on the fact he knew he was needed. The further they moved from Germany, the better chance he had to execute his own plan or even escape, if that failed.

As per Rolle's instructions to the engineer of the *Brandenburg*, the train pulled onto a side rail outside of Paris and waited for total darkness. The guards assigned to Operation Rebirth were nervous. They realized the part of their trip that would take them through Paris on the way to the port of Brest in southern France would be the most dangerous. The French Underground had been active the last several weeks, and the men on the day-watch reacted to each movement and sound with raised rifles and tensed jaws. Rolle's orders were clear; if anyone approached the train from any direction, they were to be shot. As daylight waned, the guard's nervousness increased as sound replaced sight as the means of detecting potential enemies, and every bird and cricket caught their attention. The day guards were replaced by the night watch at 8:00 p.m., but Rolle ordered all twenty-four men to remain on duty as they began their trip into Paris.

Expecting the arrival of the gold as per Rolle's plan, Becker had ordered German sentries be posted along the route east of Paris and invoked a 9:00 p.m. curfew throughout the City. But such actions alerted all Parisians that something important was happening, including the French Underground, which was trying to organize some havoc they could unleash on short notice. But unlike other German activities that could be ferreted out via bribe, spy, wiretap, or decoding of messages, whatever was happening that night was a surprise even to Germany's own occupation troops, let alone the French Underground.

The train started to move again from its position at 10:45 p.m. and reached only twenty miles per hour as it headed toward the industrial section of the City eight miles away. From that point, it would turn southeast for the final leg of the trip that would take them to Brest the next day.

Rolle stood in the area between the last two cars of the train and looked out into the darkness. For the first time since Operation Rebirth had been thrust upon him, he began to doubt himself and his plan. He agonized over the possibility that he had overlooked something. A detail so small that he would curse himself for its insignificance as he lay dying from a bullet in the brain, a knife slicing through his throat, or as he was falling from the train to his death. He cursed his own negative thoughts and tried to reassure himself that at least for now, he was neither fool nor patsy, and his famed attention to detail would serve him well when he needed it most.

After he finally regained control of his emotions, he involuntarily jumped when a volley of shots rang out from the left side of the train two cars ahead. Within seconds, hundreds of rounds were being aimed at a clearing thirty to forty yards in front of the moving train. As quickly as the shots began, they ended, and Rolle ran to the platform between the last two cars and looked into the darkness.

As it approached a gentle curve to the left, the train's headlights and the handheld lanterns of the guards focused on the targets of the earlier gunfire. Three young boys and their dogs had been cut to ribbons by the machine gun fire. One dog dying in agony was wailing, his back arched and jaws snapping at air as it flopped and gyrated on the mutilated bodies of the young boys and other dogs. A final burst of gunfire cut the dog in half, and the only sound left was that of the train as it clattered past the small mound of death.

It was not the viciousness of the attack that surprised Rolle; it was clear that no chances could be taken at that point. It was the fact that no one said a word about the boys and their dogs. It was if it had never happened. He was pleased with the professionalism of the troops that had been assigned to him.

The plan to put the train into the Paris station by 11:00 p.m. had worked flawlessly. That gave the crew one hour under the cover of darkness to add fuel, water, food, and leave Paris by midnight to continue their trip to Brest.

Rolle's orders were that no one was to leave the train for any reason except the guards who would bring on supplies. He ordered guards to man each door preventing anyone from entering the train while it was stopped in Paris. This included any nosey SS or Vichy officers.

At 11:54 p.m., the *Brandenburg* departed a deserted Paris train station and began its six-hour journey to the southern coast of France. Rolle moved to his sleeping berth and realized he needed his rest to be able to perform at his peak. He was also comforted that only a few young boys and dogs had died on the trip from Berlin. A small price to pay, he thought, for the chance to save his country.

As he was about to drift off to a comalike sleep, his last cognitive thought was, "It has been a good day."

CHAPTER 14

ARMED WITH BREAKING NEWS, JON interrupted Tom while he read a three-day-old newspaper on a picnic table in the prison yard.

"Guess what?" Jon asked.

"You grew a real dick?"

"Your penis envy is endearing. No, this is better."

"You grew a vagina?" There was hope in Tom's voice.

"Not yet, but I do think my voice is getting higher. No, they want me to be a trustee."

Finally, Tom looked up from the paper and asked, "You're kidding, right? You've been planning an escape every day for five years."

"I love irony. That's how fucked up they are. Good news is as a trustee I can be assigned off-site work details and can select my crew."

"Off-site?"

"Yeah, you know, working in parks, roadwork, picking up trash, that kind of crap."

Returning to the sports section, Tom said, "Wow, you are one lucky bastard."

"There's that jealousy thing again. But I won't hold it against you. In fact, I've already put you on a list along with those two gay accountants to do some road work."

Tom finally put down the paper and said, "Roadwork? In August? Are you fucking nuts? It'll be a 110 out there. Think I'll just stay here and wash more underwear."

"Too late. You're on my list big boy. Come tomorrow we'll be out in the real world."

"Fuck me."

"I'll pass, but you are a very handsome man" Jon said as he smiled and batted his eyes at Tom.

Normally any job that meant the inmates got to leave ASPF, for even a day, was a plum assignment. There were no full-time guards, there was a break in the boring routine, and there would be different scenery. But six days of spraying oil on a dusty road in oven-like temperatures was no day at the beach. Plus, they would be working with two boring, morose, middle-aged bean counters, who had been convicted for various forms of embezzlement and were guests of the state of Arizona for six more years.

For the four years Anderson and Baker had been in prison together, not a day went by that one did not blame the other for the two of them getting caught. While they constantly bickered, it was generally accepted that they were lovers and had probably been so before being arrested at their desks at a large Denver manufacturing firm.

What was weird about Baker and Anderson, and there were lots of weird things, was they looked alike. They were both about five foot six and weighed about 140 pounds. They both wore black-rimmed glasses and had incredibly pale skin. The only real difference was Anderson was bald as a cue ball and Baker had thick brown hair.

Of all the things Tom and Jon hated about prison, and it was indeed a long list, getting up at 5:30 a.m. was near the top. But that day, knowing they faced hours in the hot sun, they were anxious to get to the site and get as much work done as possible before the temperatures soared.

When prisoners worked off site, they would be taken by a van to the location and given the equipment and supplies they needed for their specific jobs. In addition to food and water, they would also be given detailed work orders for the week. In this case, the four men were to spray oil on a twelve-mile section of dirt road—two miles per day—that would then be tarred the following week by another crew.

But the men's secret plan for this assignment was to bust their asses in the cool of morning, get most of the work done, then take a break for lunch and have two of them work for half an hour, while the other two rested.

The four men wanted to be sure they completed their assignment exactly at 4:00 p.m. The last thing they wanted was to have the guard see them resting and the job completed. The next day he might want three miles.

After a thirty-minute drive, the men arrived at the worksite at 7:30 a.m. They unloaded the two sprayers and eight fifty-gallon drums of oil they would be using that week. After thirty minutes of filling the sprayers and making sure they fired, the men were ready to get to work.

Before he left the men and got some hard-earned rest, Jim, a skinny, chain-smoking, sideburned guard, decided to give the men a motivational speech. "You assholes got to get twelve mile of road oiled this week so we can get a paving crew up here next week. If you don't get all twelve done, you'll all be washing shit-stained underwear and dirty socks next week."

Jim's motivational speech elicited a question from Tom. "Mr. Jim, sir, if we get all this work done on time this week, do you think we could get some cold beer next Saturday night? You know like in *Shawshank Redemption*; kind of a reward for our dedication to purpose?"

"What kind of redempt... bullshit you talkin' about, you college asshole?"

"You know Morgan Freeman and... oh, never mind," Tom said.

"You know, you're a smartass, Patrick. By the way, asshole, how come you got two first names; Tom Patrick."

"I was cursed. But it gets worse; my middle name is Michael.

For a moment, it appeared that Jim the guard actually had a sympathetic look on his face at the cruelty Tom endured. Then Jim recovered. "If you want a fuckin' beer or maybe some good old-fashioned inmate love on Saturday night, I'll bet one of those CPEs next to you will take care of you."

"You mean CPAs?" Tom asked helpfully.

"Don't fuck with me, you big asshole. Now get to work all of you. I'll be showin' up from time to time and if I catch any of you not workin', y'all get sent back to the jailhouse. And you, Jon Boy, since you're in charge, it'll be your ass if these boys fuck up."

Offering to help, Jon said, "If you leave me a shotgun, I'll shoot one just to set an example."

Seriously mulling over the suggestion, Jim said, "Naw, you better not."

Just before he left, Tom asked, "Hey Jim, wouldn't it make more sense to drive us up the hill twelve miles and let us work down, rather than hauling all this stuff uphill for six days?"

Taking several seconds to let comprehension set in, Jim answered. "Yeah, I guess that would make it easier, now wouldn't it." Jim laughed, entered the air-conditioned van, rolled down his window, and told the men, "Hey assholes, you better be workin' your dicks off when I get back." Showing a nearly toothless grin to the men, Jim drove off in a cloud of dust and headed to Elsa's, his favorite greasy spoon seven miles down the road.

"What an asshole," Jon said.

"Do you think anything but an asshole would be a guard in the first place?" Tom asked.

"All I know is, I wouldn't even be here if you weren't such a greedy bastard," Baker said as he pointed the nozzle of his sprayer at Anderson.

"That's bullshit. You were the one who…"

Before Anderson could finish, Tom interrupted and said, "Guys, we've heard all this crap a hundred times before; why not just keep quiet about it?"

"We can talk about anything we want. Besides I've been a trustee longer than Jon, and I should actually be in charge here, you know." Baker said, a certain amount of indignation emanating from what was an annoying voice in even the best of times. This was not the best of times.

For several seconds after Baker's admonition of Tom, there was silence among the men. Baker looked at Tom and did not like what he saw. Holding the shovel which looked like a pencil in his hand, Tom fixed a baleful glare at Baker that made the gay embezzler's stomach turn.

Attempting to hold his verbal ground, Baker rasped, "You don't scare me, you know."

Tom said nothing, yet never moved his stare from Baker.

"He doesn't scare me," Baker repeated, as he looked at Anderson and Jon, his voice at least an octave higher.

Tom remained silent as he continued to rivet his gaze on Baker.

As Tom stared, Baker seemed to visibly shrink in size. Sensing trouble, and perhaps some serious bodily injury afoot, Jon moved slowly over to Baker's side and spoke into Baker's ear just loud enough for the other two men to hear. "Baker, there are some things you should know. Now. The big guy there, he wasn't just involved in point shaving. For three years he was a hit man for the Mafia and he's killed like a hundred people, some just innocent little kids. Real cute kids too. I've seen him lose it before, and it can get real ugly real fast. It's up to you since you're a trustee and all, but I would NOT piss him off. I mean at the very least he could hospitalize you with some serious internal or spinal cord injuries. Hell, he might even kill us all and run off to Mexico. I mean look at the guy, he's a fucking lunatic in some kind of prehistoric monster's body."

Peering over Jon's shoulder with one eye, Baker was not pleased to see the same malevolent look on Tom's face that had been there moments before. If anything, his now curled lip made him look even more frightening. "Well, you know if you let a bully like him think you're scared of him, he'll just keep picking on you," Baker said with little conviction.

Putting his arm around Baker's shoulder, Jon continued his counsel. "Baker, Baker, Baker, for the love of God, we're not talking about some schoolyard bully who might give you a bloody nose. This is a guy capable of pulling out your spleen with one hand and shoving it down your throat with the other. This guy kills for fun, so I don't want to see what he does when he's mad."

Taking his eyes off Tom and looking at Jon, Baker whispered, "If he killed all those people, what's he doing here?"

"The judge was too afraid of him to give him hard time. Besides, Tom there, claimed self-defense."

"Self-defense!? A hundred people…and those cute kids!?" Baker rasped.

"I know, I know, but you understand how lenient the criminal justice system is these days. I just hope if he does do something to you, you know, like beat you to death with a shovel, he is severely and appropriately punished for it. I guess that's all we can hope for."

Having heard most of the conversation, Eugene Anderson sidled over to Jon and Baker. "He's right, Raymond. The man is clearly demented and looking for any excuse to kill us all. Don't agitate him, for God's sake. Apologize to him right now!"

"Apologize for what? I didn't do anything!" Baker's whisper was now approaching a shout.

"I don't give a damn; make something up." Anderson said. "Your foolish pride is not worth all of us being cut up into pieces and scattered over the desert."

"Oh, you heard about that family of six over in Nevada huh?" Jon asked.

After Baker's sincere, albeit coerced apology, there were no further discussions as to why Baker and Anderson were in ASPF.

"'Fucking lunatic in a prehistoric monster's body?' That was a bit harsh wasn't it?" Tom inquired as he and Jon began raking the road.

"I was just thinking of you, big boy, and how those guys annoy you. Geez, don't be so sensitive; I was just trying to help."

CHAPTER 15

PARIS—1943

ROLLE HAD GIVEN THE ORDER before the trip from Berlin to Brest that the *Brandenburg* would not use its high-pitched steam whistle at any time on the journey. So he was still asleep when the train's lack of movement awoke him at 6:20 the next morning.

Rolle's long and deep sleep did not dull his senses. As soon as he realized the train had stopped, he rose, showered, shaved, dressed, ate a light breakfast, walked off the train, and headed for the port all within thirty minutes. Bright sunshine and a cool gentle breeze, coupled with the rest that Rolle had gotten the night before, gave him a feeling of near euphoria as he strode toward the German steamship that would be taking the wealth of Germany to a place Rolle had only read about in travel magazines. His plan was working.

The *Heidelberg* was a workhorse of the German Navy. Troops, trucks, ammunition, grain, and timber had sat on her wide decks for twelve years since her christening in 1931. Over one hundred-twenty feet in length, she made up in brute strength and seaworthiness what she lacked in beauty. Powered by four-3000 horsepower twin screw diesels, she could make eighteen knots with a full load in heavy seas. Even the load she would now take on was only a fraction of what she could carry if asked to.

The two hundred pallets were taken off the rail cars and transferred to the Heidelberg in less than four hours using two cranes and twelve crewmen. The remaining twelve stayed riveted to their posts scanning the empty dock for intruders.

By 12:15 p.m., the Heidelberg had its cargo secured under its decks and its engines murmured smoothly, ready for the journey across the Atlantic.

After having cast off one line, the process was halted by the emergence of a speeding car that approached the port gates nearly fifty yards away. Only the swastika markings on the vehicle made Rolle hesitate. He halted the ship's departure.

He signaled for two of his men to go to the gate to determine who was in the car, and what they wanted. Before the men could act on his orders, the two-and-a-half ton Mercedes crashed through the gate and tore toward the waiting ship.

Rolle did not have to tell his remaining men on the ship to be ready for anything. They had already positioned themselves to be out of sight yet have clear shots at whoever was in the highly polished Benz.

The car skidded to a stop only ten feet from the now retracted gangway. At first no one exited the car, and with its tinted glass, coupled with the shadow the boat cast on the sedan, the occupants of the Mercedes remained unseen. Finally, the right rear door opened, and a German officer unfolded from the sedan.

Peering down from the first deck of the ship, Rolle didn't like the looks of General Hans Elman.

Elman walked slowly to the front of the ship, slightly ahead of its wheelhouse, but said nothing. Instead, he looked up and down the port side of the seemingly deserted ship with its engines running and wondered what the hell was going on. He started to walk toward the aft of the ship but stopped in his tracks when he heard Rolle's voice.

"General, can I help you?"

"And who are you?"

"I am Colonel Kurtis Rolle, Director, Financial Operations, Berlin."

"Colonel, is it safe to assume that you arrived in our city by train early this morning?" "Yes, General, but I am working on a top-secret project and… "

Elman interrupted, "Is it also safe to assume you came through Paris last night on your way to Brest?"

"I must repeat myself, General, I am on a top-secret mission. If you have any further questions, I suggest you contact General Becker in Berlin."

"I know Becker and where he's located," hissed Elman. "But I have a problem." As the general spoke, two muscular sergeants carrying machine guns exited the Mercedes and moved slowly toward midship. They positioned themselves next to Elman.

"My problem, Colonel, is I have French authorities screaming at me about the deaths of three young French boys who were playing near the railroad tracks last evening. They claim they were gunned down by German soldiers from a passing train. Would you know anything about that incident, Colonel?"

Without a second's hesitation, Rolle responded, "Yes, General, I do. It was an unfortunate yet unavoidable circumstance. I regret my men may have overreacted to what they thought could have been an attack from the French underground that would have put our mission at risk."

"Sir, to say your men overreacted is an understatement of incredible proportions. Those boys and their dogs were chopped to pieces. Did your men truly believe they were under attack by two ten-year-olds, an eight-year-old, and three dogs? Or was this simply target practice and the murder of children?"

"General, I am sorry for the incident, but it was my understanding that a curfew was in place last night, and those boys should have been in their homes rather than out where they should not have been. Where were their parents?"

"Their parents are dead. Those boys lived in the orphanage just yards from where they were gunned down." The general's voice was harsh as he moved toward the port side railing and glared at Rolle.

"As I said, General, it was an unfortunate incident, yet if the French Underground was under control rather than being allowed to reign terror on German troops, my men would not have been put in position of defending our operation in such a manner."

General Elman's face turned crimson with rage as he moved closer to the railing of the ship and through clenched teeth said, "You and Becker and your soft desk jobs, what do you know of real soldiers? What do you know of what we face every day with the French? You arrogant bastards with your reckless murderous actions, you not only killed children, you have killed maybe fifty German soldiers who will now be gunned down by French snipers seeking revenge for those boys."

"General, I have given my apologies and condolences, there is nothing more I can say, except, that this ship is now five minutes late in departing and we must now cast off."

"Colonel, if you are a colonel, I must check your credentials. I insist you lower the gangway and allow me and my men to search this vessel."

"I am sorry, General, my orders are to depart at this time, and we will depart."

"Sergeants!" barked Elman, and the two armed men took aim at Rolle. "If the colonel does not lower the gangway in thirty seconds, shoot him." For fifteen seconds there was silence as the two officers stared at each other. Then in less than two seconds the general and his aides virtually disappeared, their bodies shredded by high-powered machine gun fire. Startled by the attack, Rolle had not been aware that his men had taken aim at the three men on the dock immediately on their arrival. Nor was he aware that no matter what the general had said or his purpose for being on the dock, the three men in the black Mercedes were going to be eliminated.

While the sounds of the machine gun fire echoed off nearby warehouse walls, four of Rolle's men leapt onto the deck using ropes thrown over the port side of the *Heidelberg,* and threw the three bodies into the water. The men next moved toward the Mercedes, but as they approached the car, it was thrown into reverse by its skilled driver who, after twenty yards, put the car into a 180-degree spin that allowed it to change its north/south course in less than a second.

After completing the reverse of direction, the driver slammed the car back into first gear, stomped the accelerator, popped the clutch, and the Mercedes stormed for the gate through which it had entered the port area minutes before. Blue smoke from its spinning rear tires powered by the 550 horsepower V-12 engine put up an inadvertent smoke screen that partially hid the Mercedes from Rolle's men. Undeterred, the guards opened fire at the roaring sedan, but its bulletproof body threw off the bullets like water off one of its black waxed fenders during a rainstorm.

Now kneeling, the men aimed at the car's tires and successfully hit the left front tire exploding the rubber and the blood-red spoke wheel. Seeming to ignore its wounds, the 5,000-pound behemoth continued its screeching escape toward the gate with sparks and smoke coming from the left front axle as it scraped the concrete.

From the port side of the ship, a launcher lobbed a grenade at the stricken Mercedes. While missing a direct hit, the grenade sent shrapnel and concrete smashing into the left side of the speeding car. For several moments it appeared the concussion from the explosion were going to overturn the vehicle as it rose precariously on its two right wheels. But instead, its left rear wheel and what remained of its left front axle, slammed back into the pavement. The shuddering yet still powerful V-12 found its balance and with the two rear wheels continuing to burn rubber, the shiny black Mercedes, with its red, black, and white Nazi flags on each fender flapping in the wind, sped out of port and into the Brest downtown area.

As the cacophony of the Mercedes disappeared, the four shooters, without any signal, and as one, ran for the ropes and within seconds had reboarded the ship.

Rolle, still hearing the reverberations from the bullets and grenade, was immediately struck by three thoughts: One, the men he was commanding were trained killers who needed little or no commanding when it came to protecting their cargo. Two, Germany trained its drivers very well, and three, German automotive engineering was still the best in the world.

CHAPTER 16

PRISON VAN—2012

AFTER FIVE FULL DAYS OF WORKING in the Arizona summer sun, the four men were exhausted. The trip back to the prison on Friday afternoon was depressing because they knew they still had one more day of oiling the road.

The two embezzlers were already asleep in the back of the van while Tom and Jon sat several rows behind Jim the Asshole, who was singing along with Merle Haggard on the All-Country/All-Classic radio station.

"I told you this would be a miserable week, Mr. Genius," Tom said.

"Never thought I'd miss dirty underwear," Jon mumbled.

"Next time, remember, I know everything."

"Yeah, except how to beat a six-point spread."

"Okay, I fucked up...once."

"I got an idea," Jon opined. "Why don't we tell old Jim up there that he's an asshole and we got pictures of his wife, naked. You think that might get us enough demerits to get to work in the laundry again?"

"First of all, it's stipulated Jim is an asshole by the Asshole Hall of Fame, and the very thought of what Jim's wife looks like naked is depressing as hell."

That night the four road warriors skipped TV and slept for ten hours.

Saturday was unusually cloudy for Arizona in the summer. The actual possibility of rain raised the men's spirits as they headed back to their now ten-mile oiled road. "Hey Jim, what happens if it rains, and we're stuck up on this hill?" Baker asked.

"You get wet, asshole. But no matter what, you got two more miles to get done, so get after it."

Fueled by Jim's encouragement, the men silently began the now routine tasks of unloading their equipment and beginning their exhausting work. After fifteen minutes of disinterested watching, Jim yawned, farted, belched, reentered his van, and headed back to Elsa's. Another workday done.

After Jim disappeared around the bend, Tom suddenly dropped his rake and headed for a shaded rock ledge. He took two of the towels the men had brought to wipe their sweat during the day, rolled them into a pillow, laid down, and appeared to go to sleep.

"Mr. Patrick, if I may be so bold, what the hell are you doing?" Jon asked, being bold.

"We're done."

"What are you talking about?"

"I said we're done, relax, take a load off."

Anderson and Baker looked at Tom and wondered if the heat had fried his brains, but they let Jon do the talking since they had not forgotten about the chopped-up family from Nevada and all those cute dead kids.

"Have you lost it? This is a shit job, but I don't want to end up cleaning four hundred pairs of dirty socks and no TV for the next month," Jon said.

"You've not been paying attention for the last few days have you, my learned Tiger friend from Ohio?"

"What do you mean?" Jon asked.

"I mean, you don't pay attention. You just keep your head down and rake like a bastard until someone tells you to stop. You also did not pay attention when Jim said he was going to make sure we did two miles a day, including today, and if we didn't do twelve miles by today. we're screwed."

"So?"

"Well, he's been too lazy to check out what we've done so far or too stupid to read the odometer. I'll go with stupid. But when he checks us out tonight, he'll find that we already did our twelve miles."

"No, we didn't; we've only done ten." Jon said, confidently multiplying two miles times five days.

"Nope, we've done twelve, and thus, our work is officially completed. As a result, I don't know about you guys, but I'm going to take a nice long nap, have a little lunch, maybe take a walk, and then a longer nap."

"How do you know you're right?" Anderson asked, risking mutilation.

"There are broken white mile markers that I noticed coming up the hill in the van Monday. I found them after we started working and decided to take a chance that Jim wouldn't pay attention to our mileage. So I decided we'd just keep working a little longer each day. You guys were oblivious, so the fact is we oiled about two and a half miles each day, not two miles. As a result, we're done, and we now have a paid vacation day."

"You're sure?" Jon asked.

"I'm sure."

The rest of the day some of the men relaxed. The overcast was refreshing, and for the first time in years, Jon and Tom felt almost free. No guards, no work, no fences, and eight hours of unfettered time to do anything they wanted. The problem was there wasn't a hell of lot to do.

"I'm bored," Jon said after ten minutes of looking at the desert.

"Bored? For God's sake, why don't you relax, kick back and rest," Tom said.

"Because I can't, because I'm bored."

"Well, I'm still tired and I'm going to sleep, so keep quiet in your boredom, and let me get some beauty rest."

"Unless you intend to sleep for thirty or forty years, it won't do much good. Come on, let's take a hike."

Without opening his eyes, Tom said, "You must be on speed or something. Can't you ever sit still? Besides, if Jim comes back too soon, he'll think we ran off and come after us with dogs and rifles."

"We can see down the road for miles, and if he comes, we can tell Frick and Frack there to warn us and say we're taking a crap or something."

"Okay," Tom said in a tone that indicated he knew he had no choice.

After telling the odd couple their plan, Jon and Tom went on a picnic/hike, just like they were free men.

Taking their lunch and water, they decided to go only a few hundred yards from their current position and take a circle route in case Jim came back. That way they'd be no more than a few minutes from the spot they left Baker and Anderson.

With towels wrapped around their heads that made them look like Arabs searching for an oasis, the men walked aimlessly in the desert. For the first time in five days, both men actually looked at where they were. The desert's beauty was vast, stark, and majestic. The rolling clouds cooled the air and transformed the desert into an ever changing pallet of muted tans, grays, pinks, and purples.

They followed a dried-up creek bed that no doubt flooded during the winter rains, and it meandered in a general circular path that kept the men in the direction they wanted. They felt like schoolboys playing hooky. For several hours, they laughed, drank their water, ate their lunches, and talked about nothing.

"We better start back" Jon said, "It's almost three."

"Yeah, Jimmy boy is probably ready to get back from a five-hour lunch, but I can see the road from here and we could make it back in ten minutes if we have to. Besides I have to take a piss."

Standing on a small outcropping of rock, Tom began to empty a rather impressive bladder into the creek bed. After what seemed like five minutes, he suddenly called to Jon. "Hey, look at this."

"No thanks, I've seen one before, only bigger."

"No, seriously, come here, I've found something."

CHAPTER 17

ATLANTIC OCEAN—1943

AFTER MONTHS OF RELENTLESS STRESS, the ten-day trip across the Atlantic was a welcome respite for Rolle. Yet, after seeing the performance of his men on the train tracks near Paris and the dock in Brest, it was clear that they had been given orders by someone else as it related to Operation Rebirth. He concluded his so-called leadership over the group was a sham; and sooner or later, he would be eliminated since his role as plan architect would no longer be needed.

It was obvious to Rolle the twenty-four men assigned to him had vital roles in all phases of the execution of Becker's plan, starting in Berlin and going all the way to the preliminary distribution point. After they reached that distribution point, the next step in Becker's faux plan was to have the gold trucked or flown to Canada, Mexico, Central America, Bolivia, and Argentina. That was not Rolle's plan.

While the possibility of discovery and capture by British and American navies was a genuine threat as they crossed the North Atlantic, Rolle was equally concerned about the *Heidelberg* being sunk by German U-boats, especially since the incidents outside Paris and on the Brest dock. At the same time, he assumed that there must have been some high- ranking officials of the occupation army in France who were part of Operation Rebirth, and it would be in their financial best interests to make sure the slow-moving ship reached her destination safely.

The plan Rolle had prepared for Becker, and the one he had created in his mind, were on parallel courses, and they would remain so for the next two weeks. But as each day went by Rolle wondered when he would be viewed as no longer needed and eliminated. What he needed was time. If he were able to reach the distribution point, he might have a chance.

The trip across the Atlantic was gratefully uneventful, but Rolle noticed no diminution in the readiness or focus of his twenty-four men. Along with a crew of ten, who knew nothing of their cargo or of the mission, and in Rolle's opinion, would also be murdered after serving their purpose, thirty-five men crossed the Atlantic in virtual silence.

At the end of the ninth day, the *Heidelberg*, exactly on schedule as per Rolle's plan, dropped anchor six miles east of the first stop on her voyage. For over three hours she bobbed in gentle swells and waited for darkness.

Rolle took advantage of the time to address his men when they gathered in the ship's mess hall. "Since we left Berlin nearly two weeks ago, you have been operating on day-to-day orders. I have purposely kept our long-term plans, including our preliminary and final destinations from you, until I was sure you were capable of executing your orders. All of you passed that test."

Rolle could see the pleased response from his men, who sat on tables and chairs and paid rapt attention to his every word.

"Each of you has been told of the vital importance of this assignment and the likelihood that none of you will ever return to Germany. You have also been told that many of you may die carrying out your orders. All of you accepted those risks to bravely serve the Fatherland. Now you will know the rest of the assignment. What you loaded onto this ship is German gold. This gold will be used to perpetuate the vision of your Führer decades into the future. To accomplish this goal, you men will be taking this gold to a place near Phoenix, Arizona, in the United States of America."

A collective gasp rose from the men, with one saying, "I knew it."

"Our first stop will be the city of Philadelphia where you will begin your trips by truck to Arizona. You will be divided into two-man crews, and each will take different routes then reassemble a week from today near Phoenix. I strongly suggest you spend the next several hours studying the maps that you will be given after this meeting.

Rolle went on to provide the men the details of their mission including a warning. "Greed and avarice are part of every man. You must fight such temptation. Do not trust the man next to you. If you feel he is weakening, kill him. If any of you do not reach the destination it will be assumed that you have stolen the gold in your charge. In such cases you will be tracked down by our supporters in this country and executed as traitors. Your families back in Germany will also be shot for your weakness."

A young corporal in the back of the room had a question. "Colonel, our loyalty to the Führer is sacred. But what would happen to our families if circumstances beyond our control prevent us from reaching Phoenix?"

"Each member of your family will be killed, Corporal. In your case, that means all six, including your youngest sister, Marta. I would therefore strongly suggest you reach your destination at the predetermined time."

A silence descended over the dining room as Rolle's words hung in the air like a thick fog. Before he turned and left, Rolle had a parting message: "Gentlemen, I wish you all safe and pleasant travels to the desert."

Two hours later, Rolle nervously paced the boat's deck, his face reflecting his concern. He felt his plan was vulnerable during the wait for the small boats that would begin off-loading the gold. As he waited, he looked from horizon to horizon, fearing that every smokestack he saw was a United States Coast Guard Cutter or naval vessel that would put an end to his plan before it really began.

Even though his men had changed the ship's flag from the tri-colored German flag to the red and white of Switzerland, removed the name plate from the *Heidelberg* and replaced it with the *Geneva*, Rolle was worried. He knew even his twenty-four well trained killers were no match for a curious American naval captain on a destroyer with several ten-inch guns that could sink the *Geneva* from five miles away if he refused a search party. Yet all remained quiet, and the plan entered its most complicated and dangerous segment.

At shortly before 10:00 p.m., on a warm night in September 1943, Germany began its invasion of the United States of America. However, this invasion, unlike the one that would take place nine months later on the beaches of France, would not be made with bombs or machine guns, nor would thousands of German soldiers descend on American shores. Instead, this invasion would be made with stealth, with the help of some of her own flag-waving citizens and by utilizing large sums of counterfeit American currency. Further, this was an invasion that would never be reported since no one except the invaders knew it had occurred.

The American fishermen who would off-load the gold and take it to the Philadelphia shipping dock were well aware they were going to be hauling some kind of contraband off the *Geneva*, as many had done for years as far back as Prohibition. Then they were known as "rum runners"; they would anchor off the coast and act as deliverymen for100 proof scotch made in Canada or 120 proof rum from Cuba. Some had even hauled illegal immigrants over the years, so a load involving this many of their piers was not all that unusual. All that was required was to pay off a few dock men, larger amounts to the harbor master and union head, all of whom would make sure the docks were empty when the boats returned with their cargo.

The bigger problem was contending with the Coast Guard or Navy boats that patrolled the coastal waters. However, there were holes in their assigned responsibilities. The Navy usually stayed ten miles out from the coast, while the Coast Guard focused on an area within three to five miles of the shoreline leaving a relatively unpatrolled area six to eight miles from shore. Local fishermen were also known to fish at night so their presence after the sun went down was not unusual. The fishermen saw Coast Guard boats almost every day and were seldom stopped. In many cases they had even gotten to know many of the captains and crew and waved as their boats passed.

Finally, after what seemed to be an interminable wait to Rolle, a diverse group of fishing boats and other craft could be seen queuing up in the distance and began to arrive in thirty-minute intervals. The boats pulled up next to the *Geneva,* and pallets encased in wood were lowered by crane one at a time onto the decks of small but powerful tugs, large fishing trawlers, and everything in between. In some cases Rolle feared that the smaller boats would sink under the weight of the gold. They didn't.

As the loading process wore on, Rolle continued to walk the decks of the *Geneva* and was overtaken by the reality of what he had put in motion. The theoretical penning of his plan on paper to its actual successful execution was quite different and exhilarating to Rolle. Perhaps General Elman had been correct. Too much time behind a desk can weaken a man and make him forget that the realities of actually executing a plan, compared to simply drawing one up on paper, were entirely different.

As the last fishing boat approached the *Geneva,* Rolle gathered his few items of clothing into his duffel bag, and made his way to the starboard side of the ship and awaited his transfer onto the deck of the *Lady Luck*. As usual, the placement of the pallet loaded with the gold was set on her deck and covered by a tarp and then part of that day's catch.

Thousands of cod, sea bass, and snapper enveloped the now hidden cargo and left no room for anyone on her slippery lower deck. Upon being lowered onto the aft section of the boat, Rolle nearly wretched at the smell of the remnants of years of rotting fish, diesel fuel exhausts, and the cheap cigar of the *Lady Luck's* captain Nick Zavakos.

On the ninety-minute circuitous voyage to Philadelphia, Rolle vomited almost the entire trip. His only solace was in seeing two of his men who accompanied each of the fishing boats to Philadelphia also throwing up, although they never once dropped their machine guns. Warned to ask no questions, Captain Nick said nothing as he ate raw oysters, drank warm beer, and stared at his three green-faced passengers throwing up until only bile and dry heaves were left. His toothless smile showed little sympathy.

As he gazed at the approaching Philadelphia skyline, Rolle began mentally preparing for the next part of his plan, which included the gold being out of his sight for seven days. That prospect depressed him. It also set the stage for his immediate elimination and the absconding of the gold by his men. It would be easy for his plan to now be terminated and for the gold to disappear to parts unknown with his men, who according to Rolle's plan, were supposed to truck the gold across the United States to the final distribution point.

As quietly and efficiently as the gold had been transferred from the *Geneva* to the fishing ships, it was likewise transferred from the boats onto twelve specially designed, steel-reinforced, duel-axle panel trucks, capable of hauling up to twenty-five tons each. Each steel truck door was locked with two heavy-duty bolt locks. One set of the lock keys was given to Rolle. The other held by the drivers.

Each truck carried approximately 33,000 pounds of gold comprising of at least sixteen pallets holding up to 1700 twenty-pound ingots. Several of the trucks also carried barrels of gold that had not yet been melted down into ingots. The bills of lading signed by the dockmaster described two hundred tons of Swiss machine parts that were headed for military factories in North Philadelphia, Atlanta, Chicago, Milwaukee, Denver, and other cities.

While the dockmaster and union head did not bother to open the backs of the trucks and check to confirm the contents, they did take a full five minutes to count the fifty 100-dollar bills given to each of them by Rolle's men. When finished, they nodded, and the trucks carrying Germany's future moved onto Delaware Avenue and began their respective trips west.

The plan sent the twelve trucks on separate circuitous routes from Philadelphia to a small town just outside Phoenix. Using rural back roads to avoid weigh stations and police, each truck was to take seven days to reach the rendezvous point. Each of Rolle's men were given fake I.D.'s, New York State driver's licenses, and four hundred dollars in meal and motel money, although one guard would spend each night in the back of the truck with a loaded machine gun in the motel parking lot.

At the end of each evening, the guards were to call a phone number that was different each night and report their progress and any problems. Failure to call would be interpreted as a total failure of their assignment and the assumption they had been apprehended or were stealing the gold. An immediate search would be undertaken by German sympathizers, and the men would be hunted down and killed along with their families back in Germany.

While Rolle had been concerned about such a possibility upon leaving Berlin, seeing his men perform over the previous weeks, he was convinced they would arrive on time at the distribution point, and gladly kill anyone who tried to stop them.

After he watched the last of the twelve trucks rumble onto the rutted pavement of Delaware Avenue, Rolle stood in the dark emptiness of the dock area and suddenly realized he had nowhere to go and no way to get there. Carrying his suitcase, he headed for the only light he could see, about a half mile into the distance. His salvation was Pat's Diner, an all-night establishment that catered to the dockworkers and truck drivers in and around South Philadelphia.

"What'll you be havin' tonight, darlin'?" a friendly voice asked.

When Rolle looked up from the greasy menu, he saw a surprisingly attractive blonde woman in her late thirties dressed in a blue and white checked uniform. The name "Linda" was written on a name tag.

"Coffee and eggs, please."

"Toast?"

"Rye, please."

"Well, it's sure nice to have a gentleman in here instead of the rest of you bums," Linda said as she looked around the smoke-filled diner, and the group of large men in jeans and denim jackets.

Rolle smiled and asked, "Linda, could you tell me where I could find a taxi around here?"

"Oh Lord, it's kinda late and I doubt they'll be any cabs until morning. We could try and call one but they don't like comin' down here this late at night. Lots of robbin', you know. Where you headin'?"

"To your train station. I want to catch a train to Cleveland."

"Cleveland?! Well honey, there won't be any trains leaving here till mornin' even if you could get to the station."

"That is unfortunate. Is there a hotel nearby?"

"Not too far, but all the rooms is booked with soldiers. Looks like you ain't having no luck at all tonight darlin,'" Linda said with a smile.

Rolle smiled back.

Later in Linda's room, she lay on Rolle's shoulder with her eyes closed. Rolle remained awake and stared at the ceiling. He toyed with her blonde hair. Linda opened her eyes and looked up at Rolle. "Ain't you tired? I mean I thought I wore you out."

"I fear if I fall asleep, I will miss my train in the morning."

"I love to hear you talk. Where's that accent from?" Linda asked.

"I'm from Sweden, although I thought I'd lost my accent years ago."

"It ain't much of one, but I got a good ear. Hey, I don't work tomorrow, why don't you stay over another day and I'll show you 'round town and we can have some more fun tomorrow night."

"I'd very much enjoy that, but I must leave tomorrow to attend to business."

"Well then, I guess I need to make sure you don't forget me."

Linda smiled, and slid under the covers. After several minutes, Rolle moaned, closed his eyes, and fell into a deathlike slumber.

The next morning Rolle stirred in bed. He opened his eyes not knowing where he was. He suddenly bolted up in bed and looked at his watch. He began to put on his clothes when Linda entered the room.

"There you are, sweetie," Linda said with a smile.

"Why did you let me sleep?"

"Well, I figured you needed the rest, darlin,' especially after you used up all that energy last night."

"My train…"

"Don't worry, I called the station and there's a train to Cleveland at 1:30, you got plenty of time. You go get a shower, there's a clean towel on the door, and I'll have your breakfast ready for you in a few minutes."

After a long hot shower, Rolle dressed and entered the kitchen just in time to see Linda dishing out eggs, scrapple, and biscuits. Hearing Rolle enter the room, Linda said cheerfully, "Morning, Kurtis."

Stopped in his tracks, Rolle asked, "How do you know my name?"

"When I picked up your pants to wash them, your wallet fell on the floor and some cards fell out and I saw your name. You really livin' in Berlin? I thought people were tryin' to get away from that crazy Hitler guy? By the way, you can count your money; I never took any. Last night was for free. You want some coffee?"

"Yes, thank you." Rolle sat down at the kitchen table shaken by what he had just heard.

"I have some friends who just got out of Germany, and they said it was crazy over there," Linda said as she sat down and watched Rolle eat his breakfast.

"I do work for the Swedish government but travel frequently."

"What kind of work do you do?"

"Accounting."

"Well, you finish your breakfast and I'll start washing these dishes so we can say goodbye the right way."

Linda moved to the sink, turned her back to Rolle, and began filling it with water. She did not at first hear Rolle come up behind her and was a bit startled when she felt his hands on her shoulders. He then moved his hands to her breasts. Linda moaned and leaned back into Rolle. When she did, Rolle bent down and kissed her neck. Linda's moan deepened. Rolle moved his hands up toward Linda's neck.

"Mmm, that feels real good, Kurtis, but we're gonna have to wait for a few minutes. My boss Billy will be droppin' off my check any minute since I won't be workin' today. Once he leaves, we can play some more. That okay?"

Rolle dropped his hands from Linda's neck and returned to the kitchen table. Linda rejoined him at the table and stared across at him. "Sure glad you stopped in the diner last night. Also glad all those hotels was sold out. At least I think they were sold out," Linda said with a smile. "Think you'll be back this way anytime soon?"

"I am quite certain I will, and if so, I would like to partake of your hospitality when I return."

"I just love to hear you talk. Sure, anytime you're in town you just call or hell, just stop in…anytime. I put my phone number in your wallet as a helpful reminder."

"Thank you. I promise I will return."

"You know, I got a two-week vacation saved up, but I don't guess you'd want a travlin' companion, I mean I like Cleveland…"

"I'm sorry, my business would not allow me…"

A bit embarrassed by the turndown, Linda said, "No problem. I understand."

A knock at her front door helped break the uneasiness in the air. "Must be Billy," Linda said. She opened the door, and her boss entered the kitchen. "Hey Billy, thanks for bringin' my check over. This is my friend Kurtis; he's from Sweden but works in Germany."

Billy was a short, compact man with a thick neck and powerful arms that were gilded with tattoos, some obscene.

"Hey Kurtis. I'm Billy, how the hell are you?"

"Hello, Billy."

"So you just passin' through or are you here to stay?"

"Just passing through although I will return very soon."

"You work in Germany, huh?"

"Only temporarily, I am an accountant."

Billy stared at Rolle for several seconds.

"Swedish, huh?"

"Yes, Swedish," Rolle said. "Well, I must be going, I want to make it to the train station on time."

"If you walk down to the diner, you can grab a cab there. I'll wait for you and we can walk down together," Billy said helpfully.

"That won't be necessary; I can…"

"No problem, just take your time and we can get acquainted on our walk."

"Very well. Let me get my things."

After Rolle returned to the bedroom to get his suitcase, Linda sneered at her boss. "Billy, I wanted to say goodbye to him…you know."

"I don't like that sonovabitch. You don't even know him. What if he's a pre-vert or something?"

When Rolle returned with his bag, he agreed with Billy. "Your friend is right, Linda; you can't be too careful these days with strangers." Rolle then drove his switchblade into Billy's heart four times, killing him before he hit the floor.

Stunned into silence, Linda could not at first utter a sound. Finally, she said hoarsely, "I guess you have to kill me too, right?"

"It would be best, Rolle said matter-of-factly.

"Oh…but I don't like knives…"

"Very well." Rolle grabbed Linda by the neck with his left hand and pushed her against the wall. He continued to push until her larynx was crushed. He continued to push until her eyes bulged, her face turned a dark red, then a darker blue. He pushed until she was dead, and her body slid to the floor. For several minutes he continued pushing, entranced by the expression of mild surprise on Linda's face.

Rolle's trip to Arizona was a more direct one. After catching a cab at the diner as Billy had suggested, he boarded a train at 30th Street Station to Cleveland, where he received twelve phone calls at his prearranged hotel from his men making their way across America. He confirmed their locations by return calls to numbers they gave him.

Over the next five days, he traveled through Cleveland, Chicago, Kansas City, Denver, and finally to Phoenix. Each night he received calls, made return calls, and slept in hotels near the train station.

The most serious problem encountered by one of his crews was a flat tire in Missouri. A local farmer and his fourteen-year-old son helped Rolle's men change the tire when they couldn't operate the jack. As a precaution, Rolle's men slit the throats of the farmer and his son and buried their bodies in a nearby cornfield.

As a student, Rolle had been fascinated by the United States, studying its history and geography as well as mastering English with only the slightest German accent. He remembered his father had told him that America was an "experiment" and the jury was still out as to whether its amalgamation of peoples and cultures would congeal into a true country.

Rolle knew of the race problems that plagued America and was surprised at the number of black people he saw moving with seeming freedom in the cities in which he stopped. He wondered why white Americans would work so closely with such vermin and not feel revulsion. He also wondered how Americans would want to fight and die for such a diseased and decadent country. He wished he could inform his father that the American Experiment had failed.

CHAPTER 18

ARIZONA DESERT—2012

"WHAT IS THAT?" JON ASKED.

"I don't know, why don't you go down, pick it up, and see."

"First of all, I don't want to fall on my face, and it's covered with about four gallons of your piss."

Looking down into the creek bed, Tom and Jon saw a shimmering reflection that seemed entwined in tree roots. The men scooted down the embankment not feeling the hot desert dirt on their asses. Tom reached the object first and, displaying acute archeological aptitude at the possibility of a potentially important discovery, kicked it. When that did not free the object from the roots, he kicked it again. "What the hell is that?" Jon asked, as he finally took a chance at touching the object after the arid Arizona air had safely evaporated Tom's piss.

"Whatever it is, it's wrapped tight in those roots."

On one knee, Jon tried loosening the object. It was two to three inches in width, with one inch exposed above the creek bed. Jon was almost afraid at what he thought the object to be, yet he could not break the grip of the roots on whatever they held.

"Hand me that sharp rock over there," Tom said, pointing to a flat piece of granite five inches wide with an arrowhead shape. Taking the rock from Jon, he wedged it under the root, put his weight on the thick end, and stepped down.

"Holy shit," Tom spat, as the material wrapped around the object broke loose and pieces hit him in the face.

After he picked up and examined what had flown into Tom's face, Jon said, "Hey big boy, these ain't roots."

"What is it?" Tom asked, fearing he knew the answer.

"I'd say it's what's left of someone's hand."

Moving next to Jon for a closer look, Tom moved away bone and remnants of leathered skin with a stick, then put his fingers around the object and tried to pick it up but it did not move. Reverting to leg power, he put his heel on the object and slowly his 250 pounds began to move it, like a tooth being pushed back and forth in a gum to loosen it. Again, he tried to pull on the object with his fingers, but the Arizona dirt held its grip.

"Here, let's dig away some of the dirt around it," Tom said.

"You know what it looks like, don't you? It looks like fucking gold," Jon said.

"Shut up and dig."

"Really, it looks like fucking gold."

Using their stick tools, the men exposed eight inches of "something" and suddenly stopped their frenetic action, staring at what had emerged from the desert.

Tom sat on the ground, the object between his legs. He dug his heels into the sand, put both hands on the stubborn enigma, and pulled. This time the desert released its prize. As it did, Tom fell backward against the side of the creek bed and held the ingot directly above his head. Walking over to his prone, motionless friend, Jon grasped the bar, and as Tom released it, he almost dropped it on Tom's head, unprepared for its weight.

"Ladies and gentlemen, we may have a winner." Jon whispered as he looked at the gold ingot, which shone brightly in what had become a sunny Arizona afternoon in more ways than one.

"It's gold, isn't it?" Tom almost pleaded. "Tell me it's gold. OK, even if you know it's a yellow hubcap, just tell me it's gold so I know how I'd feel if I found a bar of gold in the desert while I was taking a piss."

"It's gold." Jon said, not taking his eyes off the ingot or its lettering that said *Property of Canadian Government.*

"Holy shit," Tom whispered, as he took the ingot from Jon. "Let's look around, maybe we can find one for you too."

"What do you think it weighs?"

"I'd guess about fifteen pounds," Tom said, as he lifted the bar like a weightlifter doing curls.

"What's gold going for these days?" Jon asked, not taking his eyes off the ingot.

"Last I heard it was over fifteen hundred dollars an ounce."

"Shit, I can't even remember how many ounces are in a pound."

"Sixteen." Tom muttered as he knelt in the sand with a stick and did some quick and inaccurate calculations. "Sixteen ounces times, say fifteen pounds, is two hundred forty ounces, times fifteen hundred dollars is… around $36,000!"

"Damn, nice little nugget we just…."

"No, wait! I left off a zero. My God… that's $360,000!"

Jon said nothing at first but then whispered the all-encompassing and universally understood statement of awe: "Fuck me!"

"Tom, Jon, where the hell are you two?" Anderson's voice echoed from the road. "Jim's coming!"

Jarred from their gold lust, the men looked at each other with the same question in their eyes; "Now, what do we do?"

"We have to go," Jon said.

"I know, but what do we do with our retirement here?"

Looking around for a safe or vault and finding none, Jon finally said, "We can't leave it here in the creek. If it rains tonight, we'll never find it."

"I've got an idea, give it to me."

Handing the bar to Tom and following him back toward the road, Jon said, "You can't take it back to the farm; they'll find it during the security check going back in."

"I know," Tom said, as he climbed up an incline using natural stairs made of exposed rocks. He stumbled onto the road out of sight of Baker and Anderson. "Here, I'll put it right here under mile marker 19. We'll get on the paving crew next week and come back and put it in a safer spot."

The white marker was bent and rusted but the numbers clearly visible. Tom grabbed a pointed rock and began excavating a hole in the gravel and dirt that made up a soft shoulder at the side of the road. Burying the ingot at a ninety degree angle to the road, he covered it with a mound of rocks and loose dirt. As he put the last of the rocks on the gold, a series of long horn blasts reverberated through the valley.

"Shit," the men said simultaneously and began to sprint toward the blaring horn.

Rounding the bend in the road, still a quarter mile from the van, they saw Jim, shotgun in hand, heading toward them.

"Where the fuck have you assholes been?" Jim screamed, his eyes bloodshot reflecting the fact that five tequilas will make most men drunk and some men drunk and mean. Jim fell into the latter category. "One more fuckin' minute and I was gonna call for backup and come after your sorry asses."

"We were just looking for a place to take a piss in private, that's all." Tom said. "We were only gone a few minutes."

"Bullshit. You faggots were probably lookin' for a place to make it on work time. Get in the fucking van and keep quiet."

"We were done with…," Jon tried to explain.

"Shut up, faggot. Ya'll get into the van 'fore I shoot your asses."

"But we didn't leave the work site," Baker whined.

"I meant the other faggots…faggot."

On the drive back to camp, Jon redid the math and confirmed that the ingot they found was, on a good gold price day, worth over $350,000. But where had it come from? Being in the bottom of the creek bed, it was conceivable that the ingot, despite its weight, could have been washed downstream for miles over many years. And what of the death grip of the hand that held the bar? Whose hand? And what made him hold on even after death?

Tom and Jon said little during the hour-long drive back to the prison. They were both immersed in questions about what they had discovered. For the first time in a combined nine years in prison, both men were looking forward to their next week on the job.

Unfortunately, Jim the Asshole made sure it would be eighteen months before Tom or Jon were able to return to mile marker 19. The next day they were given jobs in the laundry and cafeteria, punished for wandering from their work assignment on the dirt road.

CHAPTER 19

UNITED STATES OF AMERICA—1943

THE TRIP FROM PHILADELPHIA TO Phoenix was both stressful, as Rolle worried about Germany's gold, and exhilarating, as he saw America for the first time in real life and not in a book or newsreel. For a country at war on two fronts, it appeared to Rolle as if America were at peace and thriving. No lines for food, everyone working, no soldiers patrolling the streets. What in God's name was it like in peace time, he wondered?

Assuming he was no longer under surveillance, Rolle realized that had he wanted to escape to save his own life, he had the perfect opportunity to do so during his trip across America. It would have been easy to melt into one of the big cities he passed through and start a new life in this strange land. But the thought was only a passing one. His life was of little consequence compared to what the gold would mean to Germany if he were able to execute his plan and return it after the war.

His country needed him now more than ever. After everything he had already given up for the Fatherland, not to return the gold would be a waste of his life, and a financial disaster for Germany. He had to try. But he needed help. He would have to trust someone, maybe even several people, if he were to overcome the odds that faced him.

Rolle's final stop was downtown Phoenix. The calls he received from his men at the end of the day reporting their positions relieved his concerns as to the gold, and the fact his men would deliver it to the distribution point as planned. All twelve trucks were now within a day's ride of Phoenix and would be given precise schedules over the next eight hours as to when they would reassemble at a location thirty miles east of town.

Rolle realized that he had only two days to initiate the most delicate part of his plan. He also realized that once the gold was reassembled in one location, he was at his greatest risk. For if he was accurate, Becker's plan for the gold did not include shipment to Reich sympathizers around the Southern hemisphere. Nor would it contain a provision for keeping Rolle alive. Rolle was certain that Becker's plan called for amassing gold in Arizona for the purpose of making dozens, or even hundreds, of German traitors wealthy Americans, after the war ended.

The first gold-laden truck was scheduled to arrive at the distribution point at precisely 6:00 p.m., almost three weeks to the day since the gold had left the Berlin train station and nearly six months since Becker presented Operation Rebirth to Rolle.

Rolle looked at himself in the mirror of his hotel room near the Phoenix train station, and hoped the gaunt, lined, exhausted image looking back at him had the strength to last forty-eight more hours. After that it would be done. Either he would be dead and the misery over, or Germany would be on a path to have its lifeblood returned to her based on Rolle's plan.

Despite his fatigue, Rolle found sleep elusive once again. He awoke the next morning as tired as he had been the night before. He lay in the too-soft bed, no doubt the cause of his aching back, and stared at a scorpion that had climbed up the curtain in his dingy hotel room. It was then he decided that this would be the first day of what he considered his plan.

With just over ten hours left before the first truck was to arrive at the truck stop four miles from his hotel, and thirty miles from the distribution site, Rolle set out to find the help he needed. He returned to a bus station he had visited the day before, where he had seen some men lying under a clump of trees that bordered the property, drinking out of brown paper bags.

A day later, ten to twelve men eyed Rolle carefully as he walked slowly toward them. Like the day before, the men began to shuffle off in different directions. By the time he arrived at where, only moments before, several men had been lounging on old tires and boxes, only two remained, both sound asleep.

Seeing an opening in the fence behind the boxes, Rolle walked around the sleeping men and peered through the hole, when he was suddenly pushed from behind while at the same time pulled by the front of his shirt. As he tumbled through the opening, he rolled down a three-foot embankment hitting face-first in the sharp scrub grass. Losing his glasses and spitting blood and dirt, he could not protect his wallet and watch, which were removed before he was able to regain his bearings. Through blurry eyes, Rolle gazed up at the four dirty men who surrounded him.

Saying nothing, one of the men walked toward Rolle, and without warning, kicked him in the stomach. Rolle moaned in pain as his breath escaped his lungs a second time in thirty seconds, and he felt the panic of gasping for air that seemed suddenly impossible to inhale.

"That's for spying on us, asshole," the smallest of the men said nonchalantly. "Now get the hell out of here."

As the four men began walking away dividing up the eighty dollars in Rolle's wallet and bickering over who would take temporary possession of his watch, Rolle, finally able to regain use of his lungs, gasped, "Wait, there's far more than that waiting for you, if you help me."

Hearing potential opportunity, the four men stopped and turned to face Rolle. With a grin on his face, the small man once again approached him, and Rolle flinched as he drew back his foot and laughed as he faked a kick to Rolle's stomach.

"You one of them queers that just likes to get beat up or what, cuz we'll beat the livin' shit outta ya for just ten dollars," the little man said as he belly-laughed. His friends laughed too.

"No, I am serious," Rolle said, as he tried to focus on the man's face. But the noon day sun directly overhead made Rolle squint, and he was wary of another kick he wouldn't see coming.

"What would you pay us, and what would we have to do?" the small man's tallest companion asked.

"I need three or four men who are not afraid of the police and want to make five hundred dollars each for one day's work," Rolle said calmly.

Suddenly the tall man moved forward and around the small man and said, "What kind of job would be worth two thousand bucks that wouldn't involve a killin'?"

Knowing he now had the men's attention, Rolle got up, dusted himself off, and replaced his glasses. "I'd think killing someone should be worth more than two thousand. The job I have in mind would require far less than murder. But it will require someone who knows this area, has a car or truck, and will perform several hours of hard labor, and the ability to keep quiet after the job."

Staring at Rolle, the four men showed no emotion, nor did they ask any further questions except the tall one who asked, "What time, where, and when do we get our money?"

After explaining the details, Rolle walked to the man who had won the right to wear his watch and said, "You can keep my money as a deposit, but I want my watch and wallet back now." The grizzled mugger smiled, looked at Rolle, then at his partners, and when the tall one nodded, he took off the watch and handed it back to Rolle, who smiled and said, "It is a pleasure to meet men who recognize a solid business opportunity."

The again watchless man smiled a toothless smile, and said, "You never know, mister, maybe you'll give us that watch again someday."

Later, as Rolle paid his daily hotel bill from a large stash of cash he had hidden in his suitcase, he was asked how many more days he would be staying at the Desert Oasis by the middle-aged woman at the front desk, as she handed him his change. "Hopefully, only two or three more nights," Rolle said, as he tried to avoid eye contact with the woman not wanting her to notice his bruised and cut face.

"Well that's fine, honey," she said. "It's nice to have quiet folks like you visit us. By the way were you in a fight or something? This is a rough neighborhood, and you should be careful."

"No," Rolle said. "I tripped and fell yesterday, I am fine."

"Okay honey, whatever you say. But get some ice on that face of yours, sugar."

At 7:45 the next morning, Rolle walked six blocks from his hotel to meet his four new partners. He carried two hundred fifty dollars per man as the first installment of the promised five hundred when the job was done.

But he was concerned that the men would rob him again, thinking one thousand dollars between them without work was better than five hundred dollars per man with work. But he had little choice. He needed the men for the next twenty-four hours. Without them, his prospects for success or a long life were minimal.

Arriving ten minutes ahead of the 8:30 a.m. meeting time, Rolle eyed his surroundings. The abandoned buildings on each corner allowed him to stay out of sight while he checked to see if he was being followed. He also carefully checked out the few vehicles that traveled the streets of the rundown neighborhood. As 8:30 approached, Rolle was seized by the possibility that his four mugger/partners would likely not arrive on time and perhaps not at all. His apprehension and nausea grew as 8:45 approached and still no men.

As he left the building on the northeast corner and began to traverse to the southeast, the four men suddenly appeared out of an empty doorway. "You were supposed to be here at 8:30," Rolle snapped as he faced the tall one.

The tall one smiled and said, "Mister, if we was a punctual, dependable bunch, we wouldn't be livin' in vacant buildin's and robbin' folks for food money. Besides, we was here at 8 waitin' for you. We saw you hidin' in that buildin' over yonder. Tryin' to spy on us again? You know what happened last time you did that."

"I wasn't hiding," Rolle said." I was trying to stay out of sight in case someone came by wanting to know what I was doing in this part of town."

"Well, it looked like hidin' to us and if we're gonna work together we need to have an abidin' trust in each other, right?"

"We are not working together, you are working for me, and if you want to earn a bonus over the five hundred dollars per man we agreed to, I suggest you do everything I tell you and your men to do."

"What kind of bonus you talkin' about for us?"

"I didn't mean the bonus was for your men, I meant a bonus for you, and a large one, if you and your men do the job that I need done."

Looking back at his three half asleep, scruffy, drinking, robbing friends, the tall one winked at Rolle and said, "Let's leave that bonus stuff 'tween you and me okay, mister?"

"Okay," Rolle said, as he handed the thousand dollars to the tall one to give to his friends.

After looking at the map of the area, Rolle pointed out where he needed to be driven and the schedule for the rest of the day. He told the tall one, named Lester, what he wanted his men to do, and it was agreed that Rolle would only interact with Lester during this operation, thus creating a chain of command.

Of the four, dirty, homeless men, Lester was clearly the leader, and Rolle figured if he offered him more money, he would take this operation a little more seriously. Rolle furthered assumed that Lester was thinking how he could not only keep his bonus from his men but also how he could steal their part of the agreed-to one thousand dollar balance.

The truck the men had somehow come up with was an old 1932 Dodge panel truck with just enough rust to keep it from falling apart. As Lester drove, and Rolle took the front passenger seat, the other three men crammed into the cluttered rear of the truck and quickly fell asleep. In addition to a noisy muffler, lack of springs, and inability to exceed twenty-five miles per hour, the truck had a fragrance that combined vast amounts of sweaty, unwashed bodies and long-lost rotted food.

"What is that stench?" Rolle asked.

"Guess that would be my boys. Kinda rich, ain't they?" Lester answered with a laugh.

The hour drive to the distribution location was hot and miserable. Lester tried to engage in conversation, but Rolle was focused on his now unfolding plan. The site they were headed to had been selected by Becker and was one of the few things that Rolle had not been in charge of. Rolle suspected that the selection criteria was based on remoteness and supposed access to Mexico, Central America, and South America via roads.

Given the staggering amount of gold and the fact that Germany may be months or even years from the end of the war, Rolle surmised that this location would be visited by Becker's traitors for years into the future to claim their share of Germany's wealth. Each conspirator could take their time knowing that they could eventually legally migrate to America after the war, win or lose, and live lives of luxury and excess.

When the two-lane paved highway gave way to a one-lane dirt road, Rolle could see why the location was selected. With only one seemingly abandoned road leading to the site, a vehicle could be seen for miles. With mountains protecting it from the east, north, and west, the huge valley that rose gradually from south to north was a perfect location to guard a country's wealth and future.

When the overheating Dodge headed up the switch-back road that led to the site, Rolle again reminded Lester and his men of their jobs and the money that awaited them when their tasks were complete. Roughly three miles from the location, Rolle told Lester to pull over to the side of the road behind an outcropping of rock so that they could not be seen from where the site appeared to be on the map. Rolle was certain there was already someone awaiting him and the trucks that were to arrive that evening.

After he gave Lester a third refresher course on the duties of the four men, Rolle opened the back of the truck, and the three men virtually fell out onto the dirt road. As he looked at this woebegone group, Rolle wondered if they could make their way up to the site over the brush and rocks. Even with the ample food and water Lester had brought and nearly four hours to cover the three miles, Rolle could not help but see the irony that the future of Germany rested in the ability of four drunk, smelly, filthy Americans to complete their tasks.

The plan Rolle had laid out made absolutely no sense to Lester. Coming into the desert and being paid all that money for what they were being asked to do seemed just plain crazy. But hell, it was a lot of money, and it was possible that what they would find at the site could lead to even more. Besides, the guy paying them was no threat and if things got tough, they could always just leave, make their way to the main road, and hitchhike back to town. At least they had the thousand dollars; that was more money than any of them had seen in years.

Despite the late start, Rolle was still ahead of schedule. He dropped Lester and his men off at around 11:00 a.m. and made good time driving the still smelly panel truck back into town. In his room before 1:00 p.m., he tried to sleep, but after an hour of tossing and turning, he disgustedly threw his pillow in the corner and gave up. If all went well that night, he knew he would be able to sleep well tomorrow night. If things did not go well, it wouldn't matter.

After a late lunch, Rolle packed his duffle bag and began his walk to downtown Phoenix. He knew it would take twelve to fifteen minutes to get to the corner of McDowell and Main, where he would be picked up by Becker at 4:00. They would then drive four miles east of the city and meet up with the first truck at 5:00. From there, they would lead the first truck to the distribution location where Rolle's four smelly and grubby "partners" waited.

The twelve trucks would arrive in one-hour intervals and be unloaded by 6:00 the following morning, the precise time Rolle assumed he would no longer be needed.

The details of the plan that Rolle had crafted, based on the nearly impossible general orders from Becker of moving two hundred tons of gold from Germany to the Arizona desert, had gone remarkably well. Of course there were the deaths in France of the children, the general, and his aides on the Brest docks, the farmer and his son in Missouri, Linda and her thick-necked boss in Philadelphia, but those losses were acceptable to Rolle, and to be expected given the importance of this operation.

Becker was late. After only five minutes, Rolle knew something had gone wrong. Or was this indeed part of the plan…Becker's plan? Becker had supposedly arrived in America through Canada five days earlier with the help of French sympathizers, and like Rolle and his men, had taken a circuitous route to Arizona. But as the minutes elapsed, Rolle was certain Becker's plan was now in effect. The question was why was he still alive?

Before Rolle could answer his own question, he was surprised by a voice that came from a black Lincoln that had pulled up to the curb. "Colonel Rolle?" Not responding directly to the question, he instead asked his own.

"Who did you say you were looking for?"

"Colonel, we have no time for games. I am Jean Dubois, I have been assisting General Becker on the project, and he asked me to pick you up and take you to the distribution site. I apologize for being late, and for General Becker for not being able to meet you personally, but we had a minor breach of our security today and General Becker remained at the site to take care of it."

Peering into the back of the car, Rolle saw no one and was undecided about whether he should run, and most probably save his life. But he knew if he ran, the gold would surely be lost forever. Without further deliberation, he walked around the front of the Lincoln and slid into the soft, deep, black leather seat.

"What kind of security breach?" Rolle asked.

"I'm not sure. All I know is I was contacted at my hotel forty-five minutes ago and told to find you and take you to the distribution site."

"What about the trucks? We were supposed to meet the first one at 6:00 p.m."

"The drivers have been contacted, and a new delivery schedule has been confirmed. The first trucks will arrive twenty-four hours later, 6:00 p.m. tomorrow."

"On whose orders?" Rolle shouted, as he realized the plan he had so carefully created for Becker and the plan he had indelibly imprinted in his own brain were now both obliterated.

"I believe the orders came from Becker's immediate superior and had to do with both the security issue and the breakdown of one of the trucks just north of Phoenix."

Rolle reeled from the collapse of his plans and tried to determine an alternative course of action during the thirty-minute drive to the site. Dubois tried to engage Rolle in conversation several times, but after receiving only "yes" or "no" answers, dropped his effort.

As they headed east toward Whiskey Junction, Rolle concluded there was little he could do until he understood more fully what had created such a colossal change in plans. Then for reasons Rolle could not explain, he felt a calm descend on him that he had not experienced since Operation Rebirth had been explained to him months earlier.

Perhaps it was the fact that for the first time he had absolutely no control over what was to occur. Whatever was to unfold in the hours ahead would come as a surprise to him. He no longer wondered if he was to live or die; he knew the answer to that question. Yet, the prospect of death did not concern him. For the first time in months, Rolle felt at ease. He let his body sink into the luxury of the Lincoln's fine leather upholstery. Rather than feeling anxiety, he instead felt curiosity. He had to see this adventure come to an end.

CHAPTER 20

ARIZONA MINIMUM SECURITY PRISON—2012

AS THEY LOOKED AT THE work assignments for the next week, neither Tom nor Jon said a word when they saw "laundry" next to Tom's name and "cafeteria" next to Jon's.

Tom broke the silence by saying, "They're going to pave that road next week and if they do any grading at all, they'll find that bar."

"I know." After several more moments of silence, Jon added, "All we can do is hope they don't, and you go back in eighteen months and dig it up."

"We could always tell Frick and Frack where we hid it, and they could..."

Jon turned to Tom with a look that said, "Are you out of your fucking mind?"

"I know, I know, that was not one of my better ideas. Do you think this is God's way of displaying a warped sense of humor, or is our luck really that bad?" Tom asked.

"Not sure, but I keep wondering how the hell a bar of gold got all the way to Arizona from Canada and who was the poor bastard hanging onto it?"

"Think there are any more bars? At three hundred fifty grand each, we find a few more, we'd be set," Tom said quietly.

"Who knows? But we have plenty of time to think about it."

The men agreed that Tom would, immediately after his release, go to mile marker 19 and see if the bar was still there. But they also concurred early on there was a high probability that the bar would be gone. They realized the pavers could certainly turn over and expose the bar if they graded the shoulder of the road before paving it.

In addition to someone finding the bar, it was also possible that the bar would be paved over, and to retrieve it would require a sledgehammer, a metal detector, and a lot of luck. In short, Jon and Tom had little hope that what they once found could ever be found again.

Over the next eighteen months, Tom and Jon were both consumed by unanswered questions: How? Who? Why? When? And were there more bars? But the questions were like an exquisite pain keeping the men alive and focused.

As Tom's release date approached, the men devised a code that would allow them to write or talk on the phone and discuss the gold without fear of having their messages intercepted. When Tom was able, he would go to the site to try to find the bar. In any case, he would call Jon the same day and report his progress. Given the low probability of the bar being there, the men spent most of their time planning more long-term strategies and how they would work together after Jon's release.

Jon dreaded Tom leaving. "It's gonna be a bitch with you not around. Why not stay another few months? No one will notice."

Even though Jon's release date was now only six months after Tom's, they would be long ones without the only friend he had ever known in or out of prison. He also remembered the stories of how jailhouse friendships never worked on the outside. Jon knew he could trust Tom regarding the bar. He just hoped that once Tom was on the outside, Tom would not forget him, or worse, associate Jon with the darkest period of his life.

Tom looked forward to his freedom and making his way to mile marker 19. But the euphoria of the ingot, especially since there was little likelihood of finding it again, had worn off. And though $180,000 per man made for a nice gift, it would not be enough to build a life around, even if the gold was still lying in the dirt, waiting to be found. Tom decided he would make his way back to Philadelphia and try to start a life there. If not, he needed to find a home. A place where he could make a living. Maybe even find a wife and raise a family.

While he would miss Jon, Tom was not certain if he would or should ever see Jon again after prison. While they spoke of somehow working together after their releases, he didn't know how if that would be possible or plausible. Yet, he had grown to love Jon like a brother, and if Jon ever needed help, he would be there for him.

The morning of his release, Tom met Jon for their last breakfast in the cafeteria. It was a bittersweet meal. "I'll call as soon as I get back from the mile marker. I still have my Visa card, a few grand in the bank, and I got my driver's license renewed by mail, so I'll rent a car and get up there this afternoon."

"No hurry, if it hasn't been found by now it'll probably be there another hundred years."

"I want this over with. We've been waiting for over a year. It's like one of those cliff-hanger TV shows that keeps you waiting over the summer to see who shot J.R."

After half an hour of awkward good-byes, Tom and Jon bear-hugged for what both assumed would be the last time.

CHAPTER 21

ARIZONA MOUNTAINS

THE JASPER SILVER MINE OPENED in 1884 after Joseph Jasper found a piece of rock laden with silver as he looked for something to wipe off the horse shit he'd stepped in while travelling from Salt Lake to Phoenix. A remarkably unsuccessful miner until that point, Jasper kept food in his stomach and clothes on his back by performing magic tricks as he went from town to town. He made some money by occasionally finding gold nuggets in California and Nevada but striking it rich was never his dream. He loved his freedom and as he saw it, too damn much money complicated a man's life.

That's why after taking his silver-laden rock into town and staking his claim, he was more than willing to sell his claim to a Denver mining company for a fraction of what it was worth if they could make a quick deal, pay him in gold, and agree to keep his name on the mine forever.

Laughed at by those who learned of the deal and called a fool, Jasper nevertheless took his $100,000 in gold and left Arizona for Northern California. Despite his concerted efforts to avoid becoming wealthy, Jasper invested some of his money in San Francisco real estate, and the rest in a local lumber company. Both were shrewd investments that made him a millionaire, and by 1905 he was one of the wealthiest men in California.

But Joseph Jasper was never really comfortable living in the big city. He would dream of the nights when he slept out under the stars and the freedom he enjoyed in his days as a miner/magician. He would cringe when his wife of ten years would announce yet another dinner, tea, garden party, or other nonsensical event he would have to attend. Wearing his tuxedo, he would remember his horse, pack mule, and denims and wonder how he ever got caught up in such a life.

His chance for escape came in October 1906, when San Francisco was leveled by an earthquake at which time Jasper was in a bar on the docks playing poker, drinking whiskey, and hiding from his wife. The wooden bar he was in collapsed in the first few seconds of the quake. A gas line ruptured and fueled a fire that devoured the structure in minutes. The flames trapped several of the patrons who died excruciating deaths when they could not escape from under the wreckage. Somehow, Jasper was thrown clear of the fire.

He attempted to get to the screaming men who were trapped, but was unable to reach them, although his hands were badly burned when he tried to pull tons of flaming lumber off his friends and drinking buddies.

Caught between burning buildings and the bay, his only escape was to jump in the water and swim for his life. After swimming one half mile north of the inferno, he came out of the water and made his way back to where the docks had been and discovered them burned to the waterline.

When he overheard his name being mentioned as one of the dead among the ruins, Jasper kind of liked the idea. After he walked to his house, found it intact, and saw his wife in the street as she talked with neighbors, he made his way to the rear of the mansion and entered the carriage house to check on his horses.

He saddled his favorite Morgan and changed into his denims and work shirt hanging in the barn. He lifted a floorboard and retrieved $100,000 in cash he kept in the carriage house for a "rainy day." Walking his horse through the devastation of the city, he slowly worked his way east, and eventually to Reno, and was reportedly last seen at a campfire by two drifters outside Tucson. He died in his sleep on July 4, 1918, in a sleeping bag overlooking the Jasper Silver mine.

Early on, the Jasper mine had made a fortune for its investors. Only forty miles from a major Western city and near rail lines, the mine poured out tons of silver per year and easily distributed it to the rapidly growing western markets. Overlooking a creek that flowed heavily in the winter and spring, the mine entrance, although large enough to accommodate horse-drawn wagons, was not easily seen from the dirt access road a half mile away.

A huge rock shelf outside the mine created an optical illusion that made it appear there was no opening at the base of the hill that led to the mine's entrance. But the most unique aspect of the Jasper was a huge cavern several hundred feet high and more than two thousand feet deep that allowed miners access to rich veins of silver deep in the mine without the laborious and dangerous drilling normally required to reach such sites.

Cool and dry, the cavern also provided excellent working conditions for the men and acted as a staging area for their equipment as they moved tons of dirt and rock each day. The cavern was a natural entryway to the silver and a barrier from the elements. Each day the men would make their way down the dirt road, enter the cavern, and then go to the shafts they were assigned to begin their day's work. In an industry fraught with danger and at times subhuman working conditions, the Jasper mine was considered relatively easy work in its protected environment.

By 1905, silver production, even with improved technology, began to taper. As a result, the Denver Mining Company sold the mine to a German cartel in 1916. Promising new investment capital and state-of-the-art techniques for extracting more silver, the new owners were apparently prepared to make good on their promises when World War I exploded across Europe. All business with German companies was suspended, and by the time the war ended the cartel had lost interest in the mine, and it closed for good in 1921.

Forgotten, the Jasper mine lay dormant for twenty-two years until its remoteness and size proved to be the perfect environment for Operation Rebirth. Its South American ownership had taken possession of the mine through an inexpensive option and notified local authorities of their intention to do some core sampling to determine if there was sufficient silver available to possibly reopen the mine. Therefore, any traffic spotted going to the remote area could be explained.

Three weeks before the first gold was to arrive, Becker had arranged for workmen to install gasoline generators for lighting, in addition to other improvements, that would facilitate the ingress and egress of Germany's wealth.

Becker had handpicked twelve men to help retrofit the mine, plus eight more who were assigned to patrol the area around the site to make sure no one interfered with the operation. The German-born crew was made up mostly of strong, young soldiers, otherwise destined for the Russian front, who were smuggled into the U.S. from Mexico via South America over a six-week period.

———————————————

As the Lincoln began its climb up the dirt road, Rolle had no idea what to expect when he reached the distribution site. Originally told by Becker not to come to the mine before the first delivery, he could not risk ignoring the order knowing that guards would no doubt be assigned to protect the site. Even bringing the four derelicts within three miles of the site had been a risk, but one he had to take.

Within one mile past the point where Rolle had dropped off the four men earlier in the day, he saw the first armed guard. Using a walkie-talkie, the guard spoke animatedly into the mouthpiece. Within twenty-five yards of the guard, the Lincoln slowed but was waved on by a second guard. Although Rolle did not see other guards, he was certain the Lincoln was being watched all the way up the hill.

Without warning, an armed guard appeared twenty feet in front of the Lincoln on a ridge above the road. In German, he said, "Follow the road another fifty meters and turn left. The road will be at a severe angle nearly behind you. Take the road to the bottom of the valley and someone will meet you." Not waiting for a response, the guard turned and disappeared behind the ridge.

Following the directions, the men still nearly missed the turn off, its angle so acute. After making a 120-degree left turn, the massive car maneuvered down the steep dirt road. Looking out the passenger window,

Rolle estimated there was at least a three hundred foot vertical drop to the floor of the valley below.

Arriving at the floor, the Lincoln was met by two more guards who immediately waved them on to the gate that lay fifty yards ahead. As they approached the gate, it was slowly opened by two more guards who directed them to the enormous cavern that had been impossible to see at any point on the steep dirt road leading to the valley floor.

While Rolle had been given the authority to select Arizona as the general area for the distribution site, it was Becker who had selected the Jasper. It was now clear to Rolle why this location had been chosen. It was inaccessible from three directions, and the fourth was totally protected by guards. It would be impossible for anything or anyone to enter or exit the site without being spotted. As the Lincoln approached the cavern entrance, General Becker could barely be seen in the shadow of the cavern. He said something to the guard, turned, and walked back into the darkness. The armed guard came out of the cavern and motioned for the car to stop.

DuBois cut the ignition. When he did, a heavily armed guard slowly approached the Lincoln with a rifle held across his chest, Rolle waited, but he was not sure for what.

CHAPTER 22

ARIZONA—2014

A CAB PICKED TOM UP at the gates of the prison at 10:00 a.m. and took him into town where he rented a van. He went directly to the Phoenician Hotel in nearby Scottsdale. After he checked in to the luxurious hotel at 11:30, he was told his room would not be ready until 2:00 p.m.. He decided that lunch by the pool was a good idea, and after a second Arnold Palmer, decided it was time for the mystery to end.

Heading east from Phoenix, Tom drove toward Whiskey Junction on State Route 60 then headed north into the hills on the paved road the men had oiled a year and a half before. As the miles ticked by, Tom realized that he was likely on a fool's errand. He also couldn't help but think of Occam's razor from a history class he took in grad school—the simplest explanation for something was usually the right explanation. In this case, Tom realized that the simplest and most logical explanation for what happened to the gold bar was it had been discovered by someone when they graded and paved the dirt road eighteen months earlier. Despite the logic of that argument, Tom had a plan if, in fact, the gold bar had been overlooked.

His plan was simple; he would drive up the paved road until he saw mile marker 19 and from that point begin a thorough search of the shoulder of the road with the shovel he had purchased at Home Depot. Unfortunately, Tom soon discovered that all the old mile markers were missing and had not been replaced, no doubt part of the paving efforts of the men and machinery months earlier. He also ran out of paved road, which meant he had already driven past the spot where he and Jon had buried the bar.

Then another depressing thought entered Tom's brain: what if over the eighteen months that Tom and Jon had been washing underwear, more paving had been done than just the twelve miles the men worked on? That thought depressed Tom even more because it would expand the area where the ingot could be; and with no mile markers, the gold bar could be anywhere.

Starting at a point where the dirt road ended and the paving began, Tom drove back down the hill. He went exactly twelve miles and pulled the van to the side and got out, hoping his mileage measurement had been accurate eighteen months earlier, and most importantly, there had been no more paving.

He tried to envision where Jim had left them off that first day to begin oiling the road, but nothing looked familiar. Locking the van and putting on some old running shoes, Tom started to walk up the hill looking for something. He found nothing.

The longer he walked uphill, the more he realized that trying to find the bar under miles of pavement was idiotic. He worried that Jon wouldn't believe him when he told him he had not found their gold.

He turned and looked back down the hill toward the van now nearly two hundred yards away and saw heat rising from the pavement. As he walked closer to the car, he saw something else behind it. It was an almost imperceptible line in the pavement maybe a twenty-five yards behind the Chrysler. Tom jogged toward the line, keeping his eye on it as he passed the van. He knew that if this was where the new pavement had been laid, it was also the spot that the four men had begun oiling the dirt road over a year before.

Kneeling down, he could clearly see a two-inch line of tar that covered the seam between the original section of road where the men began their oiling work and the new section that had been paved a week later.

Tom ran back to the van, realizing that all he had to do now to find the general area where they hid the bar was go about twelve miles up the road which would be where the men completed their oiling, and near where he and Jon had walked into the desert. It was also near his now legendary piss.

Tom slowed the van near the twelve-mile mark and saw a curve in the road. Could this have been the curve that he and Jon had run toward in their attempt to get back to the meeting spot before Jim arrived? If it was, he had now narrowed down the possible location to no more than half a mile.

On foot again, with shovel in hand, he tried to visualize how and where he and Jon had scurried up the embankment after burying the bar. He knew they could not be seen from the meeting place where the embezzlers waited. He also remembered that Jim had come running around a corner looking for them. The pieces of an eighteen-month-old memory were forming a mosaic in his brain.

Looking out over the valley below, Tom saw another familiar site—the meandering creek bed where they had found the gold. They had walked in that creek bed almost to the road because it was easier to walk in compared to the rough desert terrain surrounding it. Another piece of tile.

Tom stepped down into the creek bed fifty yards from the road and twelve feet below it. He turned back toward the road. He looked for the rocks he and Jon had climbed to reach the road right before they buried the ingot.

He saw what he thought were the stepping-stones, although there were several areas that were similar. He chose the one easiest to negotiate because he figured that would have been the one he and Jon would have likely selected to exit the desert floor.

When he climbed up the embankment, his right foot slipped, and he slid three feet backward down the slope. As he did, he tripped over an unseen a piece of metal six inches under the loose dirt.

"Damn it," Tom said under his breath as he picked himself off the ground, rubbed his bruised knee, and began another try at the embankment using the shovel for balance. After two steps up the grade, he found himself looking at the old, rusted, and now partially exposed mile marker 19, lying in the loose dirt and pointing downhill.

"Hellooo," Tom said, in his best Gene Wilder impression, as he lifted the twisted piece of metal. Tom realized this was it—the place they had hidden the ingot. He was afraid to dig. Afraid of what might not be there.

For nearly a minute he stared at the spot in the gravel as sweat slid down his face in a sheet. Finally, and with a hopeful, powerful thrust, Tom plowed the shovel into the sand exactly where he envisioned the ingot to be. The clang of metal on metal made Tom smile. He wished Jon had been there to share the moment.

Putting the shovel aside, Tom sank to his knees and dug into the loose dirt with his bare hands not feeling pain from the blistering-hot stones. He then felt it with his left hand. It was dense and heavy. As he moved the dirt away, he saw metal emerge from sand. His eyes adjusted. It was a goddamn rusted brake drum from a 1948 Buick.

"Fuck me," Tom muttered, finding yet another useful meaning for the versatile phrase while at the same time heaving the piece of rusted disappointment into the desert behind him. He was glad Jon wasn't there to share that moment.

Tom needed several moments to regain his composure, and he chugged down a sixteen ounce bottle of water during the process. He returned to the spot where he had found the brake drum and began to move away the loose gravel, hoping with each shovel thrust that he would hit something solid and this time valuable. After a few minutes of careful digging, Tom began digging furiously unable to contain his excitement.

Working an area three feet in each direction in length running parallel with the road and four feet down the side of the embankment, he moved huge amounts of dirt in several minutes. He found nothing.

Winded and sweating profusely, Tom sat on the side of the red-hot road, took another long drink of water, and tried to visualize what had happened when they paved the road. It was obvious that the mile marker sign had simply been run over by whatever paving equipment the men had used and if so, it was likely it would have been pushed up the hill a bit when the paver hit it.

Walking fifty feet uphill, Tom realized that the pavers had indeed paved at least another mile of road beyond the twelve miles that been oiled by Tom, Jon, and the embezzlers. But he also knew that should not have mattered. The bar, if it was still under the road, should be near where he and

Jon had come out of the creek bed and onto the road. And it should be just slightly up the hill and…then it hit him. The pavers would not have worked uphill like Jim the Asshole had forced them to do. They would have worked downhill, easier on the men and the equipment. Therefore, the ingot would have been pushed down the hill, not up.

Tom returned to his original dig site and began a third series of excavations, this time moving downhill in increments of eighteen inches. He spent the next hour moving what seemed to him like several tons of soft Arizona sand and dirt as he moved down the roadside.

On his first thrust of the shovel into what seemed to be his hundredth hole, Tom hit a second solid object. The clang of metal on metal made him smile. He again wished Jon were there to share in this moment. He also knew in his heart that God would not be so cruel as to fool him again with yet another rusted Buick part. He was right.

After he returned to the Phoenician, Tom called the pay phone number in the prison cafeteria more than a dozen times, only to find it busy each time. He was tempted to send a telegram or fax to reach Jon. But after thinking about it, he really wanted to hear Jon's voice when he told him. Finally, at 9:15 that evening Jon was called to the phone, and as planned, asked the first question: "Well, how was working in the yard after all this time?"

"It was good. No problems, except for this big fucking piece of metal I found."

Hearing nothing at the other end of the phone except what sounded like a soft gasp, Tom went on, "Yeah, I thought this thing must have weighed fifteen pounds, but guess what? It weighed exactly twenty pounds. Twenty fucking pounds! Damn near killed me hauling it out of there."

"So, what else is new?" Jon asked, and both men convulsed in laughter.

CHAPTER 23

JASPER MINE—1943

"WELCOME TO THE JASPER MINE, Colonel Rolle," the six foot five, 235-pound guard said when he opened the rear door of the Lincoln.

"Thank you," Rolle looked past the guard and tried to locate Becker.

"General Becker asked me to escort you to him. Would you please follow me, sir?"

As DuBois drove the Lincoln away, Rolle followed the guard into the cavern. His eyes blinked several times trying to adjust to the semidarkness. He was surprised by the abrupt change in temperature, which was at least twenty degrees cooler than the ninety plus degrees outside. The floor of the cavern slanted one to two degrees as it angled toward the various mine shafts barely visible in the shadows. Narrow gauge iron rails crisscrossed the dirt floor designed to bring the rock and silver from the depths and into the rail spur that ran adjacent to the south side of the cavern.

Rolle could see that overhead lights had been installed, but they were weak and cast long yellow shadows over only five thousand square feet of space just inside the huge cavern's arched opening.

In the southwest corner of the cavern along the left wall, near the entrance, was an old wood-and-glass office of three thousand square feet that at one time had been used by men who oversaw the loading of silver for shipping.

Finally, his eyes adjusted to the semidarkness, and he looked up and saw the enormous domelike natural ceiling within the cavern. Well over two hundred feet in height he judged, the dim yellow lights that Becker had installed, plus the natural light entering from the cavern's opening cast a muted glow that faded after only a few hundred feet and melded into blackness toward the back of the cavern.

Rolle also felt a slight breeze as he went deeper into the mine and with it an unfamiliar smell of creosote bushes that wafted from the desert floor.

Approaching the office with the guard a few steps in front of him, Rolle could see six men standing in the glow of an exposed light bulb dangling from the ceiling inside the office area. He entered the musty-smelling space but stopped in his tracks when he saw a large pool of blood in the center of the floor, coagulating under an old table with several brown metal folding chairs around it.

In the far left corner of the room he saw three bodies piled one on top of the other. The faces were bloody pulps, and it was clear each had been savagely beaten before being shot in the head. Rolle could tell immediately by their clothing and what was left recognizable of their faces that he was looking at three of the four men he had recruited in Phoenix.

Standing over the bodies were Becker and five unfamiliar men. When he saw Rolle enter the office, Becker came toward him, smiled, his hand outstretched, and said, "Colonel Rolle, please forgive this mess. I wish we could have met again under more pleasant circumstances to celebrate your successful operation. But my men found this scum approaching the cavern this afternoon. After interrogating them, we were convinced they were simply nameless hobos and not to be feared. Yet, we felt it best to eliminate all doubt."

Still staring at the pulverized men, Rolle looked at Becker and said, "Yes, it is best at this point not to take unneeded risks. I agree with your actions."

"A guard said he thought he had seen a fourth, but I dare say the sounds of our gunfire discouraged any more vagrants from lingering." Not introducing Rolle to the other guards in the room, Becker instead took him by the arm and led him out the door. As he held the door open, he turned to the five men left in the room and said, "Dispose of this debris."

Back in the cavern, Becker seemed almost euphoric as he brought Rolle up to date on the change in plans, the rescheduled gold deliveries, how the trespassers were caught, and repeated several times how grateful he was for Rolle's contribution to Operation Rebirth. Walking with Becker, Rolle said little, but kept seeing in his mind the battered and misshapen faces of the three Americans. He also wondered what they had said before they were killed and what options remained for him since the men he needed to execute his plan had been eliminated. He assumed the fourth man in the group had somehow escaped and was by now running back to Phoenix as fast as he could.

Moving from the coolness of the cavern to the outside and a still warm early evening, Becker and Rolle continued their stroll, "You look tired, Colonel. I can tell it has been a grueling trip over the last three weeks. Were there any major problems?"

"As we were about to leave France..."

"Yes, I heard of Elman. He was an ass. Do not concern yourself with that event; it has been taken care of. Any other problems?"

"No, things went as planned."

As they continued walking in the ebbing sunlight, Rolle knew that he was being debriefed by Becker for a reason other than curiosity. Becker wanted to find out if there were any more "loose ends" created by Rolle that needed to be corrected before he, too, was eliminated. Rolle didn't know exactly how much time he had left, but he assumed his life expectancy was less than twelve hours.

The men came to the edge of the huge rock face that made up part of the Jasper and looked west out over the valley to the horizon that now hid a setting sun. After several seconds, Becker said, "We have come a long way, Colonel, and are very near our goal. The Führer is aware of our efforts and asked me to convey to you his appreciation and high regard for your loyalty and dedication."

"The Führer's goals are worth any sacrifice, General. I only hope the hard work and planning that has brought us to this point is carried on by those who will receive the gold. They are the last link in the chain."

Without responding to Rolle, Becker continued to gaze out over the desert and said almost wistfully, "This part of America, away from the filth of the Negro-infested cities, is really quite lovely."

CHAPTER 24

ARIZONA MINIMUM SECURITY PRISON—2014

THE FINAL SIX MONTHS OF his term were the most difficult of the nearly eight years that Jon had spent in prison. In addition to the normal mind-numbing boredom of daily prison life, Jon was anxious to finally get on with his life. The shock of the phone call from Tom had lifted his spirits temporarily, but the frustration of not being able to be part of the discovery ate at Jon. He was also lonely. Tom's release, while good for Tom, left Jon with no one to talk, or relate to. Instead of trying to make conversation with men he would never see again, he buried himself in the library and at night wondered whose hand had been attached to the gold bar.

In mid-August Jon received his ten-day release notice. The next day he called Tom, and it was agreed that in nine days he would pick Jon up at 10:00 a.m. outside the prison gate. For reasons not entirely understood by Jon, he was becoming increasingly depressed as freedom neared. After counting down years, months, weeks and then days until he was free, he realized the strange security that prison provided would soon be gone. While he hated being incarcerated and everything associated with it, it shielded him and all inmates from what they would face on the outside.

After spending five months in Philadelphia, Tom bought a van and headed back to Arizona, feeling healed emotionally and physically. He also had a sense of purpose he had never felt before. Given that feeling of "rebirth," Tom again began to question whether a reunion with Jon would be good for either of them. As a result, he considered how he could get Jon's share of the gold bar to him without having to actually meet with him upon his release.

Jon had no idea how he would make a living after he left prison. With his Cayman money and half of what the gold bar was worth, he would have a nest egg to start with, but restarting his career would be a major challenge. But at least he knew Tom would be there when he got out, and perhaps together they could figure out their next steps.

The prison gate closed behind Jon at exactly 10:05 a.m. With suitcase in hand, he looked around and half expected to see Tom waiting for him in a stretch limo with two blondes and a keg of Coors, like they had talked about years before. But there was no limo, no blondes, and no beer. And no Tom. After twenty minutes of pacing in front of the prison gate, Jon wondered if they might let him back in to have lunch since it was Sloppy Joe Tuesday.

After ten more minutes of waiting, Jon saw a pay phone and walked toward it but realized he had no change, credit card, or anyone to call if he did. No one. That realization made him literally stop in his tracks. He looked back at the prison with a longing that he immediately knew was perverse and wrong on so many levels.

With no other immediate plans in mind, he sat down on the curb under a tree, and next to his suitcase. He didn't know what else to do.

A few minutes later the thumping sound of a helicopter came from behind the tree that Jon was sitting under. Jon ignored the sound and stared straight ahead until the chopper came directly over his head then landed across the street in a vacant lot fifty yards from where he sat.

After the chopper cut its engine, Jon saw a tall white guy casually exit and walk slowly toward him. Without saying anything, Tom crossed the road and sat down next to Jon. For a full two minutes neither man spoke. Then Jon yawned and said, "That was kind of obnoxious."

"The limo, beers, and blondes were going to cost as much, and they couldn't do what we needed done. By the way, sorry I'm late, had to get permission from the farm to land so close."

"So, what needs to be done...besides me?" Jon asked.

"We have some work to do so get off your ass and let's get going."

"Did I ever tell you I hate to fly?"

"You may have mentioned it."

Jon shrugged his shoulders, got up, and followed Tom back toward the chopper. On the way Jon thought to himself that he had never been happier to see anyone in his life as he was his tall power-forward friend.

Inside the chopper, Jon put on his earphones, shook the pilot's hand, said hello, then asked, "You've done this before, haven't you?"

"Yes sir, got my license yesterday."

As the pilot jabbed the stick, the chopper lifted six feet off the ground in a nose down attitude that made Jon's eyes open wide and his hands tightly grab the armrests. Within seconds the pilot pulled back on the stick, and the men were soon cruising at one hundred twenty miles an hour sixty feet off the desert floor.

"We going to Disneyland?" Jon asked Tom.

"Not exactly."

"Club Med?" There was hope in Jon's voice.

"Remember that thing we found, and lost last year?"

"Yeah, I remember that thing."

"Well, I think there may be more."

"Really? Why do you think so?"

"Because of the research I've been doing at the library."

"You on heavy medication?"

"Nope. Hey Bill, take us north and pass over those mines we saw last week."

"Roger."

Still close to the ground, the chopper turned left and headed north.

For the next thirty minutes the men got a close-up view of both the Jasper and Vega mines and miles of surrounding desert.

They saw the dirt road they had oiled, and the meandering creek that snaked down from at least twenty miles north of the Vega, just south of the Jasper until it disappeared on its way to Mexico.

As they turned south, Jon and Tom could see the rustic shopping area in the distance that Jim had frequented and "Elsa's" painted on the v-shaped roof of the only restaurant for miles.

After they landed twenty yards from Elsa's parking lot and near Tom's rented van, the men stood under a tree and watched the chopper head back toward Phoenix. Tom asked, "Well, what'd you think?"

"It was a fun ride, but blondes and Coors conjured up a bit more potential."

"Their names are Rachel and Brenda, and we'll see them tonight. But I want you to see other stuff first. "How about some lunch?" Tom asked.

"Think they have sloppy joes?"

"I think you need to move on."

Sitting in a small side room of the restaurant, the men ate bacon cheeseburgers and chili and talked for three hours. It was as if they had never been apart. For the first time in months, both men laughed out loud at nothing special.

After their food-filled reunion and conversation that included Tom telling Jon their gold ingot was resting comfortably in a safe deposit box in a local bank, Tom placed his laptop on the table, pulled out a large map, and lay it next to the computer.

"What's all this?" Jon asked.

While you've been washing dirty socks for six months, I was doing research on lost gold in the desert."

"You really think there's more gold out there?"

"There's too much evidence from good witnesses to ignore the fact that huge amounts of gold have disappeared around here over the years for all of it to be bullshit." Pointing to a specific spot on the map, Tom asked. "This look familiar?"

Jon stood and looked down at the map. "This is the place, huh? It does look familiar. Show me exactly where we left it."

Tom pointed to where mile marker 19 had been and explained how he narrowed down the exact location. His voice was almost a whisper, "I think there are more."

"Are you serious? I thought you were full of..."

"I'm very serious." It was the assurance in Tom's voice that caught Jon's attention.

CHAPTER 25

JASPER MINE—1943

"I THOUGHT IT BEST TO delay the delivery for twenty-four hours to ensure the security of the mine after today's occurrences. Each driver has been contacted, and we have returned to your schedule, Colonel, although a day later than planned," Becker informed Rolle.

"I concur with your decision, General."

Rolle appeared calm and collected, but his mind raced as he tried to compute how all the changes that had taken place impacted his mental plan. Did he even have a plan anymore? His thought process was interrupted when Becker told him that food was in one of the trucks that had been pulled into the cavern and Rolle could help himself at any time. Becker also told Rolle that beds had been placed in some of the private offices, and Rolle should find one and get as much sleep as possible that evening. He said he wanted Rolle fresh the next day to oversee the delivery of the gold.

Rolle's reaction to Becker's suggestion of food and rest was that he would probably be poisoned or murdered in his sleep by one of Becker's men. By 11:00 p.m. and despite his concerns, Rolle had forced down some bland food, lay on top of his assigned bed, and wondered what moves in this one-sided chess match he had left.

After he dozed off for an hour, Rolle was awakened by scratching on his locked door. Thinking it a rat or other animal, he tried to go back to badly needed sleep, but the sound persisted. Hearing voices in the background that indicated Becker's men were still working on preparing the cavern, Rolle moved to the door and when the scratching began again he quickly opened it and found Lester, the fourth hobo, on the floor, using a piece of metal as his scratching tool.

"Come in quickly." Rolle whispered as he looked into the cavern but saw no one near the office.

After he rose to his feet in the darkened room, Lester hissed through gritted teeth, "Those bastards killed my friends. They beat them near to death and then shot them in the heads like they was stuffed pigs."

"I am aware. I saw their bodies."

"What the hell is this all about, and who the hell are you, you goddamn kraut. You're all krauts, ain't you?"

"Yes, I am German, but I did not kill your friends. Those men outside did, and if I were to yell, they'd kill you too."

"Not before I'd tell them you hired us to foul up whatever it is they're tryin' to do."

Surprised by Lester's immediate comeback, Rolle hesitated and said,

"Believe me, at this point we need each other. I need to complete my task, and your help is needed to do that. As I said before there is a large amount of money at stake and you will be well compensated if..."

"I don't care about the goddamn money, mister. Money ain't worth gettin' cut up by those bastards."

"Calm down, you are safe here. But if you go back out there it is likely we will both be caught. I have some food and wine, eat something, and tell me what happened."

As he wolfed down bread, sausage, cheese and wine, Lester related what had occurred earlier. "I'd sent the boys down into the valley and told them to follow the creek bed around to the west until they could see the front of the mine. I went around to the other side where I knew some old shafts were that led into the back of the mine and, eventually, to the cavern."

"How are you aware of such details?"

"When I was a kid, my old man used to work in this here mine. My brother and I came out here and carried water for the men in the summer. I used to roam all over this mine and learned every snake hole in the damn place. We'd play down in the creek bed, up on the top where the air vents and escape shafts were dug, and even down in the mine when it got real hot. I spent over eight years here with my old man until they closed the place down."

"Go on."

"Anyways, I was working my way 'round to the other side of the mine when I see this guy with a rifle not fifty yards to my left. I slip down one of the escape shafts where I can keep an eye on this guy but he can't see me. Pretty soon I heard this ruckus from down in the valley and I see the guy with the rifle start headin' in that direction. After he leaves, I look down and see my boys being pushed up the hill by two more guys with rifles who took them into the cavern. So I move a little further to the west on top of the mine and find the vent shaft to mine Number 4 and start working my way down. I come out at the entrance of Mine Four, but off to the left, out of sight of anyone in the cavern. The guys with the rifles take my boys outta sight, but I can hear them askin' them all these questions like, 'Why are they here?' and 'Who sent them?' And stuff like that. But my boys don't say nothin'. They don't want to lose the money you promised them."

"Are you sure they said nothing?"

"Not at first. But pretty soon your friends started slappin' them around and the money don't seem all that important, and so they started tellin' the truth that some guy they don't know asked them to come to the mine and act as lookouts and all. But your friends think they're makin' up the story and don't believe them. Then the krauts start gettin' real rough and slappin' them around even more. One of my boys gets mad and from what I heard, got loose and hit one of your friends smack in the mouth. Then all hell broke loose, I heard all this yelling and screamin' and people being hit and then it's quiet. Then there's three gunshots real quick, bam, bam, bam. Then it's quiet again. Next thing I see are the five guys with rifles comin' out of that little office in front, all speakin' German and laughin'."

"Did your men describe me to the guards?"

"They tried but all they could remember was you were a tall guy from back east. But I knew you was German all along. You don't have much of an accent, but I was in Germany in World War I and know a German accent when I hear one."

"What other questions did the guards ask?"

"They asked lots of questions, but my boys didn't know nothin'. I never really told them what you wanted us to do, and they'd been too drunk to remember anything about you to tell those guards."

"The men who killed your friends are Nazis. They have been sent to this country to help in the overthrow of your government. I work for the U.S. government and was sent here to infiltrate this group so I can stop them. I needed you and your men to help me complete my job."

Lester stared at Rolle for several moments with his head cocked as if not sure what he had just heard. "That's bullshit, mister. There's some kind of shipment coming in here in the next day or so. I know my German may be rusty, but I heard the word "gold" a bunch of times today."

Rolle realized he had underestimated Lester. In the near darkness of his room, he smiled and said, "All right, you will know the truth." Rolle then told Lester almost everything that had occurred to that point over the last four months.

When he was through, Lester observed, "No wonder you could pay me a bonus."

"It seems you have many options, Lester. You can yell for the guards, and we will both be dead in minutes. You can escape back into the mine and make your way to safety. Or, you can help me with my task and become a very wealthy man."

"What are you going to do if I was to make a run for it?"

"I will stay, my job is not complete." What he did not say was that if Lester tried to run, Rolle would shoot him with the Luger he had taken from his bag earlier and hidden under his mattress, and which was only inches from his fingers. He would then go to the guards and say he was attacked by the hobo who must have been part of the group that had been shot earlier. Rolle could not risk him making good on his escape and going to local authorities. Rolle also failed to tell Lester that he would be killed even if he stayed to help him, for the same reason.

"Exactly how much would I make if I decided to help?"

"How much do you want?"

"A hundred thousand in gold." There was no hesitation in Lester's response.

"If we are successful, you will have one hundred thousand in gold. If we are not successful, we will both be dead."

"Hell mister, I've been near dead so many times tryin' for five dollars, that for that kind of money, I'll do damn near anything."

"Does 'anything' include killing the men who killed your friends?"

"I can't say they was exactly my friends, but they didn't deserve to die the way they did. It's been pert near twenty-five years since I shot anybody, but if I got the chance I'd shoot those kraut bastards for what they did to those boys."

"You will get your chance."

CHAPTER 26

ARIZONA DESERT—2014

AFTER REFILLS OF ELSA'S FAMOUS raspberry iced tea, Tom asked, "You ever hear of the Old Dutchman or Superstition mines here in Arizona?"

"Don't tell me you think that's where our bar came from?"

"I didn't say that. I just asked if you'd heard of those lost gold mines?"

"Sure, but what do they have to do with our bar?"

"Only that there've been dozens of legends over the last three hundred years about lost gold in the Arizona hills, starting with the Spanish back in the 1600s. There are well- documented stories of Indian tribes amassing gold in the hills to keep it from the white man and…"

"I still don't get how these old wives' tales are related to our bar."

"They may not be. I admit some of the info I found is pretty far out, X-Files stuff, but some of it is intriguing. For instance, in 1887, a train loaded with over a million dollars in gold for military payroll was derailed not more than a hundred miles from here and the gold stolen. In 1895, a group of renegade U.S. Cavalry troops stole over two million dollars in gold from the Mexican government in a raid at a mint in Juarez. The gold was tracked from Texas to the New Mexico Territory, and into Arizona where the trail was lost. There were several stories, and even some eyewitness reports, of Germans bringing huge gold caches into the US for safe keeping during each world war."

"Those stories sound interesting, but how do you explain 'Property of Canadian Government' on our bar?"

"I can't, but I'm working on it."

"So with all this information where do we go from here?"

"Let's take a ride."

In Tom's van, the men headed north from Elsa's parking lot. With the map spread over Jon's lap, Tom had a question. "What do you see on the map?"

Jon scanned the map again. "All I see is some land owned by some Indian tribes, a couple silver mines, some railroad lines, and the rest looks like state-owned land."

"There is also limited access to all the locations you're looking at. This road we're on now, which is also the one we oiled, is the only road for thirty miles in any direction that could possibly lead to where we found the bar."

"True, but we found the bar in a creek bed, which means the bar could've been washed down from miles away, and if so, this road could be irrelevant as it relates to the gold."

"You might be right, but if you look at the map again, you'll see those two old silver mines we saw from the chopper today both abut the creek even though one is two miles north of the other."

"But why would a silver mine spit out a chunk of refined gold that size? Are you thinking they could have been mining gold too?"

"I doubt it, but I guess anything is possible. All I know is if your theory is right that the bar washed down the creek bed, it could have come from one of those mines. And again the road we're on leads eventually to both mines. I think the mines are where we should start."

"Start what?"

"Start looking for the gold—what do you think?"

"Are you serious?"

"Of course I'm serious. I know this is all new, and I'm dumping a lot on you all at once, but there may be something to this, and I think it's worth a few weeks' work to see what we can find. Besides, what else are you going to do?"

"Well, I can tell you there are a few things that have been on my mind for eight years that I'd like to..."

"I want to show you something. The Jasper's just six miles up the road. I've been up there a few times but just peeked inside."

"Don't tell me you're afraid of the dark?

"Wait till you see this place."

––––––––––––––––––––

Negotiating a tight left turn off the road, Tom steered the van down a dirt road starting three hundred feet above the desert floor. "Damn, hope you've been practicing driving," Jon said as he looked over the road's edge.

"Nice view, huh?"

"Yeah, if you like views a million feet in the air."

Pulling the van twenty feet from the cavern opening that was not visible from the dirt road Jon noted, "Damn, that appeared out of nowhere."

As they walked toward the mine, the men could only see forty feet inside the Jasper.

"So what's in there?" Jon asked, not sure going into a huge dark mine even in the middle of the day was such a great idea.

"What's the matter, afraid of the dark?" Tom asked.

Tom tossed one of two HD flashlights to Jon, and the men entered the mine.

Looking up, the men saw a domelike roof that appeared at least two hundred feet high. The men lowered their flashlights and directed their beams to the back of the mine; despite the power of the lights, they could not see where the mine ended.

"Holy shit. You could fit a few Yankee Stadiums in this joint." Jon said, his voice in awe.

"Told ya."

The men began a slow walk from the cavern's opening toward the back of the mine. They saw iron rails on the floor and what looked like electric wires dangling from the ceiling. Further into the mine they saw empty beer cans, pizza boxes, used condoms, newspapers, pieces of lumber, broken glass, the remains of a dead coyote, and more used condoms. After walking another one hundred feet, Tom said, "Turn off your light."

After both men had done so, they were in almost total darkness. Even the large opening at the front on the cavern did not throw light back to where the men stood. They also noticed a strong breeze that rose and fell but never completely abated.

After they turned their lights back on, the men continued their stroll into the darkness and noticed the floor had a downward slope of two to three to degrees.

"I read up on this place at the local library. It was a productive silver mine for years, but then closed back in the early 1900s once the silver dried up. Since then the state tried to keep the place closed, but kids kept knocking down fences and have used it as a party spot for about ninety years. Back in the forties a South American mining company took out an option with the idea of reopening it, but nothing came of it."

After another two hundred feet, the men came to a warning line in the floor and an overhead banner that said "Danger: Open Pit One Hundred Feet Ahead."

"What the hell is this?" Jon asked.

"Looks like there's an open pit a hundred feet ahead," Tom helpfully informed Jon.

"I got that part, smartass. Did you see it before?"

"Didn't get this far. But from what I read, there's a huge hole in the rock back there. The miners used to dump trash in it, and there's all kinds of stories of men falling in and never being found."

"Let's go look."

As the men continued their stroll into the darkness, they could feel the angle of the floor descend at an ever steeper slope. They also heard, and felt, a stronger swirling wind that moved from being a tailwind to a headwind and back again within twenty feet. The sound that accompanied the wind would transition from a baritone to a soprano with levels of alto in between.

"Feel that?"

"Yeah," Tom said. "The floor's angle just dropped a bunch."

"You said kids partied in here?"

"Yep."

"That's a partying group I can respect," Jon said with admiration in his voice.

Ten feet ahead of them, the men saw another yellow warning painted on the floor of the mine, this time alerting of an open pit fifty feet ahead. Someone had stuck a small handmade sign in the ground with *"They aren't kidding about that fucking pit!"* written on it in red.

As the wind howled at their backs and the floor moved away from them more steeply with every step, Jon made an observation, "Well, you know what they say, when you've seen one gaping, howling, scary as hell black pit, you've pretty much seen them all."

"Yeah, that's a saying I've always tried to live by. Let's get the hell out of here."

Back outside the men leaned against the van, sipped their bottled water, and were quiet for several minutes as they contemplated lost gold and the Jasper.

"If I was going to hide gold, that pit might be a pretty good place to put it," Tom said.

"If that's where more gold bars are, I think one is enough."

As the men talked, a white pickup truck with tinted windows and thick knobby tires sat near the bottom of the dirt road to the Jasper. Tom saw it first.

"Don't look now, but I think someone is watching us."

Jon looked.

"Great move, Mr. Subtle," Tom said.

"I saw that truck down at Elsa's. Think they followed us?" Jon asked.

"Maybe. Let's leave and see if they follow us again."

After Tom made a U-turn and headed for the exit, the white pickup drove away.

CHAPTER 27

JASPER MINE—1943

FOR THE NEXT FOUR HOURS, in the darkness and quiet of Rolle's sleeping room, the German colonel huddled with the American bum. Despite his appearance and odor, Lester had retained some of the soldier instilled in him twenty-five years earlier. He listened to Rolle's plan, questioned some parts of it, but did not waver in his commitment to see the plan to its conclusion.

Rolle had assumed Lester was little more than a feeble-minded, robbing vagrant. And while two of those descriptions were reasonably accurate, Rolle realized Lester was not stupid. He had also assumed that Lester's sole motivation for helping him was the money he thought he would make. But Rolle also changed his mind on that issue. It appeared the men he claimed "was not exactly friends," were closer to him than he let on. While it mattered little to Rolle whether it was greed or revenge that motivated Lester, it was obvious Lester had been underestimated.

The first thing Rolle and Lester tried to determine was how many men were currently in or around the mine. They had counted six guards patrolling the outside, the guard who had opened the door of the Lincoln, and at least five to six other guards moving around the facility. There was also Becker. The total was at least fifteen, but it could be more, given the size of the mine that could hide hundreds of men if need be. That did not include the twenty-four guards who would arrive in the twelve trucks the following evening.

Rolle explained the first thing they needed was a weapon and suggested that Lester try to sneak up on one of the guards outside, overpower him, and take his rifle. "Does 'overpower him' mean split open his skull with a rock? If so, I'd rather use this here." Lester drew an old military Colt .45 from his boot. Again, he had underestimated Lester.

"Yes, that would appear to be a better option." Rolle said.

Rather than shooting one guard at a time and therefore alerting the others, it was decided that using his knowledge of the mine, Lester would try to get the drop on as many of the six outside guards as he could, disarm them, and lead them down one of the shafts leading to the cavern and the myriad of passageways and rooms throughout the mine.

"There's a bunch of old tool bins about fifty yards inside each shaft. They all have locks, and I doubt you could hear anything from them that far into the shaft," Lester said.

The inside guards, because they were constantly moving, would be more difficult to surprise and disarm. Rolle knew that the men that

Becker had brought with him were the best soldiers and killers Germany had to offer. If a fight did develop, he and Lester would be significantly outnumbered, outmuscled, and outgunned. The key would be to try to get as many of the inside guards in one place at one time as they could.

After he put down the last of the bread, Lester said, "Well, I'd better get a move on," as if he were heading home after a late night with the boys.

It was agreed that if Lester could not make good on his ambushes, he would fire three shots in the air to alert Rolle and make his escape. While Rolle didn't like the idea of Lester making it back to town alive, he had little choice under the circumstances. As Lester began to crawl out of the makeshift office turned bedroom, he turned to Rolle and said, "That was real good wine. What kind was it?"

A bit incredulous about the question, Rolle whispered, "I really don't know."

"Just wonderin'. It had a nice oakey taste. See ya later."

CHAPTER 28

JASPER MINE—1943

LESTER WORKED HIS WAY UP from the floor of the Jasper using the escape shaft of Mine 4. When he was within three feet of the opening leading to the top of the mine, he stopped his ascent, sat in the darkness for over an hour, and listened.

Earlier in the day he had seen from the floor of the valley at least one guard patrolling the top of the mine. He remembered the guard was heavily armed. And big.

From his current position in the shaft, Lester could not hear voices or the click of a guard's boots on the rock if there was a German manning his post above him. But seeing the other guards in action earlier, Lester doubted if there was a guard in place on top of the mine that he was asleep or not paying attention. He also knew that if he bolted up the shaft on top of the rocks, he would lose any chance of surprise he might have.

Taking a loose rock from the shaft, Lester tossed it as far as he could from the entrance and heard it skitter across the top of the mine for what seemed like at least ten yards. Hearing nothing, he tossed another rock in the opposite direction. Again, there was silence, which meant there was no guard, or if there was, he was asleep, or the guard had heard the rock and was very calm and patient. While Lester hoped for one of the first two options, he somehow knew the third was the case.

After waiting three more minutes, Lester was about to begin his final ascent up the shaft when he thought he caught a glimpse of a beam of light above him at the opening of the shaft. Afraid to move, Lester held his breath as a faint sound of movement caught his ear and the light appeared stronger. Allowing himself to silently slide down the shaft a few feet, Lester could not see the entrance eight feet above him but was also out of sight when the beam of light was pointed down the shaft. Easing further down the shaft, to a nearly thirty degree angle bend, Lester could not make out the garbled words coming from the top of the shaft.

Suddenly, the dirt and stone exploded around Lester as the guard pumped eight to ten rounds of automatic machine gun fire into the shaft. While the shells missed Lester because of the angle where he had positioned himself, broken pieces of rock and dirt stung his face and chest as they enveloped him in a shroud of dust and debris. After a few seconds, Lester heard a voice clearly in German, and once again the beam cast a dim light into the shaft. Burying his face awaiting a second volley of shots, Lester instead heard a grunt and felt loose stones trickle down to his position. The guard had entered the shaft.

Since he did not know the construction of the shaft, the guard quickly lost his balance and began to slide uncontrollably downward. His feet stopped at the sharp angle bend only six feet from Lester's face.

In the daylight the guard would have been able to see the numerous handholds in the shaft that were gouged into the rock and soil that could be used for someone going up or down the shaft. But at night, even with a flashlight, he could not see the handholds but had nevertheless aggressively descended down what could have been a bottomless pit.

Lester could not help but think of the guts it took for the German to jump into a black hole in the middle of a black night to check out a sound. The thought of such dedication concerned Lester as much as the weapons the guard carried.

Lester, because of his six foot four and 170-pound frame, was able to snake up and down the shaft with relative ease. But the guard at six feet and 220 pounds was having trouble squeezing down the thirty-six-inch wide opening. With his foot feeling for a path his eyes could not see, the guard poked his boot down the shaft, and found the angle that would lead to Lester's position. Knowing the shaft opened considerably wider behind him, Lester knew he had no choice.

Reaching for the Colt in his boot, he brought the small cannon up toward his face and waited for the guard to continue his downward path. But the guard stopped, and Lester could see the flashlight facing first downward, then up toward the opening at the surface. Apparently, the guard was either convinced the shaft was empty, or claustrophobia was finally taking its toll. Now seeing the handholds above him, the guard began his climb back to the top.

As the guard shoved his rifle out of the shaft and braced himself on a rock three feet below the surface to extricate himself from the hole, his spine was shattered two inches above his tail bone by the .45 caliber bullet that exploded from Lester's Colt. After splintering the spine, the shell tore through the guard's heart and exited an inch below his neck. With blood convulsing from his jugular vein, the guard slowly slid downward. Grabbing his feet as he neared the angled turn in the shaft, Lester pulled him further down several yards to the enlarged area twenty feet below the surface.

Lester moved quickly up the shaft and grabbed the guard's machine gun from near the surface. He quickly slithered down the shaft again reclaiming his original position three feet below the opening of the shaft.

Breathing heavily from exertion he was not used to, Lester sat motionless for several minutes waiting for something, but he wasn't sure for what. From below him, he was jolted by the dead guard's walkie-talkie squawking in the darkness. Moving toward the German, he found his flashlight and began going through his pockets. He found two clips for the machine gun, a compass, a Luger, and the radio. Shining the flashlight in the guard's face, he recognized him as the one who had calmly shot each of his friends in the head and later laughed about it.

The walkie-talkie sputtered and crackled, unable to operate below the surface. He knew it would be only a matter of time before more guards came looking for their comrade. Lester decided it was time to move. He quickly ascended the shaft, exited the blackness, and sat on top of the Jasper. Within seconds the static of the radio cleared, and he heard a voice calling for "Geoff" to answer.

Lester tried to remember his rusty German. He thought he heard the voice ask if the now dead guard had seen anything. Pushing the button, Lester said, "Nein". After waiting several seconds for a reply and hearing none, Lester grabbed the rifle, threw the walkie-talkie down the shaft, ran toward the east side of the rock, and hid in a stone crevice sixty feet from the mine shaft in which the dead guard lay.

Lester was certain the sound made from the now dead guard firing into the shaft and that of his Colt had carried from the top of the mine to the valley below. What he did not know was if the other guards had assumed the single shot was made by the guard or someone else. He also wondered if his "nein" had fooled the person on the other end of the radio. He doubted it.

Within seconds his questions were answered. Three guards, their boots slapping against the rock, came up behind Lester, his position hidden by the alcove four large boulders created. As the guards sprinted past, fifteen feet to his left, Lester tried to remember if Rolle had told him there had been five or six guards on the outside.

Spreading out on the huge rock, the guards searched for a sign of Geoff. They passed within ten feet of the shaft but couldn't see the opening because of the darkness and the position of rocks surrounding the hole. Even in daylight the shaft could be passed over unless someone knew it was there. But the guards were soon drawn to the shaft as the walkie-talkie squawked with static some twenty feet below the surface. Moving quickly to the hole, the guards directed their flashlights into the shaft but could not see Geoff. Calling his name and getting no response, one of the larger guards suggested that the smallest of the three enter the shaft and try to find their partner. The smaller guard wanted some time to think about going into a black hole on a black night, and a discussion among the guards ensued regarding their search for Geoff.

Because of his position and darkness, Lester could see the guards and their animated discussion but remained unseen. As the men decided what to do next, Geoff's walkie-talkie again barked, and the sound seemed to motivate the guards into action. The smallest of the three handed his rifle to the tallest guard and started to carefully descend into the shaft. He stopped briefly when his hands discovered Geoff's blood which formed a trail leading into the hole. The third guard stood with his back to the other two and directed his attention to Lester's general direction.

Lester did not think he could be seen by the third guard, but he could not be sure. Aiming the machine gun carefully, he attempted to fire a burst. The gun jammed. But the sound of his movements caught the attention of the third guard. The bullish German moved closer to Lester. Still unsure of what he heard, the guard unleashed a volley of bullets causing ricochets that echoed for miles. The dancing bullets created sparks that flew off the rocks like sparklers on the Fourth of July. The two other guards, one now in the shaft, and one crouched next to it, shouted in German, asking if the first guard had seen anything.

Saying nothing, the third guard moved toward a clump of shrub grass and four cacti that had survived in a patch of dirt on the stone and were to the right of Lester's location. Moving in a crouched position, the guard stopped briefly and appeared to be looking directly at Lester through the darkness. It was at that second that Lester shot him through the left cheek blowing out the back of his head. The second kneeling guard, seeing the flash from the Colt, began scattering bullets in the direction of where Lester had been. Unfortunately for the guard, his profile was visible in the darkness against the sky and did not provide him the protection Lester enjoyed in his position among the rocks.

Balancing the pistol on a six-inch opening between boulders, Lester squeezed off two rounds and both found their marks, hitting the guard in the side and slamming him to the ground. Recoiling into his lair, Lester avoided the barrage of bullets coming from the machine gun held in the now dead guard's hand.

After the last shell was spent, Lester did not wait. He ran at full speed toward the shaft. He wanted to get the guard who had entered the shaft before he had a chance to return to the surface. Lester could have taken his time. The guard who had emptied his machine gun in death had also taken the head off the guard in the shaft as he came up too late to help, but just in time to take two shells in the neck.

Working methodically, Lester collected the weapons and ammunition of the three Germans, dragged the bodies to the edge of the rock face, and threw them off. He had thought of putting them down the shaft but to do so would have clogged the entrance and make it unusable. He also wanted the remaining guards to know where he was and hoped they would come after him in an environment where he was comfortable and their access to him limited to only two directions.

Later, Lester sat on the edge of the shaft and pulled a plug of Redman from his shirt pocket. After chewing for a few minutes, he began spitting the juice over the side of the rock face where he had thrown the dead guards. Lester was not sure if more guards were on the way or not.

And if so, would they be coming up through the shaft or from the direction where the three had come only minutes before? So, Lester waited with a German machine gun in his lap. He also continued to spit.

Several hundred feet below Lester, Rolle had heard the volley of gun shots that reverberated over the desert rocks and filtered throughout the mine in rumbling tides of sound. He assumed Lester had been killed. This left Rolle with limited options. Without Lester to neutralize the guards patrolling the outside of the mine, Rolle would have little chance to singlehandedly take on the guards he had seen wandering around the inside of the mine. Further, in several hours the first trucks would arrive, carrying more heavily armed guards and tons of gold.

Reaching under his bed and finding his bag in his still darkened room, Rolle pulled out his Lugar and two clips and stuffed them in his belt. Peering out into the cavern, his question of whether or not the guards working inside the mine had also heard the gunshots was answered when he saw several guards come from all directions from within the cavern and assemble in a tight group around Becker. Wearing only pants and socks, Becker looked like a small, frail football coach surrounded by his massive players getting last minute instructions before the big game.

Rolle could not hear what was being said, but by the pointing of his arms and animated actions, it was clear Becker was giving orders on securing the cavern. As he spoke, another four guards came running into the shaft and approached the group. Rolle could now see more clearly what he was up against. Not including Becker, there were a total of sixteen men left in the mine who were huddled around Becker. Rolle had originally estimated the total number of guards in and around the mine at fifteen to twenty.

Whatever the true number, he realized he alone would be no match for Becker's remaining troops. He also realized more of Becker's men could still be posted outside the mine but felt the group around the general was the majority of the men he and Lester would have to overcome, if Lester was even still alive.

Rolle knew he needed more details about what was going on. Moving the Lugar to his belt at the small of his back, he opened the door of the office and began running toward Becker and his men. Thinking that because of the chaos, he could be shot at any moment, Rolle was surprised that he was virtually ignored by the guards as they listened intently to Becker's orders. Stopping a few feet from the group, Rolle could hear Becker assigning the men into pairs and telling them under no circumstances to leave their posts.

Now calm and speaking in a deliberate, unemotional manner, Becker told the men, "We have a breech in our security. Four guards are missing from their posts, and we must assume one of two things. Either those four men are traitors infected by greed and intent on compromising our operation, or they have been overcome by outside assassins aware of our operation. I want to remind you of what is at stake over the next twenty-four hours; no less than the very future of the Führer's doctrine, and to a much lesser degree, your futures as individuals also hang in the balance. I doubt you need be reminded of the financial rewards a successful conclusion means to each of you."

Seeing the look in the eyes of the men surrounding Becker reminded Rolle of the look in the eyes of another group of young men nearly twenty years earlier on a Berlin street corner. The difference was these sixteen young men were armed to the teeth and perfectly willing to die at that moment for what Becker was telling them. Rolle sensed that even Becker had underestimated these young men. They were not in an Arizona mine looking for gold or a new life in America. They were there because they still believed the promises. They believed that Becker was going to use the gold as he had pledged. They believed they were a key part in perpetuating Adolf Hitler and Fourth Reich. That belief made them far more dangerous for Rolle as adversaries than mere mercenaries. The men would also be dangerous to Becker if they learned that he intended to use the gold to make himself and his cronies very rich Americans.

CHAPTER 29

ARIZONA DESERT—2014

ON THE DRIVE BACK TO Phoenix after the aborted tour of the Jasper, Tom explained to Jon, in grindingly laborious detail, what his research over the prior six months had uncovered. This included tales regarding gold supposedly lost in the Arizona desert over the previous three hundred years.

Jon could not help but think that his former jail mate had spent just a bit too much time in the Arizona sun. The tales of lost gold had been handed down from generation to generation since the 1700s, and to Jon's knowledge, nothing had ever been found. But Tom had an explanation for that: "If you found gold, would you tell anybody?"

Excited about the possibility of hidden gold, Tom tried to fill Jon in on six months' worth of research in about an hour. Jon drifted off several times as Tom droned on about legends, tall tales, and lost payrolls. He did not want to rain on his friend's parade, but it seemed that Tom had caught gold fever and the only thing that could cure him was to let him play out some of his plans. Besides, Jon was in no hurry. It was not like he was late for a job. He decided to let Tom talk, and if need be, spend a few weeks playing gold miner before he got on with the rest of his life.

The only part of Tom's theories that Jon could not explain, and what gave reluctant credence to all his stories, was the gold bar they had indeed found. Whether it was from a lost gold mine, Spanish treasure, or had fallen from an alien craft, it had come from somewhere, and that thought alone intrigued Jon enough to humor his friend.

"By the way, how do we know the bar is even real gold in the first place?" Jon asked. "Because I broke off a small piece with a claw hammer and took it to a jewelry shop and had it analyzed. It's the real thing. But we do have a problem," Tom said.

"What's that?"

"How do two ex-cons walk into a bank or coin store and sell twenty pounds of gold worth almost four hundred grand?"

"We could say we found it in the desert while you were taking a piss."

"Yeah, and we would be back in jail the next day. I'm serious, we're going to have a problem getting rid of the bar, and if there are anymore out there, it becomes a bigger problem."

"Good problem to have. Any ideas what we do with the bar we got?"

"We could melt it down into small pieces and sell it to shops from here to New York and hope no one asks any questions, but that would take weeks. Or we could sell it to a "fence" at a discount of probably 50% and let them get rid of it in Mexico. Either way it's going to take time and cost us a lot."

"If it's going to be such a pain in the ass to get rid of the gold, why do you want to play gold miner in the first place?" Jon asked.

"Because our options as far as careers go are limited, and I believe we came across one piece of what could be more gold than we could ever spend in our lifetimes." The look in his gray eyes and tone of his voice made Jon realize Tom was deadly serious in what Jon had viewed as no more than a lark by two ex-cons with a few weeks on their hands.

"So, what's your plan?"

Without hesitation, Tom explained his detailed strategies and tactics to Jon. After thirty more minutes of listening to Tom talk nonstop about finding and getting rid of the gold, Jon was no more convinced than before of the gold's existence. However, he was sure that Tom was convinced there was gold, and the minute details of his plan indicated either brilliance or madness. Despite his skepticism, Jon could not help but be caught up in Tom's enthusiasm, and given what Jon knew of Tom's intellect, he could not simply brush off his friend's theories or the fact that Tom had done his homework.

Tom was basing his theories on the assumption that it was simply inconceivable that all the stories about lost gold in the Arizona desert were hoaxes or merely the stuff of legend. In some cases, there was simply too much documentation by historians and eyewitnesses to ignore. Of course, Tom admitted, that the further back in history he went, the less collaborative and detailed the information became. As a result, Tom had focused his investigation on the most recent stories, beginning with holdup of a Brink's truck loaded with gold that was hijacked in 1953 with over five million in bullion in it. The gold was being moved from Tucson to Phoenix by the federal government.

Using that heist as his departure point, Tom went back in time to the late nineteenth century. He carefully examined each reported incident. He subjectively measured the likelihood of the story being a fake or that the story was true, and the gold was either irretrievably lost or in fact already discovered by someone who would have the good sense to keep their mouth shut if they found a cache of gold.

Tom also surmised that the problem he and Jon faced in disposing of their gold bar, would have faced anyone else who found such a treasure. That being said, what the hell would you do with a few million dollars in gold you found lying in the desert? You couldn't just walk into town with a bucket of gold and ask for cash without attracting all kinds of unwanted attention from folks like the IRS; the state of Arizona, which would undoubtedly put a claim in for the gold if it was found on state land; and a myriad of other parties who would want to steal what you had found.

CHAPTER 30

JASPER MINE—1943

SITTING INDIAN-STYLE ON TOP of the Jasper mine under a cloudless Arizona sky, Lester could hear dimly echoed voices from below. Even though the men were speaking in German, he could understand some key words, and from the agitated tones, that the three bodies of the guards he had dumped from the top of the high rocks had been found.

Truth be told, Lester didn't like Germans all that much. He remembered how they had beaten and tortured him during his capture in 1917 in France. And he sure as hell didn't like what he had heard of Hitler and his henchman. Of course, he wasn't too partial to the U.S. Government either at that point, since they had pretty much ignored him and his veteran buddies for the last twenty-six years. Yet, if he had a choice, he would rather kill a bunch of krauts than an American, unless of course some crazy bastard really deserved it.

Perfecting his talent of adroitly spitting Redman over the side of the rocks, Lester's hope that the guards would come to him was fading. After all, he could do little to them or their plan if he remained several hundred feet above them. After nearly two hours of waiting, he realized that his choice was simple. He could leave his perch, make his way back to the main road, and let the krauts have their damn gold, or he could stay and probably get himself killed.

Of course if he left, he would walk away from a hundred thousand dollars, but that was no longer the only issue. While he wanted the Germans to pay for the deaths of his buddies, that wasn't entirely it either. It was that for the first time in nearly thirty years, Lester felt alive. The cool, smooth weight of the .45 in his hand and the adrenaline that moved through his veins made him "feel" for the first time since the Argonne Offensive.

It wasn't the killing of the guards that created the feeling. Disposing of the Germans was done out of revenge, self-preservation, and fueled by an instinct that had been dormant for decades. It was more than all that, and yet Lester couldn't quite put his finger on it. But it had to do with doing something important again.

Lester wasn't exactly sure what all those Germans were doing in the Jasper and damn well knew he couldn't trust Rolle, but he instinctively knew that walking away and heading back to town was akin to abandoning his post. A post no one except Lester and Rolle knew he patrolled.

Looking west toward Phoenix, he could see the glare of lights on the horizon. A warm breeze blew, and the quiet mesmerized him. Looking up at a blue-black sky he had forgotten existed, he thought of his father, and how thirty-five years earlier they'd come to that very spot, ate their dinners, and the same kind of breeze blew as they talked. But for the life of him, Lester at that moment could not think of one damn thing they talked about. All he knew was that the feeling of contentment and serenity he felt had been missing from his life for too long. He decided that if it was time to die, there was no better place than the Jasper.

Reaching into his pack for the last of his food, he leisurely ate some salted sausage and crackers and sipped some water. He also wondered how the hell his country could win any goddamn war when it could not even keep a bunch of Nazis from invading its heartland to divide up what sounded like a shitload of gold. Unable to answer his own rhetorical questions, he swigged down the last of his water and figured he had waited for the krauts long enough.

Moving away from the rim of the rock, he slowly ambled back to the opening where he had pulled the first guard down and entered the black hole. As he did, his hand ran over some of the blood and brain matter from the guard whose head had been blown off hours earlier.

Nonchalantly wiping his hand on his pants leg, he slid down the vent until he came to the body of the first guard that he had shot the night before. Using the guard's flashlight that he had taken earlier, he continued down for another twenty feet until the shaft opened slightly, and he was able to stand in a crouched position.

The air vents were originally drilled solely for ventilation and were too narrow save for the thinnest of men to move through. But over time, as the drilling in the mine augured further and further into the rock below, the air shafts became valuable for dropping supplies to the men, especially dynamite that would be used regularly in the mine. As a result, the vents were eventually widened to allow the supplies to be lowered more easily.

Lester recalled many occasions where he, as a ten-year old boy, used the shafts as giant slides where he would virtually leap into the abyss and slide down the thirty-five degree vents for what seemed like hundreds of feet. Of course more than once he ran into machinery or workmen that not only interrupted his fun but usually caused some serious bruising and a lecture from his father.

Lester moved more slowly down the shaft now, and it was the smells that came back to him more than any other sense as he slid into the darkness. He had never noticed the smell as a kid, but an odor of fresh dirt permeated his nostrils. He knew that no matter what happened in the next few hours, he was glad he stayed.

Before he reached the bottom of the shaft, Lester slowed his descent and stopped altogether at ten-foot increments to see if there were sounds coming from the horizontal tunnel still forty feet below him. The dozens of air shafts built into the Jasper mine angled off from the main tunnels with openings three to four feet above the floor. What Lester did not want to do was come sliding down the shaft into the lap of some German holding an automatic weapon. The problem was that Lester couldn't control the gravel that preceded him and announced his arrival at the bottom of the vent. As a result, he was prepared to hit the tunnel floor firing if he had to.

Lester stopped his slide ten feet before the end of the shaft and waited silently after he heard several pebbles hit the floor. He held his breath and wondered if anyone was awaiting his entrance. Hearing nothing for at least five minutes, he reluctantly let his feet leave the shaft and find their way to the tunnel floor. At first afraid to use his flashlight, he eventually turned on the beam and discovered he was alone in the cool darkness.

Located three hundred feet from the main cavern entrance and fifty feet inside the tunnel, the shaft had brought him to a part of the mine that was one of the first sections closed when the mine slowed production.

With three-foot-wide steel rails still in the floor of the twenty-foot-wide opening, Lester remembered that this tunnel, like several others, had been sealed off from the main entrance of the mine by huge wooden doors at least twelve feet high and eight inches thick. Unless the Germans had ideas of staying for a long period of time, he doubted they would go to the trouble of breaking down the doors just to enter a long-abandoned tunnel. He also doubted they had discovered the "secret opening" to the door that he had found as a boy. About halfway up the right-hand door, the wood frame moved slightly away from the rock, and an agile boy could slide his way into the abandoned tunnel from the main cavern through that opening.

Moving toward the wooden door, Lester saw through the cracks the muted yellow light that covered several cars, trucks, and boxes about three hundred feet from his position. He also saw several guards, weapons at the ready, in and around the lighted area. That area measured approximately five thousand square feet within the massive cavern, which Lester estimated at over a million square feet. The yellowish light created an eerie specter and cast long shadows into the cavern where an army of Germans could hide.

Looking around the cavern, Lester worried if he could actually re-enter the main area unseen and make his way to the old offices to meet up with Rolle to discuss the next part of their strategy. Lester felt trapped by what he could see in the dim yellow light. He counted six guards that stood at equidistant intervals around the lighted area. Each guard held an automatic weapon with bandoliers of ammunition crossing his chest. While they looked implacable and immovable, Lester was more concerned about the guards he couldn't *see*. They could be outside patrolling the gates and roads, hiding in the shadows of the cavern itself, or some of them could be making their way back to the top of the cave looking for whoever killed their fellow soldiers. No matter where they were, he couldn't fight what he couldn't see.

Two hundred and fifty feet to Lester's right of the lighted staging area, he saw the small offices where he had met Rolle hours earlier. He assumed Rolle was still there, but from where Lester was he had no way of sneaking into the office to make contact with Rolle. But even if he could, he wasn't sure he trusted that bastard either. On the other hand, he had little choice...for now.

Lester knew he might be able to pick off two or three of the guards in the yellow light, but that would lead the rest of them to his position, and they might be able to track him down even in the darkness of the shafts and tunnels he knew so well. Sliding down from his ledge behind the wooden door, he rested for a few minutes and noticed the adrenaline that had kept him running for the last twenty-four hours was wearing off---he was tired.

For the first time he felt the weight of the three rifles and the ammunition he carried from the dead guards. He also felt the cold metal of his Colt that he had wedged in his belt. His body was beginning to ache from too much exertion in too short a time. He knew if he waited much longer to act, he would be too tired to carry out any plan.

Turning back to the yellow light, he took one of his rifles and slid it through an opening between two thick wood slats that made up the door. He looked through the sight, took aim at the guard standing nearest to one of the trucks, and was certain he could hit the man in the chest. Saying "bang you're dead" under his breath, he moved the rifle to the guard thirty feet to the left and was convinced he could nail him as well. The other four guards were also possible targets, but their angles to Lester made them more difficult to hit. Keeping the rifle in position, he squinted when he saw a more interesting target in the yellow light.

Lester closed his left eye and looked down the barrel of his rifle. He aimed it at an area three feet to the left of the first guard, and two feet above the ground. Wiping sweat from his eyes, he again sighted his target and was sure he had at least a fifty-fifty chance to hit it.

He retrieved the rifle from its position, scooped up the other weapons, and jogged back to the shaft from whence he had come minutes earlier. If he took a shot and missed, or hit his target and he was wrong, he needed a quick escape. He figured going back up the shaft was his best chance.

After he stowed the weapons ten feet up the shaft, he returned to the wooden door and took his position. The guards had not moved. He wondered how they could stay in one position for so long. Taking aim, he laughed under his breath that he hadn't even shot a rifle in thirty years, and here he was trying to hit a target hundreds of feet away, in piss yellow light. Even if he did hit it, he wasn't sure what the hell would happen.

Lester wasn't sure if the guards even heard the shot. Or if the explosion from the right side gas tank of the large truck was the last and only sound they heard. He could not see what happened to the three guards on the left side of the truck, but the three nearest to him died almost instantly, as the forty-gallon gas tank exploded within five feet of the men. Dead in a microsecond, the men were thrown fifty feet in the air, ripped to pieces, and engulfed in flames, the remnants of the three bodies burning furiously thirty feet from the demolished truck.

From hundreds of feet away, Lester felt the heat and the thick wooden door move on its hinges. Within moments a second blast caught him by surprise when a car parked eight feet from the truck also exploded. To his right, he saw three men running from the small office area that was now engulfed in smoke. The men ran toward the main entrance to the mine, but Lester couldn't be sure if Rolle was one of them.

For the next five minutes, Lester watched as a second truck and two more cars exploded in a conflagration the likes of which Lester had not witnessed since he saw a battleship explode in France in 1917.

The acrid fumes from the fire made Lester wonder if he should abandon his position and return to the safety of air shaft he had descended moments earlier. But as the fire raged, most of the smoke and flames were making their way to the main entrance for escape.

As the flames slowly flickered out, an eerie darkness spread over the cavern. The mawkish yellow lights had been blown away by the explosion leaving only long cords dangling from a soot-stained ceiling. Small patches of fire from the remains of trucks, cars, and guards were the only light in the cavern, which became darker and darker by the second until all that was left were the embers of smoldering cloth seats.

On the outside of the cavern, Rolle, a guard, and Becker, stood behind the Lincoln. They peered into the cavern, as thick, acrid smoke curled up the face of rock into the night sky blackening the area above the entrance. Three flood lights located on the outside of the cavern were not destroyed in the explosion and emitted the only light in or out of the mine.

The explosion had blown in the windows of the office, and broken glass had virtually decapitated one of the guards in the outer office. Rolle and Becker had been knocked to the ground but had been protected from serious injury since they were in the private office thirty feet away from the front of the office.

For the first time Rolle saw a visibly shaken Becker. No longer the leader of men, he seemed at a loss on what to do next. But his highly trained guards, whom he had ordered to "stay at your posts, no matter what," had done so, except for one lieutenant who ran up to Becker after hearing the explosion. He had been ordered by his field commander to determine if there were new orders from Becker based on what the men had seen and heard.

Never having seen action before, even though he was a general in the army, Becker was not prepared to respond to a crisis of this magnitude. Screaming at the young lieutenant for leaving his post, Becker turned back toward the cavern and had no answer. Finally, it was Rolle who told the lieutenant to step a few feet away and await further orders. After several more minutes, Rolle quietly suggested to Becker that perhaps it would be a good idea to bring in the rest of the guards to ascertain they were in fact still alive and could be depended on. Becker stared dumbly at Rolle and only nodded. Rolle then gave the order for the lieutenant to bring the other guards back and rendezvous next to the Lincoln.

Two hours earlier, when the guards announced that three bodies had been discovered at the base of the rock face, and a fourth was missing, Rolle knew Lester had somehow escaped and was carrying out a plan. Rolle also knew there was no way he would be able to meet with Lester to discuss what they would do next. The explosion convinced Rolle that Lester had his own plan and was willing to risk his life to carry it out.

Although they had not spoken, Rolle knew the problems Lester faced. The most compelling would be trying to figure out how many men he was fighting. The explosion had killed seven guards, and Lester had taken care of four others earlier, but he could not know exactly how many other guards were still part of Becker's dwindling army. But at the very least, the odds were getting better.

Rolle's order to bring all the guards together next to the Lincoln would enable him and Lester, if he was watching, to see what they had to contend with over the next several hours before the trucks began arriving.

Within five minutes, the sound of boots on gravel began to make their way to the Lincoln. With Becker still reeling from shell shock, Rolle waited patiently for the last of the men to arrive from their posts and asked the major, "Is this everyone?"

"Yes, Colonel, but General Becker had ordered us to maintain our positions, and it is not a good idea to expose our men in one location."

"I understand your concern, major, but we must ascertain how many men we have left so that we can deploy them in a manner to carry out our mission."

"Sir, including myself, we have ten guards left with substantial armament, including grenades and automatic weapons."

That was more men than Rolle had hoped, but at least he now knew what he and Lester faced.

"Thank you, major." Rolle looked into the eyes of the frightened young men around him who only hours before had looked like implacable hardened killers, ready to give their lives to protect what they thought was Germany's life blood. Now, in those same eyes, he saw the toll of fighting an unknown, unseen enemy in a hostile land thousands of miles from home. Rolle saw fear.

"Colonel, do we know what caused the explosion?" The major asked, trying to ease the concerns of his men.

"I'm not sure but it must have been the buildup of gasoline fumes in the cave and the heat from the trucks. It is a setback for us, but we can still achieve our goals if we can depend on you and your men to keep your focus and let General Becker and me think through our alternatives."

While the major didn't believe the "gasoline fumes" story, he was glad Rolle used it as an explanation of what had happened and not what the major believed to have been the cause.

"Colonel, you have the total dedication and commitment of my men and me. However, I do suggest we deploy the men in a manner to protect the perimeter of the mine as we had before until final orders are given by you and General Becker."

With Becker still looking glassy-eyed and saying nothing, the major surmised that the chain of command had been, or soon would be passed, and therefore he had directed his comments to Rolle.

"Major, I agree with your preliminary plan. Deploy your men as you see fit and return here in thirty minutes for further orders. Dismissed," Rolle snapped. Turning to his men, the major barked out his orders, and within seconds the guards disappeared into the darkness. Rolle had learned the numbers of his enemy. Now he needed a plan to fight them.

CHAPTER 31

SCOTTSDALE MOTEL—2014

JON WOKE FROM A FITFUL sleep, tried to turn over, but as he rolled into the body next to him, he let out a bloodcurdling yell and fell out of bed as he twisted away from a screaming Rachel. The stereo outcry woke Tom in the adjoining room who rushed in and turned on the lights just in time to see Jon bang his head on the wall next to the bed, stub his toe on the bed frame, then begin to sob incoherently all within five seconds.

"Holy shit, what's wrong with you?" the make-up free Rachel howled, as she looked down at a clearly out-of-control Jon who was cussing a blue streak, holding his foot and head at the same time while apparently speaking in Spanish with a Norwegian accent. "This happens to convicts all the time, he's just not used to sleeping with anyone, and he must have freaked out waking up next to you." Tom proffered while smiling as he looked down at his fellow Tiger, still writhing and moaning on the carpet.

"He's crazy, and he couldn't even get it up last night," said the now suddenly less than lovely and equally insensitive Rachel, as she began to pick up her clothes that were scattered over the floor. "Brenda, one night with this loser's enough, I'm outta here, you coming with me?"

Brenda, the last of the group to be awakened by Jon's breakdown, was not quite sure what all the commotion was about, but nonetheless looked for her clothes, and within a minute the lovelies from Mesa had left the rooms, disappearing into an Arizona sunrise.

As soon as the girls left, a profound silence took over the room, and Jon, now miraculously free of all pain, sat on the edge of the bed with a proud grin on his face.

"Really? Was all that necessary?" Tom asked.

"Had a decision to make. I could waste a lot of time this morning figuring out how to get rid of her, or I could let her make the decision."

"You have to get out of this nasty habit of waking up every morning at dawn. It's okay to sleep in sometimes."

"I know, but the idea of being able to do what I want, anytime I want, is more interesting than staying in bed all morning with a Star Wars bar escapee."

"By the way, if what Rachel said was true, don't feel bad. You got to understand it'll take you awhile to get back in the swing. All cons face that. Rumor is they put stuff in the food to keep the testosterone down. It'll get better."

"God, I hope so. Did I ever tell you about this redhead I knew in New York…?"

"Yeah, about a hundred times. Since we're up, no pun intended, let's get out of here and grab some breakfast. We have work to do."

Within an hour the men headed back toward the Jasper. As they drove, they passed a white prison van carrying a group of inmates headed for a long day in the hot sun. Neither man said anything. They didn't have to.

Turning north off Route 60, Tom pointed the van up the now-familiar road and stopped near the spot where he, Jon, and the two embezzling lovebirds, had begun their work months before. As Tom fumbled over several maps, Jon got out of the van, walked over to the side of the road, and looked across the vast expanse of Arizona desert that lay before him. Although still only 8:00 a.m., the sun beat down and foretold of another scorching day.

The emptiness Jon saw before him somehow depressed him and made him realize the hopelessness of Tom's dream of finding more of the gold.

Walking back toward the van, Jon was tempted to tell Tom that he wanted out of their unwritten agreement to chase Tom's dream. Maybe even out of their friendship, if that's what it took for Jon to be able to go home, wherever that was, take whatever job he could find, and try to get his life together.

Before Jon had a chance to vent his feelings, Tom interrupted as he exited the van and spread a map across a boulder on the side of the road. "Look, this is the road we worked on, and up about ten miles is the spot we found the bar. As I said before, this is the only road that leads to the mines."

"So what?"

"I'll tell you what, I'll bet you my share of the bar that the creek bed we found that ingot in, which we know by the map meanders all the way to both mines, served as a water runoff, and maybe even some sort of trash dump for one or both mines."

"So is your theory someone absent mindedly threw out a twenty-pound bar of gold from a silver mine, and we happened to find it, even though it's at least eight miles away from the nearest mine? Couldn't it be just as likely that the locations of the mines have absolutely nothing to do with the gold bar?"

"Look out there, what do you see?"

"Not a fucking thing but sand and rock," Jon said.

"Right. Except for the creek bed, which is the closest thing to a path you can find in this place. If you wanted to hide a lot of anything, you'd need something like the mines in which to hide it, and a way to get to it without being on the road."

"You mean people used the creek bed as a path from the mine carrying one piece of gold at a time to walk it back to Phoenix where they took it to a jewelry store and cashed it in, no questions asked?"

"Damnit, I don't have all the answers, but if you're going to be such a negative pain in the ass, then I'll take you back to the motel and you can lie in bed, watch soap operas, and feel sorry for yourself in peace and quiet."

Suddenly angry, although not sure at what, Jon said, "Maybe a soap opera would have more semblance of reality than looking for a fucking gold mine in one hundred degree heat. How long do you intend to do this? Are you really serious about this bullshit? Have you lost your fucking mind?"

Staring at Jon for a few moments, Tom dropped his gaze and began looking at the map again, and said, "If we take this road to the furthest mine, it's called the "Vega," we can work our way south down the creek bed to the Jasper and see what we can see. "What do you think?"

Seeing he was being ignored by Tom, Jon was ready to explode with rage. But for some reason he said nothing more. And he wasn't sure why.

After several seconds, he moved to the boulder and softly said, "Yeah, I guess that's as good a plan as any."

Back in the van as they headed up the mountain to the Vega, Jon felt like a piece of shit for losing his cool and acting like a spoiled child. He thought about apologizing, but Tom had already accepted it by understanding that Jon's reintroduction into "freedom" was going to have moments like the one Jon just experienced, and they would have to work through them. Had Jon ever doubted Tom's friendship, he would never do so again.

A rusted dumpster lay upside down nearly blocking the entrance to the Vega. The road that Tom and Jon had traveled that started fifteen miles south ended at the mine. Beyond the mine, hundreds of miles of mountain ranges and high desert plateaus lay to the north and east.

Tom parked the van next to the dumpster. He and Jon walked the fifty yards to a shack that at one time had been the mine's office. The dirt area that led to the shack was strewn with broken beer bottles, pop cans, and rusted heaps of fencing, long since torn down by vandals. As they approached what was left of the shack, they could see its only door lying in two pieces eight feet from the office. With all the windows broken, it appeared the only thing that held the shack up was the graffiti in English and Spanish that adorned its exterior walls.

Looking into the shack from the doorway, Tom saw a scorpion scurry across the floor and under an overturned desk, its drawers long since opened, and used as target practice. Tom moved to the back of the shack, while Jon began the thirty-yard walk toward a chain-link gate due west that was secured with a large brass Yale lock.

Narrow-gauge steel tracks curved from the middle of the yard under the fence that had four "Private Property Do Not Trespass Signs" attached to it. While the fence was ten feet high and topped with barbed wire, Jon easily slid under the fence with Tom lifting a sag in the wire.

Tom required a little more time negotiating the path under the fence but joined Jon via the same route. The two men then walked single file another fifty yards from the fence to the entrance of the mine. When they approached the second barrier, it was clear that the owners were a bit more serious about keeping folks out of the Vega.

A solid iron door was secured to iron bars and welded at strategic points throughout its fifteen foot height and twelve foot width. In addition, concrete had been poured into any crevices that were created by the unevenness of the dirt road, therefore eliminating the possibility of someone slipping under the door. Graffiti covered almost every square inch of the door. "Not exactly as far off the beaten track as I thought it was given all this artwork," Tom said.

"Yeah, some of this stuff is pretty good."

As Tom shook the iron door to see if it was impregnable as it appeared, Jon noticed scrape and gouge marks near the hinges of the iron door.

"Looks like folks have tried to get in here before but didn't have much luck."

"Wonder if there are any other entrances?"

"Even if there were, what do you expect to find in there?"

"I'm not sure, but according to the local history books, this mine has been closed since 1919. If nothing else, it would be cool to get inside and see what we can see."

"Isn't this private property now? Are we going to get shot if we somehow get inside?"

"I doubt it. This place was operated by a Boston family for years after it was leased from the Arizona Territory in the late 1800s. After they closed the mine, it reverted back to the state. By the way it looks, they padlocked the place and forgot about it over the years."

"Why would that door be welded shut?" Jon asked rhetorically.

CHAPTER 32

JASPER MINE—1943

AS TOTAL DARKNESS ENGULFED THE Jasper, Lester had limited options. He could make his way up one of the air shafts to the top of the rock face, stay where he was in the relatively protected tunnel, or try to make contact with Rolle, thus risking exposure and certain death at the hands of the now nervous, trigger-happy guards.

Feeling fatigue grip his body, he based his decision on what option would offer him less immediate discomfort rather than what was either practical or basic combat strategy. The thought of trying to climb back up the air vent was not an option he considered all that much. He was just too damn tired for that. And the idea of staying where he was, in total darkness for the next twelve hours, wasn't all that interesting either. He also decided that he wasn't quite through with the krauts.

For twenty years after World War I, Lester roamed the country. Never exactly a bum, at least by normal bum standards, he was, to be kind, a free spirit. At least that was his mother's definition. His father, a silver miner at the Jasper, had another definition that was not quite so kind. Yet, they both loved their son, and were frantic when they received a telegram from him while he was on another "excursion" this time in Paris. Their concern heightened when he informed them that he had enlisted in the US Army while in France and was on his way to Germany to fight in a war they knew little about. "How could the Army take a boy of fifteen?" his mother had asked over and over.

After two years in the Army in which he had seen action in eight major campaigns, Lester was awarded the Silver Cross for bravery and several commendations for heroism in the face of enemy fire. He also had been captured by the Germans and spent four months in a German prison camp before he and two other men escaped after overpowering six prison guards. Lester got a medal for that too.

The Army would have given Lester even more medals, had they not found out that he had been a mere schoolboy when he enlisted while on a trip to France. As a result, Lester's heroics were kept as quiet as possible once the Army learned the truth. Further, Lester's career in the military was officially over as soon as he returned home. Because of the silence the Army imposed on Lester's records, he returned to Phoenix with no one except his parents knowing of his exploits. It was as if it had never happened.

Depressed and confused that the Army no longer wanted him and his hometown had forgotten about him, he decided to "hit the road" again for a while to find out what he wanted to do with his life. At first his father thought that what Lester needed was a good job in the mine, but seeing the look in his son's eyes, he knew Lester was not ready to settle down. Despite his mother's tears, Lester left Phoenix in early 1919 and made his way to California. For the next three years he traveled across the country from coast to coast, usually riding the rails until the need for a soft bed and a hot meal made him stop in a city or town and do odd jobs to earn some cash.

On several occasions, Lester ran into men he had served with in the Army. He was sometimes embarrassed by their adulation as they recalled his heroics in Germany and France. Once in the Kansas City bus station, Lester ran into a former corporal he had pulled from a burning supply truck the Germans had machine-gunned outside Paris.

"Sarge! It's me, Maloney! You remember, Corporal Maloney. How the hell you been?" a short, red-haired young man said, as he grabbed Lester's hand and shook it like it was a water pump handle. "Honey, this is the sergeant I told you about who saved my life. If it wasn't for sarge here, I'd be a buried bag of bones layin' in some shallow grave back in France."

"Hi, corporal." Lester said sheepishly. "Hi ma'am, nice to make your acquaintance." Without saying a word, Maloney's wife, clearly in the last months of what had been a difficult pregnancy, rose to her tiptoes, and kissed Lester on the cheek.

"Sergeant, I can't tell how many times my Donnie talks about you and how you saved his life, and how you were the best soldier he ever saw. It's a real pleasure to meet you."

"Well, it's nice to meet you too, ma'am, but I'm afraid Donnie here may exaggerate just a bit. He was the one who was the good soldier; you should be real proud of him. You tell that young-un' of yours when it comes, that Donnie here was a real hero and his sergeant said so."

Seeing Corporal Maloney swell with pride in front of his wife at hearing what he said made Lester feel good, even though the truth was Maloney was about a no count a soldier as Lester had commanded in those days. But it didn't matter now, especially seeing how his wife looked at him. After some more idle chatter, Lester said he had a bus to catch and said good-bye. Later that night, Lester slept off some bad muscatel in an abandoned warehouse near the bus station and began what was to become a five-day bender.

After three years on the road, Lester returned to Phoenix to find his father had died six months before, and his mother had moved to Seattle to be with his younger brother who was an attorney in a shipping company. He wrote his mother several times, but he was never sure if his brother ever gave her the letters since he disapproved of what Lester had done with his life. He never heard from his mother again. She died in 1926. Lester found out about it in 1929.

Back in Phoenix, Lester tried to find a trade that he could get into but nothing stuck. He worked in a lumber mill, a quarry, drove a truck, dug ditches, even worked in a hospital as an orderly, but he would soon become bored and leave every job. But no matter what he did, Lester had two qualities that made employers sorry to see him go. First of all, he was a tireless worker, and secondly, he seemed to command the respect of the people with whom he worked. He had an almost effortless ability to lead and direct people. Even his superiors were often prone to listen to his suggestions, and they used his leadership abilities to get other employees to get their work done.

Lester could have continued his hand-to-mouth existence for an indefinite period if it had not been for Officer Nick Quinn of the Phoenix police department. Quinn was a notorious cop with a mean streak that was often taken out on the drunks that congregated near the warehouse district of downtown Phoenix.

In the fall of 1933, Quinn was in the process of beating to death a drinking buddy of Lester's when Lester came around the corner and saw the last of what was over twenty blows with a billy club to his friend's skull. Dead after the first five blows, Quinn was insane with rage that the drunk had mouthed off to him and was ready to bring down yet another blow when Lester grabbed his arm and broke it at the elbow over his knee in a move that was as quick as it was effective. At over six foot four and a muscular 195 pounds, Lester had seen the five foot ten, 225-pound Quinn in action before and decided his days of bullying and murder were over.

As Quinn screamed in agony with a compound fracture of his left arm, he reached for his holstered pistol with his right. Moving deliberately yet with the decisiveness of an athlete, Lester kicked Quinn in the side of the head, reached down, grabbed his pistol, took hold of the barrel end, and drove the hand grip down on Quinn's broken arm again and again. The sound that emanated from Quinn was no longer a scream. It was a high-pitched wail that made him sound like a schoolgirl. A very vicious schoolgirl.

Lester dropped the pistol in a nearby trash can and calmly left the scene walking past a group of men who patted him on the back as he disappeared into the Phoenix summer night. Within three days of the incident, Lester was arrested and was initially charged with the murder of the drunk as well as assault with a deadly weapon on Quinn, who tried to convince his superiors that Lester was the killer. After checking with witnesses, it was clear Lester had not killed the drunk. But he was charged with assault, although many Phoenix cops knew of Quinn's reputation and were silently happy when Quinn had his mangled arm amputated a week after Lester's attack and was sent to prison for second-degree murder.

Lester was sentenced to six years in federal prison on the assault charge but was released after four for good behavior. During his jail time, Lester read voraciously and not only received his high school diploma, but also credit for several college courses. Literature, history, and philosophy were particularly interesting to Lester, and while other inmates listened to the radio, watched old movies, or played cards every night, Lester read. For the first time he realized what he had lost by quitting school at such an early age. He envied his brother and how his life had always revolved around books. He even inquired about completing college and getting a law degree but was told as a convicted felon no state bar would accept him.

Upon his release in November 1940, Lester was the cliché of the older and wiser man. But that wisdom did little for his ability to find a decent job. Nearly forty and an ex-con, he soon gave up on finding a career and eventually returned to Phoenix and a life filled with minimum wage jobs, some petty crime, a well-used library card, and a valuable coming to grips with himself as a man.

For several years prior to meeting Rolle, Lester had assumed a leadership role over a group of twenty to twenty-five homeless men who lived in the deserted warehouses of downtown Phoenix. Lester's leadership of the men was neither sought, nor necessarily recognized by him. He simply did what came naturally, and over time he began to feel a responsibility to the men and did what he could to help them with their precarious lives.

From the time Lester first saw Rolle on the ground behind the bus station surrounded by his men three days earlier, he didn't trust him. Even when Rolle tried to play to Lester's ego and offered him a bonus for managing his men, Lester knew there was more to the story than Rolle was telling. But most of all, Lester felt responsible for the deaths of the three men who had been mutilated by the Germans. While these men's lives were worthless by society's standards, they were Lester's friends, and he saw no difference between them and the men he had led into battle years before.

He was also curious about what was happening at the Jasper, and he felt compelled to see his mission to its conclusion, even if that meant facing the same fate as his three friends.

———————————————

Taking advantage of the total darkness, Lester decided to make his move. His plan was to extricate himself from the shaft behind the large wood doors and move to his right against the cavern walls. He would make his way to the back of the now-damaged office area where he had met with Rolle hours before. The risk was that some of the guards may have been assigned to remain in the cavern, but Lester felt that was unlikely. Anyway, it was a chance he had to take.

Trying to find the footholds he had used as a boy to climb the rocks on the right side of the huge wooden door, he stumbled several times. The weight of the weapons he carried made it awkward for him to balance on the rocks. After finding the gap between the door and the rocks, he found he had a bigger problem. Literally. He wouldn't fit. While a five feet one, 100-pound boy had slithered through the opening, a six foot four, 170 pound man could not. His plans now useless, Lester cussed under his breath and tried to think of another option. His biggest concern was fatigue. He was fading, and knew if he stayed where he was much longer, he would get increasingly sore and might even fall asleep.

As Lester sat in the cool darkness and utter silence, time seemed to bend and waft. He wasn't sure how long he sat or if he had even dozed off when he heard the sound of gravel hitting the floor of the pitch-black tunnel.

Jerked to attention, Lester at first assumed the sound was caused by a pebble being loosened by a mouse or scorpion up near the top of the air shaft and trickling down into the tunnel. Not moving and staring into the darkness, Lester heard nothing for another five minutes.

Finally, given an achy left leg cramp, Lester was about to rise and force himself up one of the air shafts when more pebbles began to trickle into the tunnel. Suddenly, the trickle became a torrent, followed by the sound of a body careening down the same shaft that Lester had descended hours before.

Remaining motionless, Lester strained to see or hear some kind of movement, but the darkness and silence were total. Whoever had entered the tunnel was also utterly silent. With only thirty feet separating Lester from the shaft and the person now at the bottom of it, Lester knew he had the advantage. He knew his newly arrived visitor was there, but whoever had just slid down into absolute darkness didn't know Lester was there. Further, whoever was there surely didn't know where he had landed. Was he all the way down the shaft or only resting on a ledge with hundreds of feet of air below him? Was he wedged in a crevice? Was he in a tunnel filled with Mojave rattlers? Whoever this man was, Lester was impressed. To slide into an abyss, be able to maintain his composure, and not turn on a flashlight or even move, was a discipline that Lester admired.

Afraid to even raise his rifle for fear of the sound it might create, Lester decided to wait out his guest. For another ten minutes, a game of nerves prevailed in the tunnel with Lester's muscles aching from their immobility. Despite the coolness in the tunnel, perspiration began to run down Lester's face, and he could feel his blue work shirt become saturated with sweat.

Then, without warning, the tunnel was filled with more pebbles coming from the shaft. As the sound of falling pebbles grew louder, Lester took the opportunity to come to one knee and place his rifle in a firing position. Within seconds the sound of a second and then a third body cascading down the shaft hit Lester's ears, and the muffled grunts of the bodies as they plowed into each other reverberated in the shaft.

Now prepared to fire into the darkness aiming only at sound, Lester was given a much better target when one of the guards flipped on his flashlight. Like a beacon on a ship, Lester fired twelve rounds at the light, which was smashed out after the second shot. Moving from the left side of the tunnel to the right after firing his deadly volley, Lester crouched in silence, the acrid smell of the spent gun powder burning his nostrils. Thirty seconds after his shots, Lester heard a gurgling sound emanating from where the light had been, and he instinctively reacted by firing another six rounds. No longer waiting, Lester ran toward where he had fired. As he neared where the light had been, he turned on his flashlight and saw three German guards bathed in blood.

The guard lying on top of the other two had been nearly cut in half at the waist by three of the fifty caliber rifle shots. The second guard, eyes opened in death, had what appeared to be two wounds in the upper chest. The third guard on the bottom of the pile was the one Lester had shot in the back hours before. Obviously, the two guards had pushed their already dead comrade down to determine if anyone was waiting below in the shaft. There was.

Behind him, Lester heard the sound of voices and running feet from the main cavern. Realizing that more guards were coming, he decided that despite his fatigue, it was time to exit the tunnel via one of the air shafts. Running past the shaft the three dead guards had emerged from, he decided it was likely at least one more guard may be waiting for him at the top of that shaft. Moving toward other shafts a hundred and fifty feet deeper into the tunnel, he reached the second of three air shafts that would eventually lead him up to the top of the mine.

The guards in the main cavern had reached the large wooden door and were calling out the names of the guards who had been sent down the shaft. Hearing nothing, they pounded the huge deadbolt that was holding fast under the onslaught of rifle butts. Finally, the major told his men to step back, and he wedged a "pineapple" grenade between the wooden slats. Pulling the pin and moving back and to the side of the door, they waited.

At the same time, Lester had found the opening he was looking for and pulled himself up into the dark shaft. Seconds later, the grenade ripped open the massive wooden door.

The sound of the blast reverberated through the narrow tunnel with such force that Lester's left eardrum, the one facing the opening, was broken, and the pain at first made him feel as if he had been hit by flying rock. Temporarily stunned, he dropped one of the rifles he was carrying, and it skidded down the shaft and hit the rock floor below. The guards were now climbing through the remnants of the door through the smoke and dust, making their way to the back of the tunnel.

Coming to his senses, Lester ascended the shaft and immediately remembered why as a child he had always preferred the other two air shafts in which to play. This shaft was narrower and steeper than the other two, and for the first time claustrophobia gripped at him as he pushed himself through a small nearly horizontal section of the shaft that led to a steep vertical climb.

The angle he was trying to traverse forced him to pull his upper body through an opening, but in doing so, he found he did not have the room to bend his legs to allow him to push himself upward. For several seconds, with a rock firmly pressing against the small of his back, he couldn't move either up or down the shaft. He fought the panic that had invaded his brain. He went limp and tried to relax. He took deep breaths hoping that when he again tried to move his body, he would be able to.

With his free right hand, he slid his remaining rifle off his shoulder and down toward his right leg, attempting to give himself more room to maneuver. With his left ear bleeding and ringing in pain, Lester tried to gather his strength for another attempt to pull himself up the shaft. Moving his feet like a seal's flippers, he began to gain some traction and inched his way upward until the rock that was at the base of his spine had moved to the back of his knees. Resting for a moment, he was snapped back into action by the sound of the guards who had now found their dead comrades and knew they were not alone in the tunnel.

Inch by inch, Lester tried to make his way past the horizontal part of the shaft, but the steep angle that his once more flexible spine had navigated years before was giving his current spine a great deal of pain. He tried to roll onto his back to make the climb easier, but his movements were again impeded, this time by his flashlight and the .45 still tucked in his belt. He removed those objects and let them slide down the shaft. Jettisoning those objects gave Lester just enough room to finally turn on his back. As he lay in the darkness and felt the rock touching every part of his body, he wondered if this would be how he would die, in the cool embrace of the rock where he had spent the happiest days of his life.

For several seconds, Lester lay still in the pitch dark and might have stayed longer if not for a second explosion that rocked the tunnel below him. Feeling the shock of the blast, Lester knew instinctively what had occurred. The remaining guards, whose steps Lester had heard in the tunnel, had fired a grenade up the first shaft where their now dead comrades had descended.

The reverberations of the blast made dust and gravel drop onto

Lester from the top of the shaft he was occupying, and again, the panic of being crushed by a cave-in or from a grenade being launched into his shaft made him somehow move the final ten inches to put him into the vertical section of the shaft. Able to use his legs again, he felt for the footholds and handholds he had used as a boy to make his way up the still snug opening.

Twenty feet from the top of the one hundred-fifty-foot shaft, Lester heard the voices of the guards below and knew what was coming. Moving his hands and feet as fast as his aching body could command them, he scrambled up the remaining distance and brought the top half of his body out of the shaft nearly two hundred feet away from the shaft he had descended hours earlier.

As he gathered his strength to pull himself out of the black hole, a deep rumble came from below him, followed by an eruption of rock and dust that spit Lester out like a cork from a champagne bottle. Flipped onto his back by the relatively quiet blast, he had to cover his face with his hands as rocks, some the size of baseballs came raining back to earth. Within seconds a second blast sent even larger pieces of rock shooting from the hole like a geyser. Continuing to roll away from the opening, Lester finally picked himself up and ran to the far north end of the rock and sought shelter in a grouping of boulders.

When the echoes from the blasts subsided and quiet returned to the top of the mine, Lester looked around and quickly determined he was alone. He doubted the Germans with their dwindling numbers would risk sending more men after him. So he stretched out on the rock and tried to catch his breath. After a ten-minute rest, Lester took stock of his situation, and his analysis wasn't good. His lungs ached from the exertion and his body, particularly his back and legs, were awash with pain. His face was cut, and his arms had deep gashes from which blood poured down his arms onto the backs of his hands. But worst of all, Lester was utterly exhausted. He decided he had to get some rest if he was to continue his war against the German Army.

He also concluded that if getting some rest meant the Germans completed their task, then that's the way she goes. He also needed a damn weapon. Both would arrive in the next six hours.

CHAPTER 33

VEGA MINE—2014

AFTER TWO HOURS OF TRYING but failing to find a way into the Vega, Tom and Jon had used up their imagination and limited rock-climbing ability. Sore and dirty from knees and palms that had repeatedly banged on the rock, they returned to the air-conditioned van and quickly emptied the two remaining bottles of Evian. "If God had really wanted us to get in that fucking mine, he would've left a key in the door." Jon opined.

"I'm not sure even God would have gotten in that son of a bitch, that door must be four inches thick, and solid iron. It weighs tons."

"The only option we have is to try and hike around to the back side of the mountain and see if there are any entry points there or come back with a fucking tank and blow the hell out of that damn door."

"Let's go eat first, before we bring in the Army."

Driving back down the mountain road, Jon was, without explanation to Tom or himself, suddenly into what had been Tom's Big Adventure. Maybe it was the rock climbing, the freedom, or even the frustration of not being able to gain entrance to the mine, but whatever it was, he was no longer an unwilling participant in the hunt for gold. It suddenly engulfed him.

"We should've packed some food and stayed up here all day," Jon said as he looked to his right as the men passed the Jasper mine on their way down the mountain.

"Rather stop at Elsa's; I'm addicted to that iced tea they serve."

"Maybe we should get a tent and just keep poking around until we get in that mine. There must be something of value in there, or they wouldn't have locked it up like Fort Knox." Jon said.

Glancing at his friend, Tom could see the long years in jail beginning to slowly melt away from Jon. Tom wondered to himself if, when the melting was complete, he would like what would remain.

For several months after his release, Tom felt changes in himself. Not just in adjusting to freedom or in returning to the person he was before he entered prison. He couldn't quite put his finger on it, but the changes were deeper than just a response to his time behind bars. He was a fundamentally different person. At first, he rejected the change but was powerless to control his thoughts, and the thought that had haunted him most was he had been a putz and had pretty much thrown away a good part of his life. He had also hurt a lot of people. For the first time in his life he was feeling regret.

As they pulled into the crushed stone parking lot near where the helicopter had let them off days before, the men were hit by a barrage of handwritten signs in white paint on black wood placards. "Beef Jerky," "Saltwater Taffy," "Cold Drinks" "Horseback Rides," "See Our Rattlesnake Pit," "Home Cooking," and "Homemade Fudge" were just a few of the attractive and sophisticated options that awaited them at Elsa's Bar and Grill.

East of Phoenix, Elsa's opened for business in 1904, the only restaurant to serve old Route 60 running from Phoenix to Tucson. It also served the Jasper and Vega mines, and for years Elsa would pack up sandwiches, her famous beef jerky, along with Cokes, fudge, apples and make at least two runs a day to feed the men at the mines all of whom had quickly tired of the dust-laden food served by the mine companies each day.

After the mines closed, Elsa's became part of a train station where passengers would load up on Elsa's cooking while the train picked up passengers and water before heading east into the molten dessert. While originally only a dining room that seated twelve with a kitchen attached, Elsa's had grown into a free form collection of buildings that now totaled over thirty thousand square feet and not only sold food, but also Indian Jewelry, cowboy boots, wallets, wine, Elvis paintings on black velvet, t-shirts, country western tapes and CDs and just about anything else a person traveling on Route 60 could use or want.

Walking up the well-worn stone steps to the main restaurant, Tom noticed a half dozen old men sitting in wooden chairs leaning on two legs against the wall of the shaded porch that abutted the restaurant. Each man held a cup that contained the remnants of several hours of well-chewed tobacco. The patch of dark-colored spit under each of their chairs indicated that their collective aims were not all that good. It also appeared that group shortcoming did not particularly bother the men.

Eyeing Tom suspiciously, one of the men snorted, "Big sonavabitch, ain't he?" The old man then spit at and missed his cup.

Tom smiled and nodded, walked over to the old men and asked, "Gentlemen, do any of you know anything about those old abandoned mines up the road?"

"What the hell do you want to know about those death traps, young man?" one of the old men who spit and missed his cup asked.

"I'm a history buff, sir. My friend and I were just up at the Jasper and Vega and from what we saw they've been shut down for some time. We were just wondering what this area was like back when those mines were operational."

Getting blank stares and no reaction from the men for several seconds, Tom was about to give up and go inside with Jon, when one of men said, "When those mines closed, this town and the little towns that had sprung up in this valley all dried up and died. But with all the men those mines killed gettin' silver out of those holes in the ground, it was high time they closed."

"How many men were killed?" Tom asked.

"Some say over a hundred were killed and buried in the Vega alone, not sure 'bout the Jasper," was the reply from one of the men who decided not to spit.

"Any of you work in those mines?"

"We're here talkin' to ya, ain't we?" one of the men said, and the rest broke up in laughter in recognition of sophisticated old man humor.

Laughing with them, Tom thanked the men for the information and went inside with Jon.

Sitting in what was amusingly called air conditioning, and smelling the cacophony of beef jerky, deep fat, and strong coffee, Tom and Jon both ordered pulled pork sandwiches and chili and grudgingly admitted it was the best either had ever eaten. Swigging down their meals with raspberry iced tea and splitting a piece of fresh baked apple pie, they now realized why Jim the Asshole had spent so much time at Elsa's.

Leaning back in his chair and stretching his still sore legs, Tom put his hands behind his head and looked out the window at the old men still in their semi-reclined position. "Those old guys are like walking history books everyone ignores."

"They've forgotten more about this area than we'll ever learn," Jon added.

"What are you boys really lookin' for?"

Taken by surprise, Jon and Tom looked up to see one of the old men from the porch standing over them, a half-chewed cigar crammed in his mouth.

"Sit down," Tom said. The white-haired man slid in next to Jon.

"Thanks."

"Something to drink?" Jon asked.

"No thanks, I've got to get going in a minute. Just wanted to know what you boys are really looking for up at those mines."

Before Jon could answer, Tom replied, "A year and a half ago my friend and I were working on a prison work gang a few miles up the road and found a twenty-pound gold ingot, and we don't have a clue as to where it came from, or if there's more of them."

Staring in disbelief at his friend and looking around Elsa's, Jon softly muttered, "Are you out of your fucking mind?"

Ignoring Jon, the old man looked at Tom for nearly a minute, alternating his gaze from the window and back to Tom. "Do you boys believe in those UFOs we all hear about?"

"Sir, my friend and I aren't crazy, nor are we making up a..." Tom said.

"I never said you were crazy. All I asked was do you boys believe in UFOs?"

"I do," Jon said. "It's hard to believe we're alone in the universe."

"How about you?" The old man nodded toward Tom.

"I believe and for the same reasons."

"Just wondered. You know stories no crazier than UFOs have been around these parts for a couple hundred years. So you finding a bar of gold isn't the craziest thing I've ever heard. Fact is, I found some gold myself awhile back up near the Jasper after a two-day rain. But it wasn't no twenty pounds. It was about the size of that coffee cup."

"Was it unrefined or part of a larger piece, maybe a gold bar?" Tom asked.

"It was refined all right, smooth as milk and had the letters 'exi' on it."

"Ours said, 'Property of Canadian Government,'" Jon said. "And we found it in a creek bed a few miles south of the Jasper."

"Do you think our finds are somehow connected?" Tom asked.

"Don't know, but there've been stories over the last fifty years of other folks findin' such things around here, but you never really know if any of it is true or not. Some folks like to make things up," the old man said.

"Do you think the Jasper and Vega have anything to do with the gold?" Jon asked. "For instance, could a silver mine produce gold?"

"It's happened, but it's rare, and it would be nearly impossible to keep that kind of thing quiet. I doubt those old mines ever produced a lick of gold."

"Then where could our gold have come from?" Jon asked.

"Look here, my name is Ben, Ben Smith. And I'm way too old to chase down gold tales and too damn old to spend anything I found, but I sure as hell believe there's gold around here and lots of it. But I came over here to tell you boys that there are as many tales of folks disappearing looking for gold as there are tales about the gold itself. You two don't look like prospectors to me, and when you go back to those hills, as I know you will, just keep a lookout, that's all."

Getting up to leave, Ben shook hands with Tom and Jon and started to move away from their table when Tom good-naturedly asked, "By the way, how did you spend the money you got from your gold?"

Smiling, the old man reached in his pocket and pulled out a leather pouch the size of a plastic sandwich bag, removed a piece of gold, smooth and flat on two sides with jagged ends. Stamped on the top of the piece were the letters "exi" with pieces gouged out before and after the letters. "What makes you think I spent it on anything?"

Staring at the broken bar, Tom and Jon both came to the same conclusion that "exi" was part of the word "Mexico" or "Mexican Government". "Aren't you afraid to carry that around in your pocket?" Jon asked.

"Not really," Ben said. As he smiled wider, he lifted up his shirt and displayed an old Remington 32-caliber revolver stuck in his belt. "You boys take care now."

"Holy shit," Jon whispered, as Ben walked away.

For the next thirty minutes, Tom and Jon tried to recall everything Ben had told them and wavered between believing he was an old man trying to feed them some local lore, or that he had somewhat confirmed that there was more gold between Elsa's and the entrance to the Jasper just a few miles up the road.

As Tom and Jon continued their conversation over raspberry iced tea, a white Ford pickup truck idled in Elsa's parking lot. Inside the truck, three young men devoid of hair but resplendent in tattoo art had seen Tom and Jon when they engaged the old men in conversation before they had entered Elsa's.

The man sitting in the middle of the bench seat, nicknamed "Mouse," was casually leafing through a recent copy of *Daily Stormer* magazine. He paid close attention to announcements of upcoming marches and demonstrations that would provide opportunities to see old friends again. After he had looked up and seen Tom and John walk up the steps of Elsa's, he offered an insightful opinion: "They don't look like no fuckin' miners to me."

"No shit, Sherlock," responded the driver named Ron, as he made a call on his cell phone. After getting an answer he said, "Hello, sir. This is Ronald, and I wanted to give you an update on those two guys we saw snoopin' around the Jasper."

CHAPTER 34

JASPER MINE—1943

LESTER WAS USED TO SLEEPING outside and was famous on the streets of Phoenix for being able to fall asleep anytime, anywhere. Stretching out, he would fold each hand under his armpits, cross his legs, put his chin on his chest, and be out like a light in a minute. Not letting a small war with the Germans interfere with his routine, Lester slept soundly for several hours before being wakened by the sun rising over the rocks. Still sore from the night before, he slowly let his eyes adjust to the half-light and decided he really needed to pee. He rose gingerly, moved to the back of the rock cropping, and peed over the edge of the rock face and looked west toward Phoenix, its lights still radiating into pink-purple sky.

Turning back to the east, he walked toward the shaft that the Germans had used to come looking for him hours before. They had now sent and lost six men in or near the shafts, and he was certain they wouldn't risk any more. Yet, he had no gun, and although he knew he had personally taken care of at least twelve of the guards between the truck explosion and the six men in the shafts, there could be fifty more for all he knew.

In the cavern below, Rolle woke from only three hours of sleep with the major knocking on the half-opened rear window of the Lincoln in which Rolle and Becker had slept. "Colonel, I've pulled my remaining six men to an area surrounding the entrance to the mine. We cannot afford further losses. I'm not sure how many men we are up against, but to overpower my men there must be at least five to six well-armed and well-trained professionals scattered throughout the mine."

Looking at Becker still asleep on the front seat, Rolle nodded and quietly opened the back door of the Lincoln, pushing himself into the Arizona morning. He had slept fitfully after the explosion in the cavern and the subsequent attempt by the guards to trap Lester in the shaft. Hearing that more guards had been eliminated by Lester, Rolle realized that he still had a partner somewhere in the catacombs of rock that made up the mine.

"Major, it is now 6:30. Within twelve hours the first truck will arrive. Make sure your men sleep in shifts, get some food, and be ready and alert for tonight. Concentrate your men within one hundred feet of the cavern's entrance. I agree it would be foolhardy to enter the shafts again looking for whoever is trying to disrupt our plans. By the way, are all the bodies of your men accounted for? It's possible a few of your men could have turned on us and..."

The major's face reddened, and he said in a low, controlled voice, "Colonel, all of my men have been accounted for. But even if they had not been, my men were chosen for their loyalty and dedication to the Führer. They would gladly give their lives before betraying our efforts."

Watching the major walk away, Rolle already knew that what he had said about his men's dedication was true. He had asked the question only to throw off suspicion as to who could be responsible for the death of the guards.

From inside the Lincoln, General Becker stirred and swung open the passenger side of the car. Seemingly revived and in control of his senses, Becker seemed unaware or chose to have conveniently forgotten his performance from the night before. Seeing the major walking away, he asked, "What did the major have to report and why didn't you wake me?"

"General, the major was simply reporting on the location of his men..."

Cutting Rolle off with a voice that hissed with anger, Becker said, "Colonel, I hope you have not forgotten that this mission is my responsibility, not yours. What other information has the major provided you that I have not been informed of?"

"None, general, the major came to me only because he was aware you were not feeling well last evening after the explosion. He felt it best you rest a bit longer this morning."

Turning to Rolle, Becker drew up his five-foot-six inches as tall as he could, looked up at Rolle, and spat, "Ever since your arrival to this mine, we've had nothing but trouble. Is that a coincidence, or has spending the last few weeks in this cesspool of a country made you forget why we're here and of our commitment?"

"General, the plans I prepared for this project had been executed to perfection until you decided to make changes without consulting me. If a coincidence exists, it is since you made those changes that chaos has taken over Operation Rebirth."

His face now crimson with rage, Becker screamed, "Consult you? Why would I need to consult you? You, a low-level bureaucrat who could never possibly understand our goals for this operation."

"You mean goals to make you and your fellow thieves rich with our country's wealth?"

"Thieves? You uninformed ass. In time, you'll learn of a group called Odessa and who makes up that group. They are men of vision, and they will soon possess the gold needed to perpetuate the Führer's vision for the entire world."

"I've heard the rumors of this group, but I know what you say is more lies. More thievery, more..."

Without further comment, Becker lunged for Rolle's throat, but Rolle deftly stepped to his right, grabbed Becker's left wrist, and twisted it behind his back. At the same time he slammed Becker's face into the right rear window of the Lincoln. As Becker crumpled to the ground stunned by the impact of his face on the thick glass, Rolle kneeled and placed his left knee into Becker's back and whispered in his ear, "Do you think I was fooled by your transparent plan? Your arrogance and the arrogance of the trash like you, think you can rob Germany of her only hope for survival, so you can live like kings."

Trying to regain his composure and dignity, Becker summoned his sincerest voice and said. "Colonel, you've been under incredible pressure for several months. I apologize for my comments. Let's go inside and revisit your plan for how to distribute the gold after its arrival."

Not loosening his grip, Rolle pushed Becker flat to the dirt and kept his knee in the small of his back. "How many are involved in your cabal, General?"

"What cabal?" We are men, good men, trying to preserve the Führer's legacy. Why have you turned against us?" Becker gasped, finding it difficult to breathe.

"I've not turned against you, General; I've never been with you. I saw through your sham since the day you presented your preposterous plan to me months ago. Do you think me such a fool that I would be taken in by such nonsense?"

"Colonel, you are insane! You have everything wrong! This gold is to build a Fourth Reich, right here in America. The Führer believes this country will one day realize his greatness, and the genius of his vision and its citizens will… "

Interrupting Becker's impromptu and desperate speech, Rolle said, "Your idiotic lies bore me, General, but you are correct about one thing. This gold will save Germany, but you will not be there to see her resurrection."

As he spoke, Rolle removed a switchblade from his pocket, flipped it open, and then calmly and deliberately embedded it into Becker's right temple. Seemingly surprised by the insertion of steel into brain matter, Becker provided no resistance, no outcry of pain, or convulsive movement. He died quietly with his eyes open in a look of curious shock.

Lifting the body, Rolle opened the front passenger door of the Lincoln and slid Becker onto the front seat, trying to position it as it had appeared minutes earlier when Becker was sleeping, with the wound side down.

In the distance Rolle could see the major still walking up the gravel road toward one of the posts his men guarded.

When the major was no longer in sight, Rolle walked back toward the offices inside the cavern. He could smell the still acrid fumes from the vehicles that had burned down to their frames the night before. He entered the glass-strewn offices and made his way to where he had last met Lester. Rolle was going use the rear exit that led into the cavern to see if Lester could be found. He needn't have bothered.

Sitting in the near darkness of the office closest to the cavern, Lester had his feet propped up on the desk and appeared half asleep when Rolle entered the room. Squinting and trying to make his way to the back door, Rolle would have bumped into him if Lester had not said, "Whoa there, mister, don't knock me over."

Startled by the sound, Rolle at first began to back out of the office until Lester turned on one of the few lights that was still working, "Turn that light out or we will be seen." Rolle whispered.

Lester hit the switch and the room returned to near total darkness as Rolle came in and shut the door. "It appears you had a very eventful evening," Rolle said.

"Well, I wasn't exactly bored, but I am a little sore and hungry. Got anything to eat?" Looking at Lester, Rolle found it difficult to believe that this, tall, skinny, dirty, middle-aged man had eliminated at least a dozen well-trained and heavily armed German guards in one evening.

"Yes, there is some fruit, cheese, and bread in the next door office; I will get it for you."

Returning with the food and a canteen of water, Rolle watched as Lester languidly peeled and ate two bananas. He then broke off some bread and cheese and made a sandwich, then washed all of it down with a long drink of water, much of which ran down his chin and made a five inch water mark on his dirty blue work shirt. Taking some water in his hands, he splashed his face and said, "Damn, I feel like a new man."

"There are still six guards left," Rolle said, as Lester stretched out in his chair apparently not all that concerned about the guards or Rolle's plans that were still in jeopardy. "I said there are still six..."

"I heard ya' the first time, mister." Staring at Rolle, Lester slowly stood up and walked toward him. Meeting his gaze, Rolle felt the Luger still wedged in his belt and wondered if he would have to use it against this man whose bearing and presence was completely different from the scruffy hobo of forty-eight hours earlier. The dirty clothes were the same, but not the man wearing them.

"Mister, I killed a bunch of men last night and while they sure needed killin', nobody would be dead today, includin' my friends, if you hadn't lied to us 'bout what was goin' on out here. I want some answers, and if I don't get them right now I'm gonna put a hole in the back of your head the size of a grapefruit." As he spoke, Lester lifted a .45 automatic he had taken from one of the dead guards. "Mister, I ain't kiddin'. You talk now or you'll be dead in ten seconds."

Rolle decided to tell Lester the truth. Within minutes he laid out every detail of the plan up to and including how he killed Becker.

Lowering the .45, Lester walked back to his chair, sat down, and picked up the remaining apple on the table and took a large, noisy bite. "First of all, I don't need all that gold for me, but I know some folks who sure could use some help. Why don't we make a deal?"

"What kind of deal do you have in mind?"

CHAPTER 35

SCOTTSDALE, ARIZONA—2014

BACK IN THEIR MOTEL, TOM and Jon discussed their conversation with Ben and realized that they had approached their treasure hunt like the city rubes they were. "Remember that old movie *The Out-of-Towners* with Jack Lemmon and what's her name?" Tom asked

"Sandy Dennis."

"Yeah, that's right. Well, that's us. We're the out-of-towners who don't have a clue about what the hell we're doing."

"Which one of us is Sandy Dennis?" Jon naturally asked.

"You are, you Ivy League slut. Hey, I'm serious."

"Look, you spent months researching the history of this area, all those legends, even the geography, what else could we have done?"

"Reading books will only get us so far; we need someone like Ben to help us get to the next level." Tom said.

"You heard him. He's not interested in looking for gold."

"I know what he said, but maybe if we could convince him to just spend more time with us, he could fill in some of the gaps in what we don't know."

Gazing out of the hotel window and seeing nothing but Arizona desert stretching to the horizon, Jon was quiet for several minutes before saying, "For over seven years I've been thinking about all the things I'd do when I got out, and I can assure you that looking for some lost gold mine in this inferno was not in my top ten. But this is like a jigsaw puzzle or a novel when you've read the ending first. We know there's gold there. But we don't know how much, where it is, how it got there, or if anybody else knows what we know, or if they know more than we do. All I do know is, I want to find out more. Even if we find out there's no gold. It would be great to find a pot of gold and retire under a palm tree on some Caribbean Island, but I know that's probably bullshit. It's just that I've never had this kind of adventure before and want to see it through to the end."

"That's how I see it too," Tom said.

"How about three months? Let's give this boondoggle ninety days and if we don't find any answers, or gold, we leave for the East Coast and the real world. Deal?"

"Deal," Tom agreed.

After a restless night, Jon and Tom headed back to Elsa's at first light and had scrambled eggs with ranchero sauce and smoked ham for breakfast by 7:30. Not seeing Ben, they dawdled in their booth till nearly 10, having several cups of coffee, and watching an eclectic group of road warriors amble through the local legendary eatery. Leather-clad motorcyclists, families, men in business suits, and various forms of cowboys and Indians created an interesting two-hour sideshow.

Not pressuring them to vacate their booth, Vicky, their waitress, kept bringing back fresh coffee and amiably chatted with Jon and Tom. Fiftyish and plump, Vicki did not let the fact she was missing several teeth on her upper left side keep her from laughing and telling some raunchy jokes. After several stops with her coffee pot, Jon finally asked her if she knew a man named Ben.

"Ben Jackson or Ben Smith?"

"Ben Smith."

"Yeah, I know old Ben. He's been round here even longer than me. I was a sweet young thing with all my teeth when I came here twenty years ago, and old Ben was here then." Laughing at her own self-portrait, she then asked Jon why he was looking for Ben.

"We're interested in this area, particularly those old mines and thought maybe Ben could help us in getting some answers for some of our historical research."

"Sounds more like you're lookin' for gold to me," laughed Vicki. "Ben must have showed you that piece of gold of his he found up in the hills years ago. He shows that damn piece to pert near everyone who gets even near this place. I don't even think that damn thing is real, but it sure gets Ben lots of attention."

Suddenly deflated by Vicki's comments about Ben and the ease by which she saw through their ruse, Tom and Jon did not see an old friend staring at them from a booth thirty feet to their right.

Glaring under a dirty felt cowboy hat and behind a scruffy beard, Jim the Asshole, and former prison guard, was trying to get his whiskey-soaked brain to remember where he had seen the two urban cowboys before. Jim was sitting with three other hygienically challenged men, all of whom were trying to eat off an all-night bender with eggs, grits, and several gallons of coffee, with little success.

"I know those two assholes over there," Jim said to his buddies, oblivious to the irony.

"Where from?" one of his associates grunted.

"Not sure. All I know is I didn't like em' before, and I sure don't like em' now."

"Yeah, they look like assholes alright," said a second informed friend, as irony reached epic proportions.

His mind now working like a rusty razor blade, Jim said, "I'll tell you what... I think those assholes work at the bank that foreclosed on my house."

"You mean the one in the trailer park?" The fourth associate asked, mesmerized by the mystery involving the two strangers who talked and laughed with Vicki.

"Yeah, I said it was my house, didn't I?" Jim responded with some irritation, as he continued to stare at Jon and Tom.

"Those assholes sure do look like bankers," the one with even fewer teeth than Vicki said.

"You know it ain't right that a man works his whole life to build a home with a satellite dish that picks up the NFL package and have some asshole bankers come and take it all away."

"How many payments did you miss 'fore they stole your house?" Jim's sympathetic toothless friend asked.

"I don't remember exactly. They said I never made no payments, but I'm pretty sure I did and the goddamn post office lost them."

Still glaring at Jon and Tom, Jim the Asshole and former guard finally decided to confront his home-takers. With his friends in tow, he walked to Tom and Jon's booth. "What are you two assholes doin' in here? Lookin' to take another man's home and satellite dish?" Looking up from their coffee, Jon and Tom did not at first recognize Jim the Asshole, nor his three rather large and half-drunk companions who now made up a large, fleshy mural surrounding their booth.

"Pardon me?" Jon asked.

"You heard me, you little asshole, what the hell you doin' here?" As he spoke, he reached down, picked up Tom's half-filled coffee cup, and drained it into Jon's lap.

"Hey, what the hell are you doing?" Jon yelled, as he tried to stand up in the booth to escape the hot coffee.

With the three men behind him laughing and providing the encouragement he needed, Jim the Asshole reached for Jon's cup with the intent of pouring his coffee into Tom's lap. Inches from the cup, his wrist was intercepted by Tom's enormous left hand and held in a grip that forced a grunt of pain from Jim's lips.

"You better let go of my wrist, boy, or my friends here are gonna start bustin' you up."

Increasing the pressure of his grip, Tom looked at Jim and calmly and sincerely said, "If they start anything, I'll snap your arm like a chicken bone. It'll be a compound fracture. There's going to be a lot of blood, and if you really piss me off, I'll keep twisting this skinny arm of yours till I rip it off. Then I'm going to stand up and beat the hell out of each of your friends with what's left of your skinny arm and put them all into intensive care. All this is going to happen just because you think we're somebody we aren't. Do you clearly understand me?"

As he spoke, Tom again increased the pressure on Jim's wrist. The vise-like grip caused Jim to moan in pain. Tom took the cup from Jim's hand, placed it on the table, and slid out of the booth feeling at a definite disadvantage in a sitting position with four men surrounding him.

Still gripping Jim's wrist, Tom reached his full six foot eight height and the three men behind Jim began to rethink their position and whether they really wanted to risk getting hospitalized over a trailer and a satellite dish, even if it could bring in all the NFL games.

"Hey Jim, this ole boy here says he ain't who you think he is. You sure they's the ones who took your house?" asked the largest of the group.

Becoming more sober by the second, Jim squinted through the tears rising in his eyes and said, "No, I ain't sure, but I know them from somewheres."

Keeping Jim's wrist in the grip of his huge hand, Tom pushed Jim toward the front door of Elsa's. As he did, the other diners had for the moment put down their forks and watched in silence. Opening the door, Tom pushed Jim down the three steps, and the former guard landed on his ass ten feet away. When he turned back toward the inside of Elsa's, Tom faced the three remaining men and for a split second thought that the short fat one, who was well over 250 pounds, might try something. Locating a spot on the fat man's face, Tom was ready to unleash a right hook that would have broken the man's jaw in several places as a similar punch had done to a mugger that Tom ran into on a Manhattan street several years before. But the fat one, seeing the sincerity in Tom's eyes, dropped his own gaze and, with the other two, headed for the door.

Vicki, the waitress, followed them outside with their check in hand and cussed at the men for trying to walk out on their bill. With all four reaching in their pockets, they finally came up with enough to satisfy Vicki, including a 20% tip.

Back in their booth after Tom had taken a bow to the applause he received from the other diners for his performance, Jon asked, "Do you know who that was?"

"Yeah. That was Jim the Asshole. Recognized him when I stood up."

"Quite a job, big guy, I was hoping the other three would have started something. Were you really going to break his arm?"

"Like a twig. He had a gun in his right pocket."

Suddenly pale, Jon asked, "Are you sure?"

"I'm sure."

"I guess you boys can handle yourselves after all. Mind if I join you?"

Looking up, Tom and Jon saw a smiling Ben Smith.

CHAPTER 36

JASPER MINE—1943

SITTING IN THE NEAR DARKNESS of the small office of the Jasper mine, Rolle and Lester came to an agreement. Rolle had realized earlier that he had greatly underestimated Lester on many levels. Yet, he realized that it was part of Lester's personality that he wanted to be underestimated. It gave him a competitive edge in dealing with people. With the men from the streets of Phoenix, he became their leader because they thought he was smarter than they were, but not a lot smarter. Had they perceived he was far different from them either intellectually or any other way, they would not have felt he was one of them. He would have been viewed with distrust, an outsider.

Lester realized the role he needed to play and took a low-key approach with his leadership position. In many cases, he let others make decisions and only if he thought they were patently foolish would he offer alternatives. That's why the men on the street respected him. While he tried to avoid reverting to violence in his violent world, Lester would never back down from a challenge or from defending those who needed it.

On more than one occasion, Lester had used his military training in hand-to-hand combat to beat senseless someone who deserved it. Once he even killed a man who had long been suspected of several beatings and mutilation murders of homeless men in and around Phoenix. When the six foot five, 275-pound man threatened to cut up one of Lester's friends, "like the others," for not giving him the last of his military pension money, Lester disarmed the man in seconds and put the knife between his third and fourth ribs. The man's body was never discovered nor missed. Coincidently, a string of slashing murders on the streets of Phoenix suddenly stopped, the cases never solved.

On the surface, there appeared to be a great number of differences between Lester and Rolle, yet the men were remarkably similar in many ways. Both tall and slender, they shared aquiline features and receding hairlines. While Rolle had far greater formal education, he recognized Lester's intelligence and ability to lead, traits he felt he also possessed. Both men were also reserved in nature, and while Lester liked country music, and Rolle, Beethoven, they both appreciated art and were avid readers. The biggest differences between the two men could not be seen.

Lester, despite the violence that had become part of his life, was a man with deep convictions and an unwavering sense of right and wrong. Rolle was far more pragmatic in his use of violence. It was simply a means to an end. Unlike Lester, Rolle would not lose a minute's sleep over someone he had ordered killed or had killed himself.

Facing each other in the darkness of the office, each man had the opportunity to kill the other, but their respective responsibilities dictated that they maintain their partnership, at least for the time being. While Lester never doubted that he was the intellectual equal of the man across the table, Rolle had only arrived at that conclusion an hour earlier. While the recognition of that fact made Lester a far more formidable adversary, it also made him a more valuable ally, even if only for the next twelve hours.

The agreement between the two men was simple. Lester would help Rolle temporarily disarm the remaining six guards at the front gate and await the delivery of the gold. After it arrived, the majority of the twenty-four guards from the twelve incoming trucks would be ordered to leave the Jasper in ten of those trucks and await further orders at a predetermined point, fifty miles from the mine.

The reality was those guards would never hear from Rolle or anyone else again. As a result, they would eventually disappear into various parts of America to start new lives or perhaps even return to Germany after the war. They would also be warned if they ever returned to the Jasper, they and their families back in Germany would be executed.

From the six remaining guards in the Jasper and several from the twenty-four delivering the gold, Rolle would select a handful to help him secure the gold until the war ended, and it could be returned to Germany. Of course, Rolle was already thinking how he could kill those guards whom he would choose because he could never risk that many men knowing the gold's exact location within the mine.

After the gold was delivered, and in exchange for his help in neutralizing the six remaining guards left in the mine, Rolle agreed to allow Lester to take one of the twelve gold-laden trucks and leave the mine.

Despite his agreement with Lester, Rolle had concluded that when the opportunity arose, he would kill Lester as well, rather than allow him to drive off with millions of dollars of German gold into the Arizona night. It was not just the gold that Lester would be taking that prompted Rolle's decision; it was also that Lester was a loose end that Rolle would prefer to eliminate, if possible. But Rolle also knew that killing the American hobo was not going to be an easy task.

Lester obviously did not trust him, and Rolle knew that. Yet, for some reason, if he was not able to kill Lester, he believed him when he said he would take no more gold than they had agreed to, and he would never tell anyone about the gold or what had transpired at the Jasper.

After making his agreement with Rolle, Lester had melted into the darkness of the cavern and embarked on the plan to neutralize the six remaining guards. Walking through the remnants of the blown-up wooden door at the back of the cavern, he entered the shaft and saw the three dead guards. Using his flashlight, Lester found his old Colt that he had let slide down the shaft the night before. He lifted two Lugers and a machine gun with five clips from the dead German guards. Lester reentered the wider of the two shafts and found his ascent to the surface considerably faster and easier than the night before given how the grenades had augured the shaft by at least six inches.

Back on the surface of the mine, Lester began to make his way down the eastern slope of the hill, one which would bring him a half mile north of where the six remaining guards, including the major, were manning their posts. Even though it was the long way off the hill, over the next hour Lester would slowly move southward, which would place him just fifty yards from where the remaining guards were positioned.

Once he was in place, Lester would wait for Rolle to order the major to join him in the cavern office to discuss the arrival of the trucks later in the afternoon. That would leave only five guards at their posts and increase Lester's chances.

Arriving on schedule and within yards of their position, Lester was unable to see the guards who were hidden in the rocks that overlooked the road. The guards were all within a fifty-yard radius of one another and made audible sounds to ensure that each was still at his position and alive. The men also talked to each other in low murmurs that carried easily over hundreds of yards in the thin desert air before fading. Sometime a nervous laugh would emanate from one of the men. Lester could hear the tension in their voices.

Picking up some of the German words, Lester determined the men were talking about home. He remembered his soldiering days and recalled that was all he and his men talked about while lying in the blood and muck of the trenches so many years before. Lester hoped the men could be disarmed without any more killing. Too many had already died.

Wedged in a cluster of rocks, Lester waited twenty minutes and finally heard Rolle's voice in the distance. All other talking stopped as the major left the others, walked back toward the mine, and engaged in conversation with Rolle who was apparently asking him to bring two or three men with him and join Rolle in the cavern. While he could not pick up all the words, Lester figured out the major objected to leaving his men and depleting his strength at their current position. Calming him, Rolle explained that he felt vulnerable in the cavern and wanted to make sure that he had some armed protection inside as well as outside. In addition, he needed to discuss the truck schedule with the major.

Hearing nothing for several seconds, Lester assumed the major was mulling over his situation and that of his men. The major was also keenly aware that an unknown group of men somewhere in or near the mine had systematically killed thirteen of his troops the night before. Whoever these men were, the major now knew they were highly trained, disciplined, and fearless. They also knew the terrain far better than his men. The major realized his men were, despite their experience and bravado, jumpy and although they would never admit it, scared.

The major finally agreed to take only one man from his post, and along with Rolle, the three men began the half-mile walk back to the cavern. Hearing the men's voices moving away from the rocks that hid the four remaining guards, Lester waited until he was sure that Rolle and the two other men were out of earshot.

The four guards that remained in the rocks soon returned to their muted conversations. By the sounds and intonation of their voices, Lester could tell they had all moved to within twenty-five yards of the main entrance and appeared even more nervous than before.

The guard closest to Lester was on his stomach facing south with a clear view of at least three miles of dirt road. Twenty-five feet to his left and twenty feet above him, a second guard could also see the dirt road and into the main drive leading to the mine. The other two guards were east of their companions and could see the dirt road heading north. While each guard could see the entrance into the mine and the dirt road in both directions, they covered a limited area geographically and more importantly, they couldn't see each other.

But Lester couldn't see them either, and while he knew their general locations, he was not in a position to get a shot at any of them. Even with the odds now only four to one, Lester did not underestimate the remaining Germans. He knew their edginess made them all the more dangerous.

Trying to get in a position where he could see at least one of the guards, Lester tried unsuccessfully to climb up a four-foot high rock. As he slid back down the slippery surface, the sound reverberated, and he knew the guards had heard him skitter down the rock face. Suddenly quiet, the guards listened for the sound to return, but Lester was motionless. Hearing muffled voices, the guards were trying to determine what to do next. Finally, echoed footsteps emanated from the position of the guard nearest Lester. The scraping of leather boot against rock indicated that the guard had decided to investigate the sound and was trying to navigate the boulders around him.

Tucked up and under the overhang of the rock he had tried and failed to climb, Lester held his position. Hearing the footsteps of the guard coming closer, Lester pulled one of the .45's from his belt. Without warning, two large feet suddenly came flying from above and landed with a dusty clomp three feet in front of Lester. Now staring at the back of two knee-high brown military boots, Lester moved quickly and from a kneeling position on his left knee shoved the barrel of the .45 into the back of the scrotum of the young German. Motionless, the soldier looked down between his legs and let out a low moan knowing the result of a .45 shell tearing through his testicles on its way to his intestines, stomach, heart and lungs.

Staying in his kneeled position, Lester moved to the left side of the guard and looked up at the tall German, smiled, and put his finger to his lips. Taking the guard's rifle with his left hand and placing it behind him, Lester slowly rose on the guard's left side and as he did so, he brought the .45's barrel upward and placed it on the left temple of the guard. With his lips next to the guard's ear, Lester whispered, "You speak English?" Nodding slowly, the guard kept his eyes forward not looking at Lester.

"That's good, 'cause my German ain't what it used to be. What's your name, boy?" Rolle asked.

"Eric." A hoarse voice whispered.

"Last name?"

"Schneider. My name is Eric Warner Schneider."

"How old are you, son?"

"Twenty-one."

"Damn I was twenty-one once, 'bout a hundred years ago. Well, Eric Warner Schneider, we got ourselves a little problem here, don't we? But if you decide to help me out, you and your friends may be able to be home in a few weeks. If you don't help me out, it's real likely you and your friends will be as dead as the rest of the men you sent after me and my troops last night."

Saying nothing, the now sweating guard continued to stare ahead. Lester was taken by how young the guard looked. While a muscular six feet five and well over 200 pounds, it did not appear that the handsome young man had even begun shaving. Yet, here he was trying to protect the future wealth of Germany in an American desert.

Motioning the guard to move from their current position to an area further east, the two men made their way up and over several large boulders and came to rest in a position that allowed a clear view of the alcove they had occupied minutes before.

With the .45 pressed in the back of Eric's head, Lester waited for some activity or sound from the three remaining guards. Finally, a half-whispered "Eric?" came from the rocks. After thirty more seconds, another "Eric" came forth, this time a bit louder. Then two of the remaining three guards, weapons drawn, leaped over the rocks into the alcove. The larger of the two landed in the same spot Eric had come down on moments before, his partner landed four feet to his left.

Lester wasted no time. He pocketed the .45, then raised the machine gun and fired a burst in the air. The two guards fifteen feet below them in the alcove froze. While he could not be seen, Lester had a clear view of both guards who were on their knees back to back with their weapons at the ready.

Lowering the machine gun and placing it under Eric's chin Lester quietly asked, "Do your friends speak English, Eric?"

Saying nothing, the young German continued to stare straight ahead.

"Eric, I could have killed you and both your friends just now. I'm tryin' my level best to get you boys back home to your mamas, but you ain't helpin' me none. Now, I'm gonna ask you one more time, do your friends speak English?"

"Yes."

"Thanks, boy."

Speaking in a calm, slow voice almost like a fatherly coach talking to his players before the big game, Lester said, "Hey boys, I think ya'll might be in a tough situation. I can see you, but you can't see me. I could shoot you both right now along with Eric here, but don't rightly want to do that. If you throw your rifles and those pistols out of that pit ya'll are in, and then tell that friend of yours to join ya'll, then there ain't no reason in the world why you boys can't be home in a few weeks."

With the sound of his voice bouncing off the rocks the two young Germans could not tell where Lester's voice was coming from. They turned their heads constantly trying to pick up the direction. The smaller of the two guards suddenly tried to scramble up the rocks and out of the alcove. Using Eric's shoulder as a platform, Lester squeezed off two quick rounds from his machine gun and the shells hit the rock the German was trying to scale two feet above his right hand. The sound of the ricocheting bullets made it sound like ten shots, not two, had been fired, and the young German fell backward on his butt at the feet of the second guard who in one motion threw his weapons up over the rocks and stood with both hands in the air.

Saying something in German to his braver but not wiser companion, the guard on the ground also unbuckled his sidearm and tossed both weapons in the same direction as the first.

"That's good, boys. Now tell your friend to join you and do the same thing."

Without having to say a word, the final guard jumped into the increasingly crowded alcove, and almost eagerly threw his weapons over the rocks.

The four tough German guards suddenly looked like four young boys who would at that moment have much rather been just about anywhere else in the world but in a hot desert in a strange land surrounded by American troops.

Moving from his position, Lester pushed Eric in front of him, and they made their way to a position six feet above the three guards now sitting in the sandy alcove. "Why don't you boys make some room for Eric here."

Motioning for Eric to join his friends, the young German jumped into the sand pit and all four guards sat in a circle and looked up at Lester in silence like boy scouts looking up at their scout master.

"Like I said before, ain't no reason why you boys can't be home soon if you all cooperate and..."

Lester was interrupted by the sound of two quick shots in rapid succession then a third and fourth several seconds later.

Reacting to the shots, the four guards in the pit started to rise.

"Why don't you boys just sit right on back down and relax." Lester said motioning with his machine gun.

Clearly shaken over the events of the previous twenty-four hours, the young Germans offered no resistance to Lester and immediately sat back down.

Maintaining his position, Lester was able to keep an eye on the four guards and still see most of the dirt road that led to the cavern. Five minutes after the four shots, Lester saw a lone figure walking toward his position. Pistol dangling by his side, Rolle walked slowly and deliberately. Calmly, he called out in German for the remainder of the guards not knowing that Lester had already neutralized them.

"Mister, over here," Lester yelled.

Rolle appeared surprised that it was Lester who had responded to him as he moved toward his position. As he walked closer, Lester briefly thought about shooting Rolle right then and there thus eliminating any potential problems that he was quite certain would eventually arise with him. Problems like Rolle killing him. But Lester didn't shoot.

Moving from the shadows of the rocks, Lester could see blood stains on Rolle's shirt and when he was in earshot he asked, "What was all the shootin' about?"

Nonchalantly, Rolle answered, "The major and lieutenant have been eliminated."

The detail he neglected to provide was that Rolle had decided on the spur of the moment to kill the two guards when they turned their back on him to look over maps that were laid over the hood of the Lincoln after they had seen Becker's body in the front seat.

As the major turned to Rolle to ask about Becker, Rolle pulled the Luger from his belt and shot him in the forehead. Shocked, the young lieutenant stood motionless as Rolle shot him once in the chest. As the two men thrashed in the dust, Rolle shot each in the temple and then walked back toward Lester and the remaining guards.

Lester had killed men before both in the heat of battle like in the last twenty-four hours and once because a man deserved it, but it wasn't something he enjoyed and often suffered nightmares about having shot a man thirty years before in the war. Rolle's apparent arrogance and indifference about killing two countrymen confirmed what Lester had believed about Rolle from the time he met him; only one of them would be alive when this adventure ended.

CHAPTER 37

AFTER THEIR CONFRONTATION WITH JIM the Asshole, Tom, Jon, and Ben spent the rest of the morning in the booth at Elsa's getting to know one another and sketching out some plans. They stayed so long they felt obligated to order lunch. As they spoke, it was clear that Ben's stated indifference about finding a large cache of gold was not entirely accurate.

However, his reasons for wanting to find gold were different than most. As he had stated to Jon and Tom before, he was too old at 73 to really care about becoming rich. That was because he was already rich. Very rich. Speculating in Southern California real estate in the thirty years after World War II, Ben had made tens of millions by the time he was forty. Later, through shrewd stock market and other investments, including going into the aviation business that furthered his love of flying, he decided to retire and take up full time his hobby of archeology. Flying throughout the world, he studied and participated in archeological digs in Egypt, Greece, Mexico, Peru, and even looked for dinosaur bones in the Badlands of New Mexico.

Since his wife had died at a relatively early age, and with only one child to raise who was now grown, Ben became a citizen of the world, and despite his age, still traveled extensively when he heard of a dig or just wanted to see a new and exciting place.

Despite his wealth, Ben liked his relatively low-key lifestyle, living on a two-hundred acre ranch outside Phoenix. Some of Ben's friends knew he had money, but even they did not know how much, nor that he had other homes in Aspen, Palm Beach, and a horse farm in Lexington, Kentucky. Ben was not being deceitful; he just felt his friends might treat him differently if they knew the extent of his net worth.

Ben had noticed Tom and Jon the first time they entered Elsa's and had accurately deduced that they were city boys trying to play gold miners. At first he was amused by their naiveté and lack of knowledge. But he was also concerned. The rumors of gold in the hills surrounding them were not new, nor were more serious stories of men disappearing while searching for their fortunes.

Some say the land killed them; the furnace-like heat, the twisting dirt roads that led to sheer two thousand foot drop-offs, or rattlesnakes and scorpions in sleeping bags were all part of the lore of how and why people disappeared. But even more sinister were the rumors of bands of thieves following inexperienced weekend gold miners into the hills and killing them for cash, equipment, pickup trucks, Rolexes, or as some suggested, to prevent them either by design or accident, from finding the gold already discovered by the killers who would do anything to protect their troves.

––––––––––––––––––––

When Ben found his chunk of gold, he had been hiking in the early morning hours in the desert several miles north of Elsa's after two days of rain. Rain in the desert, while rare, occurs more frequently than Easterners would imagine, and when it does rain, it can rain for days with a frightening intensity. Sun-baked dirt, hard as rock, does not absorb water easily, and rampaging flooding can result after even a few hours of rain. Small creeks become raging torrents that can change the contour of a desert floor. But like the sound no one hears from a falling tree in the forest, changes in a desert wilderness can go unnoticed by man.

With a desert floor that still held small pools of water after the rain, Ben had set out with some bottled water and a ham sandwich wanting to get some exercise and take advantage of a cool and still cloudy Arizona sky. After a five-mile outward hike, Ben began a slow circle that would return him to his Jeep parked off the dirt road that led north from Elsa's and ended at an abandoned mine. As he turned back to the east, the late morning sun broke through the clouds, and the desert changed from a mottled brown to a multicolored pallet of greens, tans, grays, and pinks. The colors changed by the second as clouds would reclaim the sky only to have the sun break through again and set off a new explosion of color.

Taken by the spectacle, Ben sat down on a rock to take in the beauty that surrounded him. Looking back toward the west at the endless horizon, he detected a metallic reflection fifty yards away in an area that he had just passed minutes before. Thinking it may be a pop can or piece of trash from a careless hiker, he moved toward the area to retrieve it and leave the desert as he had found it.

Walking to the spot, he at first lost sight of the glimmer as the sun peeked in and out of the clouds. Ready to forget the object, the sun broke through yet again, and the metallic object reappeared and shone brightly twenty feet ahead to his left.

Reaching the object, he found a three-inch square piece of metal that he instantly thought was a chunk of gold. Touching it first with his walking stick and simultaneously rebuking himself for such pedestrian thoughts, he kneeled to retrieve the object that rested almost completely exposed on the damp desert floor. As soon as he felt the weight in his hand, he knew his original pedestrian thoughts were correct. He had just found a damn piece of gold lying wide open in the desert, like someone had put it on a nightstand before going to bed.

For the next three days, Ben looked for more gold. He worked in ever-widening circles and spent the rest of the first day looking on the surface. On the second and third days, he brought a metal detector with him and continued his search but found nothing of value. Occasionally, especially after big rains, Ben would return to the spot but never again found gold. Over the years he, like Tom and Jon, wondered how such a piece could end up in the desert. Did it fall from the sky? Was it part of a larger cache? Was it dropped from a wagon as it lumbered across the desert? He had asked all the same questions. Until he had met Tom and Jon, he had given up all hope of answers. Yet they too had found what he had found, and for the first time in years, a new page in the mystery was turning.

As Ben listened to Tom and Jon speak, it was hard to imagine that two such bright, likable young men could have ended up in prison. He was also surprised that they were so open and honest about what they had found and their backgrounds. Ben kept looking around Elsa's hoping no one could overhear their conversation. Their enthusiasm for trying to find the gold was, he thought, borne of a desire for adventure after years in prison, the need for financial security, the challenge such an endeavor would entail, and the overriding desire to accomplish something—even if "something" was the answer to the riddle of where the gold came from and nothing more.

While the three men analyzed various theories as to where the gold could have come from, they couldn't decide on a definitive answer. But they all agreed that the gold had been refined in the twentieth century, given the size and shape of Tom and Jon's bar, and the lettering on both. They also agreed that there was more gold. The logic being that in the thousands of square miles of desert that lay outside Elsa's doors, the assumption that Ben, Tom, and Jon had found the only two pieces of gold was a virtual mathematical impossibility.

Ben also listened to Tom's theory that the silver mines north of Elsa's played some role in the gold. Ben failed to see a firm connection, but he saw how Tom drew his conclusion and agreed to visit both mines with Jon and Tom.

Tom's historical perspective and Ben's archeological experience also meshed as Tom related what he had learned in libraries, and Ben recounted his experience in excavation, impact of terrain, and knowledge of the local area. But Ben warned Tom and Jon to keep a lower profile regarding their search. He related stories of disappearances of both experienced and inexperienced gold hunters who wandered into the hills and were never heard from again. At first both young men tried to laugh off Ben's stories as mere folklore. But the serious tone taken by Ben and his no-nonsense statement that if they did not listen to his warnings he would walk away from their blooming partnership got their attention.

Finally, the men agreed on a plan. It was a plan that would prove to exhaust them physically, intellectually, and emotionally. Part of their agreement was that if they found anything, it would be split three ways. At the end of a ninety-day period, if nothing was found, they would never again pursue the dangerous fantasy of hunting for gold in the desert.

Ben added just one more condition to their agreement; he had a partner. In fact, he had two.

As Ben, Jon, and Tom wrapped up their meeting over more raspberry iced teas, tucked away in a corner of Elsa's parking lot, three young men sat in an idling white pickup truck with tinted windows. All three men were in their early thirties, had shaved heads, and as many tattoos as allowed by Arizona law. The driver of the pickup made a call to Montecito, California, on his cell.

On a golf course, an elderly man looked at his caller ID and said to his playing partner, "It's Phoenix again."

"Is he using the untraceable line?"

The elderly man nodded and answered. "Good morning, Ronald, I hope all is well."

"Yes sir, things is good."

"Splendid. What can I do for you, Ronald?"

"Well, sir, we've been following those two guys we told you about like we said we would, and it's like I said before, I think they're just tourists nosin' around the mines, you know, they look like amateurs."

"Very well. I appreciate your diligence and that of your associates, although I realize you are clearly the leader of your group. Please keep me posted if the situation changes."

"Yes sir, you bet I will."

"By the way, Ronald, how are your recruiting efforts progressing?"

"Good, sir. We got some Road Warriors and Skull Men riding in this weekend, and we should get a bunch of sign-ups from those groups," Ronald explained with enthusiasm.

"That's wonderful, Ronald. It is obvious you are a man of many talents. Stay well."

"Thanks sir and…"

The impeccably dressed old man on the golf course whose name was Armin, clicked off his phone and didn't hear the rest of Ronald's words, nor did he care to.

His elderly partner in the golf cart asked, "Any reason to be concerned, Armin?"

"Only that we are dealing with idiots."

"Isn't that the plan?"

"Yes, and the plan is working. The press and government believe what they see."

"Then you should be content to let apathy take its course."

"Yes, it always has," Armin agreed.

Back at Elsa's parking lot, Ronald basked in the compliments from the old man. "He said I was doing a great job."

Sitting next to him, Danny had a question. "What about me and Mouse here?"

"Oh yeah, he said you guys were doin' a great job too."

"Cool," Mouse said.

"Ever meet that old dude?" Danny asked.

"No. Just answered that ad online. Next thing I know I'm gettin' checks sent to my post office box just to come out here a few times a week and see if anybody is goin' into the Jasper. That's easy as shit."

"Man, you're a lucky dude," Danny marveled.

"Why's that old man so hot on the Jasper?" the ever-inquisitive Mouse asked.

"Damned if I know. But if all I have to do is give him a call every time I see someone go in there in exchange for the cash we use to get laid at one of our parties, I can dig that." Mouse had another probing question. "Ronnie, what's that old guy's name?"

"Don't know and don't care."

CHAPTER 38

JASPER MINE—1943

ROLLE WALKED SLOWLY FROM THE cavern toward Lester, pistol in hand. From several feet away, he told Lester he had "eliminated" the major and lieutenant. As he looked at Lester, Rolle continued to be surprised and inwardly enraged that a dirty hobo from this cesspool of a country could have killed and captured so many of Germany's finest.

With the automatic rifle in his hands, Lester felt secure for his own life at least for the moment, but when he saw Rolle approach, he wondered if Rolle was thinking of also "eliminating" the young guards as they sat in the dust-filled pit below him. Had Rolle raised his pistol, Lester would have shot him instantly.

The four guards in the pit, despite their swagger and imposing physical presences, were in the end, young men in or barely out of their teens who had been drafted into a mission that they were likely never supposed to survive. Most had not. Lester wondered what propaganda they had been fed to have agreed to be sent on such a suicide mission.

If the guards were to be captured by American agents, they would surely be executed as spies. Or they could be "eliminated" by the very people who drafted them when they had completed their tasks and became more of a liability than an asset. Lester knew Rolle would never allow a bunch of young German guards to be turned loose in America with knowledge of the location or existence of tons of German gold.

Lester also knew that the programming these young men underwent made them dangerous. If given a chance they would kill him without a second thought. But he also knew that they were soldiers following orders, and this war, like all the others, would someday end, and these men, if given a chance, would return to mothers, wives and sweethearts. He didn't fault them for the orders they were given to enter American soil to try to perpetuate Hitler's Germany by protecting the gold. He remembered crazy orders he had to follow years before. And while he would defend himself if they tried to overpower him, he would just as soon those boys not have to die on foreign soil, but Lester also knew his preference faced long odds.

As he rose to meet Rolle, Lester could see the confusion on the faces of the four guards as they realized that Rolle, someone whom they thought was part of their team was, somehow, someway, working with Lester, the enemy. They also had heard Rolle's comments about eliminating the major and lieutenant, and no doubt they too expected to be shot within minutes.

"It appears you have compromised what I thought were our best soldiers. It was in our best interests that these men did not live up to their advanced billing." Rolle said sarcastically.

"I don't think these boys were all that experienced, mister." Lester said looking down at the four young men.

"We can deal with these men later. In less than four hours the first truck will arrive, and we must be prepared to oversee the unloading and storage of the gold. We must dispose of the bodies that remain from last night and make sure there are no weapons or other materials that could alert the drivers of a change in plans. Don't forget, these drivers were under the supervision of Becker, and they will already be suspicious about his absence."

It was agreed that Lester would take the remaining four guards and dispose of the bodies of the other men who had been "eliminated," including Becker. Rolle would scour the area for weapons and other items that if discovered would lead to questions that would be difficult to answer when the trucks laden with the gold and more armed guards arrived.

Using an old handcart found near the back of the cavern, the surviving four Germans, under guard by Lester, took on the gruesome task of picking up the bodies from the prior evening's carnage. After an hour, the task was completed even though the tough German soldiers were on the verge of nausea especially after they retrieved the burned remains of the men killed by the exploding gas tank ignited by Lester's bullet.

The bodies were taken to an area in the back of the cavern that had been used as a refuse dump years earlier. It was a deep, forbidding chasm that had, at one time, been blocked off by a yellow and black painted gate. Over the years the gate had been destroyed and the gaping pit was now an exposed abyss that Lester well remembered and carefully approached in the half-light of two flashlights.

As a boy, the miners used to tell Lester stories about the black hole saying it was so deep that you could push a Cadillac in and never hear it hit bottom. They related tales of how Indians would use the pit for sacrifices and religious celebrations. They also told him that if he got in their way they were going to tie a rope to his leg, throw him over the side and let him dangle in the pit and he would be bait for some prehistoric monster that lived on the bottom. As he grew older and wiser to the stories of miners, he learned the truth of the pit, which was almost as frightening as the tall tales told to him.

As the guards approached the pit to dispose of the bodies, they felt and heard a swirling wind that seemed to come at them from all directions. They used a twelve-foot long piece of two-by-four to push the bodies over the edge of the pit from a safe distance. One of the guards was so terrified of the howling, gaping pit that he stood frozen, unable to move.

The chasm at the back of the Jasper had been formed millions of years earlier by a raging river that had at one time raced through the desert on its way to the Pacific Ocean. Deep canyons were gouged from the rock by the water over the eons. This was prior to the movement of the tectonic plates which forced up the mountains and rocks that existed throughout Arizona and the Southwest.

The cavern that made up most of the Jasper mine had been carved by this water, and the result of its power was at the back of the cavern in the form of an abyss forged in the rock roughly thirty feet in diameter abutting a flat, open area on the other side of the opening. A gentle slope in the floor of the cavern led to the chasm. Moving more deeply into the cavern, the slope increased from two to three degrees until it sloped to a nearly seven degree angle within twenty feet of the opening. At times wind and water could be heard emanating from the depths of the chasm, which only added to the fear that was instilled in all the miners regarding the "Pit" as it was accurately named.

Many of the men working in the mine would rather lose their jobs than be assigned to the trash detail and have to push carts of debris into the pit. Sometimes because the men were afraid to get too close to the descending path that led to the abyss, trash and debris would become entangled near the opening and someone would have to use long metal pipes to unclog the mess and push it down into the abyss.

Finding volunteers for such a job was difficult if not impossible. It was not until a local Indian boy about twelve years old, hearing of the job, volunteered and was hired by the mine for the sole purpose of keeping the opening clear. The men admired his fearlessness and dexterity in moving around the pit and nicknamed him "Pitboy," a moniker that stuck even as the boy turned into a man. When Pitboy went missing after lunch one day in 1917 and was never seen again, it was clear that he had truly earned his nickname.

After finishing their gruesome task, Lester led the four men back to the cavern office to meet Rolle who had gathered up the various weapons and odds and ends that littered the mine. As he walked into the only portion of the office not damaged by the previous evening's explosion, Lester motioned for the four guards to sit on the floor with their backs against the far wall. One of the men asked for something to drink, and while his request was ignored by Rolle, Lester gave the men two large containers of water that were sitting on a table next to the front door.

"Now what?" Lester asked.

"It is nearly 5:00 p.m., and now we wait for the first truck which will arrive in one hour. The trucks are coming in from a small town twenty miles from here, and each driver will be well armed. The two drivers will assist in unloading the gold, and these men can help us," Rolle said, motioning absentmindedly to the guards on the floor. Rolle continued, "After each truck is unloaded, I will select a few of the newly arriving drivers to assist in eventually hiding the gold in the mine. The drivers not selected will be ordered to leave and return to a site fifty miles north of here and await further orders. The last remaining truck will be used as I see fit at a later time."

"How could you have turned against the Führer and our country?" the smallest of the four guards seated on the floor asked. His name was Gregory, a six foot one, 160-pound reed-thin boy who looked to be no more than twenty years old.

A withering look from Rolle did not dissuade the young man from asking the same question a second time. As he was speaking, one of the other guards elbowed him and told him in German to "Shut up."

It was advice that arrived too late. Without warning Rolle pulled his Luger from his pocket and shot Gregory in the face. A crimson halo of blood and brain matter splattered against the olive colored wall, and in the faces of the three remaining guards. The young man slumped forward, and then fell to his right into the arms of Eric Warner Schneider, the first guard Lester had captured, and the one who had seconds before told the thin one to shut up.

Lester, unprepared for Rolle's vicious attack, moved a second too slow to throw off Rolle's aim with the first shot, but he did stop Rolle from shooting the other three, which he appeared to have every intention of doing. Lester did so when he smashed the butt end of his rifle into the lower left side of Rolle's face. The impact of the blow broke Rolle's jaw in several spots, his cheekbone, and knocked out five lower teeth. Blood spewed from his mouth and nose as he spun around 180-degrees and hit the floor facedown. Moaning while trying to regain his senses, Lester walked slowly up to Rolle still reeling from the blow and kicked him in the ribs, breaking three and knocking the remaining air from his lungs. With Rolle collapsed on the floor, Lester instinctively raised his rifle and was about to cut Rolle in half when he decided he had seen enough violence and death over the last twenty-four hours. At that moment, he vowed he would never kill another man the rest of his life, even if it cost him his.

The remaining three guards sat motionless as the American defended them against the German. One of their own. They were no longer sure of what they were doing in Arizona, or who their superiors were, or who in the hell this skinny, dirty, American cowboy who had just saved their lives was.

As Rolle gurgled blood, and spit teeth on the floor, Lester lowered his rifle that had been aimed at Rolle. "Boys, far as I'm concerned too damn many people have already died in this here ole' hole in the ground. I'm gonna try my best to see that no more die, but I'll need your help for that. Your buddy here was gonna kill everyone in this place including you three, those twenty-four men bringing in the gold, and me, if he had half the chance."

Putting his rifle on the table and sitting backwards on a chair, Lester continued talking to the three young Germans. "He and I had a deal. I was gonna help him get his gold for a small piece for myself, and for some folks who could really use some help. The rest of it was gonna be his. I didn't care what he was gonna do with it, and I sure as hell don't care what you boys do with it. You can send it back to Germany now, send it back after the war, or divvy it amongst yourselves and those truck drivers, and live like kings from here on. Like I said, I don't rightly give a damn. But some good men I knew died here yesterday and I 'spect that you boys knew most of the men who've died here since you got here. I know what it's like to be a soldier, and killin' is part of it. I sure wish I could've avoided killin' those boys last night, but they was tryin' to kill me, and that's the worst part of war. Killin' people you don't even know. People you ain't even mad at. People you might even be sorta friendly with if it weren't for some goddamn politician makin' people kill each other."

"You mean you are alone, you are the one who..." Eric began.

"Yep, it's just me, and I know it's a mistake to tell you boys that since there are three of you and only one of me, but if we work together for the next few hours, you can complete your mission, I can complete mine, and nobody needs to get their selves killed."

For nearly a minute the three young men stared at Lester and he stared back. Finally, Eric whispered to the others in German, "I think we can trust him; he could have killed us and gotten everything."

Not letting on that his German was barely good enough to understand what Eric had said, Lester was pleased that the other young men nodded in agreement with the Eric's appraisal of Lester.

Eric slowly stood and moved toward Lester and said, "There were nineteen of us chosen for this mission because of our experience, ability to speak English, and commitment to our homeland. We were told it was likely we would never return to Germany and that it was possible some would be killed. Those were risks we were willing to take for our country. Not for the Führer, but for our country. You Americans think that we do not hear the rumors of what our leaders are doing to our own people. We hear, but what can we do? What could you do if your President Roosevelt was accused of killing innocent people? Would you storm Washington? Would you rise up and kill all your leaders? Would you give up all your own freedoms, possessions, and your families to respond to rumors? I doubt it. And even if everything is true, the same question remains what would you do? What could anyone do?"

"I don't rightly know, son. But what's happenin' over there right now, true or not, will end someday, and you boys will have to make your own decisions. Like I said, what you do with this gold today, and in the future, is up to you. I'll take what's mine in one of those trucks comin' in here, and you'll never see me again. But, if you want some advice, I'd say you boys have a lot of responsibility with all that gold comin' in here. It could help a lot of folks."

Pointing to the still moaning Rolle, Lester said, "You know this ole' boy here wanted to take that gold back to Germany after the war and put it in the hands of whatever new government was runnin' things, and maybe that's the right thing to do. But if that new government is gonna be the likes of him, then maybe that ain't so good. But you boys are now in control of a whole lotta money if what this guy says is true, and those trucks start rollin' in here with all that gold."

The three young Germans looked at each other in silence after they listened to Lester. Their minds raced over the fact that within an hour they had gone from soldier to prisoner to condemned prisoner to seeing a comrade have his face shot off, to learning that one of their leaders had turned against them, to listening to a dirty American hobo giving them a civics lesson to being in control of more gold than any of them could imagine. The next hour would also be interesting.

CHAPTER 39

ARIZONA DESERT—2014

OVER FORTY-EIGHT HOURS, SPENT mostly at Elsa's, Tom, Jon, and Ben made decisions and came to conclusions. The decisions were based on assumptions, the assumptions the result of educated guesses, and the educated guesses sometimes not quite so educated. In short, far more art than science was used in the formation of their ultimate plans for searching for gold.

Ben volunteered to upfront the expedition's cost, but Tom and Jon politely refused his offer and promised they would pay Ben back when they sold their gold bar. Ben thanked them and told Jon and Tom he would accept it but knew he wouldn't.

Ben liked his new young friends and knew his days of gold searches were numbered. He also knew that if he did not help the "boys," they would probably end up lost or dead or both. Their energy and enthusiasm made Ben feel young again. He looked forward to nights in the desert, food cooked on an open fire, and the thrill of hope.

As he emerged from the 1920s era men's room in the back of Elsa's, Jon saw some local talent enter the gift shop adjacent to the restaurant. After the romantic debacle arranged by Tom with the Mesa Mensa in the motel room, whose name he had already forgotten, Jon decided to give love a second chance. He sidled up to a tall dark-haired woman but as he did, it dawned on him how much he had lost in terms of his long-held ability to strike up conversations with even the most beautiful women.

"Excuse me. Have you seen the birthday cards?"

Not looking up from the carousel of cards, the woman replied, "They're all birthday cards."

"Oh yeah, guess they are. Actually, I was looking for Arbor Day cards and..."

"Then perhaps you should try a nursery."

"Why would kids know anything about...get it? Kids, nursery. You know...get it?

The woman finally looked at Jon, but not in a good way. In fact, she shook her head in a sad way, said nothing, and moved to another carousel. Jon, showing courage over reality, followed.

"Look, to be honest I wasn't looking very closely at the cards because I was captivated by your beauty, intellect, obvious sensitivity, and the fact you aren't wearing a wedding ring."

The woman continued to look at cards, but her expression indicated she wished Jon would come up with better stuff or go away.

Jon was persistent if not creative. "Rather early in the morning for shopping, isn't it?"

The woman continued to ignore Jon but now wished he would contract a fast-acting fatal disease.

"Look, here's the deal, I was in prison for a while; nothing serious, just some money trouble, and I just got out, and to be honest with you, as I am wont to be, I suppose any woman with a pulse would look good about now, but you really do look good, I think, and I was wondering…" Jon stopped his patter as if even he couldn't believe what he had just said.

The woman slowly turned and stared at Jon for a few seconds; a look of sympathetic perplexity and amusement on her face witnessing such blatant and abject male stupidity. "So you think hitting on the first woman you see like a stag in heat is a charming approach that is likely to work?"

"Alas, I guess that depends on how smart you are."

"You mean IQ really enters into your selection process?"

"I would say yes, normally, but after eight years, I may not rate intellectual capabilities as highly as other attributes."

"Wow, it's amazing how incredibly and obliviously pathetic you are. But then again, you are a man, right?"

"Wow! That sounds like a sexist generalization if I've ever heard one, but I'll forgive your hurtful and inappropriate comments if you give me your number and…"

"My number? You *can't* be serious?"

"Wait a minute. I think I'm understanding this attitude of yours now, and I have to say it's a real stunner. Are you politely and indirectly saying that dinner and some subsequent intense foreplay, leading to sexual nirvana, is out of the question? Could that possibly be right?"

"From the looks of things, you couldn't afford the dinner and wouldn't survive the nirvana."

"Okay then, you buy dinner, and I'll bring a note from my doctor," Jon said along with a hopeful smile.

"Gee, that does sound like a great opportunity that just about any girl would jump at, but I'd rather stay home and knit."

"I can't really see you knitting, but is that a yes, no, or maybe?

The woman smiled, picked out a card, turned to Jon and said, "Good hunting, Mr. Smooth."

As she walked away, Jon did not give up, "I know, just playing hard to get, aren't you? You'll be back, just wait and see. Wait, okay, I'll buy dinner, how's that? Lunch? One taco?"

Finally, admitting utter, complete, and humiliating defeat, Jon left the shop and returned to the table with Tom and Ben.

"What'd you do, fall in?" Tom asked.

"Just trying to make new friends. What'd I miss?"

"We got most of the details worked out," Tom said.

"What time are we leaving tomorrow?"

"We'll meet here at 7, grab some breakfast, then hit the ATVs by 8." Tom said.

"Sounds like a plan. Ben, you said you had two other partners, are we going to meet them before we take off tomorrow?" Jon asked.

Ben looked around Elsa's and said, "Sam was supposed to be here… oh, here she is. Guys, say hello to my daughter Samantha, she likes to be called Sam. Say hello to Tom and Jon, Sam."

With a pleasant smile on her face, Sam said, "Oh, I've already had the pleasure of meeting Jon. Hello, Tom."

Jon shook his head, smiled, and looked down at his coffee cup.

"Sam here graduated from the Air Force Academy and served as a pilot. After her stint, she got her master's in archeology, and is living with me working in the family business till she goes back to UCLA for her PhD next spring," Ben said proudly.

"Nice to meet you, Sam," Tom said. "Glad you're going to be on our little adventure."

"Hello," Jon said.

"Hello, what's the name again?" Sam asked.

"Jon. Jon Cole."

"Ah yes, Jon. You didn't formally introduce yourself before."

"Well, that's because I'm shy. You know…always try to keep a low profile."

While Ben doubted they would find anything on their expedition, he looked forward to any event where he could spend time with his daughter.

Following in her father's aviation footsteps, Sam always wanted to learn to fly so Ben told her to do it right and get accepted at the Air Force Academy, which she did. After serving her five years flying F-15s, F-117 Nighthawks, and C-5 Galaxy Transports, Sam followed her and Ben's second passion of archeology in part to be able to spend time with him on his many jaunts around the world where he would dig up "really old stuff."

After her mother died, and Sam completed her Air Force obligation, she felt a responsibility to come back to Phoenix and take care of her dad even though he would bitch and moan and remind her he could "take care of my own damn self." Fact was, he was glad Sam had come home and was damn proud of his smart, independent daughter.

Once back in Phoenix, Ben and Sam decided to open a small aviation charter business and constructed a 7,000-foot runway on Ben's ranch that could accommodate the Gulfstream 650, King Air 350, and Beechcraft Bonanza that Sam would use to ferry well-heeled business types and rock groups around the state or around the world. The aircraft also provided the transportation for Sam and Ben on their many archeological jaunts that they both treasured. While the business did not make much of a profit, it was something Ben and Sam worked on together, which made it worthwhile for both.

Sam had had a few men in her life over the years and knew she would settle down and have a family at some point, but she felt her life was complete and did not need a man to make her happy and content. In fact, her last breakup from a guy who played football for the Arizona Cardinals had made her swear off all men. That was after she came home early from work and found him in bed with a Cardinals cheerleader. The fact that she wasn't even all that cute and dumber than a fence post pissed Sam off all the more.

When Jon and Tom first heard Sam would be joining their excursion, they expressed concern that a "girl" might slow them down. That was before they met Sam, who stood nearly six feet tall and weighed 140 pounds. While shapely in a good way, by men's standards, Sam was also "cut." Her arms and shoulders rippled with muscle as she loaded the ATVs and easily tossed forty-pound packs and heavy gear. It was clear Sam would not slow down anybody. The real question was, would the men slow down Sam? When Ben had told Sam about Jon and Tom, she expressed concern about her father taking off into the desert with convicted felons. She went to the internet and studied up on both men. Based on what she read and her belief in her father's sound judgment, she agreed that her father could go with the young men if she came along "for protection."

Ben's response was "Damn, you know you're gettin' old when your little girl needs to come along and take care of you in the desert."

The quartet met at Elsa's at 7:00 a.m. on a beautiful Saturday morning. Jon and Tom were surprised when they finally got to meet the fifth member of their ever-expanding troop. His name was Pax. He was a ninety-pound white German shepherd with blue eyes and a jovial disposition. He would ride with Ben and help with navigation. Pax never met a stranger and greeted Tom and Jon like long-lost drinking buddies before he jumped up into his seat next to Ben and patiently waited for the action to begin.

The four Hondas ATVs were loaded down with sleeping bags, fifty gallons of water, extra gas, a huge beach umbrella, and massive quantities of food, clothing, a propane gas grille, and one box of Milk Bones.

The three men, one woman, and one large dog wearing a new set of red Doggles, left Elsa's at precisely 8:00 a.m. to try to locate the spot where Ben had found his piece of gold twenty-one years before.

The group knew that their chance of finding more gold in the desert was remote but the spirit of looking for gold treasure was euphoric. Pax barked his approval.

Led by Ben, the caravan drove at fifteen miles per hour on a circuitous route that avoided some creek beds, mesas, and deep gullies.

After about thirty minutes and several stops to get his bearings, Ben raised his hand, and the four Hondas came to a stop at a nondescript area from which the group could still see Route 60 in the distance. "This is near where I found my piece," Ben announced.

Tom, Sam, and Jon shut off their Hondas and unloaded their metal detectors then spent the next four hours combing an area the size of two football fields. All they found during their search was junk. To keep their spirits high, Pax moved from person to person and delivered affectionate licks to each just to let them know their efforts were appreciated. When they broke for lunch, the group sat under the umbrella and ate dried beef, cheese, apples, crackers, and Snickers bars. In addition to the fifty gallons of water, each team member carried a canteen that Ben warned them to drink from regularly. "You can die from thirst out here before you know it. We got plenty of water so keep drinking."

The group's enthusiasm was still high despite a fruitless morning of searching. But looking at the area they had spent hours combing, compared to the utter vastness of the surrounding desert, made each one realize that even if tons of gold were buried in the desert they could see, it could take several lifetimes to find it. Nonetheless, they kept to their schedule, and after another four hours of digging up more junk in the afternoon, they had completed scouring the area where Ben had found his piece.

The next day they went to the area where Tom and Jon had found their bar of gold. Except for uncovering a fender from a 1948 Plymouth and sixteen beer cans, they found nothing of value.

By Sunday evening, and after two full days of metal detecting, the group was tired but content. While no gold was found, and most likely would not be, the idea of being alone in the desert with no prison bars, no schedules, no phones, and no immediate responsibilities created a mellow atmosphere that both Tom and Jon had never experienced. Ben and Sam knew the feeling well from their trips to archeological digs, and both hoped that Jon and Tom understood that sometimes the search was the best part of such an expedition.

Surprising Tom and Jon with large T-bone steaks that Ben had kept in dry ice, the five gold miners ate steak, whole potatoes, and beans cooked on an open fire. For dessert they had instant chocolate pudding and Oreo cookies. Tom and Jon could not remember a meal that tasted better.

That night around the campfire the group exchanged stories of their collective experiences, favorite books, travels, likes, dislikes, and hopes for the future. Sam was particularly interested in what it was like being in prison. Tom and Jon told her.

After that ice-breaking conversation, Tom felt he could ask Sam a delicate question. "So Sam, I see no wedding ring, and you're what, thirty? Any prospects on the horizon, or are you flying solo indefinitely?"

"Actually, I'm thirty-three, and if you're asking if I'm a lesbian, the answer is no, although I've thought about it after my latest experience with a man. I'm "solo," as you call it, because I don't like relationships that are confining, oppressive, one-sided, or unnecessary. Does that answer your question?"

"Wow, your bitterness is so sad," Tom said sympathetically.

"Bitterness? Just because I don't like relationships that…"

"You're right, she does sound really bitter, and obviously pre-lesbian," Jon offered.

"Failure with men? Pre-lesbian?" Sam asked, incredulous.

"Yeah," Tom said. "It's in all the books. A woman that's been dumped by ten or fifteen guys really changes. Usually end up dating women who wear comfortable shoes. Really sad."

"That's the most infantile, condescending, ridiculous…"

"No need to be defensive, Sam." Jon said gently. We still like you."

"Defensive?! Are you two completely out of your…"

It was then that Sam saw the smiles on Tom's and Jon's faces and realized she was being man-pimped.

"Okay…now I owe you guys one." Sam said with a smile.

The rest of that second evening around the campfire, four people and one sleepy dog became friends.

Up before dawn on Monday, the group kept to its schedule and headed for the Vega mine using an undulating creek bed that meandered haphazardly across the desert floor.

Pointing out rock formations and erosion markings, Ben explained how the creek, or "wash" as he called it, could contain enormous quantities of rainwater and how the narrowness of the bed would allow the rushing water to reach great speeds and with it create tremendous power. Therefore, even a metal as heavy as gold could be moved miles downstream pushed by tons of water, rock, and mud. "The gold you guys found and what I found could've come from hundreds of miles north of here and might've ended up somewhere in Mexico if we hadn't found it."

Ignoring such a depressing prospect, Sam, Jon, and Tom kept their Hondas pointed toward the Vega, the mine that had kept Tom and Jon locked out a week earlier.

As they moved northward, the terrain became steeper. Having to negotiate the ever- changing landscape, the group spent the entire morning making their way in crisscross fashion over rocks and sand until they saw a huge rock formation looming directly in front of them. Jon and Tom knew the fortress-looking structure was the Jasper. They saw its 300-foot face towering above them and the break in the rock roughly a third of the way up that the men recognized as the area that contained the cavern opening.

When the group moved to the west of the rock face, they noticed that the creek bed appeared to abut the vertical face of the Jasper for at least a mile. It then followed its contour until it split into two beds, one heading east behind the Jasper and one north toward the Vega.

Only two miles north of the Jasper as the crow flies, it took the group and their Hondas nearly half an hour of bone-rattling riding to finally see the outline of the Vega. Far smaller than the Jasper at least on the surface, the Vega looked like nothing more than a hill in the desert, dwarfed by other rock formations and mountains that were now clearly visible in the distance.

Deciding they had worked enough for one day the team set up camp before sunset, ate an early dinner, and turned in for the night soon after sunset. As the desert rapidly cooled and the stars exploded overhead, Jon wondered how many men would have this kind of experience in their lives. Not having time to answer, he fell into a deep sleep. not really caring.

In the half--light and half-consciousness that came with sunrise, Tom could hear Jon whisper his name. "Tom, don't move."

Certain he was dreaming, Tom didn't move; in fact, he tried to go back to sleep although he felt a very real need to pee.

"Tom, there's a tarantula on your left shoulder about an inch from your ear; don't move." Jon whispered, apparently believing the large arachnid had acute hearing and understood English.

Thinking this was another one of Jon's early-morning performances Tom growled, "Why don't you save this crap for your girlfriends that..." Stopping in mid- sentence, Tom felt the gigantic spider move from his shoulder onto his left cheek and hoped this was some sort of practical joke being played by Jon and Ben. As he slowly opened his left eye, he could see the hairy legs of the beast, one of which was on his left nostril.

Barely opening his mouth, Tom whispered, "Do something."

"Okay." Jon whispered again, apparently not wanting to tip off the desert monster as to his plans, "I'll get the shotgun."

Seeing through the legs of the killer spider that sat comfortably on his left cheek with no immediate plans to move, Tom could see his protective but clearly visibly-shaken partner carrying a twelve-gauge shot gun back toward his sleeping bag.

Despite what could be imminent death by massive amounts of spider poison, Tom quickly deduced that a spider bite, even by one the size of a BMW, which had moved to his forehead, would probably cause considerably less damage than a shotgun blast from two feet away. But before he had to make the final decision between receiving a fatal spider bite or having his head removed by a Remington, Sam appeared from behind Jon and calmly reached down and deftly plucked the spider off Tom's face then cradled the velvety creature in her palm.

"Ah, the poor baby, he's just a little cold that's all. He was probably in your sleeping bag most of the night, and you moved around too much so he decided to leave."

Letting out his breath, Tom stared ashen-faced at Sam and stammered, "Are you crazy, those things are poisonous."

"Nonsense," Sam said. "No more than a little bee sting if they get riled up, but they don't normally bite. Here, want to pet him?"

Recoiling in his sleeping bag, Tom looked like large eight-year-old watching a scary movie.

"By the way, I wouldn't move around too much in that bag, his mate's probably still in there," Sam casually mentioned.

Seeing Tom somehow leap vertically out of his sleeping bag from a sitting position and land on his feet while emitting a high-pitched sound of fear and loathing was humorous to Jon, who said while laughing, "I thought you were going to die of a heart attack before that damn thing bit you."

Standing up in his underwear and t-shirt, Tom looked at Jon and yelled, "And why in the hell would you grab a fucking twelve-gauge shotgun to get a spider off my face?"

"Because I didn't have a fucking howitzer, that's why. Besides, I figured if that big bastard did bite you, your face would swell up like some Black Lagoon Monster and you would've probably become permanently disfigured; and that's assuming you didn't suffer some painful noisy death over the next twenty-four hours that would've kept the rest of us awake all night hearing you go through your death throes. In other words, I was about to perform a fucking mercy killing to save you, and us, a lot of aggravation."

For several seconds, the three men, Sam, and a now-interested Pax, stared at one another in silence, with Jon's ad-lib performance still echoing in the hills. Then all four began laughing, their noisy guffaws made the area around the Vega mine sound like a sitcom laugh track.

Sidling up next to Sam, Ben whispered, "That wasn't nice."

"He moves pretty well for big man, doesn't he?"

It was going to be a good day.

CHAPTER 40

JASPER MINE—1943

WITH ROLLE TIED UP AND gagged in the darkened office, Lester and the three remaining guards decided to work together before the first truck arrived. Their biggest problem was that they didn't know what the incoming drivers knew about Operation Rebirth. Nor if the drivers were part of Becker's cabal to steal the gold, or if they would side with Rolle's plan to return it to Germany.

Given the unknowns of the situation, Lester and his new partners decided their safest option would be to act as if nothing was wrong. If all went well, each truck would arrive, take thirty minutes to unload and stow the gold in a shaft in the back of the mine. The two drivers would then leave in the truck they had arrived in, and according to the plan, go to a predetermined location to await further orders, which would never come. Simple.

Lester assigned Willy, a not very bright but imposing six foot six, 270-pound former Olympic weightlifter, to guard the road that led to the cavern with orders to give the alert when he saw a truck approach.

Willy, Eric, and Victor were the three surviving guards of the twenty who had been recruited by Becker months before. The group had made their way from Germany to Italy, into North Africa, then across the Atlantic by air to Venezuela. From there they moved by rail through Central America, Mexico, and finally by foot across an unprotected border into Arizona on what had proved to be a circuitous and deadly mission for the rest of their comrades.

The group was not aware of the Operation Rebirth scheme. They also knew nothing of the twenty-four guards who had escorted the gold from Berlin to Brest by train, across the ocean, and who were now only hours away from delivering the gold by truck to the Jasper. All they had been told by Becker was they were "serving the Führer." For most of these twenty men, that was all they needed to know.

Willy was told to direct the trucks down the dirt road that led to the cavern. Victor was assigned to join Lester in the cavern, and Eric would greet each truck and oversee the unloading process. If asked where Becker and the rest of the guards were, Eric would tell the drivers that they were scattered throughout the mine and at that very moment, several rifles were pointed at them.

At five minutes before six, it dawned on Lester that after everything that had taken place over the previous forty-eight hours—all the death, all the pain—that there was a chance there was no gold at all. It could have been a fable like the other stories of lost gold in the desert. And even if it was real, maybe the drivers, if they knew what they carried, might have decided to take it for themselves and live as millionaires in America.

At three minutes after six, the first truck lumbered up the dirt road from Route 60.

Following the signal from Willy, the thirty-foot white Ford dual-axle panel truck made the sharp left turn into the Jasper. As he watched the truck make the quarter-mile trip from the gate to the mine's entrance, Lester marveled at German efficiency, audacity, and balls in carrying out such a monumental plan. This seemed to him to be more difficult than winning the damn war. Yet here came the first of twelve trucks that contained a meaningful chunk of a nation's wealth.

Victor motioned for the driver to pull the truck into the cavern. In doing so, the driver had to maneuver around the charred remains of the trucks and cars that Lester had blown up the night before. Staring at the wreckage, the young man behind the wheel gaped like a driver looking at a three-car crash on Route 66. But he eventually followed Victor's directions to the rear of the cavern where Eric directed him to back the Ford into a position near the shaft Lester had selected to store the gold.

Deep inside the vastness of the Jasper, Lester could barely see the activity in the back of the cavern. He could make out shadows of men walking around the truck and in its headlights but couldn't make out Eric or the drivers. As he stared through the half-light, he could hear muffled voices engaged in conversation. Within a few minutes the tone of the voices increased until shouts could be heard. Something had gone wrong.

Keeping close to the cavern walls, Lester moved along the west wall and stayed in the semidarkness. As he edged closer to the Ford, he could see Victor, who had also heard the voices and had come to Eric's aid. They had their rifles drawn, facing the two drivers who had also pulled their weapons and were pointing them at Eric and Victor.

As they shouted to each other in German, Lester couldn't understand everything being said, but he did pick up a few words like "Becker" and "Rolle" that indicated not all was well with Lester's plan. But more disturbing was the sound of another voice that Lester could tell was not German, but not American either.

The voice was that of Jean Dubois, the Frenchman who had picked up Rolle in the Lincoln in Phoenix days earlier. He had come in the first truck with the two drivers. Dubois had been forgotten by the three young guards, and Lester didn't know him at all. Yet Dubois was well aware of both Rolle's and Becker's involvement in Operation Rebirth and was demanding to know where those men were before the gold was unloaded and turned over to German guards he didn't recognize.

Dubois had been sent by Becker to meet each truck outside Phoenix at a truck stop seven miles to the east and direct it to the Jasper. He would then return with each empty truck, ride back with the next, and continue that procedure until each truck was emptied.

Jean Claude Dubois was part of the French Vichy Government that helped the Nazis overtake and control his native land. Despised by his French countrymen and never trusted by the Germans, men like Dubois were betting that Germany would win the war. For if the Germans lost the war and lost control of France, the leaders of the Vichy government would be hunted down and killed by the French as the traitors they were.

Dubois liked to think of himself as a realist rather than a traitor, but he also knew he took great risks in dealing with the Germans. That is why when he was approached by Becker to become involved in Operation Rebirth, he saw it as a way to leave Europe and become very wealthy. Dubois was basically nonpolitical; he didn't really give a damn who won the war as long as he could make some money out of it and stay alive.

As Lester neared the standoff, he was able to get within twenty feet of the truck since everyone was pointing rifles at each other, unclear what to do next and not paying attention to much else. Lester had clear shots at the two drivers. He could have also easily picked off Dubois, who was unarmed as he continued to demand to see Becker and Rolle.

From the shadows Lester walked up behind the two drivers and placed his .45 behind the right ear of the taller one. Without being told to do so, the driver dropped his weapon. The clatter of the rifle hitting the floor finally made the Frenchman stop shouting as he turned and saw Lester standing behind the driver. The second driver was unsure where to aim his weapon. He kept moving it from Eric to Lester and back again. Not liking the rapidly changing odds, he too dropped his weapon.

Shock on his face, the little Frenchman began stammering in a mix of German, French, and English that Lester found both unintelligible and irritating.

"I can't understand a word yer sayin' there, partner, maybe you should talk some German so my friends here can interpret."

"Ah," Dubois said in English, as he tried to regain his composure. "An American."

"Born and raised."

"Is it safe to assume that you are not involved in our little project?" Dubois asked.

"Well, not sure it's safe to say I ain't involved, given the present circumstances, but it's safe to say I ain't German, don't give a damn about Hitler. And after I leave here, I won't give a tinker's dam what you all decide to do with the rest of the gold."

Dubois looked at Lester, and then to Eric, who was now smiling behind his retrieved rifle, and came to a rapid realization that he was likely going to be dead in a few moments and the gold he was only inches from was gone forever. Obviously, his only option was to try and switch alliances again. Quickly.

"Thank God, you have come here and discovered this plot. I never wanted to work with the Germans. I was forced to do it and was just looking for an opportunity to escape."

"Well," that's up to you, 'cause me and these boys have an agreement, and you're gonna have to deal with them from this point on."

"You mean you're the only American here? What of Becker and Rolle?"

"Well, Rolle kinda killed ole Becker, and Rolle ain't feelin' too good himself right now, so like I said, this boy Eric here and his two friends are in charge of the gold, these two drivers, and you. So if I was you, I'd be a little more friendly-like to these boys and watch what you say about Germans."

Lester walked around to the back of the truck and motioned to one of the drivers being guarded by Victor to unlock the door. Moving to the handle, the driver unlatched the double bolts, and the steel doors split open. In the near darkness of the truck, Lester could see large wooden crates in the middle of a steel-reinforced truck floor. The crates were covered by a green tarp. Loosening the ropes that surrounded the load, he pulled back the tarp, lifted the top off the wooden crate, and saw the blood of a country.

CHAPTER 41

VEGA MINE—2014

THE ENTRANCE TO THE VEGA proved to be as impenetrable as it had been days earlier when Tom and Jon tried to find a way in. "This old girl is locked up tighter than a drum," Ben said. "We'd need a whole bunch of dynamite to bust open that door."

"So let's get some," Jon said.

"The dynamite isn't the problem; the problem is we don't know who owns this mine and even if we did, we'd need permission to get inside. And then if we found anything, we'd have to hand it over since it's on their property."

"Ben's right. I found out this mine is owned by the state, but some South American trust leases her for $5,000 a year with an option to buy her for $200,000," Tom said.

"How long is the lease?" Ben asked.

"One hundred years."

"One hundred years? When was the option taken out?" Jon asked.

"1918."

"Holy shit. You mean that lease/option is still active?"

"Yep. This trust, which I tried to track down with no luck, has been paying the state of Arizona $5,000 a year for over ninety years. They mail a check to the state every April 20 like clockwork."

"What happens in 2018?" Sam asked.

"Whoever has the option can either buy the mine for two hundred grand, or the mine reverts back to the state."

Impressed by Tom's historical briefing, Sam, Ben, Jon, and Pax sat quietly as Tom went on. "Since the 1940s there's been no record of anybody entering the Vega. In talking to an old guy at the library, who knows this area, he said there are hundreds of mines like this one and the Jasper that have been abandoned for years, and the state would like nothing better than to have some mining company come in and take a mine like this off their hands and start paying taxes."

"So are you saying that even if we did somehow get in this place and find a bazillion dollars in gold, we couldn't by law take out any of it?" Jon asked.

"That's right. We really can't do anything legally here until 2018. But I wanted to come back up here and look around and at least try to get a look inside, but that doesn't look like a high probability at this point."

"Damn, I thought this was our best bet of the two. Do you think the Jasper is even worth wasting our time going through since it has been wide open for over a hundred years?" Jon asked. "After all, the only things we're likely to find are remnants of frat parties and graffiti on the walls."

"You're probably right, but who knows? There may be a connection between the mines, and since we're already here we may as well see what we can find in the Jasper," Ben said.

Jon shrugged in agreement, and the five miners set out on their Hondas via the dirt road on the half hour ride from the Vega to the Jasper.

After the group entered the Jasper, Tom asked, "Ben, ever been in this place?"

"A few times."

"We came here a few days ago but never went back to that big hole in the ground we've read about. We chickened out." Jon said.

"That pit may not be the only thing to fear in this mine," Ben said in a tone that got the attention of Tom and Jon.

Despite its size, the Jasper smelled a bit like piss. Mild piss, but unmistakably and undeniably piss. The gold-hunting group surmised that over the years, hundreds of beer parties had led to several rivers of piss being dispensed throughout the mine by thousands of drunk students with overflowing bladders.

With the front gate long ago destroyed, entering the mine was not an issue. The real issue was what could possibly be of value in a hundred-year-old mine that had been worked to death by one operator, deemed unproductive by another, and had served as a wide-open beer garden for several generations of teenagers.

As they walked to the rear of the cavern, each person carried a powerful halogen heavy-duty lantern. The sunlight from the cavern opening gave way to shadows that led to near total darkness two hundred feet from the entrance. The temperature also dropped noticeably, and Tom noticed a breeze filtering through the cavern. Odd, he thought that any breeze at all could make its way from the entrance to their current position. He also discerned a slight pitch in the floor that seemed to drop at one to two degrees every fifty feet.

As they approached the darkest part of the cavern, they saw a bright yellow line painted on the floor and a warning sign that stretched twenty-feet above them and appeared to run the entire width of the cave. In both English and Spanish, the sign read: "Danger: Open Pit 200 Feet Ahead." Even in faded light, the signs picked up the sunlight of the cave opening.

"Wonder if these signs stopped drunken college kids from checking out that pit?" Tom asked.

"I doubt it, since it isn't stopping us, and we're not even drunk," Jon said.

"Jon's right. I came here once or twice in high school, and the kids would ignore those signs and party further back toward the pit. It was scary back then and scary now." Sam said.

"You never told me that you came in this place when…," Ben said as he looked askance at Sam.

"Sorry, Dad."

Turning his attention from his wayward daughter to the fifth member of their group, Ben said, "Come here, Pax." The white dog immediately came and sat next to Ben awaiting further orders. Ben pulled a leash out of his pocket and snapped it onto Pax's collar before the group began a wary walk to the back of the cavern.

The group moved more slowly as they went deeper and deeper into the cave. They felt and heard the breeze pick up in intensity and the temperature drop another few degrees.

Approaching another group of signs that read "Danger: Open Pit 100 Feet Ahead," the group stopped as they all noticed a more precipitous pitch in the floor. "This is where we stopped last time we were here, and I think a large percentage of even the drunkest kids may have stopped here too," Jon said, as he focused his flashlight on the floor that was now angling more deeply into the darkness of the cavern.

An ominous wind also emanated from the pit with a bass voice that seemed to speak directly to the group. Whatever it said, Pax did not like what he heard and barked at it. The wind rose and fell in intensity like a zephyr through a half-opened Kansas barn door in the spring. Metallic clangs could be heard from the darkness as well as other thumps and unrecognized movement, all of which echoed in the vastness then came and went as the wind sped through the cavern.

"Kind of sounds like a warning," Jon said.

"Or a train," Tom added.

"Maybe I should stay at the front with Pax and watch the Hondas, you know, rear guard action," Jon offered.

"For a convicted felon, you're kind of a wuss," Sam observed.

"Never said I was a good felon."

"Want to hold my hand, Rambo?"

"I'm tougher than I look."

"God, I hope so," Sam mumbled.

"Likely that pit has an opening at the bottom and air from the entrance meets with air coming up from the bottom of the pit and creates that sound," Ben explained.

"Oh good," Jon said. "For a minute there I thought it was one of those famous pits where monsters climb up from the depths and eat people that get too far into this damn cave."

"I think you watched too much *Sesame Street* in prison," Sam suggested.

"Well, one thing's for certain," Tom said, "There's no shortage of other places to look in this mine before we have to go any further toward that thing."

With that, the three men, one woman, and one relieved dog spent the next two days exploring every bit of the Jasper they could. They discovered shafts that led to nowhere and contained nothing except used condoms, hundreds of beer cans, assorted trash, two stripped cars, and the bones of a dog, which got Pax's undivided attention. With every area they uncovered or air shaft that Jon or Sam ascended, they hoped that they would find something that would lead them to some answers and away from having to come back to explore the pit.

During the two evenings that the group slept in the mine, they heard the low moans of wind barrel through the Jasper. While no one made reference to the obvious, each knew that if they were serious about finding gold, they would eventually have to swallow their fear and explore the black hole lurking at the back of the mine.

On the morning of the third day, Tom and Jon awoke and found that Ben, Sam, and Pax were missing. After several minutes of calling their names and looking inside and outside the cavern, they went back to their camp site fifteen feet inside the opening to the Jasper and waited, not sure what to do next.

Ben and Sam were normally up before the two younger men, fixing something for breakfast or poring over one of several maps that Ben brought on the trip and would eventually wake the two men shortly after sunrise. Not that day. Two sleeping bags and Pax's bed were neatly rolled up along with the rest of their gear and stacked against the western wall of the mine. After another thirty minutes, Tom and Jon became genuinely concerned for the rest of their team.

The men realized how much they had become dependent on Ben and how fond they were of him. They also realized how foolish they had been to assume they could have attempted such a trip without someone as knowledgeable and experienced as he was.

The men had also grown fond of Sam. They respected her intellect, humor, and athletic prowess. Tom had particularly noticed that while Sam tried to downplay her looks by wearing glasses, no makeup, and oversized t-shirts, she was an attractive woman. She was fit and athletic, with long, toned legs. Her shoulder-length dark hair, always pulled back in a ponytail, would glisten in the sun when she let it down to dry in the warm desert air after washing it in a basin she had brought. On more than one occasion, particularly in the orange glow of a campfire, Tom found himself staring at Sam even when others were talking. Sam had felt Tom's stare, although she pretended not to notice.

Another endearing aspect about Sam was that Tom had become convinced she was the one who had placed the giant spider on his shoulder.

He laughed at the thought, and it made him even more intrigued by her.

Twenty minutes later, Ben, Sam, and Pax emerged from the back of the mine. "Morning, guys," Ben said. "Couldn't sleep any longer, and I wanted to get a closer look at that big hole in the back of this place. Sam and Pax decided to join me."

"You two shouldn't be going back there alone, Ben," Tom said, his concern etched in the harshness of his voice.

"That's right," Jon echoed. "You could start moving down that grade too fast and God knows where you guys would end up."

"Yeah, I know," Ben said, touched by the concern of the young men. "But I wanted to get a feel for just how large that damn hole is and what was it used for."

"What'd you learn?" Tom asked.

"The pit is in the shape of a half circle and at its widest is about twenty-five to thirty feet across. From the front lip of the pit to the wall behind it, looks to be maybe twenty feet. So you have about 500–600 square feet of opening.

"The three sides leading to the pit slope at least six to ten degrees. By dropping some rocks over the side, there appear to be a series of natural rock ledges on the left side as you face the hole, starting fifteen feet down that were three to four feet wide."

"Interesting," Jon said. "But does knowing the dimensions lead to any conclusions as to what the pit was used for?"

"Not exactly," Ben said. "But hearing the rocks hit metal, wood, and stone as they fell, it's pretty obvious people have been throwing stuff down that hole for a long time. And, if I was going to hide gold, I'd put it in the last place anybody would want to look, which is right down in that damn hole."

CHAPTER 42

JASPER MINE—1943

"LORD HAVE MERCY," LESTER WHISPERED. The yellowish beam from his flashlight made the shimmering gold in the back of the truck look like thick honey had dripped down the sides of the ingots.

The gold was stacked in rows on thick steel pallets. There were at least sixteen pallets on the truck, and each pallet held 100 ingots, weighing 2000 pounds per pallet. In total, there were nearly 1700 twenty-pound ingots of pure gold reflecting in Lester's flashlight. Thirty-four thousand pounds, nearly 540,000 ounces with a 1943 value of over twenty million dollars, glimmered back at Lester. But at that moment what Lester saw in the back of the Ford truck precluded him from thinking in terms of dollars. All he knew was he was looking at a shitload of gold.

"You mean there are eleven more trucks like this?" Lester asked no one in particular.

"Yes," the Frenchman said. "And each has armed guards loyal to the Reich who will stop at nothing to protect this gold. Plus they will not come to this mine unless I personally meet them at the appropriate time and place."

Ignoring Dubois, Lester pulled down the overhead door of the Ford and casually motioned the two disarmed guards to move away from the truck with his .45. "Well, like I said, my partner Eric here and I have a deal. I'm gonna take this here truck and get on down the road, and the next eleven of 'em belong to Eric and these boys. If I was you, Frenchy, I'd probably consider making a deal with them. If not, you may end up poor or dead, neither of which ain't really a good thing." Lester said as he climbed into the truck's driver's seat.

Lester nonchalantly started the Ford, then looked at Eric, Willy, Victor, Dubois, and the other two drivers through the windshield. He wondered if they were going to let him drive out of the mine with enough gold to last a hundred lifetimes. Or was somebody going to die?

As he put the Ford into gear, Lester's heart dropped when Eric stepped in front of the truck holding his rifle and stood in the glare of the headlights. Eric looked up at Lester then walked slowly around to the driver's door never taking his eyes off him. Feeling his .45 in his belt, Lester thought about trying to fight his way out of the mine if need be, but instead, he stuck his hand out the open window, smiled at Eric and said, "Well ole boy, it's been good doin' business with you. Take care of yourself now, y'hear."

Lester held out his hand for a few seconds and was almost as relieved as he was shocked when Eric shook his hand and said, "The people of Germany owe you a debt of gratitude. Be safe, my friend."

Seeing the sincerity in his eyes, Lester replied, "Thanks, boy, you stay safe too."

Looking in the truck's rearview mirrors as he left the mine, Lester wondered what the five Germans and one Frenchman would decide to do with eleven truckloads of gold. Hell, he wondered what he was going to do with one.

After he slowly exited the Jasper, Lester kept looking in his mirrors waiting for someone to come running out with a rifle and try to stop him. No one did.

As the heavy-duty Ford struggled up the steep hill adjacent to the mine, it stalled three times. Finally reaching the crest of the hill, Lester made a sharp right turn and let out a sigh of relief as he finally picked up some speed and headed down the dirt road that would eventually lead back to Phoenix. He sweated and shook as he held onto the steering wheel as snippets of the blood and carnage of the previous days flashed into his brain.

Only minutes before, Lester was not only questioning the very existence of the gold but after confirming it was real, wondered if he would be able to leave the cave without a fight. And now he was bumping down a dirt road with a truck filled with more gold that he knew existed in the world.

Over the previous twenty years, Lester's life had been a day-to-day existence. His idea of long-range planning was where he could find a free lunch. Yet, he now had untold millions in gleaming gold behind him, and he had absolutely no idea what the hell he would do next.

Several miles from the Jasper, Lester pulled off the road into the desert and drove a quarter mile into a flat area near some large boulders. He turned off the ignition and sat in the desert dusk and tried to think. So much had happened over the last three days that he wondered if it was all real. Were his friends really dead? Did he really shoot all those krauts? Was that metal in the back of the Ford really gold?

Going into the back of the Ford, he again lifted the tarp and stared. At least the damn gold looked real. And he knew his friends were dead. He wished like hell they were still around and able to share in what the gold could do.

Back in the driver's seat, Lester looked out over the desert in the fading light of a late summer evening. He was taken by the beauty he now saw before him. He was also shaken by the horror of the last few days. Suddenly, his emotions erupted, and he began to cry over his murdered friends and the realization that nothing in his life was ever going to be the same again. He knew at that moment he could no longer live his life as he had. That was no longer an option, excuse, or escape. He now had responsibility. He had decisions to make.

His first decision was to unload the gold from the truck. This was based on the fact that he had absolutely no idea what the hell he would do with seventeen tons of gold if he simply took it back to Phoenix. He couldn't just sell it on a street corner. He needed time to think. He needed a plan and he had no plan. Hell, he didn't even have an idea.

Putting the Ford into gear, he made his way further into the rock-hard desert looking for something. Turning on his headlights he made his way around rocks and cacti and washed out riverbeds to an area over a mile from the road. Moving behind a distinctive pile of rocks that hid the truck from view, Lester cut the engine and the lights and sat in the dark and quiet.

For fifteen minutes, Lester sat motionless behind the wheel of the Ford. As darkness quickly overtook the desert, he took an apple and canteen of water from his knapsack and moved from the cab of the truck to its roof.

Surrounded on two sides by rock outcroppings forged over the millennia by rushing springtime rains and hidden on a third side by tall cacti, the roof of the Ford became Lester's dining room, complete with a floor show of shooting stars across a blue-black sky. It also became his bed for the night and the place where he made the plans for the rest of his life.

At daybreak Lester awoke in a start and wondered if it had all been a dream. He climbed off the top of the truck and once again checked the contents under the tarp. With reality confirmed, Lester began to execute the first part of his plan.

He left the Ford and initiated a thorough search of the area. He checked for landmarks that he would be able to find again. He moved a hundred yards in a circular route around the Ford to determine where he could off-load the gold in an area that would not be found by the occasional fool who would wander into the Arizona desert.

While he knew he could probably stack the gold in the open and no one would find it in the overwhelming emptiness, he could not bring himself to take such a chance. After an hour of looking for someplace that could temporarily hide the gold, Lester decided to hide it in relatively plain sight. On the high ground above where he parked the truck, he found an area of soft sand nearly thirty feet by thirty feet. He found he could move the sand away by hand and sink the heavy bars into six inch holes he had dug with a flat-edged piece of stone.

For over eight hours, Lester worked to near exhaustion as he moved over 1700 twenty-pound gold bars from the Ford to their sandy burial spot by tossing them off the back of the truck into the shallow holes he had dug. He then covered the entire area with loose rocks that littered the landscape. After he was done, he was concerned that he had hidden his treasure too well. What if he couldn't find it again?

He moved back to the truck and looked for something to write out a map but found nothing. As the late afternoon sun began to bake the desert yet again, Lester realized how everything in the area looked exactly the same and how easy it would be to lose the gold forever if he were unable to somehow mark the spot and create a map of some kind.

Loosening his shirt in the increasing heat, Lester fingered a large safety pin that held the top half of his shirt closed. Taking the pin off, he opened it and decided he had found a writing utensil after all. Taking off his shirt, he spent the next hour scraping a map onto his pasty white stomach and chest. Drawing the road down his left rib cage and putting an X where the turn off into the desert was above his belt line. Drawing the creek bed north of his navel and showing two round areas representing the rock outcroppings as blood began to appear as a result of the dull pin being dragged over his skin. Lester had to stop from time to time to wipe it away and take a rest from the pain. But as time went on, he found himself digging deeper with the pin to make sure he could find his way back. As each etching was made in his skin, it also etched into his brain. He would not forget this spot. Not ever.

Taking one bar of the gold, he put it under his seat and started up the Ford. Making his way back to the dirt road, he followed the nearby creek bed and noted on the odometer that it was 1.1 miles. Scratching the information into his left arm, Lester turned right onto the road and slowly made his way another thirteen miles back toward Route 60 and his new life in Phoenix.

Several times he looked in his rearview mirror toward the Jasper and wondered what had happened with the Germans and the Frenchman the previous evening. He felt a bit guilty he had left Eric to fend for himself but shook off the urge to turn around. He was needed in Phoenix.

Less than an hour later, and within a few blocks of his lean-to/ sometimes bedroom at the back of the bus station, Lester decided to abandon the Ford. If he was seen by anyone, including cops, in that truck, they would assume he had stolen it, and then he would also have to explain a twenty-pound piece of gold under his seat.

Pulling onto a dead end street, Lester drove to the middle and he left the Ford to those who would surely find it within hours. Making it as convenient as possible, he left the keys in the ignition and the doors unlocked. He laughed to himself when he realized it was likely one of his associates would probably find the truck and sell it for a hundred dollars.

Wrapping the bar in his knapsack, Lester looked at the Ford for the last time and walked the six blocks to the area behind the bus station. As night fell, he ran into some close friends, some familiar faces with no names, and still others he had never even spoken to. He wondered why they all looked the same. He figured they did not yet know that their lives were about to change as much as his.

CHAPTER 43

AFTER A SECOND LONG AND fruitless day of searching for gold in the enormous mine, Jon had a suggestion. "We need some light before we start messing around back near that damn pit." Taking on any chore to delay working directly near the pit was okay with Tom, so he gladly volunteered to go into town to buy some lights and batteries and beer.

None of the group really wanted to go back and look into the gaping, wind-blown black hole to hell, but they realized their search for gold could not be considered a serious one if they ignored the most likely spot where someone would hide a treasure.

"Pick up a video camera while you're at it, and some nylon rope," Ben said.

While Tom was on his shopping spree, Ben and Jon sat on the floor in the middle of the cave and talked while Sam and Pax meandered around the cavern waiting for Tom to return.

"Ben, what's your ancestry?"

"Apache."

"Ever live on a reservation?"

"No, my folks moved to California right after I was born. They were migrant workers when I was growing up."

"They still living?"

"Both died in their forties, pretty much worked themselves to death, I guess. I was twelve when mom died, and dad sent me to a school for boys in San Francisco. I figured it took every penny he ever earned and saved all those years."

"Sounds like you hit the parental lotto."

"Yeah, I never realized what they'd done until I was older in college."

"Where did you go?"

"Stanford."

"I went to Princeton after I was turned down by Stanford. Where'd you end up working?"

"Always wanted to fly so I enlisted in the Air Force, and after fighter pilot training was stationed in DC flying big shots from the Capital all over the world in big jets. Pretty nice gig. Then Vietnam broke out, and I was transferred to Saigon and ordered to bomb kids and a bunch of defenseless civilians, and I couldn't take it. So they washed me out as a conscientious objector."

"That took some guts."

"If you can't sleep at night, you're not much use to anybody for anything."

"What did you do then?"

"Got into real estate for a while, did pretty well, and then decided to work on tribal affairs for twenty years, which led to the gaming business."

"Casinos?"

"I negotiated all the casino deals with the State of Arizona and federal government. I owed my people and so did the government. Plus the pay was pretty good."

The men also talked about Jon's background including his estranged parents, Princeton, and Wall Street. Jon talked about how he considered his a wasted life. They talked about all the things Jon had been thinking about for almost nine years. Ben was a good listener, not judgmental and not condescending. He nodded in agreement when Jon said he had been a jerk and maybe just a bit dishonest at times in his life.

"What you were does not have to be who you are or will be," Ben said. "You have free will. You can become anything you want."

"That's the point, I'm so messed up I don't know what or who I am anymore."

"We've all been that way at some point in our lives. You just have to decide what and who you want to be, set a compass in that direction, and do the best you can to stay on course."

As the men talked, Jon opened up to Ben as he had never opened up to anyone before, even Tom. Ben had a combination of toughness, brains, serenity, and kindness that made Jon realize he didn't need to bullshit Ben. Ben understood things. Not just the desert or how to find gold, but about people and life. Stuff that mattered, at least now mattered to Jon. They probably would not have mattered ten years earlier, but they mattered now.

Lying on the cool floor of the cave and hearing the wind blowing over them the two men, one old and one lost, took a small step of moving from friends to something more. Something that had to do with trust and understanding. While Jon had never had such a relationship before, he knew it was a good thing.

After another hour of small talk and catnaps, they heard Tom ride up on the Honda, enter the Jasper, and cut the ignition. Silhouetted against the sunlit opening of the cave two hundred feet behind Tom, they could only make out his huge body as he slowly made his way to where Jon and Ben were sitting.

"What took you so long, big boy, did you stop and..."

"I ran into the missing links in that white pickup. I think I may have killed one of them," Tom whispered hoarsely.

"What? Who were they, Tom?" Ben asked.

"Based on all the body ink, I'd say they were Neo-Nazis or some wannabes. One guy said he had friends who didn't like us looking in the

Jasper."

Tom's dazed look, bloody hands, nearly ripped-off shirt, plus assorted cuts and abrasions on his face indicated that the three men were deadly serious in their objection to Jasper visitors.

As Sam and Pax joined Tom, Jon, and Ben, Sam asked softly, "What happened, Tom?"

———————————————————

Tom, slowly and almost whispering, recounted the previous hours. After he drove the Honda back to the trading post, he got in his van and went to a local strip mall and made his purchases. He said he didn't notice anyone following him until he'd returned to Elsa's and loaded the ATV ready to return to the Jasper. That's when he saw a white pickup truck with blacked-out windows that looked like the one he and Jon had seen on their first trip to the Jasper.

When he started back into the desert, the pickup also left the parking lot but didn't appear to follow him. But about halfway to the Jasper, Tom again saw the white pickup, this time sitting about twenty feet off the rutted path Tom was using as his road in the desert. Obviously, the pickup had taken the dirt road that paralleled Tom's path and had cut across the desert from the road to intercept him. Remembering the pick- from the parking lot only minutes before, Tom at first slowed and then turned to his left fifty yards before he passed the truck. At first the truck didn't move, but within a few seconds Tom saw it suddenly lurch forward in a cloud of dust and begin to move in Tom's direction at high speed. Knowing he would not be able to outrun the truck, Tom came to a stop, dismounted the Honda, and waited.

The pickup slowed and eventually stopped, its engine idling only thirty feet from Tom. Cursing himself for not bringing the shotgun with him, Tom figured that whoever was in the truck didn't know if he was armed or not. To emphasize that fact, Tom went to the rear of the Honda and turned his back on the pickup and made it appear as if he was putting something in his belt, which he then covered with his shirttail. Tom hoped that the fresh banana, now creating a bulge under his shirt, would give the men in the pickup some pause.

Turning back to face the truck, Tom saw it slowly move toward him and could vaguely make out at least three people in the front seat. Not liking the drama unfolding in front of him, and knowing that if they were armed they could certainly cut him down from where they sat, Tom decided to take an aggressive approach and find out who was behind the tinted glass.

Walking toward the truck, Tom was surprised to see the window on the driver's side come down and a smiling face greet him.

"Hey man, what's goin' on?" a bald, tanned, thirtysomething man asked. The slender man had several tattoos including a large gothic lettered number 88 on his left arm. A Marlboro hung loosely from his lips. Tom noticed that Marlboro Man also wore several gold chains, one of which partially hid a vivid red tattoo of a serpent that wrapped around his neck, its fangs and darting tongue resting beneath the man's left ear.

The other two men who sat in the front seat, also bald with tattoos and gold chains, stayed quiet, but Tom could see them lean forward and peer at him through their mirrored metal- framed sunglasses.

"Fact is, I'm a little lost," Tom said. "Wondering if maybe you boys could help me?"

"Sure, we love helpin' folks." Marlboro Man said. "By the way, I'm Ronnie."

"Hey, Ronnie, I'm Tom. I'm trying to get back to the Vega Mine. We had a little party up there last night, and I went out to get more beer and stuff and damn if I didn't get lost."

"Really? At the Vega last night?"

"Yeah, I think that was the name…but hell you seen one mine you seen em' all, I guess."

"Fact is, you were at the Jasper last night not the Vega."

"Is that right? Well, like I said you seen…"

"Went for more beer, huh?"

"That's what I said. I hit the store to restock before we head up into the hills."

"That's cool. Kinda hot for campin' though, usually the winter's better."

"Yeah, I think you're right, first time for us out here though and we figured it would cool down the higher we go."

Shutting off the pickup's engine, Ronnie got out of the truck and walked over to the Honda. "Nice ride you got there, Hoss, guess you could go just about anywhere on that thing."

"Yeah and speaking of that I better get back to my friends; they're waiting on me."

Standing next to the Honda, Ronnie suddenly reached down and plucked the keys from the ignition. "You know, you lose these, and it's a long walk back to anywhere." "You're sure right about that. That's why I have an extra set right here," Tom said as he dangled the spare keys that Ben had insisted he put in his pocket.

Still smiling, Ronnie flipped the keys he had picked up onto the Honda's seat and started walking toward Tom. As he did, Tom could hear the other two men leave the pickup and move to his right. "Well it looks like you're well prepared for your little camping trip. Got lots of food, beer, extra keys, rope, even a VCR and lights. You gonna produce some kind of X-rated video up there in those hills?"

Since Ronnie and his friends knew what Tom had purchased, he knew they had been following him from store to store over the last two hours.

"Damn, you got me. I'm a porn producer, and we're filming a Triple X movie up at the Jasper and we're waiting for three beautiful porn stars from LA tonight to show up so we can start filming tomorrow. You guys will keep that quiet, won't you?"

"No shit?" one of the bald guys that had just left the truck said, his young man libido now palpable. "Hey, that's cool, maybe we could come up and watch and…"

"Shut up, you dumb shit." Ronnie shouted to his aroused companion, his smile suddenly replaced by a mouth full of yellow gritted teeth. "Who the fuck you think you talkin' to city boy, some shit kicker who don't know what's up? I know what's up. You and them friends of yours are fuckin' around in the Jasper lookin' for shit."

"You make it clear we can now stop our search."

"You're a real smartass, ain't you? You think since you're such a big bastard you can push folks around like you did back at Elsa's last week? That was old men you were foolin' with. You don't want to be fuckin' with us like that."

Tom weighed his options. From what he could see, Ronnie was not armed and was well dressed, which meant his two friends who were not all that well dressed were brought along to help convince Tom to get out of the mining business. Or they simply might shoot him on the spot and save themselves some trouble. Looking at the two not-so-well-dressed but sexually adventurous men on his right, Tom turned to them with a question, "You know we're gonna need one more actor up there…which one of you guys has the biggest…"

Before either could answer the question or shoot him, Tom decided to take his chance. He bolted to his right and drove his right shoulder into the stomach of the man nearest him and dragged down the second man with his right arm.

Too late, the taller of the two tried to pull a pistol from a holster in the small of his back and instead had 250 pounds of lunging Tom pin his arm between the ground and his body. The one receiving the shoulder in the stomach was also armed with both a knife and gun, but the oxygen that had left his lungs had also left his brain, and as a result he was too stunned and gasping for breath to reach for either.

Moving far quicker than a man his size should have any right to do, Tom wasted no more time with the two bald guys on the ground. Unleashing a sincere right hand, he smashed the short one into unconsciousness with a single punch. The second one needed two shots, the first that broke at least two ribs and a second to the left temple that created an ominous indentation above the eyebrow.

Seeing the odds suddenly change, Ronnie moved quickly to the pickup and was only two feet away from grabbing the rifle that hung from the gun rack, when he was stopped cold by Tom's left arm around his neck. Pulling backward, Tom yanked Ronnie away from the truck, only to lose his balance and tumble to the ground with the cowboy on top of him. Swinging wildly, Marlboro Man rained several blows on Tom's face and was more than a little disappointed when his best shots didn't have the same effect as Tom's blows had on his companions. In fact, the punches had a negative effect, in that, for the first time since their "meeting" commenced, Tom got mad.

Lifting Ronnie off him like a well-dressed mannequin, Tom threw him four feet to his right. He rose quickly and yanked the now badly dressed Ronnie to his feet and slammed him into the side of the front bumper of the pickup. Using two quick lefts to his midsection to get his attention, Tom, now more than a bit irritated by the entire episode, kept asking the Marlboro Man questions like "Why are you following me?" and "What do you want from me?" and some other questions that Ronnie may have answered if he could have talked. But the lack of air in his lungs and a jaw that felt like it had been kicked by a mule, he could only mumble some unintelligible sounds that irritated Tom even more and led to two more rib shots which did not at all help the communication gap between the two men.

Since Tom was focused on Ronnie, he didn't notice the short previously unconscious bald guy begin to stir and reach for the pistol that his buddy with the dent in his forehead still holstered. But again he was a tad late; Tom broke his arm with a vicious kick that snapped the ulna and sent the pistol flying twenty feet into the sand. As the man with the broken arm moaned in pain, Tom turned back to Ronnie who had crawled to the pickup and grabbed the rifle from the gun rack. But Tom was too quick and wrestled the rifle from Ronnie and smashed it to bits on the bumper of the truck.

Having seen the damage Tom had inflicted on his two friends, Ronnie decided to stay on the ground and instead gave peace a chance.

"That was a brand-new Winchester, you big asshole," he said with what sounded like profound sadness.

"Why were you following me?" Tom demanded.

"You were messin' around in the Jasper and some people don't like that."

"Why? There's nothing in that place except beer cans, old tires, and dead dogs."

"Maybe...but some folks feel different. You fucked up, boy."

Taking the keys from the ignition of the truck, Tom threw them into the scrub and said to Marlboro Man, "If I ever see you again, you boys won't get off with broken arms."

"You killed Johnny, you asshole, look at his head."

Fearing Marlboro Man might be right, Tom got on the Honda and drove away. He had never killed anyone before and wasn't sure how he was supposed to feel if in fact the short, bald one was really dead.

Sam used some Neosporin, alcohol, and bandages from a first-aid kit to patch Tom up as best she could. Not seriously hurt, Tom had the most pain in his badly bruised fists. But Ben didn't underestimate what Tom had been through and what it all meant. They were being watched by people who didn't want them searching in the Jasper.

"I'd venture a guess that since we were ignored when we were at the Vega, and not ignored when we came to the Jasper, the question of where any gold might be hidden has been answered for us," Jon said.

That night the team slept in a small tool bin that had only one entrance and could be locked from the inside. They also loaded the shotgun and took turns standing watch.

Before they fell into a restless sleep, Ben said, "Tomorrow, we drop a camera down that damn pit, see what's in there, and get the hell out of here." No one argued.

CHAPTER 44

JASPER MINE—1943

WHEN ERIC WATCHED THE GOLD-laden truck driven by Lester leave the Jasper, he felt utterly alone and confused. While Victor and Willy held the two drivers and the Frenchman under guard, Eric tried to mentally piece together a plan to deal with the arrival of eleven more trucks loaded with gold.

Eric was nineteen years old in 1943 and already a lieutenant in the rapidly dwindling German army. Born in a small farming village, he joined the army because he had no choice. He heard the rumors of what was happening to Jews, gays, and other political "undesirables" in prison camps in Austria, Poland, and Germany, but he entered the army with no agenda other than survival.

In mid-1943 his regiment was notified that they would soon be shipped out to replace depleted troops on the Russian front. But a week before his departure, Eric was approached by his company commander and informed of a mission he had recommended Eric for that was dangerous, secret, and voluntary. It also carried with it the possibility that he would never return to Germany even if he survived. Since the assignment was top secret, Eric wasn't allowed to tell anyone about the mission, including his family.

But based on a flimsy barracks rumor that their mission was some kind of spy enterprise in the United States, Eric took a chance and accepted the assignment, concluding that no mission could be worse than the Russian front in winter.

Eric always dreamed of going to America. Yet the things he had read about the country and its people seemed unreal. The utter vastness and diversity of its geography, the equally diverse makeup of its citizens, its movie stars, and palm trees created a tapestry of life he always hoped he could visit. But once America entered the war in 1941, Eric knew the possibility of going to the country in his books was remote.

Weeks before their departure from Germany that would eventually take them to an abandoned silver mine in Arizona, Eric and the other recruits, all in their late teens or early twenties, met in Berlin several times for briefings. Eric was impressed by the men General Becker had assembled. Each spoke fluent English, all appeared athletic, and with few exceptions, well educated. Most had attended German schools that prepared the young men for a life in the military serving their Führer. No matter what the task.

The briefings included reviews of road maps of America, its culture, new slang words, its currency, political differences between parties, its racial problems, and even the difference between the New York Yankees and the New York Giants. There was particular focus on the geography of the American Southwest.

On the last day before their departure, the men assembled in a large room on the east side of the Reichstag. Martin Bormann entered the room alone and addressed the group from the head of a large cherry table where over thirty men were sitting. "Gentlemen, your selection to be part of this mission should be considered by each of you as the most important assignment of your lives. It should also fill you with pride and self-confidence that your inclusion in this group separates you from your fellow soldiers. You are special. You are the best of our country. You are our hope for our future. Most importantly, you are the hope for our Führer, a hope that his vision will someday be shared by the entire world. The success of that vision is now in your hands."

Eric looked around the table at his fellow soldiers and saw many in tears that were born from patriotism and loyalty. The emotion in the room was palpable; even Eric was caught up in the moment of devotion to country and devotion to a man none of them had met but were willing to die for. Bormann moved from the front of the table and raised his right arm toward a large photograph of the Führer on the wall above a huge fireplace. "Heil Hitler!"

All thirty men around the table rose and, as one, repeated, "Heil Hitler!"

Now, just eight months later, Eric stood in a mine in Arizona trying to make a decision that could affect the rest of the world for decades: How and what to do with nearly two hundred tons of gold? He didn't have a clue. But the Frenchman did.

Jean Dubois talked nonstop and repeated time and again that the next eleven gold deliveries were on a tight schedule and if he was not there to greet the next truck at the rendezvous spot, the drivers wouldn't know where to deliver the gold, and the plan would fall apart.

As the minutes dragged on, Dubois's voice became increasingly shrill. Willy hit him in the stomach with his rifle butt to shut him up and give Eric some time to think. But Dubois soon recovered and resumed his grating rant.

Eric realized he had no choice but to work with the Frenchman and the in-coming drivers who would be delivering the gold. Finally, Eric walked back toward the now frantic Frenchman, grabbed him by the left arm, and moved him away from the other four men.

Speaking in French, Eric quickly made an agreement with Dubois for fifty bars of gold to be paid for his work after the last truck arrived at the Jasper. Dubois wanted a thousand bars, but by the look on Eric's face he knew he would be lucky to get his fifty and escape with his life.

The deal called for Dubois to take the Lincoln and meet up with the next incoming truck and direct it to the Jasper. He would remain at the rendezvous point until the last truck arrived. He would then lead that last truck to the mine, load up his fifty bars in the Lincoln, and melt into his new homeland with over $500,000 worth of gold. And he would, against all odds and to the chagrin of most, be alive.

Eric also cut deals with the two drivers who had brought in the first truck that Lester had driven away. In exchange for three bars each, they would help unload the gold from the next eleven trucks under Eric's direction and ensure there was no trouble with the next twenty-two drivers. While the gold was being unloaded, Victor and Willy would lurk in the darkness of the Jasper to make sure the plan was going smoothly.

After each truck arrived at the Jasper and unloaded, Eric, Willy, and Victor would thank each driver for their service, give each two gold bars for "expenses" and direct them to take their trucks in different directions miles from the Jasper and await further orders from Becker. Orders that would never arrive.

Within an hour after Dubois left in the Lincoln, the second truck arrived and quickly unloaded their gold under Eric's direction and left for a destination one hundred miles from the Jasper.

Over the next ten hours, German precision was in practice. Truck after truck entered the mine, offloaded its cargo, and disappeared back down the dirt road to separate locations to await their orders.

At just after 6:00 a.m., the twelfth and last truck entered the Jasper followed by the Lincoln driven by Dubois. After they unloaded their gold, the drivers of the last truck got their orders from Eric and prepared to head toward Mesa for further orders. As the drivers casually chatted with Victor before they left the Jasper, Eric looked back at the gold that was stacked on pallets near the rear of the cavern. While an incredible amount of gold worth hundreds of millions of dollars, Eric was amazed at how small an area was required to hold such wealth.

Ending their small talk, the drivers said good-bye to Victor and prepared to head toward Mesa for further orders. That was when the tallest of the two was shot in the left side of his skull. His brains splattered into the face of his co-driver whose own brains were a second later plastered against the back of the truck.

Stunned by the sound of gunfire, Eric dropped to one knee and too late reached for his rifle. Instead, he was hit in the back of the head by something hard and landed face-first on the mine floor, unconscious.

An hour later, Eric awoke to a screaming headache. His blurry eyes tried to adjust to the half-light of the morning sun that filtered into the cavern entrance a hundred yards away. Finally, he looked up and saw a face he didn't recognize. It was more mask than face. Deep crimson clots of blood covered a misshapen visage that tried to smile but had several teeth missing from both the upper and lower gums. The jaw itself was no longer aligned. The lower part was one inch off center from the upper half. A dark blue bruise framed an indentation below the left ear. The nose of the mask was smashed almost flat, and more blood was caked on the upper lip and seeped from the left eye.

The mask tried to talk, but Eric could not understand what it was trying to say. His attention perked a bit when he was kicked twice in the left rib cage. In German, the mask told him to stand up. As Eric slowly rose, he saw Victor three feet away, his face battered and his arms in the air. Eric also saw Willy standing behind the man who wore the mask. Willy had his rifle pointed at Eric. Dubois also held a rifle and smiled broadly as he pointed it at Victor.

In measured tones, the mask that was Colonel Rolle spoke through pain and blood with no emotion. "Lieutenant, you and the scum next to you are traitors to your country and a disgrace to the uniform you wore. But worse you have tried to steal from your county and your Führer."

Eric looked at Victor and saw the fear in his face. "This man was acting under my orders and had nothing to do with..." Before he could finish his sentence, Rolle turned and shot Victor in the mouth with his Luger blowing the back of his head out and onto the mine floor. His body fell at Eric's feet.

"He should have died trying to stop you rather than go along with a traitor. Next time he will know better," Rolle mumbled as the report of the shot echoed off the walls of the Jasper.

Ignoring the still twitching body of Victor and continuing in an almost conversational tone, Rolle said, "There is much work to do, Lieutenant, and little time. Therefore, I must ask you to assist my comrades here, and the two drivers you coerced into helping you, to overcome the problems you have caused." Still stunned by the death of Victor, Eric was not sure he heard Rolle and was paralyzed by what he had witnessed. To jolt him into action, Rolle backhanded him across the face using the butt of his pistol for emphasis.

As blood ran down his cheek and with Willy's rifle jabbed in his back, Eric walked toward the gold near the rear of the cavern. He saw the two drivers he had recruited hog-tied on the floor. The men had been beaten, and Eric wondered how he could have slept through what had happened over the previous hours. The men did not react to Eric's arrival but had heard the shot that had killed Victor and knew their lives would also soon end.

Eric was tied to the front bumper of the Lincoln and could hear Rolle give orders to Willy and the Frenchman. The Frenchman took the Ford truck and returned four hours later with twelve, twenty foot by four inch steel I-beams in addition to food, water, painkillers, ropes, a ladder, concrete blocks, mortar, six gallons of flat black paint, paint rollers, a gas generator, lights, two pushcarts and other assorted odds and ends all of which had been stored in a nearby warehouse.

When Eric and the two drivers unloaded the materials from the truck near the pit in the back of the mine, they didn't at first understand what Rolle's plan was. It appeared Rolle was going to order them to build a small building to hold the gold on the mine floor, which made absolutely no sense.

Instead Rolle directed Eric and the two drivers to slide several steel beams from the mine floor over the pit to the area behind the gaping hole that was about twenty feet wide, thirty feet deep, and ten feet high. After moving the material Dubois had brought over the beams to the area behind the pit, the plan to hide the gold became clear.

It was obvious to Eric that he, along with the other two young drivers who had come across the Atlantic via South America, would be killed by Rolle. At the same time, he could not help but grudgingly admire Rolle's ability to work through what had to have been excruciating pain to achieve his goal of hiding the gold in the Jasper until his final plans could be initiated.

Over the next two days, the gold, with the exception of one thousand bars, was moved over the pit a few ingots at a time. They were carried by hand or in a pushcart, across a path six feet wide made from the beams that were placed on the right edge of the pit, which was the shortest distance from the cavern floor to the area behind the abyss. Eric and the remaining drivers were forced at rifle point to navigate the push carts over the beams that would move under the weight of the men and material they ferried across the steel path.

Eric told the drivers not to look down into the blackness as they crossed, but the howling from the maw beneath them did not require sight to inject body-numbing fear into the men. The youngest of the drivers was so terrified that he fell to his knees and vomited while on the steel path. As he did, he lost control of his pushcart, and four bars of gold could be heard skittering down the sides of the pit.

With no order from Rolle to do so, Willy shot the young man in the back and pushed him into the pit as the young man tried to struggle to his feet.

"You may work or you may die. That is entirely your choice," Rolle said calmly to Eric and the remaining driver named Gregg. The two men decided to work.

After all the bars had been transferred to the ledge, Eric and Gregg were ordered to take four large barrels one by one over the steel pathway. At first, it appeared Gregg would defy the order as exhaustion overtook him, and he gasped for breath. He glared at Rolle, and then Willy, and it seemed he was about to charge one or both knowing he would be shot, but not really giving a damn anymore. As the standoff continued, Rolle placed the barrel of his Luger to Eric's temple and said, "Gentlemen, your work is not yet done."

Over the next hour Eric and Gregg wrestled with the large, unwieldy barrels. They tipped them on their sides and rolled them over the steel rails, twice almost losing control of the heavy loads. Even in the coolness of the cavern, the men were drenched in sweat after they finally moved the four barrels over the steel beams and stored them near the back wall of the ledge.

Rolle ordered the men to erect a block wall twenty feet wide and twelve feet high that would connect to the sides of the natural rock and an overhang above the ledge. He also ordered that a three foot by four foot opening be created at the right bottom of the wall so the men could build most of the wall from the inside away from the pit and then move out of the area back across the steel beams.

After the wall had been erected, the steel beams were realigned to expand the eighteen foot ledge that remained behind the pit and under the block wall to provide a platform for the men to paint the wall a flat black. After it was painted, it was covered with dirt and gravel then painted again.

The process was repeated five times until the wall did not look like a wall at all. It looked like mottled and uneven natural stone and created a perfect camouflage in the dim light of the cavern.

On the other side of the pit, Rolle, Willy, and Dubois seemed pleased with the results of Eric and Gregg's labor. "You can't tell it's a wall, even from this distance," Dubois said.

"True," Rolle said. "Unfortunately, the fact remains you know there is gold behind that wall which is information a traitor cannot possess." Rolle nodded to Willy who shot Dubois in the back of the head before Dubois could raise his rifle. He then casually dragged him to the pit and tossed him into the howling black hole.

After seeing Dubois shot and tossed away like yesterday's garbage, Eric and Gregg had no doubt what was in store for them. But to their surprise Rolle motioned them over the steel beams.

Eric crossed first then sagged to his knees in exhaustion. But his exhaustion was more than physical; he was also tired of seeing death. Tired of lies. Tired of pain. He was tired of every damn thing. He was done. He needed rest.

When he looked back across the chasm at Gregg, Eric saw a look on his face and immediately knew what Gregg had decided. "Colonel Rolle, küss meinen arsch du Hurensohn." Gregg then took a silent swan dive into the pit over Eric's shout of, "Gregg, don't!"

Rolle and Willy had no response to Gregg's decision other than Rolle whispered something to Willy who in turn motioned to Eric to rise and move to the front of the Jasper. What confused Eric was why he was still alive in the first place. Why had Rolle shot Victor and not him? And now why was he being led back to the front of the mine? Why not just kill him and get it over with?

After they reached the front of the mine, Rolle gently put his arm around Willy's shoulder and whispered something to him about needing rest. Willy nodded, then tied Eric's hands and ordered him to sit on the floor with his back to the mine wall as Rolle entered the offices.

For the next several hours Willy paced back and forth in front of Eric with rifle in hand. He appeared to be in a trance. Finally, Eric posed a question: "Willy, why did you turn against us and side with Colonel Rolle?" Willy did not answer. Eric asked the same question a second time.

Willy finally said in an almost gentle voice, "Colonel Rolle is right about how the gold will help the Führer, and we must make sure it is used to keep his dream alive."

Eric laughed quietly to himself when he realized that Willy still actually believed the lies. All of them. And because he believed the lies so utterly and completely, he was an extremely dangerous man.

Eric thought of trying to argue or reason with Willy, but he was just too damn tired. He figured he might as well get some rest before he died. He slept for five hours. When he awoke, he saw Willy was still pacing and holding his rifle, staring straight ahead, still following orders and still believing.

While the hours dragged on, Eric dozed off from time to time, sure that he would be shot in his sleep at any moment. But Rolle didn't emerge from the offices, and Willy continued his pacing, never varying the points where he would stop, turn, and march back to where he had started.

Later in the day, it was clear that Willy was prepared to wait for Rolle to awake no matter how long it took. Willy would follow Rolle's orders. After hearing and seeing him in action over the previous several days, Eric could see Willy had effectively lost his mind, and anything he might say or do could set him off without warning.

Willy never stopped pacing. He did not eat or drink. He did not talk other than to give Eric permission to eat dried out cheese and stale bread and drink warm water.

As day turned to dusk, Eric awoke from his latest catnap and decided to risk Willy's wrath by posing a question. "Willy, do you think perhaps Colonel Rolle left last night? Do you think he is still asleep in the office after all this time?"

"The colonel would not leave his post," Willy answered in a monotone.

"I am sure you are correct, Willy, but it has been over thirty-six hours, and the colonel has not come out; perhaps you might want to check and see if he is alright, or would you like me to check for you?"

"The colonel said not to disturb him." Willy said with a finality that Eric did not want to challenge.

As the sun set and the cave darkened, Willy turned on the lights and generator brought to the cave by the Frenchman. Eric and Willy began another night waiting for Rolle to come out of the office.

Eric was now convinced Rolle was dead, but he was equally convinced that Willy did not believe that and trying to change his mind could be a fatal exercise.

Another long night on a hard cave floor began with the backdrop of ghost-like sounds coming from the pit. Eric looked at Willy as he continued to pace and could not help but feel sorry for a young man he had known since basic training. Willy was a man who seemed to epitomize many in his country. He still believed the lies. Still thought their leaders were going to prevail, still believed a dream that was a nightmare. Not able to see the truth when that truth was too horrific to comprehend.

Eric knew he would eventually have to challenge Willy and felt his best hope was to outlast him. Sleep when Willy refused to. Eat when Willy would not. Think when Willy could not. It was a sound plan.

Then Rolle appeared in the doorway leading from the office.

Rolle was in fact not dead. In fact, he seemed more alert than before even though his face was even more grotesquely swollen and misshapen. "Good evening, Willy," he mumbled.

"Good evening, Colonel." Willy replied, his voice weakened with fatigue. "I hope you rested well."

"I did, and I appreciate your concern and following my orders, Willy." As he spoke, Rolle placed his arm around the huge young German. "You should take some food and water and get some rest." Willy nodded and stood silently next to Rolle waiting for further orders.

Turning his attention to Eric who remained on the mine's floor, Rolle smiled and without saying a word casually smashed Eric with a rifle butt to his left temple, knocking him unconscious.

Turning to Willy, Rolle said softly, "Unlike the traitors in your unit, you have performed above and beyond the call of duty, Willy. Your heroism and dedication to me and the Führer will be rewarded." Willy stood in front of Rolle, his body rigid at attention, his glazed eyes staring straight ahead as his body swayed slightly.

"Thank you, sir."

"I have one more task for you, but it is one that will allow you to rest. But to complete your mission, you must trust me, be patient, and maintain the courage you have demonstrated to me and the Führer. Do you understand?"

"Yes sir, I understand."

"Good, Willy. Very good."

Putting his arm around the waist of the huge young man, Rolle whispered his final orders to Willy, and at the same time, handed him some food and water he had brought with him from the offices.

Willy did not respond to the orders given him. Instead he nodded and did as he was told, as he always had. Just as many millions of his fellow countrymen had. Through the fog of a concussion and the pain and fatigue that wracked his body, Eric awoke and thought he heard two rifle shots. But after all he had been through the previous days, he was not sure if the sound was real, a dream, or a memory.

However, Eric was aware that at that moment he was alive and alone, and that realization made him work at loosening the ropes that had held him captive. He had been working at untying himself earlier when he knew Willy was not watching him, but now he wriggled and squirmed trying to extricate himself from his binds. He succeeded but was a minute too late.

As the ropes hit the floor behind him, Rolle appeared like a specter from the darkness of the mine alone, a Luger pointed at Eric's forehead only ten feet away. "Lieutenant, it appears you have suffered from unfortunate timing. Please sit back down."

Eric was tired of taking orders. He remained standing, staring back at Rolle with a slight smile on his lips. Rolle ignored Eric's refusal to sit and said matter-of-factly, "Lieutenant, I intend to make you die very slowly for what you have tried to do to your Fatherland. I am going to shoot you in each limb but will be careful to ensure those shots will not be fatal, though they will fracture several bones. I then will put a bullet into your groin to allow you to bleed and feel the pain you have tried to inflict on your country. Before you die, I will tie you to the bumper of one of the trucks and drag you to the pit and…"

Before he could finish his threat, Eric interrupted Rolle's soliloquy. "Colonel, I really don't give a damn if you kill me or not. What I've seen over the last few days and heard from men like you over the last three years makes death sound like a vacation in the Alps. I'm tired of living in a world that has vermin like you in it. I'm tired of a world that is inhabited by madmen like the Führer. So your threat of death holds no fear for me, only relief. But I strongly suggest your first shot is through my brain because I am only six feet from you, and you will not have an opportunity to hit my arms and legs."

Taking a step backward from the now charging Eric, Rolle aimed at Eric's face and pulled the trigger.

At a moment like that, it is difficult to understand who is more surprised— man who thought his skull was about to be invaded by a

700-mile-per-hourbullet,or the man who pulled the trigger and realized his gun has jammed. There is always that awkward, almost embarrassing second pull of the trigger, confirming that the situation had changed rather dramatically in just a few short seconds.

Rolle made a halfhearted attempt to hit Eric with the pistol, but that wasn't a threat to a man years younger, stronger, and only moments after he had been given a new lease on life.

Eric wrested the gun from Rolle and stared at the man who had been responsible for so much death. Yet, Rolle calmly, almost without taking note of Eric or the change in his fortunes, began another speech as he stood, turned, and walked toward the rear of the mine.

"The world has not seen the true greatness that will one day be Germany, Lieutenant. But it will. Young men like you will fulfill the dreams. You will do the right thing, after all, because you are one of us. You will make sure that the Fatherland will live again in the greatness that is its destiny. The vision of the Führer will be the vision of the world and his children, children like you, will lead the resurrection. It is up to you to take responsibility of Operation Rebirth and do what you must to ensure that the Führer's dream and our dream is finally realized."

As Rolle spoke, his pace quickened, and he continued his march toward the back of the cave, ignoring a neatly stacked pile of gold bars that Eric knew Rolle had reserved for himself. Eric picked up a rifle and pointed it at Rolle's back, but he knew he wouldn't need a weapon.

As he neared the pit, Rolle slowed his pace but never stopped talking, but Eric had stopped listening. He had listened all his life, and he would listen no more to men like Rolle. Men who themselves had listened to other men and other lies, and it had all snowballed into a hideous nightmare.

Eric knew Rolle had been a murderous, treacherous man, and what he was about to do he deserved, yet he could not help but think that there were even worse men than Rolle. Men who had lied to and misled a generation. Men who had killed millions. Men who still lived. Men who had to be punished. But more importantly, men who had to be stopped.

When Rolle neared the edge of the pit, he stopped but did not turn around when Eric spoke. "Colonel, I am not like you. I have never been like you. As for the greatness of Germany? It will only be realized after the Führer, and men like you are dead and hopefully forgotten by the rest of the world. I will use the gold to make sure the horror you and the rest of the Reich has created dies with each of you."

As Eric's words floated on the breeze that moved from the front of the mine to where the men stood, Rolle walked into the pit as if he were stepping off a curb. Eric heard his body slam into the sides of the walls and hit debris along his path to death. Rolle never screamed or cried in fear. Eric wondered if he would be willing to give his life for what he now believed in, as fearlessly as Rolle and others had given theirs for a madman.

As silence returned to the mine and Eric regained his senses, he sank to a crouched position with his rifle aiming into the darkness at what he couldn't see. He remembered that Willy was still in the mine.

Eric remembered the two shots he thought he had heard earlier, but he still spent several hours searching for but not finding Willy in the vastness of the Jasper. He finally concluded that the large and murderous young man had indeed been shot or had been convinced by Rolle to walk into the pit to eliminate a witness to where the gold had been hidden after Willy had sealed up the remaining hole in the wall.

In the wake of the carnage of the previous several days, Eric sat on the floor of the Jasper totally alone and entranced by the utter quiet that enveloped him. Even the winds that normally coursed through the mine were at rest.

For several hours Eric laid in the cool darkness and drifted off for hours at a time even though he was never really able to sleep soundly fearing he would be brutally awakened yet again by Rolle or Willy or even the Frenchman. He tried to reason with himself and said quietly under his breath, "They're all dead." The words calmed him for a while, and he would relax and fall into a restless sleep. But he would awake in a start, reaching for his rifle and searching in the half-light of the Jasper for something or someone. In the late afternoon, Eric decided he needed to act and make the most important decisions of his life. Decisions that not only impacted him, but thousands or even millions of people around the world.

Eric walked through the Jasper one last time and wondered if anyone who eventually wandered into the cave would smell death as he could or if it was just his imagination.

Eric loaded the one thousand bars of gold that Rolle had left on the dirt floor into the last Ford truck that Rolle had planned to use. It instead would become Eric's ticket to freedom in a new country, the country of his dreams.

———————————————————

In early November,1943, twenty-one year old Eric Warner Schneider left the Jasper mine in a Ford truck loaded with one thousand bars of gold with a value of over $11,000,000. He headed for a place called Cincinnati, a faraway city in the Midwest section of the country that was famous back home for good German beer, brats, and a place several of Eric's friends and family had immigrated to prior to America entering the war in 1941. He would spend the next forty years of his life in the city on the Ohio River.

Eric left behind in the mine thousands more ingots that had been moved from Germany to rebuild a madman's vision and legacy. He also left behind tales of lost gold that were fueled by reports of ingots, or pieces of ingots of gold, being found in or near the creek bed in the desert south of the Jasper.

Eric's fellow soldiers, who had fallen to their deaths trying to carry the gold over the pit, had taken several ingots of gold with them. Some of those ingots made their way down the 500-foot depth of the pit that emptied into a narrow funnel in the rock and then into a creek bed that angled nearly twenty miles south of the Jasper until it dried up in the vastness of the desert. Over the years, raging waters fueled by savage spring and summer rains had pushed the ingots down the creek bed as far as five miles from the Jasper.

A piece of an ingot was discovered by Ben while he hiked through the desert on a bright Sunday morning. Tom and Jon found a complete ingot nearly twenty years later. Another complete ingot was discovered by a young man who was hunting jack rabbits with a rifle when he was only fourteen. He spent the rest of his life looking for more. A couple in their late sixties from Minnesota found an ingot while camping in the desert. Being from Minnesota, they turned the ingot in to the local police department. Their discovery was not reported to the press but did lead the local sheriff to quit his job and buy a metal detector.

CHAPTER 45

DOWNTOWN PHOENIX—1943

LESTER DECIDED TO START SLOWLY. Putting the gold bar between two wooden sawhorses left behind in one of the abandoned buildings he often called home, he tried smashing the bar in two with a rock. When that didn't work, he took the bar and succeeded in breaking it in half after slamming it over a concrete step. Breathing heavily after lifting the twenty-pound ingot several times, he slumped to the dirty floor and stared at the two large chunks and small bits of gold that had been gouged off the ingot. After regaining his breath, he scooped up the half dozen bits and stuffed them in his jeans and placed the two larger pieces in his knapsack.

Given the rather casual attitude his friends had about recognizing other people's belongings, Lester felt he needed to keep the gold on him at all times. But given its weight, Lester surmised that toting the gold around Phoenix all day would hurt his back. Finally, he decided he had to take a chance. He wrapped the two large pieces in dirty old rags he found on the floor of the building and looked for a place to hide them. His choice was in the water tanks of two old toilets that had been pulled out of the walls. After placing the gold in them, he covered the porcelain treasure chest with assorted junk from the building. After his work was complete, Lester decided to see just how much this gold was worth.

Walking down McDowell Road, he decided to test the gold market at Ernie and Gwen's pawn shop. After a few minutes in the shop, he learned that both Ernie and Gwen were long dead, and he would be dealing with a short, squat cigar-chomping gnome of a man named Max Greene. "Whataya need, mister?"

"Well," Lester drawled pulling the dirty handkerchief from his pocket and opening it on the counter, "I was out in the desert last week and found this stuff on the ground. Thought it might be gold. If so, I want to sell it. That's pretty much it."

Scooting over to the counter on a chair with wheels, Max took a jeweler's loupe and began examining the six small pieces of gold, the largest the size of a man's little fingernail. "Found this in the desert, huh?"

"That's right."

"Just lyin' there?"

"Yep."

"Well, this is processed gold not gold ore, and it's pure gold, I think."

"So it's worth something then?"

"Sure."

"How much?"

"You say you found this just layin' in the dirt, huh?"

"That's what I said."

"I know what you said, but most gold found in the desert is…"

"Look fella, I'm hungry, tired, and need a bed. I found this gold and might find some more. If you want to buy it, say so; if not, quit wastin' my time."

"Easy, Slim." Max got off his chair and stretched out to his full five foot five frame. I'll weigh what you got here and let you know."

After weighing it, Max offered Lester thirty-five dollars for the six crumbs of gold.

Before giving Lester the cash, he said, "I just want you to know that I'll throw these pieces into a can with some old gold we get from time to time. When I get enough to make the trip worthwhile, I'll take it to the smelter who will give me about 30% more than I just paid you. In other words, I'm just a middleman here."

"What's the name of that smelter?"

After buying breakfast for some friends of his who needed a good meal, Lester took a ten-block walk into an even seedier section of Phoenix. It even smelled seedier, no doubt in part because of Taylor Smelting, which was housed between a pipe-fitting business and a welding shop. All three businesses emitted black smoke from their chimneys, but the smoke from Taylor Smelting smelled the worst. The sign on the front door read *Jackson Taylor, Proprietor.*

When Lester entered the shop, he was met with a chain-link fence. Behind the fence was a very large, very bald, very black man, with huge arms, sitting behind a counter eating fried chicken. The black man wore a white short-sleeve dress shirt and sported a large gold pinkie ring and several thick gold chains around his neck. The black man was Jackson Taylor just as the sign said, but he was known as J.T. to his few friends.

Calling through the fence, Lester asked, "You the man who does the smeltin'?"

"Not when I'm havin' lunch."

"Kind of early for lunch, ain't it?"

"Not when you start work at six in the morning."

"You the one who does the smeltin' when you ain't eatin' chicken?"

"Yep."

"I got stuff that needs smeltin.'"

J.T. pulled on a rope under the counter, and the chain-link fence opened. Lester walked up to the counter.

"I do all my own work. Want a drumstick?"

"Yeah, thanks." Lester lifted the leg from a bowl and took a bite of home-made fried chicken specially prepared by J.T. himself. "This is a pretty damn good chicken leg.'"

"Wait till ya taste the wings. Hey, grab us a couple beers out that fridge over yonder, will ya?" J.T. pointed to a beat-up ice box in the corner of the dingy office.

Retrieving two longneck Miller High Life bottles, Lester handed them to J.T., who opened both with a silver bottle opener in the shape of a rattlesnake head.

"What ya' needed smelted?"

Lester placed some gold pieces on the counter. Looking at the gold while shoving some chicken skin in his mouth, J.T. said, "You don't need me for that. That's already refined gold."

"I just want to sell it."

"Don't need me for that neither. There's places all over town who'll buy that kind of stuff."

"They won't buy it from someone like me without lots of questions."

"So, you're lookin' for a fence?"

"I'm lookin' for someone who can move a lot of gold and won't ask lots of questions."

"Then you lookin' for a fence. You steal it?"

"Nope."

"You got lots of it?"

"Yep."

"Here's how it'll work; you bring stuff in on Monday mornin', and I'll have cash for you by Thursday. I'll charge you a 15% service fee, but there can't be no paperwork."

"What's this stuff worth?" Lester pointed to the pieces on the counter.

J.T. weighed the gold on a new Toledo scale. "You got a little over three ounces. That's worth $120 minus my 15%. I can give you cash for this amount now if you like."

"Thanks, been awhile since I had that much foldin' money."

J.T. reached under the counter, pulled out the cash and another scale, which he handed to Lester.

"If we're gonna be doin' business, you might as well take this with you. Look in the papers for gold prices, subtract 15%, and you'll know what you got comin'. Make sure you test out the scale, so you know I won't be cheatin' ya."

"Thanks. Kinda young to have you own business, ain't ya'?"

"Worked here as a kid. Man who owned it died when I was overseas. Came back and his widow asked me to buy it, so I did. It's a livin."

"Thanks again for the scale. By the way, saw your tattoos, you in the war?"

"Navy. Got my leg shot off at Pearl. Been back a couple years."

"I was in France in WWI, infantry."

"I was a cook durin' the war. Ain't cooked nothing, but fried chicken and apple pie ever since."

"How the hell did a cook lose a damn leg?"

"Jap torpedo hit us right at breakfast time. Found out it was damn tough for a black man to swim with one leg."

"Thanks for the chicken, J.T. Maybe you could bring some of that apple pie on Monday. See ya later." Lester picked up the scale and walked out the door.

After leaving J.T.'s, Lester went to Sears and bought four pair of Levi's, four flannel shirts, six pairs of white cotton socks, one belt, six pairs of cotton underwear, a pair of boots and a wool sweater. Later he stopped at a Rexall and got some toothpaste, toothbrush, a Gillette razor, pencils, and a thick notebook with lined paper.

Finally, he went to the Majestic Hotel, got a room with a bathtub, and paid the thirty-five dollar weekly rental in advance with cash. Later, standing in the shower, he tried to remember the last time he had slept in the same bed more than two nights in a row. He couldn't.

Lester got to know J.T. pretty well over the years, including the fact that he had been framed for tax evasion for not reporting income he'd received from working part-time in a bar owned by a very white, very jealous Dallas businessman, whose equally very white wife was fucking J.T.'s brains out.

Before beginning a four-year sentence in the Texas State Prison, J.T. skipped bail in Dallas and made it out to Phoenix where he got a job in a dirty smelting plant. In the fall of 1941, after he got tired of the smell and heat, he enlisted in the Navy under a fake name where a few months later he encountered more smell and heat on a destroyer that the Japs torpedoed at Pearl Harbor. By March 1942, he was back in Phoenix minus a leg and nothing to do but go back to work in the damn smelting plant, which he ended up buying. He wanted to go back to Texas, but he knew he'd have to do time if he did. While he realized the white woman with the rich husband had not been worth all the troubles she had caused him, he also conceded she was *almost* worth it.

Over the years, J.T. had grown the business steadily by working hard and keeping his mouth shut. When small-time miners came to him with gold or silver ore, he used creative accounting to make sure they paid as little income tax on their precious metal findings as possible. After being charged with a crime he had not committed in Texas, J.T. felt the strong desire and obligation to fuck the government in general and the IRS in particular any way he could if it was possible. It was possible, and when it happened, it made J.T.'s day. He also worked with jewelers, dentists, and other small manufacturing firms that used gold in their processes. He bought and sold gold and silver on a daily basis, and business was good.

Given his work with gold, silver, and cash and the fact that his business was in a crummy part of town that the cops avoided as much as possible, J.T. got permission from the local authorities to wear a .38 caliber white pearl-handled Colt six-shooter on his hip. He silver-plated the pistol so everyone entering his shop could see it. He was also known to use the gun. Once, two young punks, seeing him all alone in the shop, tried to take back the gold they had just sold him and keep the cash. They soon found the gun was real, and J.T. was a good shot. One got a bullet in the ass trying to run away, while the other took a hit in the leg. J.T. could have killed them both but figured it would be bad for business. Word of that incident spread, and soon J.T. and his gun became famous, which helped avert further trouble.

Lester was someone J.T. trusted immediately. He couldn't say why exactly, but he just knew Lester was a white man he could believe. When Lester told him the gold wasn't stolen, he believed him. Not that it would have mattered all that much, but he believed him anyway.

Lester started his business relationship with J.T. slowly. After busting up the two large chunks of gold hidden in the toilet into smaller pieces, Lester brought them into J.T's shop one piece at a time, but each time the piece was bigger. J.T. never questioned Lester or his seemingly endless amount of gold, except once after Lester's eighth or ninth trip when he said, "Hey man, if I'm gonna be movin' a lot of this stuff, I'll need to get my friend Juan from Juarez to help me unless you want the taxman snoopin' round."

"I wouldn't lose Juan's number if I was you."

With war time prices of gold hovering around thirty-six dollars per ounce, the single bar of gold Lester had hidden in the toilet created an income stream of over $11,000, not including a 15% fee to J.T. for "processing and handling." Doing some quick arithmetic, Lester figured that the approximately seventeen hundred bars of gold that he buried in the sand was worth nearly twenty million dollars. He realized he would not be able to bring in large amounts of gold at any one time for fear of raising some unwanted attention. He was also aware that given the fluctuations of gold prices, it would be wise to pick the times when he could get the most for the gold. Eventually he and J.T. entered into an unwritten business relationship that lasted thirty-five years. It made them both wealthy men and best friends.

Between 1943 and 1980, Lester made nearly 400 trips to the desert, and J.T. always paid him a fair price for the gold. Sometimes J.T. would buy the gold himself depending on market conditions, or he would get help from Juan in Juarez or other friends around the country in the business if Phoenix was awash in gold.

But some things about Lester did puzzle J.T., "Man with all the money you got, why don't get your ass a nice place to live and a damn Cadillac? That dirty old van of yours is nasty. And for Lord's sake get yourself some clothes. I'm sick of seeing you in those old jeans and boots. And that damn shirt got holes in the elbows. C'mon man, that ain't right."

Lester would just smile and help himself to more fried chicken and apple pie.

CHAPTER 46

THE FOUR PERSON/ONE DOG team did not sleep well in the tool bin. Every sound made them jump, and the Jasper had plenty of sounds. After a quick bite to eat, they said little to each other, the usual morning banter and teasing noticeably absent.

Moving slowly out of the tool bin, they realized how vulnerable they were in the vastness of the Jasper. An entire army could be hiding in the shadows and would never be seen or heard. A single sniper could easily pick off the team, dispose of their bodies in the pit, and have breakfast at Elsa's, all in thirty minutes.

"Jon, I think you should take the shotgun and Pax, and stand guard near those old offices. Keep out of sight and don't try to be John Wayne if you see anyone. Just fire the shotgun once to warn us and then make your way to the shaft near the tool bin, and we'll meet you there and decide what to do next. Tom, Sam, and I will investigate the pit, and we'll all get the hell out of here by noon," Ben said.

Nodding without comment, Jon jogged toward the front of the cavern, shotgun in hand, with a willing Pax by his side.

Tom picked up the rope, lights, and batteries while Ben carried the video camera and Sam toted the computer. As they walked away from the natural light that poured into the front of the cave into darkness leading to the pit, the wind enveloped them and caused a precipitous drop in temperature they had not experienced before.

When they were thirty feet from the pit, Ben sat on the floor and tied the end of one of the thin nylon ropes to the video camera. Without being told to, Tom began a similar process with three of the lights he had brought with him. Tying the battery-powered halogens back to back to back, he created a 360-degree light pattern that, when attached to the video camera, would give them a look inside the gaping hole that seemed to be even louder than usual that morning. While the men worked with the ropes, Sam set up her computer and tested the images and sound after she synced it with the video camera.

While Sam waited for the men to complete their jobs, she looked up at the Jasper's high ceiling, saw its smoothness, and tried to comprehend the eons of time required to carve out such a cavern and the trillions of gallons of sea water that had poured through the mine that created the Jasper from sheer rock.

For the next thirty minutes, Ben and Tom connected the camera and lights, while Sam knotted together the five 100-foot thin nylon ropes

Tom had purchased. She used black electrical tape at twenty-five- foot intervals to mark the descent of their equipment.

After a final check of the camera and lights, they slid a twenty-foot long two-by-four they had found over the right corner of the pit and laid the other end of the wood on a ledge that stuck out eighteen inches at the bottom of the rock wall behind the opening. That positioning allowed the camera to be lowered into the pit without banging against the side walls and being smashed to bits. Tom used a metal chair he had found in the cavern as both a seat and a base. He used his 250 pounds as an anchor and slid a 200-pound boulder in front for him to use as a foot brace.

"You look like your fishing for marlin," Ben said.

"Let's hope we catch something with that camera."

As Tom slowly let out the rope, Ben noticed that the camera and the blue-white glow from the three halogen bulbs lit up the area above the pit like Times Square on New Year's Eve. The roof of the cavern came alive with phosphorescent sparkles as the bright light bounced off the stone as the camera slowly descended into the pit.

"Looks like one of the mirrored glass balls they used to have at discos in Philly years ago," Tom said.

"Wouldn't know. I was about three then," Sam said casually.

Tom tried not to smile, fearing it would encourage her.

Against the flat black wall directly behind the pit, the lights created an eerie show that slowly faded as the camera and lights were swallowed by the void. Wanting to be able to see everything they could on its descent, Ben reminded Tom to let the rope out slowly. As he did, Sam and Ben saw crystal-clear images coming from the pit.

"That's about twenty-five feet. See anything?" Tom asked.

Peering into the computer screen, Sam said, "Lots of beer cans and trash."

"Fifty feet."

"Looks like the hole's narrowing a bit. There's another ledge with some pipes and wood and fencing...Oh my God, it looks like a person...it's a young man...he's impaled on a piece of wood!"

Ben looked over Sam's shoulder and saw the young man in jeans and a work shirt.

"Wait, there's a man on the other side...Daddy, it looks like they fell yesterday."

"The lack of humidity helps preserve the bodies. Go on, Tom."

Tom let the rope slide further. "That's one hundred feet."

"Tom, move the rope to the left about ten feet."

"What do you guys see?"

"Looks like a bar of gold stuck in some trash," Ben said.

In the now swaying light, Sam and Ben saw a twenty-pound ingot with the words "Property of the United States Treasury" clearly stamped on one side.

"I'll be damned." Tom whispered.

For the next twenty minutes, Tom let the camera and light descend into the darkness. At regular intervals, Sam and Ben saw the history of the Jasper unfold before their eyes. They saw nine complete bodies, body parts that had snagged on ledges, and tons of mining equipment littering the now narrowing hole. They saw hundreds of beer cans, cigarette butts, newspapers, furniture, an old pickup truck, building materials, and the hood of a Chevy pickup. They also saw a second bar of gold and a piece of a third.

At three hundred feet, the camera and lights began to spin, slowly at first then wildly, creating a dizzying spectacle on Sam's computer screen of more flotsam that had fallen into the pit and been hooked by other trash or outcroppings. "The wind's picked up and the opening is widening," Ben said.

With camera and lights still pointing down and the rope at 450 feet, the bottom of the pit was still not visible.

"We're almost out of rope. Any sign of bottom?" Tom asked.

"No, and we're losing our signal. Let go of the rope, Tom."

"What?"

"You won't be able to pull up the camera and lights anyway, not with all those obstructions. Just let it go and maybe we can see where it lands."

Tom cut the nylon rope. Moving closer to the edge of the pit, he listened for the equipment to hit bottom. He heard nothing.

On the computer there was nothing on the screen for several seconds as the camera and lights descended into blackness.

Suddenly, a shotgun blast reverberated throughout the cavern.

CHAPTER 47

PHOENIX—1943—1979

LESTER EVOLVED INTO A CREATURE of habit. He developed routines from which he seldom varied. He ate at the same places and visited the library at the same time each day, where he would make entries in his journal. He would walk down near the public park he had funded and watch the kids run through the sprinklers. He'd buy some clothes at Sears and leave them around town in places his friends could find them.

He would spend the first three weeks of each month determining what needed to be done in and around Phoenix, and spend the last week of the month making it happen. To fund his adventures, he would drive his van out toward Whiskey Flats, park it in a rest area, and walk miles in the sand and rocks to retrieve his funding source. But as the price of gold exploded from $36.50 an ounce in 1943, to $489 by the end of 1979, Lester's desert treks became far less frequent or necessary. A gold bar worth just over $11,000 in 1943 was worth over $147,000 by 1979. Even with inflation, Lester's buried gold continued to soar in value, which he reminded J.T. of every chance he got, usually over fried chicken, apple pie, and beer.

"Did you know with the gold prices up so much since the war, the gold still in the ground after all the money I've spent, is worth 'bout five times more than all the bars in '43?"

"You're a damn conglomerate, ain't you?"

"Yep. Been buyin' up land and buildings for the last thirty years. Got so damn much money comin' in I haven't needed to get a bar in months."

"Well, it sure as hell won't rust on ya'."

"J.T., after all these years how come you never asked me where the gold was?"

"Cuz, I don't give a shit."

"Well, maybe someday I'll show you where it is."

"Remember that 'I don't give a shit' part?"

"I know, but if I was to die in bed with some young chippie…"

"Shit, seventy is young to you, 'sides, you're too mean to die."

"I'm serious, J.T. You're the only one I can trust."

"Look, Lester, I'll do anything you want. Just tell me when."

The needs in Phoenix were varied. It could be someone needing an operation, a school that needed books, a hospital that needed new equipment, a shelter that needed new beds or more food, or just a friend who needed some clothes. The fun part for Lester was to make things happen without anyone knowing it was him. He would devise elaborate ruses whereby there was a need, and then bingo, that need was met.

Of course, he had to trust some people in order to do some of the work, including an attorney, but they were sworn to secrecy and told if they wanted his help later, they had better keep their traps shut. One of Lester's biggest projects was to donate money to build a three-hundred-bed shelter in downtown Phoenix near the bus station.

Lester was in the audience with several of his buddies during the dedication of the building that featured a modern cafeteria, lending library, showers, air conditioning, TVs, and interior walls for privacy. There were hundreds of brand-new clean towels and even clothing for men who needed it. Most importantly, Lester set up a trust fund to pay for the utilities, medical supplies, and salaries for the staff. At the dedication of the building, a local minister addressed the crowd as Lester dozed off.

"Today we are proud to be able to officially open this three-hundred-bed shelter to help those among us in need. We are eternally grateful to a fellow citizen who has generously and anonymously donated the funds to allow his and our dream to become a reality today and into the future."

Nudged awake by one of his friends after the speech, Lester rose with the rest of the men and began to leave. Another friend had an opinion. "I ain't never stayin' in no damn shelter."

"I don't know, looks pretty nice to me," another friend noted.

"How 'bout you, Lester? You gonna use that shelter? Or you gonna stay in that fleabag joint you live in?"

"I'll move to the shelter if you boys do."

"They gonna have that cable TV thing I've heard about?"

"I have a feeling they will," Lester said. "They surely will."

As the crowd dispersed, the minister came up to Lester, whispered in his ear, and then hugged him. Looking around and embarrassed, Lester nodded to the minister and caught up to his friends to discuss new rooming arrangements.

Later that afternoon, Lester, as usual, walked five blocks to his favorite diner called Maxine's. As he waited for the light to turn green at the corner of McDowell and North 19th Avenue, a white Buick Electra 225 drove slowly past him. The driver of the Buick looked at Lester and then parked on the street a block away. In his rearview mirror, the driver of the Buick watched Lester enter a little diner across the street. After he exited the car, the handsome older man, who wore an expensive linen suit and sunglasses, leaned against the Buick's front fender and gazed at Maxine's.

When he entered the diner, Lester went directly to "his booth" at the back near the kitchen. Lucille, his favorite waitress, was of an age that you really couldn't tell how old she was, and she sure as hell wouldn't say. Some would call her a faded beauty, but Lester just liked the fact she was friendly, gave him "trouble," and always had a big smile every time she saw him. She also had really big tits that she wore proudly and with distinction, which Lester also admired.

Handing Lester a copy of the *Phoenix Times* left by a previous customer, Lucille said, "You're late."

"Had a meeting."

"You're never late."

"I was today."

"I had to go hide the meatloaf so you'd have some."

"Is it Tuesday?"

"You forgettin' the days now? Damn, you're gettin' old."

"Not too old to ring your bell, young lady."

"You've been threaten' to turn me every which way but loose for twenty years now, Lester. I'll bet that old thing of yours don't even work no more."

"Careful now, if I turned the python loose on you, you'd drop all those other boys you got."

"Lester, they ain't no other boys. You want cherry or peach pie for dessert?"

"I'm rich. I'll take both."

"How do you stay so skinny?"

"Countin' all my money."

"That why you wear that same damn plaid shirt all the time?"

"Just careful with my cash, darling. That's why I'm rich."

Lucille smiled and walked away, but as she did, she had a warning for Lester.

"Don't you be lookin' where you shouldn't now, old man."

Lester smiled and continued to look at Lucille's butt.

As Lester read the paper, the man from the Buick entered the diner and sat next to the window at a small table. He scanned the menu but glanced up several times to look at Lester.

Not having noticed the man noticing him, Lester finished his meatloaf dinner ,including two pieces of pie, left Lucille her usual five-dollar tip, and was about to leave when the well-dressed man approached Lester and stood next to his booth.

"Lester, may I join you?"

As he looked up at the tall, slender well-dressed man that stood next to his booth, Lester immediately recognized who it was. "Well, I'll be damned."

"Hello, my friend."

"Sit on down here, Eric."

Eric slid into the booth across from Lester and was finally face-to-face with the man he had diligently been searching for over three decades.

"It has been a very long time, my friend-" Eric said.

"Did it all really happen?"

"Sometimes I wonder. But the nightmares are vivid at times. I still see the faces," Eric said.

"I know. Every time I go out toward the Jasper, I think of my buddies from that first day and all the stuff that happened."

"You look well, Lester."

"For an old fart, I guess. You look healthy and rich, Eric."

"The years have been kind to me and my family."

"So what the hell brings you to Phoenix?"

"You do, Lester."

"Me?"

"I had a private detective try to track you down years ago, but for the longest time he had no luck. Finally, he found a filing for an apartment building you bought but didn't believe it was you based on where you lived. To his amazement. his research then discovered that you're worth over twenty-five million dollars."

"Closer to fifty, not includin' the rest of the gold."

"You have done very well, my friend."

"I'm hangin' on. You lookin' for some cash, Eric?"

"No, I'm not. Like I said, I too have done well. The detective said you have donated much to the people of this city but have done so quietly."

"If people think you got lots of money, they treat you different-like. More fun to do things that surprise people."

"I understand, Lester."

"Eric, one thing I was always curious about was what happened after I left that night?"

"There was more death. I was the only one that survived."

"How about all that gold?"

"You don't know?" Eric asked.

"How would I know?"

"I thought you would have returned to the mine and..."

"Never wanted to set a foot in that damn mine again." Lester said.

"Nor did I." Eric agreed.

"So what the hell happened to all that gold?" Lester repeated.

"I don't know. There is always the possibility it's still there."

"Good Lord, I figured you came back and got the gold years ago." Lester said.

"After you left the mine, I dealt with the remaining trucks and Rolle..."

"Rolle? You mean that crazy sonovabitch wasn't dead?"

"No, but that is a story for another time. After I left the mine with one thousand bars of gold, I made it back to Cincinnati, got into business with my uncle, and raised a family. I tried to forget what had happened, but the nightmares..."

"You mean you took just a thousand bars for yourself?"

"Yes, and I have donated most of the proceeds to Jewish charities. I know it's not enough but…"

"No, that was a real good thing you did, Eric."

"Like you, I prefer to do things quietly."

"That means between us we took about twenty-seven hundred bars but accordin' to Rolle, there were over twenty-thousand bars, and some barrels full of stuff. What happened to all that?"

"Like I said…I don't know."

"You said you came to Phoenix to see me, how come?" Lester asked.

"I had assumed you had eventually gone back to the Jasper and figured out a way to take the gold. I wanted to see you again and commend you on what you had done with it. But hearing now that you didn't retrieve the gold creates a bigger question. If the gold is still there, what do we do with it?"

"I'm sure too damn old to do much of anything, but you're right, it's time somethin's done with it."

"I am afraid I will not be much help however. Another reason I wanted to see you again is I'm dying. My liver cancer has spread and…"

"Damn, Eric, I'm real, real sorry. You're still a young man. How much time ya' got?"

"Six months. But I feel healthy. I still jog each morning although my doctor said that will soon end."

"So what do we do, Eric, I mean about the gold"?

"The first thing we need to do is determine if the gold is still in the mine."

"Can you walk a few miles?" Lester asked.

"Yes."

The next morning Eric and Lester parked the Buick in a rest area off Route 60 and walked into the desert. Lester toted his army surplus backpack while Eric wore a sweat suit and tennis shoes.

"No roads to the Jasper?"

"Before we go to the Jasper, I want to show you somethin' first. It ain't far."

After forty minutes of walking, the men approached a large cluster of Stonehenge- type rocks adjacent to several large cacti.

"This is it," Lester announced proudly.

"Is what?"

"My bank."

Lester moved to an indistinct area of loose sand and gravel, moved away some sage brush and got down on all fours. He reached into the sand and pulled out a twenty- pound ingot, and simultaneously displayed a big smile on his face.

"You mean you keep your gold out here in the open like this?" Eric asked, incredulous.

"Well it ain't exactly out in the open, but I couldn't think of a better spot for it."

"What if someone followed you?"

"That's why I walk out here. Easier to see if anybody's around."

"You mean you carry each bar from here back to the car?"

"Yep, made about 500 trips so far. Used to go more often but with gold prices goin' up and…"

"Dear Lord, that means you've moved over…"

"Five tons, about 160,000 thousand ounces, damn near forty million dollars."

"But how can you walk all that way with a twenty-pound ingot?"

"Oh, it ain't that hard. Besides keeps me mean and lean."

"How many bars are left?"

"Over 1100."

As Eric tried to calculate the numbers, Lester beat him to it.

"At today's prices there's about a 150 million dollars here in the ground, give or take. Want some?"

"Oh, my God! No, Lester, like I said…I don't need…"

"I know it's kind of crazy to hide it out here, but fetchin' it a bar at a time over the years worked. People never suspected nothin'."

"But what if you had died?"

"I have a diary back at the shelter that, they keep in a safe for me with a map in it, and instructions on who to give it to if I kick over."

"Smart idea."

"Yep. But you know what? I think gold prices is goin' higher. Wouldn't surprise me none if gold is at $1,000 an ounce someday. They ain't makin' no more of it. You ready to head up to the Jasper?"

After they walked back to the Buick, the men drove north to the Jasper. The closer they got to the place that had occupied their nightmares for nearly four decades, the quieter they became. When they pulled up in front of the cavern, two coyotes slinked passed the Buick and disappeared into the rocks.

Seeing Eric's face, Lester said, "Hell, Eric, we don't have to go in that place. It really don't matter if the rest of the gold is in there or not. If it's there. we're too old to get it. And if it ain't, it's gone forever anyway."

"I need to at least find out if the place it was hidden has been discovered."

"How will you know?"

"If the spot is how I left it that last night, the gold is there. If it has been returned to its original state, then someone has discovered the gold."

After Lester and Eric exited the Buick, they leaned against the front bumper of the car and talked. They also saw a rusted sign that said *Arizona Mining LTD. No Trespassing.*

Pointing to the sign, Lester said, "I heard about that mining outfit. They came here right after the war. Said they was gonna start mining again, but nothin' ever happened. In fact, I was wonderin' at the time if you was part of that group?"

"I never heard of that company. Do you think it was a ruse to gain access to the mine and to try to find the gold?"

"Don't know, but I wondered that too," Lester said.

"I did some research after the war about the twenty-four men who drove the trucks and delivered the gold here to the Jasper. Five died in the mine. I knew many of the remaining nineteen men and contacted all their families after the war,". Eric said.

"Any of them still alive?"

Thirteen of the men eventually returned home. But by 1955, each was dead."

"They were still young men."

"Many were killed in accidents. Several became mysteriously ill and died. Two shot themselves," Eric said.

"Do you think they were all murdered?"

"Without question."

"What about the six that didn't return to Germany?" Lester asked.

One died in a plane crash, but the other five, according to their families, never returned to Germany. They all remained in this country, raised families, and became very successful."

"You know where they live now?"

"It appears one is in South America and the rest in California." Eric said.

"Did any of the drivers who went back to Germany ever mention the gold they had delivered to the Jasper?"

"Constantly. In fact, I think that's why they were killed. They'd get drunk and talk about all the gold they delivered years before. Most folks thought it was just war stories the men made up. But I think some people believed them," Eric said.

"You think that Odessa outfit I've heard about all these years killed those men to keep them quiet?"

"The existence of Odessa has never been confirmed. But if it did exist at one time, it was led by the very men within the German government who arranged to have the gold moved to this country. But most of those men did not survive the war or spent decades in prison."

"If Odessa didn't kill those thirteen boys who delivered the gold, who did?" Lester asked.

"I suspect it was the men who stayed in America after the war. I believe those men formed a solemn pact to say nothing of the gold while quietly taking steps to find it."

"Like taking a lease on this place?" Lester asked.

"Yes. At the same time, they systematically eliminated the men in Germany. After their deaths. the stories of lost gold would become a thing of legend and soon forgotten."

"You think those truck drivers who remained in this country ever found that gold?"

"I don't know. But I can give a better opinion after we go inside," Eric said.

"One more thing Eric, all twenty-four of those drivers saw you when they delivered the gold. Did anyone ever come lookin' for you?"

"I don't know. My parents and two sisters died during the bombing of Dresden near the end of the war, and I had no other relatives that were living in Germany. So there was no one to contact. I changed my last name when I moved to Cincinnati, so there was no way to trace me. I assume they thought I had been killed like everyone else in the Jasper."

After several moments of silence, Lester asked, "You ready to go inside, Eric?"

Eric nodded.

When the men entered the Jasper, the smell hit them first, registering in their brains and sending both of them back in time. Fifty feet inside the cavern, Lester looked up and to his right and saw the black soot still visible on the south wall from the inferno he set off by shooting a hole in the truck's gas tank.

Eric looked to his left and saw the area near the old offices where Rolle shot his friend in the face.

As they walked deeper into the mine, the wind began to gust, and a low moan encircled them. The beams of their flashlights caught beer cans, old newspapers, animal bones, and other debris. The floor of the mine began to slope as the old men carefully negotiated their way toward the pit that they could never, and would never, forget.

Twenty feet from the gaping abyss, Lester said, "Ain't nothin' changed I can see."

"Look more closely, my friend."

Moving his flashlight from the floor to the ceiling and turning in a full circle, Lester could see no difference in the mine from what he remembered decades earlier. Then his flashlight caught something that had not been there in 1943.

"That's it, ain't it?" Lester asked.

Eric nodded.

On the drive back to Phoenix, Eric said, "I too have often asked myself if it had all been a dream. And if it was real, how could I have been so foolish to have believed what they were telling us?"

"You wuz just a kid, Eric. Besides, lots of people believed that man, but when you discovered the truth, you did something about it. That's all that counts."

"You were very brave to have done what you did."

"I have bad dreams too. Figure I'll be doin' a stretch in Hades for my part. But if you and me hadn't done what we done, the world might be a whole different place right now."

"Lester, you did what you had to do. We were fighting the same war that was being fought in Europe and the Pacific, only no one outside that mine knew it. You protected the world from those who would have tried to create the reality of a Fourth Reich. With the wealth that was brought from Germany to the Jasper, they would have had the resources to grow the evil we destroyed."

Nodding in silence, Lester looked at Eric with a sense of relief that his actions from so many years before that still made him wake up in cold sweats were justified. Hearing someone else articulate what he had always silently hoped was the truth lifted a burden that Lester had been carrying for decades.

"You think the gold is still there?" Lester asked.

"Yes. If the wall had not been there, then obviously the gold would have been gone. But the wall is still there, and there would have been no reason for someone to rebuild it after taking the gold."

"That makes sense, Eric. So what the hell are we gonna do about all that damn gold behind that wall?"

"I am afraid that will be up to you, Lester. I am going to spend my remaining months with my family, but I wanted to find you, thank you, and share what I knew. Maybe it is best to let the gold stay where it is until a younger generation can deal with it. Obviously, it's hiding place has stood the test of time so far."

"Yeah, maybe you're right. Besides, I have enough to deal with in doing stuff with the gold I got in my bank out yonder."

After a long dinner of good food, drink, and overdue conversation, Eric and Lester took a stroll to walk off the apple cobbler. On their walk, a half dozen men passed Lester, smiled, and said hello. Eric noticed the warmth in their smiles. "Lester, why haven't you let the people around here know what you've done for them? You'd be a hero, my friend."

"I done some things in my life I ain't real proud of. Things that still keep me awake at night. Figure doin' what I been doin', quiet-like, is maybe a payback. Makin' things right, sorta."

"I understand. And like you said before, it can be more fun to do things and just see how people react not knowing it was you who did them," Eric said.

"Yep."

After several more blocks, the men stopped in front of the shelter that Lester called home along with a couple hundred of his best friends, a block from Eric's Buick.

When the old men warmly shook hands, Eric said. "Goodbye, my friend. I will never forget you."

"I won't forget you neither, Eric. You done real good and I'm proud you're my friend."

The men from a WWII battle in 1943 embraced on a street corner in downtown Phoenix in 1979. After he watched Lester amble toward the shelter on a warm Arizona night, Eric got in his white Buick and drove back to Cincinnati where he died four months later.

A rabbi delivered the eulogy.

CHAPTER 48

JASPER MINE—2014

HEARING THE SHOTGUN BLAST, BEN, Tom, and Sam moved into the darkness of the cavern along the northern wall and headed for the prearranged spot near the tool bin they had slept in the night before.

Without being asked, Jon told the others that he had seen four men walking down the path from the dirt road. When he fired his shotgun and made himself and Pax visible to them at the entrance to the cavern, they stopped, returned to their Benz, and drove away.

"Well, it's good they saw you and know you're armed," Ben said.

"Could you get a good look at any of them?" Tom asked.

"No, except they were all well-dressed and they were old guys."

"Nice to be so popular, isn't?" Tom said sarcastically.

For the next two hours, the team stayed in the tool bin, sipped some water, ate, and told Jon what they had seen in the pit.

"I don't think there is any more gold in this mine," Tom said.

"What about the bars you guys saw in the pit?" Jon asked.

"I'm not saying there wasn't gold in here at one time but…"

"Not sure I agree, Tom," Ben said. "We know there has been gold in this mine at some point because of what we saw in the pit. The question is, is there more? And if so, where?"

"Daddy, this mine has been wide open for a hundred years, and we've looked all over this place and haven't found anything, and I'll bet a bunch of other people have looked too."

"I agree, but someone is concerned about us being in here, and the only reason I can think of why that's the case is they believe the gold is in here, but they can't find it either," Ben said.

"Do you guys think anyone would just chuck gold into the pit?" Jon asked.

"Why would anyone just throw gold into a bottomless pit?" Sam answered.

"Could you think of safer place to hide it?" Ben asked.

"No…but if you can't get to it, what good is a safe place?" Tom reasoned.

"Look, we can debate all this later, but I think after we do a final look-see, we need to wrap up this expedition today," Ben said.

"Why?" Tom asked.

"This place doesn't feel right. There are spirits in this cavern that speak of true evil."

"Evil spirits from a guy who went to Stanford? C'mon, Ben," Jon said with a laugh.

Ben turned to Jon and said deliberately, "Don't let your whiteness discount the possibility that things you can't see do exist."

"I was never very religious," Tom volunteered.

"I'm not talking about religion. What I'm talking about is real and tangible. You simply need to open up a part of yourself and learn to feel what's around you. The silence will speak to you if you learn to listen."

"What are you hearing, Daddy?"

"I know it'll sound melodramatic to all of you, but there's also a feeling of sadness in this mine. It's real. I've felt it since I first walked in here. There's a feeling of dread as well. The spirits of the dead are at war in this mine," Ben said somberly.

For nearly a minute, no one spoke as Ben's words resonated in the silence. Finally, Tom rose to his feet and responded, "I think Ben's right; let's get out of here. We've looked in every nook and cranny of this place and haven't found a thing except in that pit. And if gold is in there, then that damn pit can have it."

"Before we go, I want to conduct an experiment," Ben said.

Following the old man, the group walked to the back of the mine within twenty feet of the pit. With the howling wind as a now-familiar background, Ben picked up several golf ball-sized rocks lying on the right side of the pit. Moving back toward the group, he gave one of the rocks to Tom and pointed to the right side of the pit. "Throw this against that wall."

"What?" Tom asked.

"I said throw that rock against that wall, and listen, all of you."

Tom threw, and they all listened. It sounded like a rock hitting rock.

"Again."

It sounded the same.

"Again"

The same sound.

Five more times Tom threw, and the sound was just like a rock hitting rock.

Ben picked up several other rocks and had Jon throw them against the wall on the left side of the pit. The sound was the same as Tom's throws.

"Now, Sam, throw a rock at the wall behind the pit."

She only threw once. That's all she had to throw for everyone to hear the difference. It was a hollow sound.

For the next thirty minutes, the four of them threw more rocks, then listened, theorized, hoped, laughed, and finally decided that they had found a man-made wall behind the pit. Beyond that, they didn't know what the hell to do about it. If they could get through the wall, what was behind it?

"To break through that wall, we're going to need some equipment, and we're going to have make some noise. Then if we find anything, we're going to have to figure out how the hell we get whatever might be in there out of this place with the boys from Deliverance and AARP nosing around," Tom said.

Jon suggested, "Maybe I should drive into town and get a U-Haul truck…"

"Wait a second, guys." Sam said. "If there is gold behind that wall, it has been in a real good hiding place for a long, long time. My suggestion is we make a hole in the wall small enough to see what's behind it. If something is in there, we can patch it up and make it look like it's looked all these years until we decide what to do."

"That may not be so easy," Jon noted. "How do we get over the pit to put a hole in the wall to even look inside at whatever's in there?"

"If it was easy, it wouldn't have been a good hiding place all these years," Ben said.

For the next two hours the group made suggestions, offered opinions, argued, speculated, planned, ditched it all, and started all over again. In the end, they decided they would go to town, get some four-by-sixes, and build a small wooden platform at the far right corner of the pit. Then one of them would walk onto the platform and use a hammer to put a small hole in the wall, look inside with a flashlight, and find out if they had hit the biggest lottery in the history of the world.

It was a good plan, except they weren't sure who might be watching their every move or who might walk in during their search. And if they did find anything, how would they get it out of the mine and where would they take it? Having no immediate answers to their own questions, they waited and did nothing for a week.

Nothing, except assemble the platform in Ben's garage and develop a plan that would allow them to enter the Jasper at midnight, put the platform in place, put a hole in the wall, look inside, and get the hell out of the mine as quickly as possible.

On a late Sunday evening, the group entered the Jasper in Ben's pickup and dropped Pax off at the front of the mine with orders to "stay and watch." The big white, blue-eyed dog sat down and riveted his focus on the entrance of the mine and seemed to embrace the responsibility that had been thrust on him.

Ben drove to within twenty feet of the pit. The group quickly unloaded a nine-foot by twelve-foot wooden platform, slid it over the edge of the pit and anchored it on an eighteen-inch ledge that was exposed under the back wall. They lay ten-50-pound sandbags on the edge of the platform that was placed on the mine floor to help stabilize it.

It had been decided that Jon, because he was smaller than Tom and stronger than Ben, would be the one to walk onto the wooden plank, take a hammer, and punch a hole through the wall and see what, if anything, the wall hid. Sam had a different opinion.

"I'm lighter than all you guys, and let's face it, I'm in better shape. Whoever goes onto that plank needs to be light, strong, agile, and coordinated. Looking at you three, I just don't see it."

Tom started to argue, but Ben stopped him. "Don't even try, Tom. When she gets this way, it ain't no use. Just like her mother."

By 1:00 a.m. the platform was in place over the right corner of the pit as planned, but there was a difference in the level of the mine floor and the level of the eighteen-inch ledge behind the pit. As a result, the platform was neither flat nor particularly stable despite the anchor provided by the sandbags.

For further protection, two ropes were looped around Sam. One was tied to Tom, and the other tied to the bumper of Ben's pickup.

After the ropes were secure, Sam nonchalantly and with no ceremony walked out on the platform and made for the wall to begin her work. With a six-pound sledgehammer in one hand and a flashlight in the other, she began an assault on the wall.

Initially making no headway, she increased the power of her blows until on the fifth whack of the hammer, she broke through what appeared to be solid rock but was in reality cement block painted with a half-dozen coats of flat black paint. Trying to keep the hole as small as possible, at first she couldn't break through the other side of the block so she had to smash two more to give herself room to break completely through. After several more attempts, the head of the hammer finally broke through the other side of one block and then two more. Sam moved the pieces of block and dust away. She knelt and put her head through the hole and shone the flashlight through the twelve-inch opening.

The guttural sound Sam made echoed through the mine. At the same time, she pulled her head and arm out of the hole and stumbled backward falling dangerously close to the edge of the makeshift wooden floor. The flashlight flew from her hand into the pit. Seeing her sudden movements, Tom pulled on the ropes that held Sam, and Jon ran onto the platform and helped her back to the mine floor.

Kneeling next to Sam who was now sitting on the dirt floor, Ben gasped, "Honey, what in the world did you see?"

"A man. There's a man in there," Sam whispered hoarsely.

CHAPTER 49

THE DAY AFTER ERIC LEFT, Lester spent several hours in the library detailing their conversations and trip to the Jasper in his journal. Seeing Eric had profoundly affected Lester, mainly pointing out that he was getting old as hell, could die at any time, and then what would become of the gold? He also realized that aside from the men in the shelter, he had no family and was alone. He figured he would change all that starting at Maxine's Diner.

"At least you're on time tonight," Lucille said.

"Just came to say I ain't eatin' here tomorrow night."

"And why not?"

"Cuz, you and me are goin' out for dinner tomorrow night, that's why."

"Oh really?"

"Yep."

"I have to work tomorrow night, and besides you can't afford to be takin' anyone out to dinner."

"First of all, I decided I wanted to get into the diner business, so I bought this place today from Maxine's boy."

"You crazy old man, what are talking about?"

"I mean you're workin' for me now, and I'm orderin' you to take off work tomorrow night. I want you all dressed up. We're gonna have ourselves a time, girl."

Lucille looked up questioningly at her former boss behind the counter who gave her a thumbs-up and nodded.

"Lester, that is very sweet, but I really don't have anything to wear and…"

Lester pulled out three hundred dollars and gave it to Lucille.

"Here's some cash. Get your hair and nails done, buy a new dress, some shoes, and some fancy perfume. I know where you live, and I'll pick you up at six."

"Are you okay, Lester?" Lucille said with concern.

"I'll be just fine if you saved me some meatloaf."

The next night Lester pulled up in front of Lucille's modest home in his ten-year-old van wearing a new blue suit at least two sizes too big, a new white shirt, and a wide red and white tie. He had shaved, and his freshly cut hair was slicked back and smelled of Clubman hair gel. He had also poured what seemed like half a bottle of Old Spice aftershave on every possible body surface. He looked real slick.

Lucille had purchased a dark green print cotton dress, dark brown shoes, and a white shawl. She wore the corsage that Lester had bought for her. She looked real pretty.

Despite knowing each other for nearly twenty years and talking most every day, Lucille and Lester sat stiffly in the van on the twenty-minute ride to the restaurant trying to think of something to say.

"You look real pretty," was the best Lester could do.

"Thank you. Here's the change from the money you gave me. It was way too much."

"You should have spent it all. Just keep it. After all, you're missin' all your tips tonight."

Shoving the change in his coat pocket, Lucille said, "I can't do that, Lester."

When Lester pulled up in front of the Biltmore Hotel in Scottsdale, two young valets ran up to his van to greet him.

"Good evening, Mr. Jones. We were expecting you," one of them said as both van doors were opened simultaneously.

"Evenin,' boys."

"I didn't even know your last name was Jones," Lucille said.

"Yours is Wilcox. Lucille Marie Wilcox."

The maître d' saw Lester enter the restaurant and moved around four other patrons to greet him. "Mr. Jones, so good to see you again. We have your table ready."

On the way to their booth, Lucille whispered, "Lester, what the hell is goin' on here?" Lester just smiled.

Once seated, two waiters poured water, unfolded napkins, and placed them in Lucille's and Lester's laps. Menus magically appeared, and a wine list was given to Lester.

After a few minutes, Lester asked the waiter, "How's the lobster?"

"Flown in fresh today, Mr. Jones."

"You like lobster, Lucille?"

Before she answered, Lucille looked at the menu, saw the cost and said, "Lester, I ain't orderin' anything that cost seventy-six dollars even if rice and salad is included. That's crazy."

"We'll take two lobster dinners, some of your best white wine, and make a couple of those chocolate soffly things."

"Yes sir, Mr. Jones, two chocolate soufflés."

"Lester, you tell me what's goin' on here right now, or I'm gonna get up and leave."

"Remember all those times I told you I wuz rich? Well, I am rich. Damn rich. In fact, I may be the richest son of a bitch in this whole state."

"Oh Lord, Lester, I wish you wouldn't make up such things. All these new clothes, this fancy restaurant, this fine hotel, you can't afford all this."

"First of all, I eat and sleep here for free, don't pay a damn dime…"

"That's it, Lester. I can't bear to hear you say such…"

"Lucille, darlin', I eat and sleep here sometimes for free cuz I own this whole kit and caboodle. The hotel, the restaurant, the golf course, everything. Told ya' I wuz rich."

Lucille shook her head and started to slide out of the booth but stopped when Lester pulled out an old notebook and handed it to her.

"What's this?"

"It's a story. But I swear it's all true, every damn word of it. It'll explain why I get free food here."

Lucille took the notebook and started to thumb through it, but Lester said, "You can read it later, I got some other things to talk about with you."

Lucille set the notebook down and turned to Lester. "Like what?"

"Well, I've been thinkin'…I know I'm old as hell, and you're just a young thing, but how 'bout if we wuz to get married? I've been meanin' to ask you for a while, hell, guess it's been ten years now, but never got up the nerve. I know you're past child bearin' age, but that's okay with me, it'd be just you and me."

"You're crazy, Lester."

"Nope, just figured you and me get along real good, and I ain't got all that much time left, and maybe we could just be happy awhile, and you wouldn't have to work. Maybe we could travel and see the world."

"Lester, you are very sweet to ask but…"

"Tell you what, you read my journal there and maybe it'll convince you I ain't crazy. Another thing, I ain't askin' that you love me none, cuz if you want to know the truth, I love you enough that I could get by with you just likin' me a little bit. Hell, I've been lovin' you for twenty years now and not sure I could stop if I wanted to. But I'll understand if you say no as long as we can still be friends, cuz I like ya' too, not just love ya, if ya know what I mean, and would sure hate to never see you again just because I told you I was lovin' you. Aw hell, that don't make no sense at all, does it?"

Lucille reached over to Lester and stroked his cheek. "It makes all the sense in the world, Lester. I don't know what's in this old book, but whatever's in it, is you. And I guess I've been lovin' you for a long time too, 'cause you're the nicest, sweetest man I've ever known."

When the waiter approached the table with the white wine, he stopped when he saw Lester and Lucille in an embrace, tears running down both their faces. The wine could wait.

CHAPTER 50

JASPER MINE—2014

"IT COULDN'T HAVE BEEN A man. You must have seen something else," Tom said as he put his arm around Sam's shoulder.

"The first thing I saw was what looked like canvas-covered boxes. When I moved the flashlight to the left I saw this man in a uniform sitting on one of the boxes holding a rifle. He was staring right at me."

"Did he move or say anything?" Ben asked gently.

"No, he just sat there and stared at me."

"We just said the other day, there are probably a hundred ways into this place and maybe someone is guarding whatever's behind that wall." Jon said.

"You said he had on a uniform. Could you tell what kind, was he a cop, a guard, or maybe military?" Ben asked.

"No, but he carried a rifle, that's all I can remember. Oh, one more thing, there was a canteen sitting next to him." Sam said, as she quickly regained her composure, although she made no attempt to move away from Tom's arm that remained around her shoulder.

"A canteen would indicate it's a military man, but what would he be doing here?" Ben asked.

"Sam, could the man have been dead?" Tom asked.

"No...I mean, I don't think so. His eyes were open, and like I said, he was staring right at me. His eyes are blue."

"We need to get inside that wall once and for all and find out what's in there. I think we should do it now before we get another visit from the local Welcome Wagon contingent," Tom said.

Without waiting for agreement from his partners, Tom rose and walked toward the platform.

"Tom, wait," Sam said.

"Tom, don't," Jon said.

But Tom wasn't listening. He walked onto the platform, picked up the hammer Sam had dropped, and began smashing the black wall. Within a minute, he had opened up the hole enough for him to stick the upper half of his body through. As he scanned his flashlight behind the wall, he saw the guard that had scared Sam. But Tom didn't retreat. He crawled through the enlarged hole and disappeared from the view of the other three.

"Tom, you okay in there?" Ben asked.

"I'm okay."

"What the hell's in here?" Jon asked.

After several seconds of silence, Tom nonchalantly said, "A really dead guy...and a bunch of gold."

"Quit screwing around," Jon said.

From behind the wall, Tom asked calmly, "Isn't there an intergalactic rule that says whoever finds the gold first owns it all?"

Ben and Sam looked at each other and smiled.

"If you're kidding around, I'm gonna cut off your..." Jon said.

"Tom, can we take a look?" Ben asked.

"No! No! Its mine...its alllll mine!" Tom stuck his head out of the hole, a big grin on his face.

Sam and Ben moved to the platform after Tom came back across it. They took turns and peered inside. Their reaction was surprisingly muted as if they were looking at the inside of a Walmart.

"Let me see," Jon said. After a few seconds behind the wall, Jon stuck his head back through the hole and exclaimed, "Holy fucking wow! Yes! Yes! Yes!"

Tom, Sam, and Ben smiled at Jon's euphoria.

"There's thousands of ingots back here! They must be worth a billion dollars! What's gold selling for today, close to $1,500 an ounce? Holy shit!"

"Before we leave, we should take an inventory of what's back there. I also saw four large barrels," Ben said.

"That place is too cramped for me," Tom said. "Jon and Sam can squeeze in there and see what we have."

"Good idea," Sam said. "I'll take my camera and record everything we find."

"Sam, you okay going in the hole with Jon?"

"Sure."

"Be careful, honey," Ben said.

Armed with flashlights and a camera, Sam and Jon squeezed into the hole made by Tom and disappeared behind the black wall. Even though they knew the man behind the wall was dead, they both recoiled at seeing the hulking figure who sat on the edge of a wooden barrel, his rifle in his hands and at the ready. The man's face had a look of melancholy, his blue eyes wide open, his skin flawless.

"He looks like one of those dummies in a wax museum," Sam whispered almost in fear of waking the young man.

"How could he die just sitting there like that?"

"Daddy and I have seen people, especially from dry locations, who died standing up, leaning against a wall."

"He looks like a young man. I think he's wearing a German uniform. I can see how you'd think he's alive."

"He looks sad," Sam said.

"Well, he is dead."

Sam sat down on a barrel next to the dead German and stared into his blue eyes. His eyes seemed to follow her movements, which mesmerized Sam. "He looks alive, even from this closeup."

"Maybe he's the guy you've been looking for. Tall, young, handsome, blue eyes, and really quiet."

The hole in the wall behind Sam allowed a slight breeze to enter, and the dead man's hair fluttered. Sam took her hand and gently moved his hair back into place; it reminded Jon of how Barbra Streisand had stroked Robert Redford's hair in *The Way We Were.*

As Sam moved her hand away, she accidently brushed the dead man's rifle. It discharged with a flash and deafening roar in the enclosed space. The bullet passed under Sam's right armpit and smashed into Jon's left thigh.

The recoil from the rifle seemed to fold the dead man in half. The upper part of his torso fell slowly, almost in slow motion, toward Sam, who slid to the floor to escape the dead man who continued to inch toward her. His blue eyes looked directly into Sam's.

Instinctively, Sam raised her arms and tried to ward off the dead German. But as he hit her outstretched hands, they penetrated his chest, and a fine dust erupted from his torso through his brown uniform and enveloped Sam's body. Sam tried to cry out, but she inhaled the dead man's dust, and it gagged her into silence.

Seeing Sam disappear under the dead man, Jon yelled, "Sam, are you alright? Sam?!"

Lying on her back, Sam continued to hold up the lifeless corpse as it slowly disintegrated into a fine dust and drifted onto her like brown snow. Sam could see his intense blue eyes inches from hers. The flawless skin from his face began to crack and fell away from the skull, the blue eyes tumbled out of his head onto her face and chest.

For several seconds, she was virtually paralyzed and couldn't make her body react. But then Sam began to punch the corpse. Each time a blow landed, a dust plume erupted, sending more of the dead man's dust onto her until she could no longer breathe. She felt his hands on her—they moved! His hands pulled on her, pulled her up toward his eyeless skull. She punched the dead man again and again.

"Sam! Stop it, it's me, Jon! Calm down, you're okay, calm down, Sam."

Suddenly Sam stopped punching, realizing that the hands she felt on her were Jon's.

"What happened?"

"Well, it appears you just got hit on big time by a dead Nazi who shot me in the damn leg."

As she coughed and wiped dust from her face, Sam's brain finally deciphered what Jon had said. "Oh my God, you've been shot!'"

"Yeah, I think I mentioned that."

Seconds later Ben thrust his head into the dust-filled room and yelled, "Sam, Jon, what the hell happened in here?! Are you guys okay?"

"Jon's been shot."

"By who?"

"By him." Sam pointed to the now-flattened dust-covered uniform."

"Let's get the hell out of here and get Jon to a hospital," Ben said.

"Bullshit. The bullet went all the way through my leg and into the wall. I'm not leaving here until we find out what's in here."

Having replaced Ben on the platform wall, and having seen Jon's injury, Tom said. "Don't be an idiot. You could bleed to death. Get the hell out of there."

"I'm not bleeding that bad, and it didn't hit a bone. I'm okay. Sam, you ready with that camera?"

On her feet, camera in hand, a dust-covered Sam said, "Ready."

Jon limped to the nearest pile and pulled back the green tarp. In less than a minute, Jon had uncovered billions of dollars in gold. Gasping for breath from the exertion, pain, and dust, Jon turned to the exposed gold and whispered, "Fuck me!"

As Sam clicked away on her camera, Ben and Tom entered the tight space and gaped at the impossible.

"Where could all of this have come from?" Tom asked.

"Given the uniform that pile of dust is wearing over there, I'd say Germany," Ben said.

"It does look like a Nazi uniform," Jon said.

"It is. His rifle is WWII vintage," Ben said.

Still dusting herself off, Sam asked, "What would a Nazi soldier be doing in Arizona? And do you think he's been sealed up in here since WWII, Daddy?"

"Looks like it."

Breaking the spell of historical possibilities, Jon asked, "Do you guys have any idea how rich we are?"

"Pretty rich," was Tom's answer.

"Pretty rich? We are disgustingly, arrogantly, stupidly rich."

"Yeah, I guess that too," Tom agreed.

As she knelt and touched the now-flattened uniform on the floor, Sam had a question. "Why would this man allow himself to be sealed up in here until he died? He had a rifle, and it looked like he could have broken down the wall with his bare hands."

"Look over there." Ben pointed toward several concrete blocks, a bag of mortar, and a trowel. "I'd say this young man sealed himself up, and someone else just threw some paint and dirt on the outside to blend with the rest of the wall."

"Maybe he didn't think he'd be guarding something until he died. Maybe he thought he'd just be behind the wall for a short time. You can see he had some food and water, even a candle over in the corner," Jon said.

"Whoever convinced him to go behind this wall must have convinced him they'd be back for him later," Ben said.

"That was one hell of a salesman," Jon offered.

"But he must have realized at some point no one was coming for him," Sam said.

"Some men are trained to follow orders. I suspect our friend here was one of those who did exactly what he was ordered to do, even if it meant he would die," Ben said.

Tom asked, "If this guy was really a Nazi, does that mean the gold came from Germany?"

"That's the most logical answer, but who knows? My bar said Mexico on it and yours Canada."

"When I was doing my research on all those tales of lost gold, I read that the Nazis moved massive amounts of gold from Germany during both world wars to protect it from being confiscated by the Allies. But how could they get all this gold from Germany to Arizona?" Tom asked.

"It would have been difficult," Ben said. "But with enough money anything is possible."

"Daddy, could the gold have come in from Mexico or Canada?"

"Not sure, but I'd bet there are a bunch of countries' names stamped on these bars."

Jon and Sam moved to one of the stacks of gold.

"This one says U.S. Government," Sam said.

"This stack says Australia," Jon said. "And here's Brazil."

"Looks like they were thinking ahead as to where the gold was ultimately going," Ben said.

Still euphoric over his newfound riches, Jon said, "It doesn't really matter where the hell this stuff came from, it's all ours now. Unbelievable."

Tom pointed to the barrels in the back of the space and asked, "Jon, did you open those barrels yet?"

"No, toss me a hammer."

Jon took the hammer and limped over to the first barrel where he wedged the claw end into the edge of the rim. The wood squeaked as Jon strained to pry open the lid. Suddenly the lid flew into the air, and Jon fell to the floor as the lid landed at his feet. Jon slowly rose, looked into the barrel, and said softly. "Ladies and gentlemen, we have a winner."

"What's in there?" Tom asked.

"Looks like about ten thousand loose rubies, diamonds, emeralds, and some notebooks," Jon said. "Hey, Ben there's something else, a gift you can give to your grandkids." Jon then tossed a small red toy truck to Ben.

Ben caught the toy, smiled, and spun the wheels of the truck with his fingers. But then Ben suddenly grimaced and dropped the toy like it was a hot ember then uttered, "Awl...no!"

"Daddy, what's wrong, you okay?"

"That toy... it's..."

"It's what?"

"Never mind."

Jon moved to the next barrel, opened it, and discovered more thick notebooks, gold plates, and silver place settings. The third barrel had notebooks, watches, and gold jewelry. After each discovery of treasure, Jon looked like a kid on Christmas morning, no longer able to speak but instead showing his utter joy by his ear-to-ear grin.

"I think we need to get out of here," Ben said.

Jon ignored Ben and instead moved to open the fourth and last barrel. The expression on his face moved slowly from glee to curiosity as he stared into what looked like black tar. Then the jellied substance gurgled, and an air bubble rose to the top of the barrel and belched out a putrid odor that enveloped the space.

"Holy Christ, what is that stuff?" Jon said as he fell back from the barrel and landed on a pile of gold, covered his nose, and coughed.

Sam helped Jon to his feet with one hand and covered her nose with the other, as she peered into the barrel. Sam gagged at the vile odor that had drifted near the opening in the wall where Tom and Ben stood.

"Jesus," Tom said. "What the hell is that smell?"

"Tom, hand me that piece of wood over there," Sam said.

Using the stick as a stir, Sam churned the black goo with one hand while she kept her mouth covered with the other. After her third stir, something short and black fell out of the barrel onto the floor. Jon used the claw part of the hammer, picked it up and examined it.

"What is that thing?" Sam asked.

"I dunno, but this part looks like a gold ring."

"Oh my God," Sam gasped. "It's a finger."

"Holy shit," Jon dropped the finger to the floor.

Suddenly, the contents of the fourth barrel began to churn and bubble; items floating to the surface of the black mixture. As she looked into the barrel, Sam saw human remains. There were ears, jaws, bones, teeth, fingers that were part of a viscous, rotting liquid that took on the appearance of a ghastly, hideous soup. The airtight barrel had prevented the contents from drying up; instead the body parts seeped blood that had turned black over the decades.

"I've got to get out of here," Sam said as she climbed through the hole in the wall, sprinted across the platform, and vomited on the mine floor.

"Jon, put the lid back on that barrel and get the hell out of there now. That stuff could be toxic," Ben shouted.

On his way out of the space, Jon grabbed two of the large leather binders he had found in one of the barrels. At the same time Ben pulled mortar and black-trim house paint from the pickup, and the men replaced the broken blocks. Within thirty minutes of patching, painting, and dirt throwing, the wall had regained its camouflaged look.

Later, as the group sat on the mine floor, Jon said, "I heard about the Nazis pulling teeth for gold but never thought it was true, how could they...?"

"They got gold anyway they could find it," Tom said. "Hard telling how much they took that way."

"Do you think they put that gold we saw in the barrels into the ingots?" Sam asked.

Ben replied, "Years ago I read a story, that claimed Himmler set up a false identity and bank accounts with the Reichsbank under the fictitious name of Max Heiliger. They would melt down the gold fillings and jewelry taken from those exterminated in the concentration camps, put it into gold bars, and sell it on the international market. They would take the cash and put it into those bogus Heiliger accounts. I remember the name because I had a friend in college named Mack Heiliger, and I thought of him when I read the article. So, in answer to your question, is it possible some of the bars inside that wall contain gold from concentration camp victims? I'd say yes, it's possible if not likely."

For several minutes, the four treasure hunters sat in silence on the floor of the Jasper and tried to grasp the golden and dark reality that lay behind the black wall. Each also mentally asked the question, "Now what the hell do we do?"

"The first thing we do is get Jon to a hospital," Ben said.

CHAPTER 51

BILTMORE HONEYMOON SUITE—PHOENIX—1980

LESTER AND LUCILLE WERE MARRIED by a justice of the peace in the recreation room of the Phoenix Men's Homeless Shelter. Two hundred of Lester's best friends showed up, some of them sober.

Lucille agreed to the location after Lester agreed to build a shelter equally as nice for homeless women and children. "Sure, I was gettin' around to that anyway," Lester told Lucille.

Lester's best man was J.T., who gave Lester a fancy gold keychain in the false hope that Lester would finally attach the chain to the key to a new Cadillac. But he knew better.

A week before the wedding, Lester had led J.T. to his gold stash in the desert, and the men talked at length about the things Lester wanted to see done with the gold if he were to drop dead in the heat of passion. J.T. laughed but agreed to make sure all those things would be taken care of and even had some ideas of his own that Lester agreed to.

Lester also took J.T. to the Jasper and told him about the gold that he suspected was behind the black wall. "If it really is there, that's too much for me to handle, even with Juan's help," J.T. told Lester. "We best just let that stay put for a spell."

On their wedding night, Lester and Lucille laid in bed, with smiles on their faces. "I'll say this, Lester, you're full of surprises," Lucille said with genuine contentment in her voice.

"I told ya not to get the python all lathered up."

"You call him the python?"

"Yeah, but you can call him anything you want."

"How about my new best friend?"

"Whatever you call him, he'll answer to it."

Snuggling into Lester, Lucille said, "That's good to know." Then she asked, "Lester, do you really own this hotel?"

"I'm too old to lie about stuff."

"That's good to know too. I read most of your journal last night."

"Yeah? What'd you think?"

"Who else have you shown it to?"

"Just Eric and J.T."

"Can you trust them?"

"Sure, Eric could have come after the gold years ago and never did. And I had to drag J.T. out to see where my stuff is. He's already worth lots of money and don't want to be bothered with it. By the way, ole J.T. will take care of you after I'm gone. You won't want for nothn'."

Lucille kissed Lester on his shoulder and said, "You ain't going anywhere for a long time based on tonight's happenings."

"Well, Lucy girl, I'm afraid that ain't so true."

"What do you mean?"

"I was feelin' poorly a few months back and went down to the free clinic. They sent me to a specialist and, well I got the same damn cancer Eric has. Damn liver cancer. Looks like a big ole baseball in there."

Lucille sat up in bed. "You mean you're dyin'?"

"Not tonight."

"When?"

"They didn't give a day and time."

"How long?"

"'Bout a year."

"A year?! Why in the world would you marry me and not tell me you were dyin'?"

"Cause you might not have married me."

"Lester, that's dishonest."

"Well it's not like we were gonna have some twenty-year marriage anyway. Hell, I'm old, girl. Besides, I wanted to make an honest woman out of you and spend my time with someone I cared for, and someone who would maybe watch over me for a few months."

"I'd watch over you whether we were married or not. You should have told me, Lester."

"Maybe so, but look at it this way, when I'm gone, you'll be the richest woman around these parts and will be able to do any damn thing you want. No more servin' meatloaf for quarter tips."

Lucille looked at Lester with tears in her eyes. She put her head on his shoulder and caressed his face. "Does it hurt?"

"Naw, just a little pinch in my back."

"You know, we should've gotten together years ago. All those years we were alone."

"Can't worry about all that stuff now, girl. We got to figure out how we handle all that gold still in my bank out in the desert. And then what the hell we do with all that gold behind that wall."

For the next six months, Lucille and Lester had themselves a time. They lived in the honeymoon suite at the Biltmore, ate good food, drank good wine, and even drove over to the Grand Canyon. "Damn thing's pretty big," was all Lester would say when he looked down at the immense canyon floor.

They also made plans on how she would handle the responsibility of Lester's real estate assets, cash in the bank, gold in the desert, and even more gold behind the wall after he was gone. They decided J.T. would, if need be, fetch the gold just like Lester had done for over thirty-five years, and together they would carry out Lester's wishes. They made a plan.

After an afternoon where they walked around downtown, said hello to a dozen of Lester's buddies, and had dinner at Maxine's, they went back to their suite and watched *Wheel of Fortune*. Lucille could tell Lester was tired. As she laid next to him on the king-sized bed, Lester turned to her and said, "I think it's time, girl."

"Okay, I'll shut off the TV."

Weakly, Lester said, "No, I mean…"

"Oh no, I'll call the doctor."

"No, don't do that, honey. Let's just lay here a spell."

Lucille put her arm around Lester's shoulder. "Does it hurt, sweetie?"

"Just a little."

"You know, I loved you for a long time," Lucille said.

"Figured so. Like I told ya, I loved you too but was too scared to tell ya."

"Never thought you was scared of nothin.'"

"Just you, girl."

"You damn fool."

"I know, but these have been a real good six months."

"You promised me a year."

"I 'spect I was fibbin' there just a bit."

Lester looked up at Lucille and saw the tears and hurt on her face.

"I never wanted you to have to see me like this," Lester said. He closed his eyes and drifted off to sleep.

The next morning, Lucille, who had stayed up most of the night concerned about Lester, reached over and felt for him. He wasn't there. Thinking he was perhaps in the bathroom, she called out for him, but there was no answer. She called the hotel front desk and was told that Lester had left early in the morning and had driven off in his van.

Lucille hung up the phone, sat down on the bed, reached for Lester's pillow, and held it against her chest.

After a slow early-morning drive through downtown Phoenix, Lester dropped in and said hello to his best friend.

When he saw a frail and gaunt Lester, concern came over J.T.'s. face. "How you feelin', man?"

"Feel good. Think I might take up golf. Hell, I own a damn golf course."

"I know you do. Good idea, if you do, I will too."

"I'll let you play for free."

"Want some chicken?" J.T. asked.

"Yeah, I'll take a leg."

For several minutes, the men sat in silence as Lester nibbled on his drumstick.

"You remember how to get out to my bank?"

"I remember."

"Well, don't forget. And don't forget my attorney's name and number; she handles all the real estate and business stuff."

"I got it, don't worry, Lester." J.T. said.

"I know you got it. Ain't worrin', just kinda remindin', that's all. Well, J.T., guess I better get a move on."

"C'mon, man, you just got here. Have another leg and a beer."

"I'd like to, but I need to go somewhere," Lester said.

"Then I'll come with ya."

"Thanks, but I got some business to tend to."

"Okay then, I know you're busy. But hey, Lester, remember when you came in here that first time back in '43 with those little pieces of gold?"

"Yep, I remember."

"Do you know what I was thinkin' that first day?"

"Nope, sure don't."

"I was thinkin', that's a good man there," J.T. said.

"You was always a lousy judge of character."

"I know, but I just want you to know…"

"I know, J.T. Feel the same way. Thanks for…well…"

"Yeah, I know, Lester."

As Lester struggled to rise from his chair, J.T. resisted the urge to help his friend, knowing that pain would be worse for Lester than what he was feeling in his back. Finally standing, Lester said, "Guess I'll see you around."

"Yeah, see you around, Lester."

From his office window, through the tears that flowed freely down his face, J.T. could see Lester as he walked slowly to his beat-up van and drove east toward Whiskey Flats.

CHAPTER 52

PHOENIX—2014

A WEEK AFTER FINDING THE gold behind the wall in the Jasper, Ben, Jon, Sam, Tom, and Pax sat around, or under, Ben's kitchen table with pens, calculators, computers, and a water bowl in front them.

"Jon, you estimated 17,300 bars. At twenty pounds each, that's 346,000 pounds or 5,536,000 ounces. At today's price of roughly $1400 an ounce, that's $7,750,000,000 give or take, and that does not include the gems, silver, and loose gold," Ben announced without fanfare.

The resulting silence in the room lasted over a minute.

The previously euphoric and stupidly rich Jon was the first to speak. "I don't want anything to do with it," he announced, to the surprise of the group.

"Why not?" Ben asked.

"As much as I like money, and I like it a lot, knowing where that gold came from would taint anything I'd buy with it. Besides, I read through those binders last night, and there were the actual names, ages, and addresses of thousands of people in it, plus an itemized list of all the stuff the Nazis had taken from each of them. It made it all the more real. It was depressing as hell."

"Tom, how about you?" Ben asked.

"I feel the same way. I haven't slept for a week thinking of what we saw in those barrels. This has been a great adventure, and we found one of the most valuable treasures of all time, but I think we should leave it where it is, and I, at least, need to get back home, find a job, and move on."

"I can understand how you boys feel. As I said when this all began, I'm too damn old to worry about making more money at this point. I got in this thing for the fun of the hunt. I really didn't think we'd find anything. But since we did, I don't think we should just ignore what that amount of money can do if used in the right way. But more importantly, what happens if the wrong people get hold of that gold?" Ben asked.

"You mean like the guys I ran into in the desert last week?"

"Exactly, Tom. You said they all had Nazi tattoos."

"Yeah, they did. And they also said there were some people who didn't like the fact we were snooping around the Jasper."

"So, what are we supposed to do? Go get the gold and turn it in to the government so they can waste it on another war or piss it away on bullshit?" Jon asked.

"I'm not sure anyone is suggesting we turn it over to the government, but I don't think we want to risk letting it get into the wrong hands either.

That amount of gold could do an incredible amount of good or incredible damage in the world. As much as none of us want to benefit from that gold, we have a tiger by the tail here, folks."

Again, the group of four sat in silence, stumped by the dilemma of too much gold and not enough ideas of what to do with it.

Finally, Sam said, "Let's give it back."

CHAPTER 53

LESTER HAD DECIDED HE WANTED to make one last trip to his "bank" in the desert and then go back home to Lucille and tell her how much he loved her, until it was time. He wasn't quite sure why he wanted to make a last trip other than he wanted to make sure all the gold was still there, where it was supposed to be. All eleven hundred bars of it. And he wanted to retrieve one more bar for old time's sake. He figured he would give it to some stranger when he got back to town and make that person's day.

He also figured he had one last hike in him. At the same time, he really didn't want to die in front of Lucille. That would be kind of rude and embarrassing.

Taking the now-familiar route to the rest stop that would be his intermediate destination before his walk into the desert, Lester thought back to that first trip he took with his three buddies and Rolle. He wondered what would have happened if he and his boys hadn't come across Rolle in the back of the bus station. Maybe his three friends would still be alive. But what would those Nazi guys have done with all that gold by now?

He thought about what the gold he had driven off with that night had meant to all those people he knew in Phoenix. How many people were still alive and healthy because of that gold? How many had gone to college? How many lives had been touched? He thought of Eric. He smiled at his thoughts and memories.

Lester was glad he had stopped by to see old J.T. on his way to the desert. He'd never tell him so, but he loved that big man like a brother. He figured J.T. felt the same way. He regretted he hadn't stopped by the shelter and said good-bye to his buddies. But hell, that could have taken all day. Or maybe a week. They knew how he felt about them anyway. They were his family.

Lester's faded blue van pulled into the highway rest area off Route 60 east of Phoenix. He lingered in the idling vehicle for a few minutes. He needed to gather his strength. He knew that once he left the van's air-conditioned coolness, he would face hours of unrelenting heat and utter exhaustion.

Finally, he switched off the ignition and gathered up his army surplus backpack that was loaded with a canteen and his usual lunch. When he stepped out of the van onto the simmering asphalt of the rest-area parking lot, Lester took a breath but the searing dry air instantly parched his throat. He coughed several times before a drink from his canteen allowed him to breathe again. But the cool water did not assuage the pain in his back. Nothing would. Not now.

But it would just be one more trip. One more last trip.

CHAPTER 54

BEN'S HOUSE—PHOENIX

AFTER SAM'S SUGGESTION HUNG IN the air for few moments, Tom asked, "You mean give the gold back to Germany, Sam?"

"No, I mean give it back to the people it was taken from. Jon just said he has the names, addresses, and ages of some of the people the Nazis robbed, and an itemized list of what was taken from them. I see all those ads on TV about family trees and ancestry websites. It looks like it wouldn't be all that difficult to track down some descendants of those killed and return to them what was taken from their families."

"Sam, that's a romantic idea, but there were millions killed, and in some cases entire families wiped out. It would be nearly impossible to track down either survivors or descendants and then calculate what would be owed to them. I like the idea, but I don't know how we would carry out such a plan. Hell, I don't even know how we would get all that gold out of the mine in the first place," Tom noted.

Ben added, "There would be another issue we'd have to deal with here too. That gold legally belongs to whomever has a lease on that mine. It looks like an outfit called Arizona Mining Ltd. has had a lease in place since the 1940s and according to what I found, they have been making regular lease payments since that time."

"Sounds like the same thing that's happening up at the Vega as well, only that lease has been in place even longer," Jon said.

"That may explain why people like those skinheads didn't want us snooping around the Jasper. Maybe they believe there is gold in there, and they just haven't been able to find it yet," Tom added.

"Given all the new technology out there, it's just a matter of time before someone does find it behind that wall, if they're convinced it's in the Jasper."

"Ben's right," Jon said. "If those guys who jumped Tom are part of a larger neo-Nazi group, they've undoubtedly heard the rumors about lost Nazi gold and won't stop until they find it. And if they do find it, God knows what they would do with that amount of wealth."

"So what the hell do we do now?" Tom asked.

"What we can't do is let that gold remain where it is," Ben said. "That would be irresponsible and dangerous. Given the dead soldier we found and the skinheads who attacked Tom, it's likely, if not probable, there's some kind of Nazi connection going on here. So it seems to me our first job is to get the gold out of there and stash it somewhere that will be safe and secure until we determine what we do with it."

Tom asked, "Why not give it to one of those large Jewish organizations?"

"If we do that, they'd have to know where we got the gold, and then there is the IRS, the state, and all kinds of bullshit we'd have to deal with," Jon said.

While the men were exchanging ideas, Sam was busy tapping on her iPad. After several minutes, she made a statement. "You guys are a bunch of negative pains in the ass. We have no choice of what we have to do with the gold. None. We have to return it. It is our moral obligation to begin with."

"Tell us how you really feel, Sam," Tom said.

"Okay, I will. I just looked up this Arizona Mining Ltd. outfit that has the lease at the Jasper. Guess where they are based? Brazil. They're part of an international conglomerate. Guess where that conglomerate is based? Germany. That same conglomerate through another holding company also has the lease on the Vega through another South American firm with German connections as far back as the 1920s. Based on that evidence, it's clear there are Nazi fingerprints all over this gold, and I don't think we should have any second thoughts about absconding with it...if we can."

Tom said, "Sam's right," and added, "There's always been a connection between Brazil, Argentina, other South American countries, and the Nazis. After WWII, it was confirmed that many high-ranking German officers headed there even before the war was over when they knew they were going to lose. It was proven after the war that those high- ranking officers also moved valuable artwork, cash, and gold out of Germany so they could retrieve it after the war. It was an operation some called the Rape of Europa."

"Okay, let's assume Sam and Tom are right about the Nazi connection and the gold we found. So what? Who put the gold behind that wall doesn't answer the question of what we do with it now," Jon said.

"Yes, it does, Jon," Sam said. "The fact that it is highly likely there is indeed a Nazi connection with the gold answers the question very clearly. Especially given what appears to be a re-emergence of the neo-Nazis and other hate groups in this country and around the world. We have no choice but to secure the gold. But then take the next step and do the research to return it to those it was taken from. I know we can't find everyone, but we can certainly find some."

"Sam, do you realize what this kind of commitment will mean in terms of your time and your life?" Ben asked.

"Yes, I do, and I'm not asking you guys to jump off this bridge with me. But, as Daddy said, we simply can't allow a group of crazy skinheads or other hate groups to find that amount of wealth, period. But we also have a responsibility to at least, in some small way, undo part of what the Nazis did. It won't heal the pain or take away the horror, but it's just the right thing to do, and I'm going to do it with or without you guys."

After more silence, Tom had a question. "Hey Ben, has Sam always been such an opinionated, bullheaded, walking, talking migraine?"

"Yeah, pretty much."

"Okay, Sam, if we're all on this bandwagon, I assume you have a plan, right?" Jon asked.

"Give me a week. In the interim, I have some homework for each of you."

"Of course you do," Tom said.

CHAPTER 55

PHOENIX—1980

WHEN LESTER DIDN'T RETURN TO their suite the next day, Lucille knew he was dead. She also knew he had wanted it that way. Over the years, she tried to imagine what had happened to Lester after he had left J.T.'s that morning and headed east. While she accepted his death, every time she went to Maxine's for dinner and sat in Lester's booth, she expected to see him amble in and ask for his meatloaf.

For months after last seeing Lester that morning, J.T. rode his ATV into the desert a dozen times trying to find his friend, but the vastness of the Sonoran can swallow a man, aided by wind-fueled dust storms and raging rains. J.T. knew his search was hopeless, but he felt closer to Lester when on his searches into the endless sand and rock.

Lucille and J. T., with the help of Lester's attorney, carried on Lester's legacy of using the gold to help the people in and around Phoenix, particularly the poor, who never knew where the clothes and food came from that they would find scattered around the city, as if placed there by magic. They never found out who funded training and work programs in modern air-conditioned buildings or who provided medical care and food at no cost.

Eventually, the poor and homeless friends of Lester died off, and his memory faded, but J.T. and Lucille never stopped their work. They even set up a foundation that would carry on their giving after they were dead and gone.

A week after Lester disappeared, Lucille found a white envelope in her underwear drawer. She recognized Lester's handwriting.

For some reason Lucille was afraid to open the envelope and read whatever Lester had written to her. Was it something about the gold? What to do with it? Was it going to be some kind of confession? Something he had been afraid to tell her? What if what he had written soiled her memory of him?

After several sleepless nights, Lucille decided it was time. The first thing she noticed when opening the envelope was the date on the handwritten letter. It was years before Lester died.

"Dear Lucille,

My name is Lester Jones. You just served me the best damn meatloaf I ever ate. And the peach pie weren't bad neither. I've decided I want to marry you. Not now, mind you, but some time. You're real nice to me, but I know you don't love me or nuthin' like that, but I startin' lovin' you first the time I seen you last week. Love you more this week. 'Spect I'll love you more next week. By the way, I'm a rich son of a bitch and figure I could get you to love me just 'cause I'm rich, but that wouldn't be no good. Wouldn't last. So, I guess I'll take it slow and easy like. Also need to tell you, I like the way you walk. Kinda smooth like. Figure I can sneak a look now and then, and you won't know I'm a lookin'. Not sure when I'm gonna give you this letter, maybe I'll just keep it to remind me when I started lovin' you. Maybe I'll give to ya when I know you love me. Hope it won't be too long. Your future husband, Lester Jones. P.S. I really am a rich bastard but hope you love me 'fore you find that out for sure.

Lucille carefully folded the letter and placed it back into the envelope. She looked at it for several moments and said to no one, "You could have given it to me after that first meatloaf, Lester."

CHAPTER 56

DESPITE HIS ADVANCED YEARS, J.T. was still a physically imposing man, someone people didn't mess with. It was more than the silver-plated .38 he still wore on his hip each day in his shop that had kept the bad guys from the neighborhood at bay for over fifty years. It was J.T.'s reputation for helping people who needed help that gave him "street cred" that was based on respect, not fear.

Maybe it was helping someone who needed surgery, or a deserving kid who needed college tuition, or a mother with too many kids and not enough food. Whatever the neighborhood needed, J.T., in his own quiet and sometimes gruff way, was there to help.

J.T. could afford to help. He had saved millions from his days working with Lester and never forgot the skinny white man whom he had grown to love like a brother. He missed their conversations over fried chicken, beer, and apple pie. He missed the only friend he ever had.

He often wondered what happened to Lester that last morning he saw him in 1980 when he had visited his shop then drove away heading east to the desert. J.T. hoped that Lester's last hours were peaceful and often spoke with Lucille about the man they both missed. They also spoke of Lester's diary and what he had written so many years before. Was it all true? Could it be true?

J.T. knew the gold part was true because he had visited Lester's "bank" in the desert a few hundred times since Lester's disappearance. However, with Lucille's permission and encouragement, he did so by utilizing an ATV he would load onto the back of his Ford F-P450 Platinum pickup truck before venturing into the desert in the early morning. He had told Lucille, "It makes carrying twenty-pound bars a lot easier on an old man."

J.T. also got permission from Lucille to begin moving the gold out of Lester's not-so-well-hidden hiding place in the sand. They realized it would take some time but figured J.T. would get the job done within a few years. They were both afraid that at some point someone would stumble across the gold or hear the endless rumors about a treasure, and it would suddenly be gone. Lucille trusted J.T. and told him to do whatever he thought was best to protect Lester's secret.

So they agreed that on J.T.'s trips to the desert he would retrieve at least two to three bars at a time, so he would slowly move the gold to a safer place. They decided that safer place was in a series of safe-deposit boxes at several Bank of America branches in and around Phoenix. On his trips,

J.T. also deposited something into the desert that he hoped would convince gold hunters from continuing their searches. Every time he did, it made him smile.

Lucille and J.T. opened scores of safe-deposit boxes using over a dozen fictitious names, which gave them both safety and easier access to the gold when they wanted to sell the bars to generate cash for some worthy cause.

To eliminate any suspicion, J.T. would in many cases melt down the ingots at his shop into smaller sizes he could sell more easily. It took more time, but both J.T. and Lucille slept better.

Despite J.T.'s concerted efforts over the years to move all the gold bars from Lester's "bank" in the Sonoran Desert, nearly twenty-five bars remained in the sand with a value of between $10 and $12 million. J.T. hoped he lived long enough to get all the bars to the safety of the B of A.

But there wasn't a time J.T. ventured into the desert that he didn't think of the incredible amount of gold that could still be in the Jasper. He hoped that if the trove really did exist and was ever found, it would be by someone who would put it to good use. But he worried that if the wrong hands got hold of that amount of wealth, what havoc they could wreak. He lamented he was too damn old to do anything about it.

On a Thursday night right after closing the shop, J.T. was about to leave and go home for the night when his front doorbell rang. When he looked into the monitor of his hidden camera that showed who was at his front door, J.T. saw an elderly man in what looked like an expensive dark suit standing next to a younger tall blond man with short cropped hair and a scar on his face. Through a microphone, J.T. said, "Sorry, I'm closed. Be open tomorrow morning at seven."

Looking around for the camera, the old man said, "Oh my, we are looking for a Mr. Taylor and have flown in from San Diego to introduce ourselves to him at the suggestion of Juan in Juarez. He said you were someone with whom we could conduct confidential business."

"I'm Jackson Taylor. What kind of business you talking about?"

"I would prefer not to discuss it here on the sidewalk. We can come back tomorrow. Thank you for your time." The two men began to walk away. J.T hit the intercom button again.

"Hold on. Since you came all the way from San Diego and know Juan, come on in for a few minutes."

After J.T. opened the steel door, he greeted the two men who entered his shop. "Thank you so much for seeing us at this late hour, Mr. Taylor. My name is Armin Martin, and this is my associate, Jagr."

"Evening, Gentlemen, so how's Juan doing these days?"

"I am afraid I am the bearer of sad news, Mr. Taylor. Juan passed away rather suddenly last week. It was quite unexpected."

"Juan's dead? How? He was in good shape and…"

"Juan fell. From a great height."

"Fell? What about Maria and his boys?"

"They all fell. From a very great height."

"What the hell you talking about? What's your name again?"

When J.T. moved to his desk to try to retrieve his silver-plated pistol he had put away for the night, he was a step late. Jagr pulled his own gun, with a silencer attached, and pointed it at J.T.

"Mr. Taylor, I would greatly appreciate it if you would please sit down so we can have a discussion."

Taking a seat, J.T. said," If you guys are looking for money, I don't keep it here."

"Mr. Taylor, through some research with friends in Mexico, we have learned that you have had a many decades long working relationship with a gentleman named Juan Montez. Is that accurate?"

"You with the IRS, Mr. Martin?"

"No, Mr. Taylor; we are simply businessmen curious about the relationship between you and Juan."

"No big deal, when prices around here dropped some, I'd call Juan and he'd sell it for me in Mexico if the prices were better there."

"I presume you met Juan a few times?"

"Yeah, a few times, so what?"

As Dr. Martin and J.T. spoke, Jagr moved next to J.T. and placed his pistol on his shoulder next to his ear.

"Mr. Taylor, Juan was an uneducated and seemingly unemployed man, who along with a relatively large extended family, lived rather lavish lifestyles in Mexico. During our conversation with Juan, before his terrible accident, he indicated you were his biggest client."

"So?"

"To be more accurate, after further inquiries from Jagr, Juan, and his wife admitted you were his only client."

"Well, I'll be damned. Never knew that."

"Such knowledge would of course lead one to wonder things. Like where did you get the gold that you sent to Juan, on what appears to be a regular basis for decades?"

"Juan exaggerated. Never sent that much to him. Just a few ounces here and there."

"Mr. Taylor you are far too modest. When Jagr searched Juan's home after his untimely death, he found two gold bars worth nearly a million dollars. Hardly a trifling amount for a poor Mexican gentleman with no apparent income source."

"Damn, you got me. Maybe Juan made his money selling drugs? Or he was a real good saver."

"A possible conclusion, except Juan kept remarkably good, albeit handwritten records. And those records indicated he and his family had received over 200 twenty-pound gold ingots over a period of more than sixty years. Further, that those gold bars came from a gentleman in Phoenix named 'el moreno Jackson.'"

"Small damn world. My name's Jackson too. Like another few million folks in this country. Pretty common name."

"Quite. However, I don't believe in coincidences, Mr. Jackson."

"Guys, I told you all I know about Juan, and what I sent him and …"

"Jagr, please shoot Mr. Taylor in the left leg right above the knee."

Without a second of hesitation, Jagr shot J.T. as directed, the silencer making the shot sound like a "whomp" rather than a "bang."

"Ahhh… what the fuck are you doing, you crazy bastard?" J.T. fell to his right on the couch as blood seeped from the wound and through his fingers.

"Mr. Taylor, I really don't believe you are taking our interest in the gold you sent Juan very seriously. But perhaps I am at fault here because I have not been specific enough. So to avoid any further misunderstanding and needless pain, please tell us where you got the gold to send to Juan."

"I don't know what the hell you're talking…"

"Dear me, Mr. Taylor, I fear my friend here has far more bullets than you have limbs. Jagr, please shoot Mr. Taylor in the right elbow."

Jagr fired again, shattering J.T.'s elbow. "Oh my God…!! Stop it, stop it!!

"Mr. Taylor, the leg wound you have is one that will lead to major blood loss, and absent treatment, death will come in less than thirty minutes. The wound to your arm will not bleed as much, but is, as I am sure you will agree, far more painful. As will the next dozen nonlethal wounds you will be forced to endure if you don't tell us what we ask of you."

"Okay, okay, stop shooting." Through gritted teeth, J.T. said, "This Chinese guy comes in here once a month. He told me he'd been a miner years ago and found a lot of gold over in California. He wanted me to fence it for him. That's it."

"Mr. Taylor, please don't assume me a fool. A miner would have found ore, not refined gold ingots stamped with the names of countries on it." Dr. Martin nodded at Jagr. "Please remove Mr. Taylor's left ear."

Too late, J.T moved his arm to protect his ear. The bullet severed his ear, and it landed in his lap. He passed out.

After several seconds, Jagr splashed water in J.T.'s face until he awakened in agony. "Ow, good God!!"

"My dear sir, I am afraid the next several bullets will remove any vestige of your manhood, although they will not unfortunately, be fatal."

Gasping, J.T. said, "Look you fucking cocksucker, you're gonna kill me one way or the other no matter what I tell you, so I ain't telling you nothin'. So go ahead and shoot my dick off, I ain't using it no more, I have a fucking brain tumor and I'll be dead in six months anyway, so kiss my sweet black ass."

"You are a brave and honorable man, Mr. Taylor. But unless you tell us who brings you the gold that you sell in Mexico, my assistant will make, at my direction, your final moments ones of unspeakable agony. We will also bring into your shop some of the children we saw outside and allow you to witness their equally painful deaths. All this because you will not cooperate with us."

J.T. grimaced in pain and breathed heavily as he looked at Dr. Martin and then to Jagr. "Ah shit, I guess it don't matter anymore. Give me some pain medicine and some water, and I'll tell you an interesting story."

Dr. Martin nodded to Jagr, who removed a vial and syringe from his coat pocket. He injected its contents into J.T.'s left arm. J.T. laid back on the couch and closed his eyes; his breathing became less labored and his pulsed slowed.

Jagr handed J.T a large bottle of Perrier he had retrieved from the refrigerator. J.T. unscrewed the cap and put the bottle to his lips. "That's better," he said right before he slammed the bottle into Jagr's face, knocking him to the ground and breaking the green bottle. J.T. took the remaining neck of the bottle and cut his own throat from ear to ear. Blood erupted from his jugular vein and quickly covered his white shirt with a deep red hue. A smile came over his face. He gave Dr. Martin the finger seconds before he gave in to the darkness.

CHAPTER 57

BEN'S HOUSE—PHOENIX

AS PROMISED, A WEEK LATER Sam had a plan. It was detailed and predictably brilliant. The three men she submitted the plan to originally thought it was a stupid plan, fraught with danger and likely to fail. Sam politely told all three they could go screw themselves. She further suggested, in the kindest terms possible, that they could become part of her plan, or she would find three women to help her execute it.

Her sweet talking, Tom and Jon called them threats, worked. The men eventually bought into Sam's plan because it was, after all, both detailed and brilliant. They just needed a little time to become smart enough to understand it. It took a bit more time for that to occur than Sam had hoped.

"Does the Gulfstream have the range to fly all the way to Europe?" Tom asked.

"It has a range of 7,000 miles and fully loaded with fuel can carry an additional 1800 pounds. Of course if we strip her down she can carry far more weight."

"I don't like to fly, Jon reminded everyone.

"Then maybe you can take a train to Germany," Tom suggested.

Ignoring both men, Sam had a question for Jon. "Any luck in tracking down some people on your list as test cases for us?"

"Some. For better or worse, the Germans did take copious notes on just about everything they did. Some of the people on the list I worked on were from Poland and Hungary. I didn't have much luck in tracking down any of those names. Our best bet will be to focus on families from Berlin or Hamburg. It appears that after the war, some of the people who survived the concentration camps went back to the cities they were from and tried to start over, Jon said.

"That makes sense," Ben said.

"Yes, but many of those people who did go back were sole survivors of the camps, having lost entire families. If they were children, they ended up in orphanages or moved in with friends from the old neighborhoods, or in some situations, just lived on the streets. In any case, most changed their names, so it was hard to identify people and where they ended up," Jon said.

"But you found some, right?" Sam asked.

"I think so. The ones I feel pretty confident about were those who immigrated to the United States right after the war. The record keeping was good, and it was easier to follow a name and family tree," Jon said.

"Of those you found, are any still alive?" Tom asked.

Jon replied, "I found ten people that as of last year were still alive and well, living in the U.S.. Some were small children when they, along with their families, were sent to Treblinka or Auschwitz-Birkenau in Poland, or Bergen-Belsen or Buchenwald in Germany. Most of them are in their late seventies to mid-eighties at this point."

"Tom, were you able to determine from those notebooks what their families had lost?" Sam asked.

"In some cases I found very detailed records of what was taken from their families and was able to use some present value and inflation analysis to come up with some numbers of what the Nazis took. In other cases, the details of what was taken was less clear, mainly because the Germans had no idea what some of the stuff they took was worth," Tom explained.

"I think it would make sense to focus on the ten names Jon found living here in the U.S. before we begin going to Europe. That way we can beta test and fine-tune our tactics and see what works and what doesn't," Ben said. Tom, and Jon nodded in agreement.

"Okay then, I'll continue to work on my list and see if I can get phone numbers and addresses for the ten I selected. Then we can decide next steps," Jon said.

"Good," Sam said. "But we do have that little issue of how we get a couple hundred tons of gold out of a mine that some neo-Nazis are watching on a regular basis, but I have some ideas."

"Of course you do," Tom said.

Ignoring the snide comment, Sam said, "Many of my ideas have come from this." Sam held up the well-worn journal that Lucille had left with her and Ben at the library.

"What's that?" Tom asked.

"It's a story about two WWII heroes no one has ever heard of."

Over the next four hours, Sam shared some of the details of Lester's handwritten journal with Tom and Jon. She told them the incredible story she and Ben had already read. It included how Lester hid his truckload of gold in the desert and conveniently provided a map pointing out in detail where to find it.

"A World War I vet named Lester Jones and a young German soldier named Eric Schneider single-handedly stopped the Nazis from forming a Fourth Reich here in the U.S. It appears they killed over forty Nazis in and around the Jasper back in 1943. If they had not, who knows what this country and the rest of the world would be like today."

"My God," Tom said after reading Lester's account of blowing up the trucks and cars in the cavern with a single rifle shot and how he was nearly trapped in the mine shaft after the Germans shot pineapple grenades up one of the shafts. "Do you think this stuff is actually true?"

"If not, Lester should have written scripts in his spare time because this could make a hell of a movie," Jon said.

"After meeting with his wife several times now since she showed up at the library, I believe every word Lester wrote. As she said, 'Lester weren't no liar.' She was also able to update us on some other information that we were dying to hear about," Ben said.

"Hey Tom, remember when we found our gold bar…"

"I know what you're thinking, but what are the chances that could have been Lester's hand around that bar?" Tom asked

Ben answered. "There's no way of knowing who was holding that ingot, but it's a fact that where you guys found your bar was directly between Lester's "bank" in the desert and the place he'd park his van at the rest stop. Besides, I'd like to think Lester was intentionally passing that gold on to you boys. Maybe he knew you were the right ones."

After a steak dinner and some excellent merlot, the group discussed specifics of how they would remove the gold and secure it before some bald guys with Nazi tattoos beat them to it. "According to Lester's journals, it took a dozen heavy-duty trucks to move the gold into the Jasper, then it took several men, some of whom fell to their deaths, ten hours to move it into the area behind that wall where we found it," Sam pointed out.

"I see why they used so many trucks. Getting the gold onto a single truck that could navigate the access road would be impossible even today. No matter how we do it, it's going to take several trips in and out of the Jasper to get the gold out of there," Jon said.

Tom added, "There is no way we could haul that stuff out of there an ingot at a time. It would take months, and we'd have to fix the hole in the wall each time. Sooner or later the bad guys would be there when we were there."

"Tom and Jon are right, Sam. Physically removing the gold is the easy part, but doing it and not being seen will be the challenge. I suspect that mine is being watched on a daily basis."

"What if we let the bad guys find the gold?" Sam asked.

CHAPTER 58

JASPER MINE

EVEN THOUGH J.T. HADN'T PROVIDED the information requested, Dr. Martin had learned through his Mexican connections that gold ingots, like the ones that had been delivered to the Jasper in 1943, had been moved from Phoenix to Mexico.

What Dr. Martin didn't know was exactly how many gold bars had originally been delivered to the Jasper in 1943. He knew the truck he had driven contained approximately 34,000 pounds or around 1700 ingots of gold. He assumed the other eleven trucks contained approximately the same amount but couldn't be sure.

The biggest uncertainty was even if there had been 200 tons of gold, what had happened to it over seventy years? Had it been discovered, and through men like J.T., slowly distributed around the world? Or was the gold discovered in Mexico just a miniscule portion of the original gold stashed by Rolle, which remained hidden in the Jasper?

No longer waiting for the input or approval of his partners, Dr. Martin decided to act. He purchased sophisticated equipment to once and for all discover whether the gold was still inside the mine.

Dr. Martin and Jagr stood at the entrance to the Jasper and saw the flurry of activity, heard the clatter of jackhammers and the hum of other equipment as more than two dozen miners, scientists, and laborers attacked the Jasper and her secrets. Dr. Martin felt an expectation like when he was a boy awaiting St. Nick to arrive. He knew in his heart that his life-long wait was nearing an end that would, ironically, marshal in a new beginning. A beginning long overdue.

Temporary halogen lights exposed nearly every corner of the massive mine. Men with portable X-ray machines looked behind stone walls or into floors. Men dropped cameras down the pit and in doing so discovered six gold bars that they retrieved by dropping a man attached to a harness down into the abyss. Word of the ingot's discovery heightened Dr. Martin's hope and enthusiasm. If need be, he would send men deeper into the abyss or even find an outside access to the bottom of the pit, although such an enormous and highly visible engineering undertaking was not a step he wanted to consider...yet.

CHAPTER 59

BEN'S HOUSE—PHOENIX

"WHAT DO YOU MEAN LET them find the gold, are you crazy?" Jon asked.

"According to Lester's notebook, none of the twenty Germans protecting the gold or the twenty-four guys who delivered it knew exactly how much gold was in the Jasper. And since it was delivered in 1943, no one has any idea how much of it has been removed from the mine over the years. All anyone knows for sure was some amount of gold was shipped from Germany in 1943 to the Jasper. Only Rolle, Becker, and eventually Lester and Eric, knew the exact amount of the gold, and they're all dead."

"Are you saying we should let them find some of the gold?"

"Kind of." Sam explained...not really explaining. "I agree with Tom we can't be opening and closing the wall a hundred times taking out small amounts of the gold or someone will be there on one of our trips, and they'll discover the entire amount. So, I suggest we lure them away from the Jasper."

"To where, with what?" Tom asked.

"Let's head out to the Jasper, and I'll fill you guys in on the plan. Showing will be easier than telling."

On the surface, Sam's preliminary plan made sense, although it would take days of planning and detailing before it could be executed. But the plan was shot to hell when the quartet was flagged down by an armed security guard who stood where a vehicle would normally make a tight left-hand turn down to the opening of the Jasper. Sam ignored the waving guard by rolling down her window and sweetly asking. "Is the mine closed? I used to party down there in college, and I wanted to show my friends how cool that mine is."

"Sorry, miss, this is private property, and there's a couple dozen guys down there doing core samples and all kinds of stuff."

"Oh, darn. I wanted to just show my friends..."

"You're gonna have to move on, Miss; some trucks will be arriving here any minute with more equipment."

Sam smiled, rolled up her window, and continued to drive up the road past the Jasper.

"I'll be damned," Jon said. "They've found it."

"We don't know that," Ben said. "Maybe they're just bringing in more equipment to conduct a search."

"Whether they find it now or find it later, it sounds like they're real serious this time. It's only a matter of time before they do," Tom said.

"We have no choice then," Sam said.

"What do you mean no choice?" Ben asked.

"We have to execute my plan now."

"That's nuts," Tom said. "We'd need at least a week of planning to..."

"We don't have a week," Sam said. "We have today. Right now."

"Before we try to pull off a half-baked plan, we need to know if the gold behind the wall has already been found," Ben said.

"The only way we can do that is to get into the mine and look at the wall. If it's still there, so is the gold. If not, some neo-Nazis are really, really rich," Jon said.

"Daddy, is our equipment still in the back?" Sam asked.

"Unless you took it out, it's all in the rear storage area."

"Remember what Lester wrote about gaining access to the Jasper by going down those shafts at the top of the mine? You know, where he shot those guards that first night?"

"You can't be serious, Sam, that was almost seventy years ago, no telling what happened to those shafts since then," Tom said.

Thirty minutes later, the group of four was standing on top of the Jasper. Tom and Jon carried the equipment from Ben's Jeep. From below them the sound of pounding jackhammers and other assorted machinery wafted upward along with muffled men's voices.

"According to Lester's diary, this was the spot he fought his first battle with the Nazis," Sam said.

"Look over here. This could be the shaft Lester went up and down that first night. It looks pretty narrow. He must have been a skinny guy," Tom said.

"Look, this might be the access to the Jasper, but it's way too dangerous for anyone to try and enter the mine using this shaft," Ben said. "We have to find another way or come up with a better plan."

"Daddy, there's no time for a better plan. We have ropes, a harness, a radio phone, flashlights, and three strong men to hold onto my..."

"Not a chance Sam. If anybody goes down a shaft, it'll be me," Jon said.

"Jon, your leg's still bothering you. You can barely walk on it. Daddy, let's face it, you and Tom just won't fit."

"What do you expect to do if you can get into the Jasper? There could be fifty guys down there, probably armed like that guard we saw," Jon noted.

"All I'm going to do is drop into that horizontal area Lester talked about that had the big wooden doors..."

"You mean the ones the Germans blew all to hell?"

"According to Lester, I'll be able to see what's going on from that location. I'll just zip down there real quick, take a look, and give you guys a tug on the rope, and you can pull me up. It'll take five minutes. Then based on what I see, we can either come up with a new plan, or if I see they've discovered the gold, we can head down to Elsa's for lunch."

Without waiting for approval or a response to her explanation of next steps, Sam slipped into the harness. She threaded one end of the rope through the metal clips and handed the other end of the rope to Tom. "Tom, tie this around your waist and I'll pull on it if I need help coming back up."

"What if this rope isn't long enough? What if you run into some snakes down there? What if…" Jon's questions made Sam smile.

"Jon, I'll be fine. I was in the military, you know. I've had training."

"You had snake training? Thought you were a pilot," Jon replied.

"Be careful, honey," Ben said, knowing any argument with Sam at that point would be futile.

"Don't worry guys. I'll be back in five minutes."

They didn't see Sam again for twelve hours.

CHAPTER 60

JASPER MINE

"DR. MARTIN, WE'VE RETRIEVED SIX gold bars from that pit by going down 150 feet. If we go any further, we'll need more rope."

Responding to the leader of the engineering team, Dr. Martin replied, "Thank you for the update, Thomas. Let's continue with the X-ray units for the time being and see what we come up with."

"Yes, sir. But if that gold is buried in this dirt and rock floor, it will take us weeks to cover it all. And that doesn't include what could have been stuffed in the walls then covered over."

"Do your best, Thomas. If you require more equipment, please advise."

"Yes, sir, I'll let you know by the end of the day."

As the engineer moved back into the bowels of the Jasper, Dr. Martin had a feeling that this was going to be the day. The day that nearly seventy years of questions would be answered. He could feel it. It was palpable. He only wished the Führer were here to see that his vision and brilliance was soon to be rewarded.

CHAPTER 61

ON TOP OF JASPER MINE

AFTER SAM CHECKED HER EQUIPMENT for the last time, Jon approached with advice. "No need to be a hero down there. Just take a quick look and get your butt back up here."

"You're not worried about me, are you?" Sam asked with a grin.

"So what if I am? You know how you girls are, so weak and helpless."

"Careful. I might hit you with a sexual discrimination suit."

"Oh good, I thought you might just beat me up," Jon said.

"Wouldn't want to embarrass a tough felon like you."

"Be careful, sis, and watch out for snakes."

"Roger, that."

Sam double-checked her ropes and harness and put on her head-mounted radio that connected to the one Ben wore. "Daddy, do you copy?"

"Copy."

Sam nodded, and maneuvered into the same shaft Lester had entered to do reconnaissance decades earlier. Within ten feet of her entry into the darkness, Sam saw a snake. It was curled up on a rock and ignored her presence. Sam quickly slid past the reptile while she shook her head, and thought of Jon. "What are the chances?" she whispered to herself.

After descending thirty feet into the shaft, she came to a turn and a small opening. Sam turned off her light and discovered she was already in total darkness. The angle of the shaft cut off the light from above. After turning her light back on, she wondered if Lester had a light source back then. If not, he was an even braver man than she gave him credit for being, and she already gave him a lot of credit.

As Sam descended into the shaft, she immediately felt the decreasing temperature. She could smell the ancient dirt and rock that enveloped her. At one point she felt her shoulders touched by the rock that now seemed to want to embrace her. For several seconds, Sam had to choke down the feeling of claustrophobia. After moving past the narrow section of the shaft, Sam tested her radio. "Daddy, do you copy?"

"Roger. But you're breaking up just a bit. You okay?"

"Okay. Shaft's narrower than I thought. Very cool in here. Hear sounds from Jasper."

"You have plenty of rope left, Sam."

"Roger."

"Be careful."

"Roger...whoa..."

"What's wrong?"

"There was a steep drop that moved me down about twenty feet. Sounds getting louder."

"Sam, you're breaking up. Say again?"

Ben's words were garbled.

"Daddy, I'm getting interference on my end, not sure you can hear me."

After thirty more feet and another steep angle drop, Sam's feet dangled over the edge of the exit of the shaft. With her light she could see the horizontal shaft below her. She turned off her light and dropped to the floor. On her right she saw the large wooden doors that Lester had written about and the damage done by the German grenades.

"Sam, you okay? Come back."

"Daddy, I see the doors Lester shot through to hit the trucks. There are three armed guards at the entrance of the mine near the offices where we slept."

"Sam, did you say armed guards?"

"Roger, and the rest of the mine is lit up, looks like a couple dozen guys with all kinds of electronics all over the floor."

"You're still breaking up."

"I think I can climb through this door into the main cavern and get close enough to see if they're working on the wall over the pit."

"Sam, stay where you are! Don't go into that cavern. You copy? Stay where you are. Sam? Sam, get back up here! Do you copy?"

"Daddy, can barely hear you. If the wall's still there, we'll know the gold is still behind it."

"Sam, we're going to start pulling you up."

Sam ignored Ben, unhooked her harness, and began climbing though the hole in wooden door. She turned down the speaker on her headset. Ben, Tom, and Jon began pulling on the rope. There was no resistance; no one was attached.

After sliding through the hole in the door, Sam moved along the northern wall of cavern. It was less well-lit and in heavy shadow. In the distance over a hundred yards away, she could see more than a dozen men scouring the floor area in front of and on either side of the pit with X-ray machines. The wall behind the pit was undisturbed.

Sam flipped on her headset and whispered, "Daddy, the wall behind the pit is still there. I'm on my way back."

Ben could only hear static from his radio. "Sam, we can't hear you. Come back up the shaft, now!"

As Sam turned to make her way back to the shaft, she ran directly into the chest of a smiling Jagr, who stood in front of several other men.

"What are you doing in here?" Jagr asked.

Surprised by her unexpected introduction to Jagr, Sam sputtered,

"Oh, I'm…I'm a spelunker, and I climbed up the walls of that pit. Who are you?"

"A spelunk…?" Jagr asked, the smile still on his face.

"Someone who explores caves," Sam offered.

"Who were you talking to on this radio?"

"To the twelve U.S. Marines doing exercises here in this mine. They'll be coming up the pit walls any minute. By the way, do you guys have permission to be in this mine?"

"We work for the ownership of this mine and you are trespassing." Jagr explained.

"Gee, sorry about that, this is the first time I've ever seen anybody in this place. Well, I guess I better get going. Promise I won't trespass ever again…"

When Sam started to walk away, one of the men behind Jagr stepped in front of her with his rifle pointed at her chest.

"You were talking to someone on your radio. Who was it and why are you in this mine?"

"Like I said, I am a spelunk…"

Without warning, Jagr viciously backhanded Sam knocking her to the floor.

"I suggest you answer me truthfully before my superior arrives. He is not nearly as patient as I am."

Sam wiped the blood from her mouth. "It's not nice to hit a girl."

"Unless you tell me why you are here, I can assure you there are worse things than being hit…for a girl." The men surrounding Sam laughed at Jagr's threat.

"I ask you one last time, what are you doing in this mine?"

"I come here all the time. I run in the desert, climb up the pit walls, and run back to my car. Didn't know this was private property."

Jagr reached down and ripped off Sam's University of Arizona sweatshirt. She tried to cover herself, but two of the men grabbed her arms and lifted her off the ground. Jagr approached Sam and pulled down the straps of her sports bra. The men behind him and those holding Sam cheered. Sam stared defiantly into Jagr's eyes. When Jagr reached for Sam's breast, she kneed him in the groin. Staggered by the blow, he backed away. With a smile on his face, he recovered and hit Sam in the stomach with a powerful blow that knocked her to her knees while the guards continued to hold her arms.

"So, the bitch is also a tigress." Turning to his men, Jagr asked, "Which of you men would like to go first?"

A tall, young, dark-haired man stepped forward with a smile on his face. "Hey, today's my birthday. I guess this is my present."

The rest of the men laughed and cheered as the dark-haired man undid his belt. The men holding Sam lifted her off the ground and pulled down her black stretch leggings. A third man forced Sam to her knees. One of the men sliced off her panties with a long blade, while the dark-haired man positioned himself behind Sam, the smile on his face wider.

As he was about to enter Sam, the dark-haired man gave a thumbs-up to the other men and said, "I think I'm going to remember this surprise birthday present."

At that moment, a bullet hit the man between the eyes. He had a look of surprise on his face, and as if in slow motion, fell straight back onto the mine floor. The other men raised their weapons but lowered them just as quickly when they saw who fired the shot.

"Jagr, I am surprised at you for allowing something this unseemly to occur on your watch," Dr. Martin said.

"She refused to talk, sir."

"Jagr, help this young lady dress herself."

Jagr handed Sam her torn sweatshirt and helped her raise her leggings. After Sam was again dressed, she smiled at Jagr, and without warning, unloaded a right cross that knocked him backward almost off his feet. A look of rage appeared on Jagr's face. He took a step toward Sam who stood her ground and threw a left hook that planted Jagr on his ass. Blood trickled from his mouth.

"Next time, keep your fucking hands off me, you missing link."

Jagr reached for his pistol.

"Jagr, no." Dr. Martin's voice was calm but firm. "You have disrespected this young woman and earned her wrath." Dr. Martin moved between Sam and Jagr.

"My dear, I am truly sorry for this lack of courtesy and disrespect. Please accept my apologies."

"What do you want from me?"

"Would you care to join me in our offices for a drink and some conversation?"

"No, I would not. What I want to do is get the hell out of here."

Sam tried to walk around the men. Dr. Martin nodded and one of the men placed a rifle in Sam's back.

"Young lady, perhaps you are not aware you are trespassing on private property, and I believe, as the owner of this mine, I am entitled to know why you are here. If you don't want to talk to me, perhaps you would prefer I contact the local county sheriff and we can discuss your trespassing with him."

"C'mon mister, no need to call the sheriff. I've had enough trouble with him already," Sam said.

"Well then, I again, with the utmost respect and sincerest apologies, ask you to join me in a brief and private conversation. Assuming of course you will not take your pugilistic abilities out on a poor man of nearly ninety years of age."

Sam looked at the armed men around her and suddenly became agreeable.

"Well, since you ask me so nicely."

"Splendid. Shall we?"

Dr. Martin led Sam to the front of the mine and into the offices where she, Jon, Tom, her dad and Pax had slept during their inspection of the Jasper. Sam noticed that the armed guards, who had been cheering on her assault ten minutes earlier, were now standing watch outside the offices Dr. Martin had led her into.

"Please have a seat, my dear. May I offer you something to drink?"

"No thank you."

"I'm sorry, but I did not catch your name before."

"My name's Samantha, but my friends call me Sam. You can call me Samantha."

"Of course, and I quite understand. But perhaps we can change all that after we have a little chat."

"I doubt it."

"Well Samantha, your presence in my mine is quite surprising since we have all the entrances we know of guarded quite well, as you can see. Would you mind telling me how you got inside the Jasper, so we can improve our security?

"Sure, I climbed up the pit walls."

"No, you didn't, Samantha. Having seen the inside of the pit with our digital camera, that would have been utterly impossible."

"Okay, you got me, mister. Here's the deal, I found a bunch of gold near here a while ago and thought maybe there's more inside this mine. I mean where else could the gold have come from? So from time to time, I come in through some old air shafts, snoop around in the nooks and crannies, and see if I can find more gold. I didn't know you'd have an army waiting for me in here today. This place is usually deserted."

Dr. Martin was visibly shaken at what he heard from Sam, but he quickly regained his composure. "Did you say you found gold? How interesting. Did you find the gold here in the Jasper?"

"No, the gold I found, I mean, the gold me and my boyfriend found, was in the desert not far from here."

Dr. Martin seemed unsure on how to proceed. Sam sat quietly and looked around the office.

"May I ask how much you found?"

"Lots."

"You realize if you found the gold on my property…"

"Then it would belong to you. But we didn't find any gold in your property, at least not yet."

"How do you know it wasn't my property? I own substantial land holdings in all directions around the Jasper."

"Because my boyfriend and me checked with the county after we found the gold and they told us it was state-owned land we were on."

"You didn't tell the state you found…"

"Are you kidding? Think we're stupid?"

"Of course not, Samanatha."

"Hey, you have a bathroom in here I could use?"

"Of course, my dear. In the next room on your right."

Sam moved to the next office leaving her radio phone on the desk next to Dr. Martin. In the bathroom, Sam retrieved her cell phone from inside her running sock and sent Ben a text. *Daddy, I'm okay, DO NOT TRY AND USE RADIO, CALL OR TEXT ME ON MY CELL!! I'll contact you when I can. Stay put!! Love you, Sam.* She deleted her text and put the cell back in her sock.

On top of the Jasper, Ben felt his cell vibrate and saw the text from Sam. "She says, she's okay, and we should wait for her to contact us."

"You've got to be kidding. You think she's down there with the Boys from Brazil having lemonade?" Jon asked.

"Not sure, but we have no choice but to sit and wait here for a while," Ben said flatly.

After her text, Sam flushed the toilet and splashed her face with water before re-entering the office and taking her seat.

"My dear, I am fascinated by your story. How did you possibly stumble on such a cache?"

"Well, it was the craziest thing. My boyfriend Bruce and I were out walking in the desert after a rainstorm. About fifty feet in front of us we saw a reflection of something shiny after the sun came back out. So we walk over there and saw part of what turned out to be a big twenty-pound gold ingot. It was just lying there; we couldn't believe it."

"It was just lying there in the open desert?"

"Well, it was surrounded by some big rocks, but yeah, it was pretty much just lying there in the open in front of God and everybody."

"What did you do with the ingot?"

"Oh, there was a lot more than just one ingot."

"What do you mean? How many more?"

"I don't know yet, we keep finding them all the time scattered all over that area near those big rocks."

"Do the ingots have anything stamped on them?"

"Why? I found them. They belong to me and my boyfriend."

In a more impatient tone, Dr. Martin asked. "What was stamped on them?"

"Names of countries; Mexico, United States, Canada, and some more."

"How many are left?"

"I dunno, like I said, we keep finding them. Why do you care how many there are? They're mine."

Dr. Martin walked away from Sam and stared out into the Jasper. He saw the flurry of activity and felt a rage well up inside him. For nearly a minute, he fought to hold in that rage. Finally, he turned back toward Sam with a wry smile on his face. "Samantha, I am quite certain you have discovered something that belongs to me, my dear. Something that I have been searching for a very long time. How it got to where you found it, I have no idea but…"

Sam could see sweat bead up on Dr. Martin's flushed face.

"I don't think so, mister. You know what they say, finders keepers…"

"You certainly deserve a reward for what you have found, but that gold you discovered does not belong to you; it belongs to me."

"Really? How do you figure that?"

"Samantha, while you certainly have the advantage of possession of the gold…"

"Actually, we don't have possession of all the bars, just three of them, but that's, like, a lot of money, you know? Like I said, there were so many of them we left the rest where we found them. The only thing is we don't know where to sell them, you know?"

"You mean the gold is just lying there in the open?"

"Well, we've found the bars scattered over about a half mile of desert. Some here some there, you know, but we didn't know what to do with the three we found, so we thought it was just a good idea to leave the rest of them where they were. Not likely anybody's going to find them out there in the middle of nowhere."

"I understand. Like I said, I am perfectly willing to make you and your boyfriend…"

"Bruce."

"Yes of course, Bruce… very wealthy for finding my gold. But if you don't cooperate, I am afraid I will be forced to call the sheriff to report my gold stolen, and let the law handle this situation."

"It's our gold—we found it!"

"Samantha, if I call the sheriff, it is likely that you and Bruce will be arrested for trespassing and possessing stolen property. What you already have will be confiscated, and you will end up with nothing."

"You're a prick."

"If you show me where the gold is, I will let you have an additional three bars. If my math is correct at today's prices that would mean you would have, with the three bars you already possess, over $ 2.5 million dollars tax and aggravation free. That sounds like a nice finder's fee for you and Bruce."

Sam rose and walked around the room in thought for nearly a minute. "Five bars."

"I'm afraid three is my best offer, Samantha."

"Five, or no deal."

Dr. Martin was silent for several moments, pretending to weigh an offer he would not live up to. "You drive a hard bargain, young lady. Okay, we have a deal. You show me where the gold is, and you will get your five additional bars."

"Okay, but you have to promise me you won't ever call the sheriff, and you won't kill me after I show you where the gold is."

"You have a very active imagination, young lady."

"Promise?"

"I promise, Samantha."

"Okay, do you have flashlights?"

"Yes, of course."

"Alright, after I pee again, I'll take you to the gold."

In the bathroom, Sam sent another text: *"Leaving Jasper, going to Lester's cache. Meet me one mile south in two hours."* S.

CHAPTER 62

ON TOP OF JASPER MINE

SAM'S TEXT EASED BEN'S MIND, for about ten seconds. She was okay, for now. Then the worry began to mount again like a series of lead weights that were being placed on his shoulders one pound at a time.

After Ben told Jon and Tom about the text, he suggested they sit down and remain patient for another couple hours. Ben went over to the edge of the cliff on which the men were perched and looked out over the western horizon. He saw the yellow lights of Phoenix shimmering in the purple dusk.

He chastised himself for worrying about Sam yet again. But he always worried. But she always came back to him.

But Sam knew how much her father loved her and worried about everything. And while she hated putting her dad through such angst with her aggressive risk-taking lifestyle, she also knew he wanted her to live a full, rich life. He wanted her to have complete unobstructed freedom. He wanted her to be happy. Just happy. She was.

When Sam came home from the war, she jumped at the chance to go into the aviation business with her dad. Ironically, both of them downplayed the event, yet both were overjoyed at the idea of flying around the world together on the spur of the moment, taking trips to archeological digs, historical sites, hikes in far-off woods, or going to New York to see the latest Broadway show.

They did actually do chartering work and enjoyed meeting the interesting people who would utilize the air charter services of Apache Aviation, LLC. But the business was secondary to them just being together.

The thing Sam cherished most about her dad was his humor. He was really funny in a droll sort of way. He would make a comment, and it would take a few seconds for it to sink in, but when it did, Sam would burst out laughing, sometimes at inappropriate times and places. There were times Sam would hear a funny joke, call her dad, and without even saying hello, tell the joke then immediately hang up knowing her dad was laughing his butt off halfway around the world. That would make her smile. His laughter.

As the purple in the western sky faded to a dark blue then to a star-studded black, Ben knew Sam would be okay. She had to be okay.

CHAPTER 63

JASPER MINE

AFTER RETURNING FROM THE BATHROOM, Sam said, "Okay if you want to go now, it'll be easier to find the site in the dark if we take the road, rather than going cross country."

Dr. Martin nodded, ordered Jagr to round up the men still working in the Jasper, tell them to stop what they were doing, grab their equipment, including battery- powered halogens, and form a five-vehicle caravan.

Sam entered the lead Suburban and sat in the second row seat next to Dr. Martin. Behind them sat Jagr and two armed guards.

Sam hoped she could see all the landmarks that Lester had put in his diary given the moonless night. As the huge SUV turned right and headed down the dirt road, Sam leaned forward and told the driver, "Let me know when we've gone 1.6 miles."

The driver nodded and set his odometer.

"We need to look for a pile of rocks about three feet high on the left side of the road. When we see that, we turn right into the desert in another fifty yards."

Dr. Martin said, "Very well." After almost seventy years, the thought of finally seeing the gold, the German gold he had delivered so long ago made his heart race. He hoped he would not succumb to a heart attack just minutes before seeing what he had so long sought. But he knew fate would not be so cruel to him. He thought of all the years that had passed and of all the dreams to resurrect the visions of the Führer that were now within reach.

He began thinking ahead about how they would dispose of the stupid girl who was leading them to the fulfillment of a destiny that was over a hundred years old. But given the endless desert that lay outside the windows of the SUV, that wouldn't be a problem. Of course he would let Jagr amuse himself with the girl and then offer her to the other men for their pleasure before deciding where to bury her.

"We have gone 1.5 miles," the driver said.

"Okay, slow down...there, there are the three rocks. Okay, take it slow now, just a little further, and...there, turn right as soon as you pass those two trees."

The caravan of SUVs turned right into the pitch-black desert. "Now just go about another mile or so until you see a big rock formation on your right," Sam directed.

The SUV moved in silence over the rock-hard dirt, occasionally passing over small gullies and rises on the desert floor.

"There, on the right. Those are the rocks I'm talking about," Sam said excitedly.

The caravan slowed to a stop, and Stonehenge-type rocks could be seen in the glare of the headlights.

"It was around here somewhere we found our first bars."

Without saying a word, Dr. Martin opened the door of the SUV and stepped onto the desert floor. On cue, fifteen others stepped from their vehicles into the darkness that was within minutes transformed into near daylight. Towers of lights were immediately erected, and blue-white light exploded onto the rocks, sand, shrubs, and trees.

Turning to Sam, who had exited the Suburban, Dr. Martin asked, "Where, my dear, did you find your gold bars, exactly?"

"Well, if I remember we found the first few in that flat spot over by those rocks, and then some more down in that gully over there."

Immediately, six men with metal detectors sprang into action in the areas Sam had pointed out. In less than a minute, a distinctive beep was heard from one of the detectors. Then another. Then another. "Dr. Martin, please, over here quickly." When Dr. Martin arrived at the site, a smiling guard held up a gold bar, and handed it to him. He stroked the bar like it was his lover. He felt its smoothness. He could sense its power. He touched *"Property US Government"* stamped on the bar. Dr. Martin smiled and said to himself. "Not anymore."

"Dr. Martin, here!" Twenty feet away, another guard held up a bar.

Over the next thirty minutes, the men found more bars and stacked them in front of Dr. Martin's Suburban. As they did, a look of satisfaction came over his face, and he turned to Jagr. "Go get the rest of the men from the mine along with their equipment." Jagr nodded.

A few yards behind Dr. Martin, a man in a white coat dropped nitric and hydrochloric acid onto a half dozen of the bars. After several moments, he smiled broadly and gave two thumbs-up to Dr. Martin, who returned the chemist's smile.

Sidling up to Dr. Martin, Sam asked, "When do I get my five bars?"

"When our task is finished here."

"I want my bars now. I want to go home. Bruce will be worried about me."

"I said when our task is completed, not before."

"If you don't give me my bars now, I won't show you where all the other bars are. There's like twenty spots like this one all around here, especially down in that valley you can't see in the dark. In fact, this is the smallest one. You should see all the bars buried about four hundred yards from here in that old creek bed."

"Show me."

"Now?"

"Yes, now."

"Okay but watch out for the rattlesnakes. They come out at night."

"We will drive."

"Suit yourself."

After getting back in the SUV, and with Dr. Martin in the back seat with her, Sam directed the driver to the second location. Within minutes, guards and technicians had located a dozen more bars.

"Did you say there are over twenty more locations like this one?" Dr. Martin asked.

"We found at least that many, and we didn't even have metal detectors. Like I said, this whole valley in every direction has tons of those bars either laying on top of the dirt or just under it."

"How are you able to find those bars?"

"Wouldn't you like to know?"

"Samantha, we have a deal. You lead me to all the gold you have found, and you will become very rich, and I won't call the sheriff."

"That damn sheriff's a prick too. We never did what he said we did. Okay, I'll give you my map."

Dr. Martin was incredulous, "You mean you have a map of where you found the gold?"

"Of course. Think I'm stupid?"

"Where is the map?"

"C'mon, you think I'm gonna give you the map before I get my five bars?"

"Where is the map?" Dr. Martin repeated.

"Well, I don't have it on me. I think your men proved that."

"Where is the map?"

"I'll bring you the map if you give me my five bars."

"I will give you your five bars when you produce the map."

"Like I said, mister, I don't have the damn map with me. I'd have to go get it, but I don't trust you. What if I get the map, bring it here, and you don't give me my five bars and then you kill me, and keep my bars and my map? That would not be cool."

"Perhaps I can offer a solution to our conundrum..."

"Our what?"

"Our problem."

"Oh."

"I'll send Jagr with you to retrieve the map, and you can bring young Bruce back with you to insure that you will get your five bars and be protected."

"I don't want to ride with that creep. What if I just bring the map back tomorrow?"

"I'm afraid that is my best offer. Take it or leave it. If you chose to leave it, I will have my men hold you here until the sheriff arrives."

"You are a prick. Guess I don't have much choice."

"As soon as Jagr returns with the rest of the men, you can go with him and retrieve your map. Until then, I must insist you remain in the vehicle."

"So, I'm like, under arrest?"

"No, my dear, we just want to make sure you are safe and sound until Jagr arrives. By the way, how long will it take for you to retrieve your map?"

"About an hour."

"Then once you leave, I will expect you to return within the hour. At which time you and Bruce will be a wealthy young couple, and free to go."

Dr. Martin opened the back door of the Suburban and exited, then motioned for two armed guards to stand watch over the SUV.

Within ten minutes, Jagr had returned with the rest of the men from the mine and more equipment. Sam could see Dr. Martin talking to Jagr. As she watched, Sam slipped her cell phone out of her sock, dropped it below her knees and typed out another text. *"Meet me one mile south of Lester's cache area in 20 MINUTES. When you come down road, turn off head lights. At 1 mile past cache area, go ¼ mile west into desert and wait. I may not be alone." S.*

Sam slid her cell back into her sock and waited. She continued to see Dr. Martin speaking with Jagr.

"I want you to take the young lady to where her map is. Her boyfriend may be there and insist on coming back with you. Once you return with the map, you will be free to entertain yourself with either or both as you deem appropriate. I am sure you will be creative. When you are sated, dispose of them in a safe spot and return here."

"Yes, sir. I look forward to enjoying the charms of the young lady. It will be particularly enjoyable with her young man watching."

"As you wish, Jagr, but make sure you bring the map back here first."

"Yes, sir."

Through the windows Sam could hear the beeping of the now dozens of metal detectors as they uncovered scores of bars and stacked them in front of the SUV and under the blue-white halogen bulbs. Dr. Martin stood next to the growing pile, transfixed by what he was seeing.

"Tom, Jon, c'mon let's go. Sam just texted me." The men rose in unison, grabbed the remaining equipment, and jogged to the Jeep.

"Is she okay?" Tom asked.

"I think so. But we may have trouble waiting for us when we meet her." As he spoke, Ben reached under his car seat and pulled out a military style Smith and Wesson .45.

"Exactly what kind of trouble are you expecting?" Jon asked.

"Not sure, but I want to be prepared. You know, like the Boy Scouts."

"Wish we had that shotgun." Tom added.

"Look under the back seat. The shells are in the spare tire well."

Tom retrieved the Remington and the twelve-gauge shells.

"Sam said to turn our lights out going down this hill. So open the windows and let me know if I'm going off the road. I can't see ten feet in front of me."

As the Jeep moved down the road at ten miles per hour, more bars were being discovered. Sam could not see exactly, but it looked like over two hundred had been discovered and stacked in the sand.

The Jeep, in darkness and silence, moved past the turn-off area where Lester's cache had been discovered. To their right the three men could see the halogen glare emanating from the site. A mile further down the road, Ben, as directed, turned right into the desert, but stopped just a few feet off the road. "Tom, take the shotgun and wait here. I think Sam may be heading this way. Jon and I will continue a bit further."

"Okay. You guys be careful."

"You too, big boy. Can you shoot that thing?" Jon asked.

"We'll see."

"Watch out for the snakes," reminded Jon.

"You and your damn snakes."

Jon and Ben drove into the darkness for approximately a quarter mile, turned off the Jeep, and waited in the darkness.

"You really have a thing about snakes, don't you?" Ben said.

"I hate snakes."

"You sound like Indiana Jones."

"I hate them even worse than he did."

"Ever see one? I mean up close and personal," Ben asked.

"No, but I've seen them in zoos and on TV. I mean, I really hate snakes."

Ben shook his head in wonder. "Sam said to wait here for twenty minutes."

A mile north of their location, Jagr entered the driver's seat of the SUV. He looked in the rearview mirror at Sam but didn't speak.

"Head out to the main road and turn right," Sam directed.

Remaining silent, Jagr maneuvered the SUV and headed east toward the dirt road.

"You owe me a sweatshirt and some underpants, jerk."

"It appears you will be able to afford a new wardrobe."

"It just feels weird not wearing underpants."

Jagr looked back at Sam again.

"Back in college, I'd wear these short skirts and no underwear. Made me feel hot all day. Sometimes, I'd sit in class and give the guys a show. Know what I mean?"

"You did not seem to like it today when one of our men tried to…"

"No woman likes it if somebody tries to take it. They have to ask for it. You know, say please."

"Is that all it takes…someone just has to 'say please'?"

"Well, he has to be good-looking, have a good body, and be, you know, sexy."

"I'd think a man must also have the equipment and know how to use it, to earn your favors."

"Yeah, that too."

As they approached the dirt road, Sam said, "Turn right here."

After several seconds of silence, Jagr said, "Perhaps if I were to 'say please'…"

"I might…but we have to be back in an hour or your boss might get upset. I wouldn't want you to get in trouble."

"I don't think he would mind if we were a few minutes late."

"You promise you won't tell my boyfriend?"

Tom could see the Suburban's headlights moving slowly down the dirt road toward him. He hid behind a tall cactus hoping the SUV would turn into the area where he was waiting. But the Suburban drove past Tom for nearly a quarter mile before it slowed and finally turned into the desert.

Tom began a slow jog through the cacti and ground cover toward the taillights of the SUV which stopped two hundred yards off the road.

"We can fold down the seats and make it more comfortable," Jagr said with a grin.

"Oh, I don't know, it's a beautiful night, what about outside?"

"You are an adventurous lady."

"You're not boring, are you?"

As Tom approached the SUV, he could see Sam slide out of the back seat and walk around in front of the vehicle where she met Jagr in the glare of the SUV's headlights.

"I think you should remove your clothing," Jagr said, his voice thick.

"You've already seen me. I want to see you. It's your turn—you go first."

Jagr smiled as he began his strip by slowly removing his pullover shirt. "Wow, looks like somebody hits the gym," Sam said. Jagr's smile widened.

After awkwardly removing his shoes and socks, Jagr loosened his belt and let his pants fall to the ground. "Don't believe in underwear, huh," Sam noticed.

"I like movement, and to be ready for action at any moment."

"Looks like you are certainly ready for action."

"You inspire me."

"Lean against the hood, shut your eyes, and quit talking," Sam said as she pushed Jagr against the SUV and sank to her knees.

"American women are very dominating and…"

"I said quit talking."

Obeying Sam, Jagr closed his mouth and eyes , and leaned against the warm hood of the Suburban. Sam moved her hands up each of his legs. She heard him moan in pleasure and felt him quiver in anticipation.

Within two seconds, Jagr's moan turned to a wail of agony when she slammed her fist between his legs four times before he fell to the ground, where he landed in a fetal position. His moans were not those of pleasure.

In a single motion, Sam grabbed his clothes, shoes, and socks and threw them in different directions into the black desert. She ran to the driver's door of the SUV, found the keys still in the ignition, fired up the Suburban, threw it into reverse, and began spewing up dirt and dust while looking into the rearview camera. It was then that she saw a tall man carrying a shot gun, not twenty feet behind her. Sam slammed on the brakes, rolled down her window, and calmly asked, "You order an Uber?"

After entering, Tom looked at Sam and said, "Wow, you're a tough first date."

"Oh no, are you saying he may not call me again?"

CHAPTER 64

DESERT---ONE MILE FROM JASPER MINE

TWO HOURS AFTER JAGR HAD left with Sam, his men were still finding gold even without a map. Over two hundred bars with an aggregate value of nearly $90,000,000 had been pulled from the sand and neatly stacked in several piles in front of Dr. Martin. While this amount of gold represented a small percentage of the number of bars that had been delivered to the Jasper in 1943, it was, according to Dr. Martin, a "promising start" to recovering that which had been lost for so long.

Dr. Martin was not sure why Rolle would have risked placing the gold in the open desert so long ago but concluded the strategy had worked. If only three bars were missing, found by the stupid American girl and her boyfriend, from the original 20,000 bars, along with those that had been seen in the pit, then Dr. Martin was ecstatic that what remained in the ground would allow him to carry out his plan. The plan he had worked so hard to execute. A plan that would, once and for all, rid the world of an insidious pestilence.

His only concern was why Jagr was late in returning with the girl and the map. While the bars were still being uncovered in the sand, the pace had slowed, and Dr. Martin recalled the girl saying the valley beneath where they were now working contained even more bars. He was already planning to move his team to the valley the next morning and had devised a work schedule whereby one team of workers rested, while the others searched the sand with metal detectors. A job made easier with a map.

At 2:15 a.m., a cut, bruised, and naked Jagr stumbled into the work area. His feet and legs were bleeding, and he limped badly. "What happened to the map, Jagr?"

"There was no map. The bitch pulled a gun on me, forced me off the road then ordered me to take off my clothes then threw them into the desert."

"How did a woman…"

"She put a pistol to the back of my head, it was a Sig Sauer, I think, she then ordered me to…"

"Jagr, did your cock betray you? Did you succumb to the young woman and she outsmarted you?"

"No sir. I never touched her. I don't think there was a map."

"Nonsense. The woman would not have walked away from over $2,000,000."

"If there is a map, maybe she plans to return and take far more than just the five bars she was promised," Jagr said.

"Jagr, you have disappointed me. Your actions have put our operation in jeopardy."

"I am sorry, sir, deeply sorry. Please forgive me."

"Of course, my son. After all these years of loyal service, I will give you another opportunity to redeem yourself, but do not disappoint me again. Now, have someone take you back to the Jasper, find some clothes and shoes, take some nourishment, and return here in forty-five minutes. We have much work to do."

"Yes sir. I will not disappoint you again."

As Jagr turned and walked away, Dr. Martin drew a pistol and shot him in the back of the head. "I know you won't, Jagr." He shot him three more times. The sound of the gunfire echoed in the black desert and got the immediate attention of the workers still pulling bars from the sand. "I want some of you to get rest now, then return to relieve those who will stay. Our work here is only beginning." As he spoke, two guards dragged Jagr's body into a gully and tossed him down an embankment. Dr. Martin didn't seem to notice.

CHAPTER 65

BEN'S HOUSE—PHOENIX

AFTER TOM AND SAM FOUND Ben and Jon in the desert, thanks to a few calls and texts, it was almost dawn when the four finally returned to Ben's ranch. Despite the hour, Sam and Tom made a breakfast of scrambled eggs, sausage, hash browns, French toast, and fresh-squeezed orange juice. "Let's eat now, get some rest, and talk when we get up and our minds are fresh," Ben said.

After eating in near silence, the quartet retired to separate bedrooms and slept until late afternoon. Later, sitting around Ben's pool, the conversation began with a question by Jon, "Now what the hell do we do?"

"We wait," Sam said.

"Wait for what?" Tom asked. "Once they find there's not much left of Lester's stash, they'll probably just head back to the Jasper and start their search all over again in there. That group doesn't strike me as one that will give up."

"Maybe what they found will be enough," Jon said, unconvincingly.

"Wonder what they're doing up there now?" Tom asked.

"Let's go look," Sam said as she smiled at Ben.

Twenty minutes later the group was flying north toward the Jasper at 2,000 feet in Ben's favorite Mooney. They did not have to fly directly over the area to see Dr. Martin's crew of two dozen men hard at work inside and along the banks of a meandering creek bed. The men could be seen working south from the Jasper in military precision. "Are you guys aware that I don't like flying?" Jon reminded the group as he looked out the window.

"Looks like they do have a plan," Tom said.

"That's what I was afraid of," Jon said.

"We have a plan too," Sam said, as she smiled at her dad.

"We do? Besides letting them take the last bit of Lester's gold, what kind of plan do we exactly have?" Tom asked.

"Just look down there and tell us what you see," Sam said.

Tom and Jon peered out the Mooney's window.

"I see about a million square miles of sand and two dozen guys with metal detectors digging up lead bars," Tom said.

"Yeah, that's what's I see too…wait a minute…oh shit, are you fucking kidding me?" Jon asked in a whisper.

"I don't kid," Sam said.

"She doesn't kid," Ben agreed.

CHAPTER 66

DESERT NEAR JASPER

AS THE SUN SANK IN the west, a group of eight ATVs, carrying sixteen heavily armed men and women dressed in black military fatigues, came across the desert at forty-five degree angles. They drove slowly, with purpose and discipline, maintaining their distance from each other and moving inexorably toward their target. The ATVs at first created an almost imperceptible humming sound that led Dr. Martin's men to initially look skyward to determine where the sound was coming from. They saw only one small single-engine plane.

As the ATVs moved across the desert, they kicked up dust that could be seen from the Mooney. The circle tightened around Dr. Martin's men like a large noose. They were oblivious to what was heading their way and continued to work in and around the creek bed.

Colonel David Green, a twenty-five-year member of the Jewish Defense League, rode in one of the ATVs, an Uzi in his lap and his eyes covered with Oakley Gator Sunglasses. While he wasn't trying to look cool, he did. He also looked scary, as did the other fifteen special ops soldiers who had volunteered for a "special assignment" over 7,000 miles from their homes in Tel Aviv. After hearing the details of the assignment, over 110 former Israeli soldiers had volunteered.

The driver of Colonel Green's ATV had his Uzi draped over his shoulder. In fact, every ATV contained two soldiers armed to the teeth. If someone was interested in starting a mini-war, Colonel Green and his troops were more than happy to oblige.

Through a series of international contacts that included encrypted messages, satellite phones, and coded texts, Sam had reached out to fellow pilots around the world, including Israeli pilots she had trained with, and explained her proposal. A deal of sorts—*you help us, and we'll help you,* kind of deal. The Israelis with whom she spoke thought it was a damn good plan and immediately accepted the proposal.

As the ATVs moved to within a half mile of the creek bed, they could be heard by Dr. Martin's men. But not heard by Dr. Martin who was asleep in one of the Suburbans.

He was awakened by a knock on the window: "Doctor, someone is coming." Exiting the Suburban, Dr. Martin could now hear and see Colonel Green and his approaching troops, only 200 yards away. Many of his men were still in the creek bed looking for gold bars.

"Men, grab your weapons, we are under attack!" Dr. Martin shouted.

"What did he say?" one of his men digging in the creek bed asked of anyone who might know the answer.

When he reached for his weapon, it was shot out of reach by six Uzi rounds from one of Colonel Green's troops. Within seconds, most of Dr. Martin's men dropped their weapons and raised their hands. Three did not. When they instead raised their weapons to fire, they were shredded to ribbons by at least five Uzis.

For over a minute, the Uzi's smoked, the air reeked of nitroglycerin, and the desert was silent. Dr. Martin's men stared at Colonel Green's troops, not sure what to do next other than keep their hands in the air. They looked toward Dr. Martin who had instinctively positioned himself between the gold bars and Colonel Green's troops, apparently hoping that a nonagenarian could not only hide but also protect what had been found.

Finally, one of Dr. Martin's men uttered, "Fuck me."

"An interesting offer, young man, but I would prefer to know how many other men await us in the mine." Colonel Green asked softly as he approached the twenty-two year old.

Colonel Green's soft tone and smiling face scared the hell out of Dr. Martin's guard. He thought about running. He thought about screaming. He thought about not talking. As he contemplated other useless options, Colonel Green slapped handcuffs on the heavily tattooed young man then whispered in his ear as he simultaneously pulled an eight-inch serrated blade knife from his waistband. "You have ten seconds to answer my question. Only ten. If I get to eleven, I will disembowel you with this knife, and you will be forced to catch your intestines and other organs before they hit the ground. It will take you over an hour to die. One…"

"There are no men in the mine; everyone is here. We don't know that old dude over there. We were told we could make some coin if we…"

"Thank you, that is far more information than I need," Colonel Green said, maintaining his smile, then added. "If I discover you have lied to me, your death will be even more painful than I previously described. Do we understand each other?"

"Yes…I mean, yes sir."

After leaving the young man, Colonel Green approached Dr. Martin from the rear and placed his Uzi at Dr. Martin's back. "Hello, you must be Dr. Armin Martin."

"I am."

"I believe you are trying to find some things that belonged to my grandparents. They would like those things back."

CHAPTER 67

BEN'S MOONEY

BEN SENT THE MOONEY INTO a wide circle pattern around the Jasper, which allowed the team to see Colonel Green and his troops cram Dr. Martin and his remaining men into the back of the Suburbans driven and guarded by the Israelis. The SUVs were then surrounded by the ATVs, and the vehicles made their way up the dirt road that led back to the Jasper.

In the Mooney, Tom had a question:, "How many lead bars did J.T. bury?"

"Hundreds according to Lucille," Sam said. As she spoke, a "ping" was heard in the plane. Then another. Suddenly, the right rear window shattered, sending pieces of plexiglass over the cabin, mainly over Jon. Hot Arizona air filled the cabin as two more pings were heard over the wind noise.

"We're being shot at, Daddy." As she spoke, Sam texted and gave coordinates. Within sixty seconds, two of Colonel Green's troops split off from the caravan and tore back toward where Dr. Martin's men had been digging.

Ben banked the Mooney to the left and dove the plane toward the desert floor. An acidic smell filled the cabin, and a thin stream of oil could be seen coming from the right side of the engine housing.

"We're losing oil pressure," Ben said calmly.

"Can we make it back to the house?" Sam asked.

"Don't want to land around here."

"Did I ever mention I hate flying?" Jon asked.

"At least there are no rattlesnakes up here," Tom said.

Below the Mooney, two of Colonel Green's troops had located the lone remnant of Dr. Martin's group who had been peeing among the rocks while his cohorts had been loaded into the Suburbans. He had three AK-47s with him and kept firing round after round toward a now-disappearing Mooney. His bald head with a red swastika tattooed on it made him an easy target.

Major Sylvia Weissman knew she needed only one shot. She took four.

CHAPTER 68

BEN'S HOUSE—PHOENIX

DESPITE OIL SPLASHING ON THE windshield, smoke pouring from the engine, and Jon puking in the back seat, Ben made a perfect landing of the smoldering Mooney at his private field. Fifteen minutes later, Ben, Tom, Jon, and Sam were sipping iced tea in Ben's kitchen.

"When do they arrive?" Tom asked.

"Within the hour," Ben said.

"Have you heard if..."

"We agreed, no communication. We just have to wait."

For nearly two hours, the four sat in virtual silence.

CHAPTER 69

INSIDE THE JASPER

GIVEN HIS ADVANCED YEARS, DR. Martin was provided a chair. The rest of his men were directed to sit on the floor of the Jasper in a semicircle, facing the pit, twenty feet from the edge, their hands tied behind their backs.

In front of the men were the 250 bars they had pulled from the desert dirt and sand. Dr. Martin was within five feet of the bars. He stared at them like a lost lover. His heart wanted them back. His brain knew better.

For nearly thirty minutes there was absolute silence in the Jasper. At one point, one of Dr. Martin's men raised his hand and said, "Excuse me, can I...?"

Without answering, one of Colonel Green's men looked at the man with sincerity on his face, put his finger to his lips, and slowly shook his head. There were no further questions.

At first, the sound was muffled. Like summer thunder. As the volume rose, the sound became that of an approaching commercial jet. When the trucks began to enter the Jasper, the roar was deafening, and the image of the behemoth trucks with their headlights glaring, diesel exhaust pipes belching, produced a rumbling that made the floor of the mine vibrate. It also scared the hell out of Dr. Martin's men who were already wishing they were somewhere, anywhere else.

Colonel Green greeted the drivers of the trucks, who had shut down their engines and began unloading what their trucks carried. After conferring with the six drivers, he walked to the bars that sat in front of Dr. Martin. The colonel was joined by two other men who began a chemical analysis of each bar. Most of the bars analyzed were then absent mindedly tossed into pit and could heard clattering down the sides of the mine on their way to the darkness. Each time a bar was thrown into the abyss, Dr. Martin winced, his body physically reacting to his loss. With each tossed bar he seemed to wither.

The bars that weren't discarded were set six feet to Dr. Martin's right. As his men continued their analysis, stacking, and disposal regimen, Colonel Green approached Dr. Martin. "My dear Dr. Martin, it appears you are confused by our actions. It's very simple, really—the vast majority of the bars your men found last night were nothing more than lead bars painted gold. You were fooled, Doctor. Fooled by a man named J.T. and a young woman who allows me to call her Sam. Doctor, your men tested the wrong bars. Your euphoria and gold lust led to an erroneous conclusion. However, I thought you would like to see what it is you have apparently spent decades looking for." Colonel Green then nodded to one of his men.

With military efficiency, Colonel Green's men began their performance by sliding a piece of one-inch steel measuring 12 inches by 14 inches over the edge of the pit. In less two minutes, three of men using eight-pound sledgehammers had completely broken down the wall, tossing the remnants into the pit.

As what was behind the wall was revealed, Dr. Martin's eyes widened, and he stood at his seat in awe. "Ah, there it is. How lovely. How clever Rolle was." Dr. Martin also began to laugh and cry at the same time.

With Dr. Martin watching every move, Colonel Green's men, using reinforced electric handcarts, moved over 17,000 gold bars and four barrels from behind the wall into the back of the six heavy-duty trucks, each capable of carrying 80,000 pounds. It took less than an hour.

As each handcart moved past Dr. Martin, he gazed longingly, his tears never abated.

After their doors were shut, the trucks again roared to life, and within minutes, left the Jasper in deafening silence.

Dr. Martin had returned to his seat and sat with his shoulders stooped, looking at the now nearly empty space behind the wall. Then his eyes caught something in the corner of the space. It was gray-green. At first he didn't realize what he was looking at. After several moments, he had a question. "Colonel Green, would you indulge an old man one favor?"

Seeing what Dr. Martin was looking at, the colonel nodded.

Dr. Martin slowly walked over the steel plate and moved to the very back of the area behind the pit. There he picked up a gray-green uniform. It was very large. He brought the uniform to his face and inhaled the dust that embedded it. "Willy, my dear Willy."

For several moments, Dr. Martin stroked the cloth and held it to his chest.

"Thank you, Colonel. Your indulgence is greatly appreciated." Then without hesitation, Dr. Martin walked into the pit. He made no sound as he bounced off the rubble that tore and broke his body on its journey.

CHAPTER 70

BEN'S HOUSE—PHOENIX

AFTER THE GOLD HAD BEEN unloaded into the underground bunker that Ben had constructed on his ranch, Ben, Sam, Tom, and Jon stood among the colonel's troops, shaking their hands.

"Did you retain the number of bars we had agreed to, Colonel Green?" Ben asked.

"It is better that all the gold be returned to those who lost everything. My men and I will be eternally grateful for what you and your team have decided to do. It is an honor to assist all of you. It is time for reparations. But beware, Dr. Martin is not alone. Others will follow and try to find what you have. What you have in the ground is their Fourth Reich. They know the gold exists and will stop at nothing to possess it."

CHAPTER 71

INSIDE THE GULFSTREAM 550—TWO WEEKS LATER

IT WAS, ADMITTEDLY, A BIT CRUEL, but Tom, Ben, and Sam knew it had to be done. After all, Jon had been whining for days when he heard of the cross-country trip in Ben's Gulfstream 550 to visit their first "client." "I really don't like to fly," he had said about a hundred times leading up to the trip.

"Yeah, we get it," Tom said. "But just have a few glasses of wine, go to sleep, and Ben and Sam will try to avoid the Rocky Mountains."

As soon as Jon nodded off, Sam pulled out a half dozen perfect replica toy rattlesnakes. She paid extra for the battery-powered ones that rattled. She placed a couple of them on the seat next to Jon and a few more at his feet.

The sound Jon made when he woke up and first heard then saw the plastic reptiles was almost ethereal. Certainly not the sound that would come out of a grown man. To his credit, he did not jump from the jet. Nor did he even acknowledge that the incident occurred. Once he was sure the snakes were just toys, he put them into a storage bin and came up to the cockpit.

"Hi Jon, how'd you sleep?" Sam asked.

"Oh fine. Feel like a new man."

"That's a refreshing thought." Sam said.

Jon mumbled something obscene that Sam could not hear, returned to the passenger compartment, and took a seat next to Tom. Tom did not acknowledge Jon and continued to pore over what looked to be old documents with the State of Arizona seal at the top of each page. "What-cha reading?" Jon asked.

"Just looking at some interesting ownership records of mines in Arizona and comparing them to some of the things I read in Lester's diary about gold shipments during the war. And I found other records on the internet about rumored gold shipments during the war that sound like what we found.

"So what's the problem?"

"Well, there are a lot discrepancies in what Lester said was delivered to the Jasper and other accounts about gold being taken from Germany and delivered to the US. In fact, the descriptions I've read based on supposed eyewitness accounts don't match up in terms of the amount or even the location. I mean it doesn't sound like the Jasper."

"Let me see." Jon took a stack of papers Tom and been reading and began perusing them. "Says here that over 150 tons of gold and silver bullion and coins were taken from Germany then delivered to the U.S. through Mexico. It claims the gold and silver was stored in a mine in Arizona." Jon said.

"I saw that too, but we didn't find any silver. Or any coins. And the description of the mine certainly isn't the Jasper."

"It sounds like the Vega." Jon said.

"Holy shit, you're right."

"But Lester never mentioned any coins or gold at the Vega." Jon noted.

"Maybe he didn't know anything about what could be in the Vega. Maybe it was the wrong war."

"You mean those eyewitness reports were talking about WWI?" Jon asked.

"What else could explain it? I read earlier that Germany and her allies had shipped gold over here as far back as 1916. That would explain the German 100 year lease of the Vega. A lease that's still in place."

Sam joined Tom and Jon in the passenger compartment, and noticed what Tom was reading. "Catching up on history?"

"I think we've found our part-time summer job."

"Hey Sam, what would you have done if Dr. Martin's crew would have dug up some lead ingots first?"

"Lucille had told me J.T. had dug up all but twenty-five real gold ingots in Lester's hiding place, so I went out there a few days before and moved them in places where I thought I'd be able to direct Dr. Martin's men to dig first. I saw his men do some testing on some of the first real gold they dug up, and just hoped they wouldn't test any more. I think seeing all those bars stacking up in front of them made them gold crazy."

"If J.T. hadn't taken the time to plant all those gold-painted lead bars in the desert this would have never worked." Jon said.

"He was a smart guy. He figured someone, sometime, would eventually run across Lester's cache, so every time he picked up one of Lester's gold bars, he'd drop about 10 lead bars on the desert floor." Sam explained.

Lucille said J.T. loved Lester like a brother and wanted to protect his gold. He did." Sam said.

"Hey Sam, ever hear from your boyfriend from the desert? Tom asked. "You two looked like a real happy couple until you tried to de-ball him with some good right uppercuts."

"No, the bastard. You know men. They say they're gonna call and never do."

After arriving at La Guardia in late afternoon, the group headed to the Sofitel in Manhattan, took a nap, ate Italian that evening, then went to see the musical *Beautiful*.

The next morning they met for breakfast and discussed in detail their upcoming meeting. They had done their homework on their client by combing over the records they had recovered from the barrels in the Jasper to ascertain what had been taken in 1939. As best he could, Jon had done the financial analysis and arrived at a number he felt was fair. But all four knew nothing was really fair. No number or financial calculation would ever be enough—not for what had been taken.

They took a cab to the Upper East Side and rang the bell of a beautiful townhouse. A trim, elderly woman peered through the window, smiled, and opened the door.

"Hello. I have been waiting, please come in."

"Hello ma'am. My name is Samantha. This is my father Ben and our friends Jon and Tom."

After shaking hands with the men, the old woman said. "When I received your letter, I thought it was a hoax. I could not understand how you found me and how you could know so much about…about what happened."

Over the next three hours Ben, Sam, Tom, and Jon told the old woman an incredible story. They introduced her to Lester, Eric, Lucille, and J.T. They told her the story of Rolle, Dr. Martin, and those unnamed who remain committed to a virus that began a hundred years before. A virus of hatred, stupidity, and intolerance. They also told her of the gold.

"The reason we are here today is not just to tell you a story, but in some small way recompense you for what you and your family lost so many years ago." Ben said as he handed the woman a check for $2.6 million. "This amount is based on what we believe the Germans took in terms of real estate, cash, stocks, bonds, and other assets from your family. We have calculated as best we could what those items would be worth today."

The old woman looked briefly at the check but remained silent.

Tom opened a small travel case and began pulling out items one by one. "Based on the Nazi records we found, we believe these personal items are at least some of the things it appears were taken from you family." On the table in front of the old woman were several watches, rings, bracelets, and other assorted jewelry. There was also a red toy truck.

Gazing for several moments at what Tom had laid out in front of her, the old woman reached over the jewelry and picked up the truck. "Ari," she whispered. "He was only four. He was such an imp. Always running all over the house. This was his favorite toy. Of all the toys he had, this little toy truck was his favorite. He would say 'Anna, where is my red truck?' And I would say, 'Under the couch, Ari, where you always leave it.' He would giggle and then retrieve the truck. It was a game we would play."

Ben, Sam, Jon, and Tom knew at that moment the trip from Arizona had been worth it.

"After a few years, we all knew what had happened to mother, father, and Ari. We prayed we were wrong, but we knew. But everyone around us had lost family so we banded together to survive the horror. I can't tell you how much I will be forever indebted to each of you for what you have brought me today. But I have one more favor to ask of you. I would like this check and this jewelry to go to the Holocaust Museum in Washington, DC, in my parent's and Ari's names, so people will never forget. My family and I don't need the money as much as we need people to never forget. Do you understand?"

"Yes, we understand," Ben said. "We will be happy to do as you ask."

"I would like to hold on to this." Anna picked up the red toy truck and cradled it in her hands.

On the flight to DC, Jon asked. "Tom, so who's next on the list?"

"After Washington, we visit a Dr. Martin Sporn. He lives in Miami. He survived Auschwitz, but his entire family died there."

"Good thing I love to fly, and we have a jet." Jon said. Pax wagged his tail in agreement.

Next stop Miami.

ABOUT THE AUTHOR

FOR MARK DONAHUE, 30 years in senior management at two Fortune 200 firms was enough. So, he quit and decided, at long last, to write. The result was five novels released in 2020 and eleven screenplays, three of which are in pre-production as feature films. "Guess I should have left commercial real estate sooner." His readers wholeheartedly agree.

Mark resides in Ohio with wife Marsha, Mika, The Wonder Dog, and boss of the house, Rocky the Cat. Much missed, and immortalized in Mark's first novel, *Last at Bat*, the late great Wheaten Terrier Carly, watches over all of them from an honored perch on a bookshelf—where else would a writer's dog be?

www.DonahueLiteraryProperties.com

DONAHUE
LITERARY PROPERTIES

Made in the USA
Monee, IL
12 October 2021